A Second Humorous Erotica Collection

STAND UP, LIE DOWN COLLECTION

A Second Humorous Erotica Collection

CHASTITY VELDT

4 Horsemen
Publications, Inc.

4 Horsemen
Publications, Inc.

Published By: 4 Horsemen Publications, Inc.

4 Horsemen Publications, Inc.
PO Box 417
Sylva, NC 28779
4horsemenpublications.com
info@4horsemenpublications.com

Edited by Kris Cotter

Library of Congress Control Number: 2024950037

Paperback ISBN-13: 979-8-8232-0733-1
Hardcover ISBN-13: 979-8-8232-0734-8
Audiobook ISBN-13: 979-8-8232-0736-2
Ebook ISBN-13: 979-8-8232-0735-5

Table of Contents

Francis
in Fargo

TABLE OF CONTENTS

CHAPTER 1

"Man, is there anything to do in this town?" Jake Nilsen mumbled as he navigated his pickup down Main Street. He was in Fargo, North Dakota, on a Wednesday morning, on the first stop of his Wacky Wild West tour. At least that's what his agent was calling it, even though Jake hated it.

"I'm not calling it that," Jake had told him during a rare face-to-face meeting in Chicago.

"Oh, come on, man," said his agent, Kurt. "Don't you get it? You're a comic? You're going out west? The wild west?"

"You know, you keep asking questions as if I don't know the answer. This isn't the Socratic Dialectic."

"The what?"

"Socrates. He would ask questions to get people to see his side."

"So? It works, doesn't it?"

"Yeah, but they killed him for it."

"Eww. Fucking Ancient Greeks," said Kurt.

"Look, I get what you're saying, but the slogan's about as overdone as a redneck's steak."

"Do rednecks get their steak overdone?" asked Kurt.

"How the hell do I know?" said Jake. "I needed something to complete the simile, and it was the first thing I could think of." Jake ran his hand through his thick blond hair and adjusted his glasses. People often remarked that Jake looked like Tony, the first German terrorist to die in *Die Hard*. He was also a former swimmer who had come *this close* to making the Olympic team.

After washing out, he turned his eye toward standup comedy, although he was still a fiend about working out, whether swimming at a local pool, running, or lifting weights. He had a membership at a 24-hour fitness place with locations all over the country, and he would visit them whenever he visited a new city.

Kurt laughed at that and said, "Regardless, I'm going to book your gigs as Jake Nilsen's Wacky Wild West tour. And I'll have Angela do all your social media with that."

"It's not going to be that dramatic if I'm only opening and middling on this tour, you realize. It's hard to hype a tour when I'm the 15-minute schlub middling the night," said Jake.

Middling means working as the second comic in a three-comic night, between the opener and the headliner, Jake said as an aside to the reader. Then, he winked at you, and you felt yourself go a little weak in the knees.

"Are you saying you can get me all headlining gigs?" he said, returning his attention to Kurt.

"Absolutely! Now, they won't be big cities *per se*," said Kurt, using the only Latin he knew. "But they'll be in sizable cities. I can get you into Vancouver, BC, Reno, El Paso, and Tucson. I might even be able to get you gigs in Portland, Oregon and I've got a club in Dallas that just opened and is still trying to get bigger names. But right now, we fit their budget. By the time you get there in 2023, you'll have a chance to really polish your act, and you'll be landing some big venues."

"I am whelmed."

"Is that even a word?"

"Absolutely."

"Whatever. Plus, Angela has been giving me some ideas about posting videos of your show on YouTube and Instagram that can build up your crowds."

"Sounds good to me," said Jake, who tried to avoid social media as much as he could. He would sign into his accounts to see what Angela had been up to, but he left the actual management of them to her and Kurt.

Kurt had been his agent ever since Jake had joined the comedy circuit. The two had been in the same comedy troupe at the University of Minnesota, even while Jake was on the swim team. But while Jake had gone into standup, as well as making some smart real estate investments that made him nearly wealthy, Kurt and his girlfriend-now-wife, Angela, moved to Chicago and went into talent management and booking, handling the bookings and promotion for several comics, bands, and actors around the Midwest. Kurt also handled the bookings for Curtis Sanders, another friend of Jake's, and a fellow comic. The two would often exchange tales of sexual exploits whenever they were in the same city.[1]

---

[1]   See *Stand Up, Lie Down #3: Lydia in Louisville*

Now, after spending a few weeks at home with his family in Mankato, Minnesota, Jake found himself back on the road, starting just across the state line with Fargo, North Dakota.

Jake drove down Main Avenue, before pulling over and grabbing his phone. As was his other habit with any new city, in addition to looking for a place to work out, he always looked for a bookstore and a coffee shop to spend most of his downtime between nightly shows.

His GPS took him to a used bookstore on 1st Avenue, which Jake decided was a good store. He was a fan of bookstores, especially the used ones, because there were so many pleasant surprises to be had.

Jake didn't like new bookstores as much because the offerings were always so predictable: Every best seller in the last five years, including every James Patterson book ever printed, plus a few that were from the future.[2]

His favorites were old mysteries and pulp fiction stories, especially the ones by little-known authors. Jake kept a list on his phone he called his mystery book wish list. He would find the books on his list, read them while he was on tour, and when he had accumulated about twelve or so, he would ship them back home and ask his brother to unpack them and put them on his shelves. Whenever Jake went home for a visit, he would sort and catalog his books. After nearly two years on the road, he had accumulated quite a collection of mysteries.

Jake kept a small notebook of coffee shops and restaurants he visited on his travels. It was more like a travel diary than an actual journal, where he would write reviews of his experiences and rate the meals. It wasn't anything he published online or shared with

---

[2] Don't ask.

other people, it was just a nice way he could remember the cities he visited and the sights he saw.

He also had a code for some of his more erotic encounters on his travels. As Jake bounced from city to city on his tours, he had often hooked up with one or two women in each city. Rather than spell out all the sexy details that might accidentally be discovered by a future girlfriend or, worse yet, his mother, he simply wrote a line along with each woman's name as a reminder.

"Had dinner with Irene," "went for drinks with Natasha," "ate brunch with Carrie."[3]

However, Jake did work with a ghostwriter to recount eight of his most recent erotic encounters on the road, the first volume of which is now available at fine online bookstores everywhere.

"Hello, and welcome to The Next Chapter," said a young woman behind the counter. "Is there anything I can help you find?"

Jake looked around for a few seconds before he focused on the woman. "Oh, no. I'm just here to see what I can discover."

"Ah, a fellow seeker," said the woman. She was tall, about 5'10", pale, had shoulder-length black hair, and wore a flannel shirt tucked into a pair of tight-fitting jeans. Jake could tell she was fit by the way she stood. She looked like most female swimmers he knew because they tended to be broad across the shoulders and narrow-waisted, which she was.

"Seeker?" Jake asked, worried he was appearing in an urban fantasy book or was about to be recruited to join a Quidditch team. "What's a seeker?"

---

[3] See *Stand Up, Lie Down* books: *Irene In Indianapolis (#2)*, *Natasha In Nashville (#4)*, and *Carrie On Campus (#6)*

"Sorry, that's what I call the people who come in here just to browse. They're not looking for anything in particular, they just want to see what they can find. They like the, uh…"

"Serendipity?" asked Jake.

"Yes, the serendipity of discovery. There's something special about used bookstores because you never know what you're going to find."

"That's what I love about used bookstores," said Jake. "I like old mysteries, usually anything before 1980, and the best bookstores always have a few shelves of old pulp novels and paperbacks."

"Then you're in luck," said the woman. "We have a huge selection of old paperback mysteries. My boss is something of a mystery nut, and she buys all kinds of mysteries off eBay and from Goodwill, so she's got some unusual ones."

"So, this isn't your shop?" *I've been through this once before. I don't think I can have my heart broken by another bookshop owner,* Jake thought, recalling Molly, a bookstore owner he had a sexy good time with in Milwaukee. A few weeks later, she told him she was seriously dating Ted, a stuffy accountant her aunt had fixed her up with.[4]

"No, I just work here part-time."

"You're not dating an accountant, are you?"

"Huh?" She looked a little confused. "No, I don't have much time for a social life."

Jake breathed a tiny sigh of relief.

---

4 See *Stand Up, Lie Down #1: Molly in Milwaukee*

"I'm getting my graduate degree in exercise science at the university." The woman smiled a little, and he decided he liked her smile.

"Were you an athlete?" he asked.

"I was a swimmer as an undergrad," she said.

"No kidding? I was, too!"

"Seriously? Where was that?"

"I graduated from the University of Minnesota six years ago."

"I just finished up at Moorehead State University two years ago."

"Wow, fellow Minnesotan. What's your name?" Jake stuck out his hand. "I'm Jake Nilsen."

"Nilsen?"

"N—Er, yes," said Jake, surprised. Most people misheard his name, pronouncing it Nelson, Nilsin, or Nielssen unless they were from Minnesota. Jake's heart gave a little flutter.

"I'm Tess." She shook Jake's hand, and his heart melted a little at her firm grip and long fingers.

"So, are you a mystery fan, too?"

"Oh, a little," said Tess. "I actually like creative nonfiction more. Essays, memoirs, what they call 'new journalism.' But I read mysteries now and again." She listed off a few of her favorite authors, including one Jake had never heard of, E.C.R. Lorac.

"I don't know him."

"Her. She was a British crime writer and wrote several dozen books under a few different names."

"Well, I'll check her out. Which way to the mystery section?"

"Follow me," said Tess. She walked down one of the long aisles, and Jake had a chance to check her out from behind. He liked what he saw, but made sure not to look too long because a gentleman never stares. Good thing, too, because she turned around to see if he was looking at her ass, and bit her lower lip.

Tess brought him to the appropriate shelves and bent down to find some books. Jake risked another quick glance at her shapely ass and marveled at its heart shape in those jeans. He snapped his eyes back up as she stood up and handed him a few paperbacks.

"These are some of Lorac's books, including her debut novel, which is what made her famous."

"Thank you," said Jake, flipping through them and looking at the covers. "I'll take them all."

"Ooh, great. Thank you. Come on back to the counter, and I'll ring you up." Tess returned to the front of the store, and Jake swore she was putting a little more swish in her hips on the return trip.

"So, is there a place to swim around here?" Jake asked after Tess rang up his purchases. "Or even a decent weight room?"

"There's a fitness place about half a mile from here," she said, naming the same place Jake had a membership to, but we won't name here so we don't get sued for using their name in an erotica novel. Let's just say, it's a whole *planet* devoted to *fitness*.

"Oh, I have a membership there already."

"Cool. I'm heading over there in a few hours if you'd like to work out together, and then maybe we can get an early supper."

"That would be great. I have to go check into the club and then check out the apartment situation," said Jake.

"Club? Are you a DJ?"

"No, I'm a standup comic. I'm headlining at Cookie's for the next four nights."

"A comic, eh? Mama always said not to get involved with no circus folks," Tess said, adopting a slight Southern accent.

Jake laughed. "Tell Mama you're safe with me."

"Yeah, but I don't always do what Mama said," Tess said, biting her lip again.

Jake turned red as Tess laughed at him. She texted him the address, and they agreed to meet at 3:00 for a workout.

A few minutes later, Jake walked into Cookie's Comedy Club and found his way back to the manager's office. "Hi, are you Katelyn?" he asked when a woman opened the door.

"That's what my mom said," said an older woman, holding half a doughnut in one hand and her mobile phone in the other. "Let me call you back," she said into the phone.

"You want a doughnut?" she asked, offering up a box with a couple left.

"You know, normally I wouldn't, but I'm going to work out after this, so I think I can manage it." He selected a plain old-fashioned and closed his eyes as he savored his first bite. "I usually don't indulge, so this is a real treat."

"Yeah, it shows, hot pants," said Katelyn, roaring with laughter. "I'll bet you leave a lot of broken hearts in your wake."

"Uh, no, I uh—" Jake stammered, thinking of his last eight-city tour, in which he had sex with gorgeous women in every one of them. And you can read all about it in the first volume of *Stand Up, Lie Down*, available now on Amazon.[5]

Katelyn laughed even louder. "Settle down, Chief. I'm just bustin' your balls." Katelyn had a loud, rough laugh, and Jake realized he would love to have ten of her in any audience. She would be a real ego boost to any semi-decent comic.

"So, what's the housing situation for the club?" Jake asked, trying not to seem too pushy.

"Well, stud, I don't think my husband would like it if I brought you home." She laughed again. "So we're going to put you up in a hotel. Will that be okay?"

"You don't have an apartment?"

"Oh sure, but we don't put our headliners in that shithole. No, that's only for the openers and middlers. We treat our headliners like royalty around here. At least as royal as you can get in America's farmland. You'll be staying at the Holiday Inn off the interstate. It's just about 10 minutes from here. We already got a reservation in your name, so just tell 'em who you are."

Jake thanked Katelyn for the chance to perform, and for the doughnut, and he headed off to check in at the hotel.

---

[5] Just go to https://bit.ly/ChastityVeldt or search for my name on Amazon.

CHAPTER 2

"**M**an, my muscles are going to be screaming at me tomorrow," said Jake. "I haven't worked out like that for a few weeks."

"Seriously? You look like you work out every day. You've got a great physique," Tess said, using the fancy exercise science word for "delicious, yummy muscles."

"Well, I try to. I run every day that I don't work out. And I try to swim two or three times a week. And if I can ever borrow a bike, I'll go for a long ride."

"That explains soooo much," said Tess, a little breathlessly.

"What?"

"What? I mean, that explains why you're so, um, built."

"You look great, too," said Jake, who had been raised to give a compliment when you receive a compliment. Now that Jake could see her in her exercise clothes, he was even more turned on. Not only did Tess have broad shoulders and a tapered waist — sort of a female version of Jake — but she had large breasts that stretched her sports bra beyond the capabilities of mortal sports bras. She was now covered up in a loose-fitting t-shirt and shorts, but the memory of her breasts still lingered in Jake's mind. It was 5:00, and they were finishing their early supper at a local diner Tess had recommended.

"Tell you what, I'm taking a class on sports massage therapy and I have to get in so many hours of massage practice to pass the class. If you'd like, I can give you a rubdown so you won't be so sore tomorrow."

"That would be great," said Jake, who always loved a good massage. Hell, he even loved a mediocre massage.

"Perfect. I've got my portable massage table in my truck because I have to do a session with one of my classmates. It will help me catch up if I do you before I do her."

"Uhh..." said Jake, turning red.

"Oh God, sorry! I didn't mean *do* you," said Tess, forgetting she was in an erotica book, and we all knew where this was going anyway, so don't act like I just spoiled this for you. "I meant, give you a massage."

Jake took a drink of his Coke and mumbled something about knowing what she actually meant.

"Wow, you turned really red there, Jake. Are you one of those good conservative Lutheran boys who still gets red when he says 'boobies?'"

"Lutheran, yes; conservative, no. And I just have trouble discussing ... sexy things without getting all red and embarrassed." This had long been Jake's problem. He had trouble discussing sex in person or over the phone unless he was actually having sex. Then, his dirty talk was sheer poetry compared to his awkward blatherings at times like this.

"What like all the time?"

"Uh, not all the time."

"Hmmm. You'll have to tell me more. Let's go do you... your massage."

Jake made himself comfortable on Tess's table, which she had set up in his hotel room while he showered. When he came out of the bedroom, he saw that she had set up a small Bluetooth speaker and played some relaxing yoga music through her phone.

"I've got a few different oils to choose from," said Tess. "I've got lavender, peppermint, CBD, juniper, and ginger."

"Seriously? I thought this was a sports massage."

"It is. You need oil for lubrication. Juniper and ginger bring oxygen to muscles, and peppermint is cooling and an analgesic." Which is a fancy exercise science word for "pain reducing."

"I like peppermint. Let's try that."

"Sounds good." Tess put the bottle of peppermint oil in a small hot pot filled with water and turned it on. "We'll let the oil warm up a bit while you get ready. Strip down to your comfort level, and you can get under this towel."

Jake did as he was told, wrapping a towel around his narrow waist before slipping off his underwear and climbing onto the table. Unlike Tess, Jake remembered he was in an erotica book, so he figured he'd save some time.

"Alright, here we go." Tess had stripped down to her workout short-shorts and sports bra. "I don't want to get oil on my clothes," she explained.

Jake groaned as she dug her strong fingers into his back muscles. She poured oil onto Jake's back and rubbed it in, focusing on his cannonball shoulders and thick back muscles. Her fingers dug into Jake's lower back, slipping under the towel. With each pass, she went slightly lower under his towel until her fingers were touching the top of his ass cheeks. Jake could feel himself getting harder and wondered what he was going to do when she had him turn over. Jake had an eight-and-a-half-inch penis, and he doubted the towel was going to be heavy enough to keep him from pitching a tent.

Jake tried thinking of unpleasant things to make it go down — car accidents, guys getting hit in the groin with footballs, this book's audio reader saying words like "seepage" and "gurgle" — when Tess switched ends and started working on his calves and feet.

Good God, her fingers are strong and *magical*, he thought.

His unpleasant imaginations were working, and he felt his cock begin to subside until she started working on his thighs and going up under the towel, making it swell to its previous glory.

"Is this okay?" Tess asked. "Am I using enough pressure? Do you want it harder or softer?"

"I think it's plenty hard enough," Jake stammered. Tess snickered and worked her hands higher up his legs until she was lightly brushing his cock with her fingertips.

"You *are* a bit, er... tense," she murmured. "You should turn onto your back, and we'll see what I can do for you there."

Jake did as he was told and tried to tuck his cock between his legs, but his thighs were still slippery from the peppermint oil, so it popped up and lifted the towel with it.

"Oh, my!" she gasped. "Is that for me?"

Jake said nothing as she slowly lifted the towel. Her eyes widened as she took in Jake's eight-and-a-half-inch cock in all its glory. She ran her fingers down his rock-hard abs and traced the V-muscles[6] that traced down toward his pubic region before she finally wrapped her long fingers around his thick shaft. She stroked his cock with her hands still covered in peppermint oil, the coolness of it making him gasp.

"I'm surprised you were able to swim with this thing in your suit," she said, licking her lips.

"I wore the long shorts. My cock bulged out of the Speedos."

"I'll just bet it did," said Tess, wrapping her other hand around his dick. "This looks incredible." She lowered her mouth to his dickhead and gave it a small kiss and then another. Then, with a *schlurp*, she sucked him into her eager mouth, using the suction to pull herself down on it. She sucked until she had a little more than half of it in her mouth and then released it with a gasp and gurgle.

"That thing is so thick, I don't know if I can get it all in without hurting my jaw," she said. "But I'm going to try."

"Yeah, baby, suck my cock. Let me see you take it in your mouth." He felt much more comfortable talking dirty now.

---

[6] That's called the Adonis Belt. See, this book is both sexy AND educational!

He put his hand on the side of her head and combed her black hair with his fingers. She returned him to her mouth, sucking hard as she did so. She slid it back out and then back in, bobbing her head, working to take more and more of his cock. As she sucked, she jacked him with her hand, using both her mouth and fingers together to stimulate his entire manhood.

"Let me see your tits," said Jake. Tess raised up and peeled off her sports bra, freeing her 32D breasts. He held one in his large hand, kneading it and massaging it. He pulled her closer and sucked a hard nipple into his mouth. He kissed, licked, and sucked both her tits even as she slowly stroked him.

"I'd love to fuck your beautiful tits," he said. "Slide my cock between them." Tess obliged by placing his prick into her cleavage and squeezing her tits together, sliding them up and down around his shaft.

Jake groaned his approval as she continued her ministrations. "That feels amazing," he said after a few minutes. "But now I want to fuck you."

"Oh, fuck," moaned Tess. "I want this monster in my pussy. How do you want me?"

"Bent over the table," growled Jake. She released his cock from her grasp and took off her shorts as he moved behind her. He held her hip with one hand and guided his dick toward her wet pussy, rubbing his cockhead between her lips. She moaned and breathed harder as his fleshy invader pushed her swollen lips apart.

"Fuck me, Jake. Put that thing inside me and fuck me. Make me your slut!"

The peppermint oil, Tess's saliva, and her pussy juices let Jake slide completely inside her with one push. Jake grabbed her waist with both hands and drove himself deeper inside her eager cunt. He slowly pumped himself into her, thrusting deeply with each push.

"Oh, fuck, Jake. That's amazing. Holy shit, your dick is so big. Oh God, I'm so full. My pussy is so full! Oh, God!"

"I love your pussy, Tess. You've got such a hot pussy, and I love being inside you. This is incredible."

"Don't go slow! I need you to fuck me hard. I haven't been fucked in months, and I need you bad!"

Jake obliged, and Tess's big tits swung in circles while he pistoned into her hot pussy, pulling her back as he drove forward, their bodies slapping together. He reached around and squeezed one of her large breasts as he pounded her from behind.

"Rub your clit," he said. "Rub your clit while I fuck your beautiful, wet cunt. Holy fuck, your pussy feels amazing. It's like a velvet glove wrapped around my cock. Oh, I love your wet velvety pussy."

Tess did as she was told and rubbed her clit with her middle finger as Jake drove himself over and over inside her.

"Ohhhh! Ohhhh! Ohhhh!" Tess wailed with each thrust. "Oh fuck, I'm going to cum, Jake. You're going to make me cum." Jake normally used the proper pronunciation of "come" and not "cum," but he wasn't going to complain. Not that he was picky, he just preferred the more traditional pronunciation.

Their bodies continued to clap together as Jake grunted and Tess shrieked. She rubbed her clit faster as Jake pounded her more furiously.

"Ungh! Ungh! Ungh!" he grunted, as she neared her orgasm.

"I'm going to cum, Tess. You're making me cum." Jake switched to her pronunciation so she wouldn't feel awkward, then grabbed her shoulders with both hands and drove himself as deeply as he could, holding himself firmly in place inside her pussy.

"Oh, God, Jake, cum inside me! Fill me up while I cum. Cum with me. I'm going to cum! I'm cumming! I'm cumming! I'm—HOLY FUCK, I'M—AAAAHHHHHH!"

The two lovers experienced simultaneous release, Tess's knees buckling when she came. Jake held onto her waist to keep her from falling even as he fired shot after thick shot of jizz into her tight cunt.

"Ohhhh, fuck. I feel it, Jake! I feel it! I can feel your hot cum inside me," she panted, her back slick with sweat. Jake folded himself over her, wrapping his arms around her waist to keep her from falling.

The two lovers stayed in that position for a few minutes, panting, until Jake shrank and slipped out of her, followed by some of his ... seepage.

"Let's get on the bed," she said. "I need to relax. That was my second workout of the day."

"Me too. I may need another massage," he said.

Tess snuggled up to him, pressing her breasts against his torso, and laying her head on his shoulder. "That can be arranged, but let's skip the regular massage part and get straight to the fucking. Plus, I want you to eat my pussy."

"That can be arranged, too," he said, kissing her forehead.

"We need to hydrate, of course. It's important to stay hydrated," said Tess, using a fancy exercise science word for "drinking plenty of water."

CHAPTER 3

Three days later, on Saturday morning, Jake was at a Farmers Market in one of the parks, strolling around and taking in the sights and smells. He stopped by different booths and food trucks and bought a loaf of bread. He was on the lookout for tomatoes because there's nothing better on a Midwestern summer night than tomato sandwiches.

He stopped by one farm table that bore a large sign, "Fran's and Sheila's Organic Farm," and checked out their vegetables and other items when he heard someone speak. "Anything I can help you with?"

Jake looked up and saw a woman in her late 20s or early 30s, wearing work shorts, hiking boots, and a t-shirt that said, "Farmers do it in the dirt." She was about five feet, five inches, and had shoulder-length straight brown hair pulled back into a ponytail. Her hips were narrow, and her breasts stretched the front of her t-shirt. Jake struggled to maintain eye contact with her.

"I'm just looking for some tomatoes," he said.

"You've certainly come to the right place," she said, and Jake could have sworn she puffed out her chest.

"How, uh, how big are they?"

"Well, you can see for yourself," said the woman, smiling. "They're right in front of you."

Jake thought he was going to come in his pants until she pointed and said, "We have a wide variety of Roma tomatoes, heirloom tomatoes, and my favorite, beefsteak tomatoes."

He looked down and saw that there was, in fact, a wide variety of Roma, heirloom tomatoes, and beefsteak tomatoes on display.

"Oh, uh, yes. There they are. All the tomatoes. From your garden."

"Farm."

"Yes, farm. Tomatoes from the farm. That's what I meant."

"What size do you prefer?" asked the woman, sticking out her chest even farther, a twinkle in her brown eyes. Jake felt his face get hot, and it took everything he had not to glance down again.

"I'm not picky. I like tomatoes of all sizes and kinds. I love anything that I can get my hands on." Jake blushed even deeper and stammered, "Er, that is, I just want something for tomato sandwiches. 'Tis the season, you know. Do you have any you recommend? It's hot in here. Is it getting hot in here?"

The woman laughed at Jake's discomfort. "I happen to like beefsteaks for a tomato sandwich. Just a couple of thick slices with some cheddar cheese, and I'm set for the night."

"I usually just get tomatoes from the grocery store, but I'm on tour and just had a hankering for them today."

"Tour for what?"

"I'm a standup comic. I'm performing at Cookie's this weekend."

"I've been there with friends. It's a fun place, but I don't get to go too much during the summer, of course. But I go during the fall and winter after the season's over."

"Ah, so you're a farmer, too?"

"Too? I thought you were a comic."

"I am. But my parents have a farm, and I worked on it until I went to college. I'm Jake, by the way." He stuck out a hand. She had a firm handshake, and he could feel how strong her fingers were.

"Frances Jacobsen," she said. "You can call me Fran, though."

"Jacobson?"

"No, Jacobsen."

"Hi Fran, it's great to meet you. I'm Jake Nilsen."

"Nellson?"

"No, Nilsen."

"Ah, I thought so. You're from Minnesota, I'll bet. So, are you in the mood for tomato sandwiches right now?" she asked.

"Yes, I just need to find some mayonnaise and salt and pepper."

"Well, I see you have some bread there. I'm done in 10 minutes. If you can wait for me, I'll share my tomatoes if you'll share what you've got."

Jake's face turned bright red once again. "Uh, uh, uh..."

Fran laughed. "Bread. Share your bread. I've even got cheese. And mayo, of course. I like something creamy on my tomatoes." *There! She did it again! I'm* NOT *crazy!* Jake thought as Fran stuck her chest out one more time.

"It's a deal," said Jake, trying not to fall on the ground in a quivering, embarrassed heap. "I'll even help you tear down."

When everything was finished and Fran's truck was loaded up, she grabbed a small cooler and cutting board, and they made their way to a picnic table under a tree.

Jake sliced the tomatoes and prepared the sandwiches. As he worked, Fran shared her story about how she became an organic farmer after college.

"I went to Minnesota State in Moorhead, just over the state line, and got my degree in English literature," she said. "I tried being a high school teacher, but kids just don't want to learn about Walt Whitman and Sylvia Plath in rural North Dakota. So, I gave up teaching and decided to try my hand at organic farming.

"My aunt and uncle owned a farm, but they died in a car accident, so they left it to my sister and me. She is still going to college, so I handle most of the farming. We lease most of the land out to a neighbor, and we manage a couple of acres for organic farming. Both of us work regular jobs to pay the bills, and we grow a lot of our goods over the summer and sell them to restaurants and at the farmers market."

"Well, if these tomatoes are any indication, you and your sister are doing great work. These are amazing. Certainly better than any grocery store tomato."

"Thank you, the secret ingredient is cow manure."

Jake stopped chewing and looked like he wanted to spit out his food.

Fran threw her head back and laughed once more. It was a hearty laugh, and Jake loved how she looked as she laughed from her soul. "I'm kidding! I'm just kidding. You're not allowed to put animal manure on human crops."

"I knew that," said Jake, who didn't actually know that. "But I don't know enough about organic farming to know what you can get away with."

"No, the rules are the same. You can put manure on food that's intended for animals, but not people. No, we use a lot of mulch and yard waste."

The two chatted for a while as the farmer's market continued to empty and people strolled by with their pets and children. An alarm beeped on Jake's phone, and he said, "I have to change clothes and get ready for my show tonight. Would you like to go?"

"To watch you change?" Jake was sure she puffed out her chest again. Her nipples hardened, and he could glimpse a faint outline of them under her shirt, but he quickly looked away. *A gentleman never stares*, he thought, remembering the admonition from Chapter 1.

"Uh, uh, no, I mean, you would, that is, I thought—"

Fran laughed again. "I can tell you're a Minnesota farm boy. You sure do blush easily."

"Oh, and you North Dakota farm girls are so genteel and urbane?"

"Watch it, Gopher. I know what those words mean."

It was Jake's turn to laugh. "Touché. I did mean to go to the show, though."

"Like this? I mean, I should change, shouldn't I?"

"I mean, I'm not one to tell a woman what she should wear. I think you look great. But if you would like to change, the show doesn't start for two hours. I do two sets tonight at 8:00 and 9:30. And if you'd like, we could go out for dinner afterward. Are there any places open after 10:00 here?"

"Yep, there's Flanagan's, the microbrewery near campus. They're open late on the weekends, and the kitchen stays open until midnight."

"Perfect. Do you want to come to the later show? I'll leave a ticket for you at the box office."

"I'd love to. It's a date."

The two hugged before they left, and Jake could feel her large breasts pressed against his stomach. He imagined them to be as large as beefsteak tomatoes and just as firm. She held onto him for a few seconds as he smelled her hair; it smelled like lavender. Jake could feel his cock begin to swell as the two stayed clenched together, and he was sure Fran could feel it, too.

"Someone sure loves tomatoes," she said, giving Jake an extra squeeze so she could push up against his dick. "Maybe I can give you some more later." She winked.

Jake blushed and stammered his goodbye and said he would see her at the club. She stood on her toes, gave him a short-but-not-too-short kiss on the lips, and walked away, turning back to wave at him as she did so. He admired the view and loved watching her tight ass as she walked away. But he didn't look too long, because gentlemen still don't stare.

Jake went back to his hotel room to change and shower, jerking off his eight-and-a-half-inch cock, imagining Fran under him, moaning as he thrust his hard cock in and out of her wet pussy.

"Oh, fuck, Fran!" he groaned as he aimed his spunk at the shower drain. "You're so fucking hot. Take all my come." He hoped that would hold him over. At least he had pronounced "come" the right way.

CHAPTER 4

Jake's show was a big hit to the good people of Fargo, North Dakota, and the crowds, though a little light—"About 80% capacity both shows," Jake texted to Kurt immediately afterward—were extremely enthusiastic and laughed at all the good bits. Jake had recorded both sets, which he would listen to in his truck as he drove to his next destination in Vancouver, BC.[7] Comics often did this so they could figure out which jokes needed work.

And now, he was on foot with his new friend, Francis the farmer, to Flanagan's Fermentables in downtown Fargo. She had greeted him after his second show with a big kiss, slipping her tongue into his mouth and giving him a hint of her intentions.

"Hey, Franny," said the server, as they sat down.

"Hi, Jessica, how's it going?"

---

[7] See *Stand Up, Lie Down, vol. 2: Vanessa in Vancouver.* If you're reading this now, you can just start that one up after you finish this one.

"Oh, you know, college brew-bros being obnoxious douchebags, stiffing us on tips. Same old shit."

"Well, I promise we won't do either," said Jake.

"Speak for yourself," said Fran. "Jessica knows what a handful I can be." The two women laughed.

"Do you remember the end of finals week junior year?" asked Jessica.

"My God, yes! I puked so much, and you lost your shoes," said Fran.

"And we both uh... ended up ... with Bobby Stampfer."

"Oh, yeah," remembered Jessica. "What's he doing now, I wonder?"

"I think he's a youth pastor in Minneapolis. His wife is a dentist."

"Who knew a youth pastor could do all that?"

The two women sighed and appeared lost in their memories with Bobby Stampfer, before shaking themselves out of their reverie.

"Anyway, what'll you have?" asked Jessica.

"I'll have a hefeweizen," said Fran.

"I'll have the same," said Jake.

"Two hefeweizens and I'll leave you alone with the menus," said Jessica. "And each other," she added with a wink.

"So, I'm guessing you two know each other fairly well," said Jake.

"Yeah," said Fran, her cheeks turning a deep red. "We've known each other since high school, and then we both went to college together. She was also an English major, and we lived together on campus for three years. She's married now, and her husband sells insurance."

"Interesting."

"No. No, it's not," said Fran, smiling. "And he's not. He's my insurance agent, so he's given me the lecture on having enough insurance on my farm and making sure I've got the right kind of health insurance. He's really quite boring, but he makes Jessica happy."

"Have you decided what you want?" Jessica asked, popping up out of nowhere.

"Uh, I need a second," said Jake.

"I know what I want," said Fran, looking deeply into Jake's eyes. "Just the house burger with tater tots."

"A burger sounds good. I'll have the BBQ bacon cheeseburger and Caesar salad on the side."

"Great choice," said Jessica, taking the menus from them.

"Nerd," said Fran.

"Hey, more job security for you, right?" said Jake.

The two chatted about their favorite books, their work, and what it was like growing up on a farm. As they ate their cheeseburgers and talked, the restaurant emptied, and Jessica cleared their plates and refilled their drinks, but otherwise left them alone.

After they were finished, they stood outside and noticed it had gotten a lot chillier in the last hour. Fran checked her phone to see the temperature.

"Thirty-six degrees! Fuck, it's cold. I was expecting it to stay in the fifties tonight. And I've got to walk back to the club to get my car!" Fran was wearing a skirt, blouse, and light sweater, something suitable for a warm fall evening, not the early cold snap of winter.

"My hotel is ten minutes over that way. I walked over for the exercise. We can get my truck, and I'll drive you back."

"That's a deal," said Fran. "I just hope I don't turn into a block of ice first. You'll have to carry me over your shoulder." Fran squeezed his shoulder to see if it was up to the task. Her eyes widened as she felt the cannonball under Jake's jacket.

Jake took off his sports coat and draped it over her shoulders. "Never let it be said that Jake Nilsen is so ungallant as to let a lady freeze," he said in a bad British accent.

"Won't you be cold?"

"Cold? Bah! Mine Viking blood shall fend off winter's icy fang!"

"Why are you talking like that?" Fran said, laughing.

"I don't know. I think it's Shakespeare."

"Yes, *As You Like It*."

"Well, yes, I do like it."

Fran laughed her lovely, hearty laugh again. "No, the play. It's from the play, *As You Like It*. It's one of my favorites. Duke Senior said:

"*'Here feel we but the penalty of Adam,*

"*'The seasons' difference, as the icy fang*

"*'And churlish chiding of the winter's wind,*

"'Which, when it bites and blows upon my body,

"'Even till I shrink with cold, I smile."[8]

"Wow, that's impressive. How do you know that?"

"Like I said, it's one of my favorites. Plus, my sister made a needlepoint of that for a pillow at our house a few winters ago when it was really cold. It's on our couch."

As the two walked, the wind picked up, and it began to rain.

"Oh, fuck, I'm freezing!" fussed Fran. "Fucking Fargo forecasts!"

The two ran to Jake's hotel, but even so, it took several minutes, and by the time they arrived, they were both soaked to the skin.

"Oh, shit, I haven't been this cold in a long time," Fran said as her teeth were chattering. "You must be freezing without your jacket."

"I'm not too bad, but yeah, I'm cold. You're a little blue, though."

"Well, it's seasonal affective disorder, but I have a full-spectrum lamp at home."

Jake laughed in spite of their situation. "No, I mean, you look a little blue. Let's go upstairs. We've got to get you warmed up."

"Why, Mr. Nilsen, are you trying to get me out of my clothes?"

"Actually, yes, but not for that reason. Your temperature could drop dangerously if you stay in cold, wet clothes."

"Oh," said Fran, looking a little disappointed.

---

[8] Wow, sex AND Shakespeare? How many other erotica books do that for you? Except maybe "Twelfth Inch."

"I mean, we'll have to get you warmed up while your clothes dry, of course," Jake said with a sly smile.

"I like the sound of that," said Fran. "Lead the way, my Viking warrior."

CHAPTER 5

"Quick, take your clothes off and hang them up in the shower," said Jake, handing Fran some clothes hangers.

"Mr. Nilsen, you're trying to seduce me. Aren't you?" Fran said, teeth still chattering.

"Well, no, I hadn't thought of that. I feel very flattered," answered Jake, repeating Anne Bancroft's response to Dustin Hoffman.[9] "Okay, maybe a little."

"Well, I wouldn't say no," answered Fran.

"Uh..." Jake's brain stalled for a second and then regained its footing. "Either way, you can put on one of my t-shirts while we figure it out." Fran went into the bathroom while Jake slipped into a dry pair of tight boxer briefs and turned the heat up on the in-room thermostat.

---

[9] It's from the the film, *The Graduate* (1967). Google it.

"Ooh," said Fran when she stepped out of the bathroom, Jake's shirt hanging down to mid-thigh. She admired Jake's six-pack abs and his Adonis belt all the really sexy fit guys have, which invariably guides the eye down to…

"My eyes are up here," said Jake, smiling. "Here, get under the quilt and sit on the couch. I'm going to hang up my clothes and get dressed."

"You don't have to do that on my account."

"Yeah, but I want them to dry quickly."

Fran laughed. "No, I mean the getting dressed part, you big goof."

Jake stammered and blushed before he ducked into the bathroom. He returned in a pair of running shorts and a workout shirt, which he insisted on getting a size too small. (Jake wasn't vain by any stretch, but he did like the looks he got when he wore those shirts at the gym.)

"Aren't you cold? You should get under the blanket with me."

Jake quickly complied, and the two snuggled up together. Jake put his arm around Fran and pulled her in tightly, even as she couldn't stop shivering.

"I'm not warming up," she said. "I can't get warm."

"Well, I've heard that if you're really cold, you need to get your body up against someone else so you can exchange heat. We need to get as much of our skin together as we can."

"So, like a seated hug? I like the sound of that," said Fran.

"Sure, like that," he said, his voice getting husky.

Fran straddled Jake and faced him. He put his arms around her and held her close for a few minutes.

"That's helping," she said, still shaking, "but I'm still not warming up very fast."

"I can imagine. You still feel cold to me. We were out in the cold longer than we should have been."

"Skin to skin. We need to be skin to skin," whispered Fran.

Jake took off his shirt as she raised up and took hers off, but was still wearing her bra. Jake noticed that her bra had left wet spots on the shirt.

"At the risk of sounding like a perv, you should take your bra off. It's still wet, and that's going to keep you cold."

"Well, isn't that convenient for you?" Fran said, smiling.

Yes, it is, Jake thought, silently thanking the author.

"Fine. Close your eyes." Jake did as he was told—sort of—as he narrowed them to slits, watching Fran remove her bra, releasing her breasts. He almost popped his eyes open at the sight. *Mmm, they really* are *like beefsteak tomatoes*, he thought, remembering how she repeatedly thrust out her chest at him when they first met.

She snuggled back into him, and he could feel her naked tits pressed against his chest. Jake's cock hardened quickly, pressing against Fran's vulva. She buried her face into the nape of his neck and pressed her lips to his skin. She gave a tiny little moan as she felt the pressure of his dick against her. Fran began grinding herself into Jake's hardness, working her hips back and forth, rubbing her covered lips on his hidden prick.

"It's working," she said. "But I need more. I need to be closer to you."

"We're as close as we can get, aren't we?"

"No, closer." Her voice was hoarse with desire. "Skin to skin. Everything." Fran stood up, letting Jake see her beautiful breasts. Her nipples were a beautiful rose color and stood out like pencil erasers. She removed the shorts she had borrowed from Jake and stood before him, completely nude. She had shaved her pubic hair except for a thin vertical strip, guiding the eye downward to paradise. Jake stood up and removed his shorts, his eight-and-a-half-inch cock springing out and pointing straight at Fran.

"Ooh, did I do that?"

"You did. I've been like this since I met you."

He sat back down and tucked his prick between his legs, while Fran resumed her old position on his lap again, pressing her chest against his. Jake shifted his legs a bit, and his shaft popped up and lightly smacked her vulva. Fran slid her hips back and forth once again, rubbing her naked cunt against his cock, her juices making it slick.

"Ohh, this is better. I'm definitely getting warmer," Fran moaned. "Ohhh, yes."

The two kissed deeply for several seconds, tongues darting in and out of each other's mouths. Jake turned his attention to licking her ear and neck, and Fran gasped when he tongued a specific spot on her neck. Jake focused on that area, and Fran breathed heavily.

"That's so good," she moaned. "I love that. But I want to be closer."

"How can we—?"

"Closer!" Fran slid off Jake's lap and kneeled before him, holding his cock in her strong hand. "I want your big cock inside me; if I can get it to fit. That's as close as two people can get. But first, I want to suck that big monster and taste you."

With that, Fran slid Jake's cock into her eager mouth as deeply as she could. Jake groaned in appreciation as she sucked it like she was trying to drink a thick milkshake. She raised her head, sucking hard along the way, and then dropping her head down again, going a little deeper each time, repeating the process until she had nearly six inches sliding into her throat. It was a rare woman who could suck Jake that deeply into her mouth.

"Holy fuck, I love seeing you suck my cock," said Jake. "God, you're sucking it so deep in your hot mouth. I love your sweet mouth. Suck me in deep, baby. Suck my big cock."

Fran eased up on the suction and bobbed her head up and down on Jake's thick meat, using her hand to jack him off at the same time. She shoved it in as deeply as she could, hitting the back of her throat over and over. He could hear the "Gluk. Gluk. Gluk." as she bottomed out on his dick.

"God, I love that sound. Now I want to fuck your mouth." Jake stood up, and Fran moved to accommodate him.

"Yes! Fuck my mouth, you fucking stud," Fran gasped, jacking him off. "Shove that thing down my throat."

Jake put his hand behind her head and drove deep into her eager mouth, again and again, listening as he hit her gag reflex, "Gluk. Gluk. Gluk." He paused occasionally after shoving his dick as deep as it could go, holding it there until she tapped his thigh and he pulled out. Then she would grab his tight ass again and bob her head back and forth, fucking her mouth with his thick dick once more until she pulled him in and held him there, repeating the process.

Thick ropes of saliva spilled out of her mouth, coating his cock and falling on her naked tits and thighs. Each time she released him, she stroked his shaft, using her honey saliva as lubricant.

"Oh, fuck, I'm going to come," Jake warned, using the proper pronunciation of the word instead of "cum." "I want to come in your hot mouth. Are you ready?"

"Shoot your load in my mouth, stud. Fuck my mouth and come down my throat," she begged. "Give me all your come!" Jake was pleased to note that she also said "come," and not "cum."

Jake resumed his throat-fucking until he moaned, "Get ready, baby. Look at me. Let me see your eyes when I come. Here we go. OH! FUCK! I'M COMING!" She grabbed his ass and held him in place while he fired his hot wad into her eager mouth.

He grunted as the first shot hit the back of her throat. A second and third load followed, and Fran held them in her mouth while Jake stroked his dick a few more times, firing a fourth and fifth shot on her tongue.

She made a big show of rolling his come in her mouth before she swallowed it and then opened her mouth again to show him it was all gone. "Mmmmm, that's so good," she said. "Sweet and salty."

"Ohhhhh, fuck. That was amazing."

"Now I want you to fuck me with that big monster," moaned Fran.

"I'll need a few minutes to recover," Jake said, smiling. "But I'm going to spend it eating your pussy."

"Ooooh, that sounds wonderful." Fran sat down on the couch and pulled her knees up to her chest, holding them and spreading her legs. "Eat my wet pussy, stud. Drive your tongue inside me."

Jake kneeled down before Fran and gave one long lick from her taint up through her wet folds, and flicked it off her clitoris. Fran gasped and smiled as Jake looked up at her, repeating the process, two, three, four more times. Fran's pussy was already wet from grinding on Jake's dick, and he savored her taste as she got wetter and wetter.

"Oh, fuck!" she groaned when Jake sucked her lips into his mouth and pushed his tongue into her heavenly folds. He released the pressure and drove his tongue in and out, fucking her with it. "Oh, my God! You're so good at that. Ohhhh, that feels amazing."

Jake turned his focus to her hard clit, flicking it with his tongue as he slid a finger in between her swollen pussy lips. He fucked her with his thick digit and continued tongue-flicking her pink pearl. She let go of her knees and rested her heels on his muscular back.

"Oh, Jake. I'm almost there! Please make me come, stud. Don't stop doing that, I'm going to come! I want to come in your mouth. Can I come in your mouth?"

"Mm-hmm," said Jake, his mouth full of her lips. "I want to taste your come." He switched his attention to her sopping pussy, driving his tongue back into her folds and rubbing her clit with his thumb. She pulled him deeper toward her.

"OH, SHIT! THAT'S IT! THAT'S IT! I'M GOING TO COME IN YOUR MOUTH! YOU'RE MAKING ME COME! HERE I—AAAAHHHHHH!"

Fran thrashed as her first orgasm crashed over her as Jake continued his frenzied ministrations. "I'M COMING AGAIN, BABY! LICK UP MY JUICES! I'M COMMMIIIIINNNNNGGGG!"

Jake eagerly lapped at the delicious wetness that greeted him, gripping her thighs even as she pulled on him with her heels.

"Oh, fuck! No more! I can't take it. My pussy is sensitive!" Jake released her from his oral grip and smiled up at her, his face shiny with her juices.

"I've never come a second time like that," she gasped. "Hell, I've never had anyone make me come like that a first time! That was amazing!"

"I endeavor to provide gratification, madam," he said in his best British accent (which really wasn't very good).

Fran was now red-faced and sweating, all memories of being cold gone. "I can't believe I came that hard, and you still haven't fucked me. Let me catch my breath for a minute, but I don't want to lose the momentum. I've got to have that prick deep inside me as soon as you can."

"I'm ready when you are," Jake said, leaning back and revealing his re-hardened cock.

"Take me any way you want me."

"How do you feel about doggy style?"

"It's my favorite way of fucking!"

"Get on the bed, then. I'll fuck you anyway you want it."

Fran quickly crawled onto the bed and pointed her ass at her lover. "Ohh, take me, Jakey. Fuck my pussy. Fuck me like an animal."

Jake kneeled behind her and placed one hand on her hip, using his other hand to slide his cock up and down between her labia, wetting his head between her folds. "I've wanted this all day," he said. "I imagined this as soon as I met you."

"I wanted it, TO—OHHH GOD!" she shrieked as he drove himself home, encasing himself in her wet velvet. "Holy fuck, you're so big. Shit, you're going to split me in two! Hold on for a second."

Jake grabbed her hips to hold her still and thrust himself deeply into her wet snatch. She was already wet enough that he slid in without any resistance. He drove himself to his root and held it as she got accustomed to his fleshy invader. She readjusted her position and wiggled her hips, feeling his cock deep inside her. Fran flexed her cunt muscles and squeezed his hardness, making him gasp.

"Now, we're close," she gasped. "This is as close as two people can get, and I wanted this when I met you, too. Now, fuck me with that big dick!"

Jake slid his massive tool out until just the head was nestled between her lips, and then he slammed himself back into place.

"Hoooooooly fuck!" Fran gasped again. "Oh shit, that feels so good."

Jake repeated the withdrawal and driving, slowly at first, his pelvis clapping against Fran's supple ass, causing it to shake with each impact.

"Ohh! Ohh! Ohh!" Fran moaned with each forward thrust. Jake continued pounding her pussy as Fran groaned every time he re-buried himself. He gripped her hips more tightly and pushed her away from him before pulling her back onto his cock.

Soon, he was using her momentum to pull her onto his prick, holding his hips steady, fucking himself with her. The hard rocking motion caused Fran's tits to swing and sway, twirling in circles, which was mesmerizing if someone else had been underneath Fran trying to catch them with their mouth.

"Unnh, unnh, unnh, unnh." Fran's face was slick with sweat. It beaded on her back and dripped off her swirling mounds, even as sweat poured down Jake's face and nearly hairless chest.

"Let's ... change ... now," said Fran, between thrusts. Jake withdrew, and Fran's pussy ached at his absence. She flipped onto her back, spread her legs, and grabbed the back of her thighs to offer herself to her Viking stud.

Jake easily slid back home and pressed his mouth to hers, where she welcomed him with another groan into his mouth. The two kissed, tongues eagerly exploring, giving hints of the other's come as they kissed. Jake felt Fran's wondrous tits pressed against him again as their sweaty bodies slid against one another. She wrapped her legs tightly around Jake's slim waist as he drove his cock deep into her tight pussy.

"Oh, fuck me, you fucking stud! Yes, like that! Please fuck me forever!"

"I'll fuck you as much as you want!" promised Jake, sweat dripping from his face onto hers. "I'll fuck your beautiful pussy forever."

"I'm going to come again, lover! Your cock is going to make me come! Oh, God! I'm coming! I'm ... COMING! OHHH, FUUUUUCK!!" Fran shuddered and shook as her body was wracked with her third orgasm of the night. As she came down from the high, she said, "Come for me, Jakey. I want you to come for me now."

"Where do you want me to come?" he gasped. "I'll come anywhere you want."

She smiled. "What are my options? Where do you want to shoot your load?"

Jake slowed down to make this moment last. "I could fill up your hot, wet pussy. Or I could jack off and finish on your stomach or your beautiful tits. I could shove my cock into your mouth again and jizz down your throat. Or I could fuck your tits until I give you a hot facial."

"We're going to try all of those tonight, but right now, I want your jizz on my stomach. Come on my belly, stud."

Jake jammed himself into Fran several more times before he pulled out and scrambled to his knees. Fran rested her heels on his shoulders and grabbed his cock, jerking him off and pointing him at her.

"That's it. Come for me, baby. Come on me. Shoot your hot come all over me. I want your come on me. Give me that big loa— Oh, fuck!"

"GAAAAHHH!" Jake shouted as he fired his first burst onto Fran, where it landed between her fleshy tits. His second shot nearly reached her chin, leaving a long trail from her chin to her strip of pubic hair. The third shot matched the first one, and he shot two more times, both of which led up to her belly button, pooling in it.

"Hhhhhhholy fuck, that was incredible," said a more-than-satisfied Jake, falling onto his back next to a very happy Fran. "That was amazing. You're amazing." He leaned over and kissed her, then licked her sweaty cheek. Jake tenderly wiped some wet hair off her forehead and kissed her deeply once more.

"You sure know your way around a cock, milady," once more with the bad British accent.

"And you're pretty handy with a pussy, my dear sir," replied Fran, equally badly. "That was wonderful. And I'm finally all warmed up." She blew up at some hair that was still in her eyes. "In fact, I may be a little too warm now."

"I've got an idea," he said. "How about I turn the heat down, and we take a shower to cool off?"

"That's a great idea. But not too cold, because I want you to fuck me again and deliver on your come promises."

"You've got a deal, Fran Jacobson."

"Jacobsen," she said with a laugh.

Vanessa
in Vancouver

Table of Contents

CHAPTER 1

"**W**elcome to Canada, and welcome to Vancouver," said the passport official, handing Jake's passport back to him.

"Thank you very much," said Jake Nilsen, smiling and returning the passport to his backpack. He walked through the Vancouver International Airport, looking up at the signs that directed him to the car rental desks.

As he walked, Jake thought back to his conversation with his manager, Kurt, before he left.

"You're sending me to Vancouver? That's actually pretty cool," Jake said.

"I know. We're able to call this your North American tour, and now you can say you're an internationally known comedian," said Kurt.

"I don't know if I'd go that far," said Jake. "That makes it sound like I've performed in Europe or Asia."

"Do you want me to book you in Europe or Asia?" Kurt asked, somewhat seriously.

"I wouldn't say no, but let's see how this tour goes. Maybe the author will have it in her to write a third series."

"What?"

"What? Never mind. I just said the narration out loud." Jake waited through an awkward silence. "Anyway, so where am I playing this weekend?"

"You'll be at a club called Doughnuts."

"Donuts?"

"No, Doughnuts. You're in Canada, so that's how they spell it. I'll text you the information, and your car is equipped with GPS so you'll be able to navigate there. It's in a part of town called Dickens."

"Oh, really? Do you think I should do a joke about—"

"No. They had a comic there a few months ago who did that, and they fired his ass. No dick jokes."

"I was going to say Charles Dickens, you ass."

"Oh, that's okay then. Yeah, just no dick jokes in Dickens. They get—"

"Pissed off?" Jake said and then laughed out loud at his own joke.

"Seriously, dude. Just don't."

"Did you tell Curtis?"

Kurt said that yes, he had informed Curtis Sanders, one of Jake's good friends on the comedy circuit. Kurt had booked the two comics at a few of the same places during Jake's Wild West tour, with Jake headlining some of the time, and Curtis the others. The two often worked together and had a long-standing tradition of sharing stories of their sexual conquests, as you will see in Chapter 2. Whoever told the steamiest story, the other person bought dinner.

Jake found his rental car and punched the address into the GPS, following the directions until he reached the Doughnuts Comedy Club.

"Hi, I'm looking for Caitlyn," Jake said to a passing server. It was 2:00, and lunch was winding down, with just a couple of tables occupied.

"I can take you to her. What's your name?"

"I'm Jake. Jake Nilsen."

"Neilsen?"

"No, Nilsen. I'm the headliner this weekend."

"Hi, Jake-Jake Nilsen. I'm Vanessa, I'm the front-of-house manager." She extended her hand.

Vanessa was five feet tall and Asian, with short black hair in a spiky cut, and several earrings in each ear. She wore yoga workout pants and looked like she kept in shape. She was thin and not curvy, but looked strong. Jake had noticed that her thighs appeared especially muscular. Being a swimmer and workout fiend himself, he tended to notice things like that.

"It's nice to meet you," said Jake, shaking her hand; her fingers could barely wrap around his palm. She eyed him up and down, taking in his 6'3" frame, blond hair and glasses, and swimmer's build with wide shoulders and a tapered waist. As their hands touched, she flashed a vision of Jake wearing Viking clothes and wielding a mighty sword.

"Have you ever been to Vancouver, Jake-Jake? You seem a little familiar."

"No, I haven't, but I get that a lot."

"What, people think you've been to Vancouver a lot?"

Jake laughed. "No, the looking familiar thing. I look like Tony, the first terrorist to get killed during *Die Hard*."

"That's what it is!" Vanessa said, snapping her fingers and pointing at him. "Your feet aren't as small as his, are they?" She looked down at Jake's size 13s and remembered the old adage about men with big feet. Her eyes widened as she imagined the possibilities.

"No, not at all. I get asked that a lot, too."

"And the 'Ho Ho Ho' thing?"

"I went as him to a Halloween party once. I wrote 'Ho Ho Ho' on a gray sweatshirt and then just sat on a chair in bare feet the entire night."

Vanessa laughed at the image and said, "I'll bet you were real fun that night."

"Yeah, I don't like big crowds, so it was a great way to be at the party without having to talk to a lot of people."

"But you're a comic. Don't you want big crowds?"

"There, yes. Because I'm only on stage for an hour, and then I can leave and hide out in the back until they all leave."

"I'm the same way. Working here is fun, but it drains my energy. Let me take you back to Caitlyn so I can get back to work." Vanessa guided Jake through some tables to the restroom hallway and went to the farthest door in the back. She knocked and opened the door.

"Caitlyn, Jake-Jake Nilsen is here to see you."

"Neilsen?" asked Caitlyn.

"No, Nilsen," said Vanessa.

"Hi, Caitlyn, it's great to meet you. I'm looking forward to this weekend."

"Me too," said Caitlyn. "Sorry, I'm just finishing lunch," she said, sticking a forkful of waffles in her mouth. "Want a bite?"

"Um, no, thank you. But that does look good. Are you guys still serving lunch?"

"Sure," said Vanessa. "I can take care of you. Just come out and find me when you're done in here." She smiled and headed back out to the dining area.

"She's so great," said Caitlyn. "She was already working here when I bought the place, and when I saw how good she was, I kept her on and made her the front-of-house manager. She's a competitive skier, too. Skis early in the morning and then works the lunch and dinner shifts."

"She seems pretty nice."

"Oh, she's a sweetheart." Caitlyn took another bite of waffles. "So, you want the key to the club apartment, I'll bet. There are towels in the linen closet, and both beds have been made up. Curtis got there earlier today, so you can fight over who gets the big room. He's emceeing the open mic tonight, so I hope you don't mind that."

"No, that's fine," said Jake. He hated open mics but recognized that this was how every comic got their start. Plus, the emcee usually got 50 bucks for their effort, so he was willing to suffer through them whenever he middled; the headliner never emceed an open mic. Jake even liked to talk with the seasoned amateurs and give them some advice and feedback, but that was rare.

"So, did you fly in or drive in?"

"I flew up from Portland and left my truck at the airport."

"I don't blame you. It's about 500 kilometres, and traffic's a pain in the ass," said Caitlyn, using the Canadian spelling of "kilometers."

The two changed a few more pleasantries before Jake headed back out to the dining room for a late lunch.

"So, you ready to eat, Jake-Jake?" asked Vanessa. She guided him to a table.

"Sure, what do you recommend?"

"Oh, it's all good, but I love the burgers. Let me get you a menu."

"No need. Can I just get a cheeseburger with peanut butter and jalapeños? And some fries and a side of mayo?"

"Peanut butter and jalapeños? That's an unusual pairing."

"I tried it when I was on tour once and loved it. So now that's my standard go-to burger. Of course, I shouldn't get the fries, but I need to go for a run tonight, so I figure I can spoil myself a little."

"Are you a runner?" asked Vanessa.

"No, I'm actually a swimmer, but I run whenever I can't find a pool."

"There's a YMCA not too far from where I live, and they've got a pool. I'm going there this evening to work out. If you want, I can take you as my guest."

"That would be great. I haven't had a good swim in a couple of weeks."

"Excellent. I'll get your number from you and text you the details." Vanessa went off to place Jake's order and take care of the remaining patrons still in the restaurant. When she brought Jake's burger out, she handed him a card with her phone number and an address on it.

"I'll get there at 6:00, and I'll probably hit the weights. If you'd like, we can shower there and go out for a drink afterward."

"That sounds great. I'd love that."

After lunch, Jake said he was looking forward to the evening, and he stuck out his hand to shake hers, but she held her arms out for a hug, so he leaned over and embraced her. She was so small that he had to bend way over to give her a proper hug, which saved him the embarrassment of rubbing his crotch on her.

"I'm looking forward to it, too," she murmured in his ear.

Jake found the apartment without any difficulty and parked in the assigned spot. He got off the elevator on the right floor and found the apartment.

"Jakey Nilsen, is that you? I've got a good story for you this time!" he heard a voice call. "I hope you're ready because I'm feeling especially hungry."

CHAPTER 2

CURTIS IN CEDAR RAPIDS

Jake and Curtis hugged the way men do: sharp thumps on the back and squeezing each other as tightly as possible, to show they aren't actually gay because this isn't that kind of book. If you're looking for that, check out Dominic N. Ashen's great *Steel & Thunder* series.[10]

"So, what've you been up to, Jakey Nilsen?" Curtis asked. Curtis was Black, skinny, and stood nearly as tall as Jake. His long, gangly arms and legs made him look more like an awkward teenage nerd than a 28-year-old man, which he used as part of his act.

The two talked and shared stories of the road and discussed their upcoming plans—Curtis was also represented by Jake's agent, so they were booked in a few different places together.

---

[10] *Rowr!*

Finally, they got down to business.

"It's contest time!" said Curtis. "Whatcha got for me?" The two comics regularly traded stories about their sexual adventures whenever they met up. Whoever had the hotter story, the other person had to buy dinner. Right now, Curtis was leading the competition, five to two.

Jake settled into the couch, making sure to cover his crotch with a throw pillow because he knew this was an especially hot story. Considering he hadn't seen Curtis for several months[11], he had several to choose from, but he needed the win. So, he relayed the entirety of Chapter 2 from *Stand Up, Lie Down: Carrie on Campus* in a brazen attempt to get you to go buy a copy.

In it, Jake met Lynn and Krissi at a local restaurant, received a blowjob from them both, and then ate both women's pussies until they came from his hot oral ministrations. All while in the parking lot against Krissi's car.

"And then we went back to Krissi's place and fucked all night," Jake concluded. "At one point, Lynn was laying on top of Krissi, making out and mashing their tits together, and I was fucking one and then the other, switching between the two."[12]

"Wow, that was a good one," said Curtis. "I may not be able to top that one. But I'll try."

This is Curtis's story:

So you remember my girlfriend Anna and her friend, Debi? Yeah, this doesn't involve them. We're all living together in Louisville

---

[11] See *Stand Up, Lie Down, volume 1: Alyssa in Atlanta*

[12] That part wasn't in the original book. I added it here for your enjoyment. You're welcome. —CV

now. I'm on the road a lot, but when I'm home, we fuck like rabbits. We have an open relationship, so I get to enjoy myself when I'm on the road, and they get to find someone and enjoy themselves, too.

No, this time, I was in Cedar Rapids, Iowa about three months ago. It's not a big city, only about 130,000 people or so, and they've only got the one comedy club. But when I was there, I was a goddamn celebrity. I headlined for a three-day weekend and got the royal treatment.

Anyway, it was my second night, Friday night, at Chuckle Chunks, and this bachelorette party was there. These six women are getting hammered during my set, and they're laughing their asses off at everything I'm saying.

No, not just because they were drunk, Jake. I'm fucking hilarious!

Anyway, it was my last set of the night, and the bachelorettes asked me to join their party. I figured I had a pretty good shot at scoring with one of them, and they were all pretty hot. I like my women with some meat on their bones, and I was in Heaven.

No, I didn't score with all six. This isn't some stupid-assed Literotica story. But I did hook up with this one girl, Alice, and one of her friends, Jesse. Alice was a White girl, blonde, tall, very curvy with huge tits. She was a high school teacher, and yeah, she was the bride-to-be. Okay, this is like a stupid-assed Literotica story.

I finished my last set at 10:00—they close 'em up early in Cedar Rapids—so we headed out to a bar. We were doing Jager bombs at a bar near the college, and people were coming and going until it was just me, Alice the bride, and Jesse, her maid of honor. Jesse was short and skinny, with brown hair and brown eyes, and she wore glasses. She was kind of meek and mousy and teaches art at the same school as Alice.

They didn't want the party to end, so we Ubered back to the club apartment. By this time, Jesse was into me. Shut up, man, she was!

It must have been the alcohol because she had been real mild-mannered all night. She laughed at my jokes during my set, but real quiet like. But as the night went on, she got a little crazier and was laughing out loud at everything. I could tell she wasn't used to drinking because it only took a few shots to get her out of her shell. And she'd say shit like, "I've never had this much to drink before" and "I hope I don't get too crazy." But this chick's idea of crazy was wearing a funny hat at a bachelorette party, so I don't know what I was expecting.

Anyway, she sat next to me whenever she could and rubbed her hand on my thigh. She'd graze my cock on occasion and once even kissed me full-on in the bar. We started making out in the backseat in the Uber, and I swear the driver was watching us in the rearview mirror. She didn't look like she approved of a Black guy and a White girl together, so when we got to the apartment, I winked at her. I still gave her a good tip though, 'cause I ain't a dickhead.

We get up to the apartment, and I sit down on the couch. Alice goes to the bathroom, and Jesse plops down on my lap, facing me. We start making out again, and she starts grinding her pussy on my dick, which is already hard as a rock. She's wearing a skirt, so there's not much separating us.

I figure we can do this until Alice comes out and wants to leave again, so I immediately go for Jesse's tits. They were kind of small, but she was into it. I reached up under her blouse and undid her bra. I start massaging her tits, and her nipples get hard, and she starts moaning into my mouth.

"Oh, God, that feels so wonderful," she says. "I love that. Keep doing that." She unbuttons her shirt without ever breaking off from kissing me and shrugs out of it, then takes off her bra. She had some small tits, maybe a B cup, but I don't care. Her nipples were like pencil erasers. I ran my thumbs over them, and she starts moaning louder. She's grinding on my cock harder and is breathing harder, and I think she's about to come.

Then I hear this voice behind me. "What the hell, you guys?" We look, and it was Alice. I think she's gonna get all pissy and leave. Instead, she says, "That looks so fucking hot," and she climbs onto the couch next to us and starts kissing me.

Jesse says, "What about John?"

"I don't give a fuck," says Alice. "I think he's sleeping with Shelley." And she starts making out with me. Jesse starts licking my neck and my ear, which really turns me on. Jesse's still grinding on my cock, so I grab her ass and keep moving her.

Alice stands up and takes off her dress and is just wearing her bra and panties, a black lacy number. She's got some monster titties, must have been a double D, and she's got a big booty, so I'm in love.

I say, "Let me see those beautiful titties," and she takes off her bra. I start sucking on those tits and kissing and licking them all over while Jesse's going after my neck. Alice starts moaning because I'm sucking on her hard nipples like I'm trying to get a milkshake through a straw. I guide Jesse's head to Alice's other tit, and she hesitates.

"Do it," Alice says, and she grabs the back of Jesse's head. Jesse kisses Alice's nipple a few times and then sucks it into her mouth very delicately. Alice throws her head back and moans. She says, "I'm so wet right now."

I reach down and feel Alice's pussy through her panties, and she's soaked. I rub her pussy a few times and then move her panties aside to slide in one of my fingers.

"Oh, fuck. Fuck, that's so good," she says. By this time, Jesse is totally into sucking Alice's big tits because she's holding one in both hands and massaging it while she's sucking. She looks at what I'm doing to Alice's pussy, so she stands up and takes off her skirt and panties.

"Do that to me," she orders. I put my other hand down on the couch, and she mounts my finger and starts fucking herself on it. "Oh, my God. That's wonderful. This is so naughty. I love it."

Now Alice takes off her clothes and then helps me take off my pants. Jesse is still riding my finger, and she's grabbing my arm to steady herself. When Alice gets my underwear off, I hear her gasp, and she takes my cock in her hand. She kneels down and takes me in her mouth. She really goes to work on it, jabbing her mouth down on my cock like she's punishing one of us, me or her, I don't know. I could feel my cock hit the back of her throat and she's going "Gulk, gulk, gulk" as she's jamming my cock into her mouth.

Meanwhile, Jesse is humping my hand as I'm rubbing her clit with my thumb and she's moaning louder. She's going, "Oh, fuck, I'm gonna come. Oh, fuck, I'm gonna come," and then her body tenses up, and she squeezes my arm like she's about to fall off a cliff and chokes off a scream. She buries her face in my shoulder for a few seconds. She's all sweaty and her hair is plastered to her forehead. She finally looks up at me, my finger is still buried in her cunt, and she says, "That was amazing. I've never come like that before."

I say, "Have you ever done anything like this before?"

"No, not at all. I've only ever had sex with one guy before, and that was in college. We were both virgins, and we were pretty bad at it. He would come, but I usually had to finish myself off in the bathroom. We only dated for three weeks before I broke it off with him."

All that time, Alice is still sucking my cock, going "gulk, gulk, gulk." Jesse kisses me hard on the mouth and says, "I want to try that." So she pulls herself off my finger, and I look her dead in the eye while I suck her juices off my finger. She gives a little shudder and kneels down next to Alice.

"Let me have some of that," she said to Alice. So Alice sits back and holds my cock for Jesse.

"Have you ever done this before?" she says.

"Only one time with Jacob, and he came in my mouth immediately."

"How was it?"

"I gagged because I was surprised, and spit it out, but the aftertaste was pretty good. But he never wanted to do it again because he thought it was dirty."

"It's supposed to be dirty. That's the whole point," Alice says. "Let me help you." And she guides Jesse's head down to my cock.

Jesse wraps her fingers around my shaft, which looks like a monster in her tiny hand. She kisses the tip and then gives it a lick while she's jacking me off. She licks the tip a few more times and then takes my cock head into her mouth and sucks on it for a few seconds. "Like this?" she says.

"Yes, but take as much as you can without gagging," Alice says.

"Also, try not to use your teeth," I say because I'm helpful that way.

"Sorry," Jesse says and then returns to my cock. She's able to take about two or three inches into her mouth—this time without teeth, thank God—and gets a good rhythm going.

Alice puts her hand on the back of Jesse's head and pushes a little bit each time so Jesse is able to work in another inch, and she's nearly halfway down my shaft.

Yes, it *is* eight inches, jackass! Well, seven-and-a-half.

Anyway, Alice stands on the couch and positions her pussy right over my face, so I do what any good man would do and start tonguing her pussy. She was completely shaved, and I go to town, lapping up her wet cunt and sucking on her fat, meaty lips. She's got her hands on the wall, holding herself up, and I start licking up her pussy and over her clit. Alice is moaning like a horny ghost, going, "Ohhhhhh. 'Ohhhhhh." Then she starts swearing at me. "Oh, that's it, eat my fucking pussy, goddammit. Lick my cunt, you motherfucker, I'm gonna come on your fucking face." It was so hot that I started shoving my tongue into her cunt and rubbing her clit with my thumb. Her legs are trembling a little bit because I'm good at this. Meanwhile, Jesse's gotten into a really good rhythm on my dick, sucking it and jacking off my shaft.

I look down at Jesse and keep rubbing Alice's clit with my thumb. I warn her, "I'm gonna come, Jesse. Get ready, I'm gonna come in your mouth, baby," but she speeds up and starts shoving my dick deeper. Pretty soon, I shoot my first shot into her mouth.

I hear her go, "Mmf!" but she seals her lips around my dick and holds on like a champ. Another one fires out, and she goes, "Mmf!" again, and then does that for a third and fourth shot. She raises up, and my fifth one gets her right on her chin. She looks up at me, my come dripping from her chin, and looks like she's wondering what to do with a mouthful of come. After a few seconds, she swallows hard and blinks a few times.

"Ohhhhh, fuck. That tastes amazing," she said, smiling like she was surprised. "That was sooo good. I'm gonna want that again." She scoops my come off her chin and pops it in her mouth, sucking on her finger to get it nice and clean.

"Hey, don't forget about me. I still want to come on your face," Alice says. So I turn my attention back to her bald pussy hanging over me, and I start eating. Jesse kneels on the couch and starts sucking one of Alice's tits again. Alice is moaning and grinding her cunt on my face, so I keep eating and rubbing her clit while Jesse is sucking her nipples.

Pretty soon, Alice is breathing hard and moaning, "This is it, you guys. I'm gonna come. Curtis, I'm gonna come on your face. Oh my God, here I come!" and she throws her head back, and her pussy floods right into my mouth. Man, she had some sweet juices, and I lapped them all up. When she finishes, she climbs down, and I kiss Jesse so she can taste Alice on my mouth. She slides her tongue in and out of my mouth, groaning the entire time.

The three of us cuddle on the couch, and I take turns kissing each of them as we cool down. I ended up fucking them both a few times before the night was over—Jesse was especially into it. She was so tiny I could barely get my whole cock into her, but she was finally able to take it all, and I buried myself balls deep into her. Turns out that little mousy girl is a real beast when she gets going.

Me and Jesse ended up fucking all weekend while Alice went home. She confronted her fiancée about Shelley and told him about us. Jesse texted me and said that rather than breaking up, those two decided they wanted an open relationship. They still got married, and Jesse joins them on the weekends. One time, Alice and Jesse joined Shelley, and they all fucked the shit out of John. Then Jesse put on a strap-on and fucked both girls. Turns out, she's now the dominant one in that relationship. Who knew that mousy little girl would end up being the dominant one?

"Wow, that was a great story," admitted Jake, hiding his throbbing erection under the throw pillow. Curtis was similarly covered with his sweatshirt. "I think it's a close call this time. I'd almost call it a draw."

"Yeah, but you ate those women *and* got a double blowjob outside in public. I think the tiebreaker goes to you."

"That makes it five to three, you," said Jake. "Finally! I didn't think I was ever going to get another win."

"Clearly, the secret is to fuck two women," said Curtis.

"Remind me to tell you about what happened in Birmingham.[13] It was especially hot."

"Don't spoil it for me! Wait until next time we're together."

"Definitely. Although I may just keep that story to myself."

The two made plans for dinner now that it was Curtis's turn to buy. Jake headed off to the shower and jacked off while he was in there, remembering Krissi and Lynn and dreaming about heading back to Abraxus Tasker College for a repeat performance.

Meanwhile, Curtis locked the door in his room, took a picture of his cock, and sent it in a text message.

------

[13] See *Stand Up, Lie Down: Betty In Birmingham.* It's my favorite! —CV

"Thinking of you," Curtis wrote.

A photo came back of a pink pussy with a thin brown patch of hair above it, a pair of fingers holding the lips wide open.

[Thinking of you, too. Can't wait to get you back to Cedar Rapids and buried back inside my wet cunt. Alice says hi.]

Curtis jerked off into some paper towels, moaning Jesse's name, and buried the evidence in the kitchen garbage can.

Chapter 3

J ake met Vanessa at the Y at 6:00, and they greeted each other with a quick hug. Jake was carrying a small gym bag, and Vanessa was already dressed to work out—black yoga shorts and a navy-blue sports bra—carrying her own bag.

"If you want to swim, I can sign you in, and you can do your own thing. Then we'll meet back in the lobby at 7:30. Will that work?" said Vanessa.

"That would be wonderful," said Jake. "I haven't had a good swim in a few weeks. Then do you still want to get dinner?"

"Sure, there's a French bistro nearby. I'm friends with the owner; I'll text her about saving us a table."

Jake began his workout at the pool, dressed in his long bike short-style suit called swim jammers. The pool was fairly empty, so he picked a lane and began his warmups. Jake's strokes were smooth and clean, born of years and years of practice at his middle school, high school, and college pools.

Jake had been a competitive swimmer growing up in Mankato, Minnesota. His family owned a farm, and he had to work with his father most mornings. By the time he was in high school, Jake realized that he could get out of his farm chores if he focused on being a long-distance competitive swimmer, specializing in the 1,500-meter events.

That meant getting up at 4:00 a.m. every morning and practicing for two hours before school, followed by regular practice after school. He thought he was pulling a fast one on his dad, except his dad knew that by working to get out of his chores, Jake was working much, much harder than he would have if he had just stayed a farmer.

As Jake reflected on all of this, he was struck by the same realization his dad had, and he stopped and treaded water as he let that moment of cognitive dissonance settle over him. Then he smiled and continued on.

Jake had been one of the best high school swimmers in Minnesota and a top-notch swimmer in college at the University of Minnesota. But being the best swimmer in Minnesota is like being the best oboe player in Alabama.

Still, Jake was just a fraction of a second from becoming an alternate on the Olympic swim team. Not that it bothered him too much. He had also started investing in rental apartments in college, and by the time he graduated, he was making a six-figure income from his rentals.

A few years later, with some investment help from his old high school teammate, Alan, who had gone on to become a financial advisor, Jake was now a part-owner of two car washes in Miami and a strip mall in the tourist section of Savannah, Georgia. So he wasn't rich, but he could see rich from his house.

Not that Jake ever had much time for a house. He was on the road as a working comic nearly nine months out of the year, going home between tours and for holidays. He kept all his stuff at his parents' house and just rented long-term Airbnbs when he wasn't traveling.

Jake loved to read, and visited used bookstores in every city he visited, buying old murder mystery and science fiction paperbacks. Whenever his truck started getting too full of books, he would pack them up and ship them back to his parents in Mankato.

Jake churned out lap after lap, his body feeling good, although he knew he was going to pay for it tomorrow. He felt like he was in training again, so he kept going, kept up a near-race pace, counting in his head: *17... 18... 19...* all the way to 30 laps. He stopped and held onto the side of the pool as he checked his time. He was only two minutes slower than his personal best, but reminded himself that he hadn't picked up the pace until he was nearly halfway through.

He briefly wondered if he still had what it took to get back into competitive swimming. He still had the build for it: slim waist, broad shoulders, and a set of abs you could grate cheese on, including the hot little V found on the cover of most romance novels. Then he remembered what it actually took to compete at that level, and he decided he liked his current life a lot better. He got to see different parts of the country, he got to make people laugh, and there was no more of this up-at-four-in-the-morning bullshit.

Plus, there was the sex. Such great sex. Oh, sure, he'd had sex in college. How could you be an athlete and not have sex? His favorites were the swimmers from the women's team.

But Jake's coach had been one of the old-school guys who believed that sex sapped your energy, and he had his swimmers on a strict "no sex during the season" rule. Jake didn't strictly follow it, but it was still a pain in the ass. Now, he could wake up when he wanted, have sex whenever he wanted, and make a whole lot more money than competitive swimmers ever did.

His thoughts drifted to Vanessa, his new friend, as he got out of the pool. He padded to the locker room and began to shower. There were private shower stalls, so he could let his thoughts drift wherever they wanted. They drifted over Vanessa's body, and he imagined the petite Asian woman straddling his cock, squeezing him with her powerful skier's thighs, his hands cupping her small breasts. He grew hard as he imagined her impaling herself on his eight-and-a-half-inch cock, her head thrown back, ass slapping on his thighs, and small breasts bouncing as she fucked him cowgirl style.

Jake wrapped his long fingers around his shaft and began to jerk himself off. If he was going to have sex tonight, he wanted to make sure he got his first orgasm out of the way. He always lasted much longer the second time around.

In Jake's mind, he and Vanessa changed positions. Now she was lying on a table as he was standing up—hey, like the name of this series!—holding her ankles and driving his thick cock into her pussy. The table was rocking, and Vanessa was moaning with every thrust as he drove himself into her tight cunt.

Jake stifled a grunt as he came, aiming his jizz jets at the shower drain, hoping no one was around to hear him.

The coast was clear as he stepped out of the shower and dried off. He got dressed and met Vanessa in the lobby. She was dressed in black leggings and a t-shirt emblazoned with the name of a ski brand, plus a puffy vest to ward off the fall chill. She also wore lightweight hiking boots, which looked almost too heavy for her shapely, slender legs.

"How was your workout?" she asked, extending her arms for another hug. He bent over and squeezed her lightly, trying not to snap her back as she contorted backward to accommodate his height.

"Great. I'll be paying for it tomorrow, but it felt good. I haven't put in a swim day like that in months. It reminded me of my days in college."

"Cool. I did arms and back, plus I rode the bike."

"Oh, yeah, Caitlyn says you're a skier?"

"Yep. Not quite a pro, but I'm pretty competitive in the amateur circuit around the province."

"Do you ever want to go pro?"

"Oh, I might. I mean, I get some sponsorships and things like that now, but I can never quite crack that line. So I'm pretty happy just doing what I do. I'll probably head back to grad school in a year or two and study exercise science so I can be a ski coach. In the meantime, I just enjoy the ride and live in the moment. So, are you ready to eat? Celine said she's saving us a table."

CHAPTER 4

It was already dark as the two took Jake's truck to Celine's Bistro, where they were shown a table in the back corner. They perused the menus, and Vanessa asked, "Do you want to split some oysters? I hear they're good for your libido."

Jake's face grew hot. Could she tell he had jacked off in the shower?

"Sure, I mean, if that's something you think you need."

"Oh, my libido is just fine, Jake-Jake. I'm just looking out for you."

"My libido is pretty good, er, Van-Van. Bleah, that doesn't work."

Vanessa laughed. "My friends usually call me Vanny or sometimes Nessie. Like the Loch Ness Monster. But please call me Vanessa. I like the way you say it."

"It's my Norwegian Minnesota accent. Some people think I'm from Canada."

"Oh, no way, not sounding like that. I mean, you sound a little bit Canadian, and I see why most Americans may think so, but we can spot the Minnesotans and the North Dakotans a kilometre away," she said, using the Canadian pronunciation of "kilometer," again.

Their oysters arrived with all the accouterments, and Vanessa showed Jake how to eat them with a little hot sauce and lemon. Afterward, she ordered a chicken salad sandwich, while Jake ordered the grilled salmon.

"So did they work?" Vanessa asked, resting her hand high up on Jake's thigh. Jake's dick stiffened as she squeezed his thigh a few times.

"Well, they're not *not* working," he said. He placed his hand on her thigh and slid it up toward her pussy. Jake wondered if all Canadian women were all this forward.

"No, we're not all this forward," she said as if reading his mind.

Is she reading my mind? he wondered. *Or is she reading the narrative?*

The author assured him that she wasn't reading his mind and that she couldn't read the narrative either—it was just a lucky guess on her part.

"It was just a lucky guess on my part," Vanessa said with a laugh. "I know you're only in town for a few days and I didn't want to waste time with that silly mating dance ritual bullshit. You're only here for three nights, and I didn't want to waste any time. Besides, Curtis told me you were a good fuck."

"Whoa!" exclaimed Jake just as the food arrived. "First, thank you, Curtis. Two, how does Curtis even know? And C, did you ask him, or did he just offer that up out of the blue? 'You should meet my friend, Jake. He's a good fuck.'" He stuck his hand out and introduced himself. "Hi, there. Jake Nilsen, damn good fuck."

Vanessa laughed a deep, throaty laugh that was surprisingly big for such a small woman. "No, I slept with him the last time he was here. We had a good time, but I didn't want to turn it into a repeat performance. I like variety."

"It's the spice of life," quipped Jake, wishing he hadn't sounded so lame.

Vanessa rested her hand on Jack's stiff cock and squeezed it through his jeans. Even through a layer of denim and cotton underwear, Jake could feel the strength of her grip. She squeezed up and down the length of his dick and inhaled sharply when she realized its size.

"One of the other waitresses wanted a crack at him this weekend," she added. "Besides, I think you're much bigger and I'm going to enjoy feeling this slide into my pussy."

Jake choked on a bite of his salmon and washed it down with a slug of his beer. "I mean, do I get a say in any of this?"

"Sure. Do you want to have sex with me tonight?"

"Absolutely," he said without hesitation.

"There, you had a say." She took a bite of her sandwich, set it back down, and returned to massaging his erection through his jeans. "Look, I don't get hung up on sex. I enjoy it, it feels good, and I like to do it for recreation and pleasure. I like skiing and going fast down a mountain. I drive fast, and I ride my mountain bike fast. And I believe in telling a guy when I want to sleep with him, rather than drawing a relationship out to the third date only to find out he's a total dud or lives with his mommy. So if you're ready and willing,

I want to take you back to my place and ride you like I stole you, because Curtis is probably boning Therese at the comics' apartment by now. My pussy is wet, and I want to fuck you right now."

"That sounds like a great plan, and I'm excited to be a part of it!" Jake half-shouted and then looked around to see if other people heard him.

Vanessa waved down their server. "Check, please."

CHAPTER 5

"Have a seat," said Vanessa, pointing at her couch. Her apartment was small, with the kitchen and living room in one big space, with a door for a bedroom and a bathroom. It was clean but cluttered. There were skis stacked up against the wall, poles hanging from a hat rack, three pairs of ski boots in the corner, and a pile of skiing magazines on the coffee table.

Jake sat in the middle of the couch while Vanessa turned on the stereo in the living room and poured two glasses of wine.

"Forgive the decor," she said over her shoulder. Jake admired her toned ass and legs as she walked around. He couldn't wait to see those legs wrapped around his waist. Or neck. "If I'm not working, I'm skiing. And rather than spend money on rent for a bigger place or a garage, I just keep my stuff in my house. I rarely have anyone up here, so I'm not too worried about how it looks."

"It looks fine to me. I'm on the road so much, I don't even have a place. I just stay in a long-term Airbnb when I'm off."

Vanessa handed Jake a glass of wine and took a big drink from hers. "Curtis said you're rich though. Why don't you have a big-assed house or something?"

"No, not rich, just okay.[14] I don't want a house that I don't live in nine months out of the year."

"You know what? I'm bored. I wanna fuck." Vanessa set down her wineglass and kneeled down in front of Jake. "If this thing is as big as I think it is, I can't wait to get my mouth around it." She undid Jake's belt and unzipped his pants, fishing his hardening cock out and gazing at it.

"I was wrong. It's bigger." Vanessa slowly stroked his prick and studied it closely, kissing it lightly in different spots. Her hands were small, so she had farther to stroke, which suited Jake just fine. "Oh, yeah, it's *much* bigger."

Vanessa licked the underside of his cock, from balls to tip in one stroke, then kissed the head a few times. She stuck her tongue on Jake's slit and cleaned off the first drop of pre-come that had formed there.

"Mmmm, sweet." She raised up, took off her shirt and sports bra, and Jake admired her body. Her abs were tight, and he could see a faint outline of a six-pack on her flat tummy. Her breasts were small, but her nipples were already hard. He reached out and gently pinched them both before massaging her tits in his large hands. He then took off his own shirt and slid his pants and underwear off. Vanessa stood and did the same. She bent over to slide her leggings off over her ankles, and Jake could see her tight ass and her vulva peeking out between her legs. Her pussy glistened with her juices, and Jake reached out to touch it.

---

[14] Jake's just being modest. He's rich.

"Ah, ah, me first," she said, turning to face him. Jake saw that she had shaved her pussy so that her remaining pubic hair formed a lightning bolt. She noticed him staring.

"My own little joke. I like to go fast," she explained.

"Me, too."

"Not too fast, I hope."

"Yeah, that gets awkward and embarrassing."

Vanessa pressed her finger to Jake's lips. "Shhhh, no more talking." She kneeled back down and held Jake's cock between her tits, holding it in place with her hands and sliding up and down with it against her chest for a few seconds. Jake loved the sensation of the underside of his eight-and-a-half-inch dick against the soft skin of her chest. It felt like satin rubbing against his shaft, and he wondered how long he could last before spurting his come on her chest and chin.

He never found out because she sucked his head into her mouth and pulled off again with a pop. She repeated the process one, two, three more times, popping his dickhead out of her mouth each time.

Finally, she took as much of his cock into her mouth as she could manage, which was only the top three inches, just past the circumcision scar. She drew it out of her mouth slowly, sucking hard as she did so. Jake gasped at the pressure, watching Vanessa's cheeks hollow out. As she sucked, she used both hands to stroke his shaft.

Vanessa alternated between sucking and licking up the sides of his dick like an ice cream cone, or sucking his balls, resting his cock on her face as she did so.

"Oh, this is so good," moaned Jake. "I love how you suck my cock, Vanessa. Ohhhhh, suck my hard cock, Vanessa."

Vanessa responded by shoving more of Jake's prick into her mouth and holding it. She took a few breaths through her nose and then slid it even farther down her throat until almost half of it disappeared. She continued jacking his cock with one hand and fondled his heavy ball sack with the other.

Jake was also a believer in being appropriately groomed and shaven, so his pubic hairs were short above his cock, and his ball sack was completely hairless. Inspired by Vanessa's lightning bolt, he tried to distract himself from coming by wondering if he could groom his pubic hair into the shape of a dolphin.

He should have been thinking about baseball though, because he could feel the pressure building up in his balls and groaned his approval. "I'm going to come, baby," he whispered. "I'm going to come." He thought he would set the expectation and pronounced it "come" instead of "cum," just in case she needed a little hint on what he preferred.

Vanessa eased his cock out of her mouth and began licking up and down, lubricating the lower half with her spit, returning to her previous position and jacking him off faster.

"Oh, this is it, Vanessa. You suck me so good. I'm going to come in your hot mouth. Ohh, fuck, I'm gonna come. I'm coming, I'm— AHH! AHH! AHH! AHH!"

He jetted one burst of come into Vanessa's mouth, and she grunted in appreciation. It was followed by a second, which she swallowed. She quickly pointed Jake's cannon at her chest as shots three, four, and five erupted over her tits, hot come dripping down over her tits.

"Ohh, yeah, lover. That was so fucking good. And you taste delicious. But I love to feel hot come on my body, too. I'm gonna do that a few more times so I can get some more of both."

Jake could only nod as he panted, his hairless chest glistening with sweat, more sweat running down his cheeks. Vanessa wiped his come off her tits with her finger and scooped it into her mouth, catching each drop and sucking her finger clean.

"Now, how about you, lover? Do you eat pussy?"

"There's nothing I love more. Except maybe fucking it."

"You're in luck then, because I want you to eat my wet pussy and then fuck it. Lick it, then stick it," she said with a laugh. She flopped back onto the couch next to Jake, and he kneeled down in front of her. He kissed her on the mouth and poured a little of his wine onto her tits, then licked them off, making her moan.

"Oh, suck my nipples, lover. Take my hard nipples into your mouth." Jake did as he was told, sucking each nipple and as much of her breast as he could fit into his mouth.[15] As he sucked on one, he played with the other one, switching back and forth a few times.

"Ohhhh, Jake-Jake, you have an amazing mouth. Suck my titties, Jakey. Suck them hard." He continued sucking while she ran her fingers through his thick blond hair, massaging his scalp and pulling his head down to her chest.

---

[15] In case you were wondering, and I'm sure most of you were, Jake *did* set the wineglass down onto the table and on a coaster. I just didn't want to interrupt the sexy narrative. "Jake sucked Vanessa's nipples, pausing only to carefully set the wine glass on a coaster so as not to leave a stain on the rich cherry wood. Speaking of wood, his cock got even harder." See? It just doesn't work.

Jake reached up and rubbed his thumb over her hot cunt, sliding it up over her clit, causing her to gasp. He began to rub her clit with his thumb, and she moaned and wriggled her hips.

"Eat me, Jake-Jake. Eat my wet pussy. Take me in your mouth and taste my juices."

Jake didn't need to be told twice, so he lowered himself between her legs and kissed the lightning bolt thatch that guided him down to her beautiful lips. He licked up her slit, bottom to top, sliding his tongue over her pink pearl, and she gave a little squeal.

"Oooh! Do that again!"

He licked her pussy again and a second time and a third, Vanessa squealing each time his tongue came in contact with her bud. Then he clamped down on her clit with his lips and lightly sucked it, darting his tongue over it. She laid her legs over his shoulders. He curled his arms around her thighs, holding them open as she tried to squeeze them together in ecstasy.

After a few minutes, he lowered his head a few inches and slid his tongue into her pussy, sucking her lips into his mouth.

"Holy shit, you *can* eat pussy. Oh God, that's so good." Jake didn't tell her that he had gotten quite good at eating pussy over the last year, which you can read about in *Stand Up, Lie Down, Volume I*, now available on the publisher's website.[16]

He continued fucking her pussy with his hard tongue and reached up to rub her tender clit with his thumb.

---

[16] https://4horsemenpublications.com/our-authors/chastity-veldt/

"Ooooooh, fuck! That's so good! I'm gonna—oh fuck! I'm gonna come, Jake! Ohh, I'm gonna come in your mouth. Eat my come, lover! Here I—Here I—ohhh, fuuuuuuck!"

Vanessa squeezed her thighs together, arched her back, and clutched Jake's hair as she felt a wave crash over her. Jake continued to tongue fuck and flick her clit as she rode the wave, shrieking and moaning. He was rewarded with a shot of her tangy juices, which he held in his mouth, savoring the taste as she came down from her orgasm.

Jake released his grip on her thighs and moved his mouth, giving her a chance to catch her breath.

"Oh, my God, that was amazing," she said. "I think I squirted a little."

Jake made a point of swallowing what was in his mouth. "Yes, you did," he said, smiling. "And it tasted wonderful."

"That was sooo good. I haven't come like that in a while."

Jake sat next to her on the couch, and she crawled onto his lap, facing him, and lay against his muscular chest. The two stayed there, listening to each other breathing, listening to the music coming from the stereo.

Vanessa's breathing slowed until she nearly fell asleep and she bolted up and said, "Shit, I can't fall asleep just yet! We haven't actually fucked. Do you want to eat something?" She went into the kitchen, completely unself-conscious about her nudity.

"Well, I already did," Jake said, smiling.

"Yes, and you did it very well. Do you want anything else?"

Jake joined her in the kitchen and said, "There's only one thing I want in here." He held her by the shoulders and turned her to face him. She smiled as he leaned over and kissed her hard on the mouth. She reached down and gripped his massive cock, which was already hard again.

"Me too," she said. She kneeled down again and sucked his cock into her mouth, driving as deeply as she could and soaking it in her thick saliva. She bobbed her head back and forth several times and stroked him until he was good and wet, strings of saliva stretching between her mouth and his shaft.

"Now, shove that thing inside me and make me come." She stood up and bent over, resting her elbows on her small kitchen table and spreading her legs. Jake eagerly complied, taking a position behind her, spreading his legs to line up with her, and pointing his dick at her pussy's opening. He slid the head up and down between her lips a few times, sliding it in a little farther until he had slid the tip into her moist folds.

"Uhhhhhh," Vanessa moaned. She tried to shove herself backward, but Jake had hold of her hips and held her in place.

"Patience," he said, smiling. "I want to enjoy this."

"Please fuck me! Please! Shove that monster cock into me."

Jake oh-so-slowly slid his cock farther into her pussy, watching her engorged lips part and move aside as more of his dick slipped gently into her.

"Oh, God, yes! That's it. Get it in there. As far as you can!"

Jake was about two inches from being completely inside her when he couldn't go any farther.

"Oh, fuck! It's so thick! Give me a minute. I need to get used to this."

Jake was happy to wait and made his cock jump.

"Oh, shit, what was that?" Vanessa said, laughing.

"Guy Kegels. We have our own Kegel muscles." He made his cock bounce again a few times, and Vanessa cracked up, interrupting it with moans at every bounce.

"Okay, I'm ready. Slide it in slowly, and let me get accustomed to it." Jake slowly slid out of her tight pussy until only his tip was nestled between her lips, and then just as slowly, eased it back into her.

He slid it out again, and she moaned as she felt her pussy empty of her new friend. She moaned again at its return, enjoying the feeling of being filled up once again. Jake repeated the process, a little faster this time. Out, in. Out, in.

As he slid back inside, he pushed a little farther each time, sliding more of his meat inside her eager cunt, making her whimper with each push. "Ohh! Ohh! Ohh!"

Jake drove himself deeper and deeper. After several thrusts, he was finally fully inside her, buried up to his hilt. He held himself there to let her get used to the feeling again, and she sighed as he waited, occasionally bouncing his prick and making her giggle.

Jake loved feeling her wet, velvety pussy walls embrace him, and he tried to think of other things to keep himself from jetting inside her too quickly. This time, he thought about baseball and was able to hold off from coming much longer.

"That's it, Jake-Jake. Fuck me with that big dick-dick." Jake pulled out again and quickly drove back into her.

"OHH!" she shrieked. "Again!"

Jake pulled out once more and thrust himself back into her once more.

"Ohh! Yes!"

Jake pulled out and pushed in again, speeding up with each thrust.

"That's it! Fuck me, you big-dicked Viking! Fuck me with that big cock!"

Jake grabbed her hips and pulled her back toward him even as he slammed forward, shoving his cock as deeply as it would go. He kept a steady rhythm of pulling and thrusting as his pelvic area clapped against her ass. Soon, all Jake could hear over the music was Vanessa grunting —"Unh! Unh! Unh!"—as their bodies slapped together. He could feel the familiar sensation in his ball sack, but he wasn't ready to come just yet. He wanted to keep fucking this beautiful woman.

He pulled out and commanded, "Get up."

Vanessa did as she was told, a little confused. Jake grabbed her under the arms and lifted her up. She quickly understood and wrapped her arms and legs around him, holding herself up. He reached around and maneuvered his dick into position. Once in place, she lowered herself onto him and took him fully inside her. She raised herself up by squeezing her thighs together, and he put his hands under her ass and helped lift her up, so she was bouncing up and down on his thick cock.

Vanessa let out a long moan as she rode him. "Oooooooohhhhhhhh." The two kissed deeply, tongues sliding in and out of each other's mouths, sweaty faces rubbing together. Jake carried her over to the wall and pushed her up against it, and continued driving up into her dripping cunt. He could feel her juices cooling on his cock and running down his balls.

"This is amazing, Vanessa. You've got a beautiful pussy. It's so hot and tight, and I love how it feels gripping my cock."

"I love your cock, Jake-Jake. I'm so full right now. I don't know if I want you to shoot your hot come inside me or cover me with it."

"I'll do both," he gasped. He continued thrusting inside her as she bounced up and down on his dick, moaning as each thrust drove him up inside her. She clawed at his back and kissed him wildly all around his face and neck, writhing in ecstasy.

"I'm cumming, Jake-Jake! Your big dick is making me cum! Ohh, fuck, here I CUUUMMMMMM!"

Vanessa screamed and writhed as another orgasm crashed over her, so overcome with ecstasy that she accidentally used the wrong pronunciation of "come," and Jake was enjoying it too much to notice. She continued to bounce on her Viking lover as she shook from the second orgasm of the night.

When she stopped, Jake carried her back to the table and very gently laid her down on it, without ever removing his cock. She gasped for breath as Jake held still, staying inside her. With a final shudder, she looked up at him and said, "Now, you. I want you to come for me."

Jake lifted her legs so they were pressed up against his chest, curled his arms around her knees, and began thrusting himself inside her once more. He rocked back and forth, sliding his cock in and out of her dripping cunt as it gripped his cock and seemed to grab it each time he drove home.

"That's it, baby! That's it! Fill me up. Fill me up and say my name. I love how you say my name," Vanessa moaned.

"Oh, fuck, your pussy is amazing, Vanessa," he moaned in return. "You feel so, so good. You're so fucking tight and wet, Vanessa. I love being inside you."

He moved his hips in rhythm to the music on the stereo, driving deeply with each thump of the bass drum until he felt himself approaching the edge again.

Vanessa could sense it too because she said, "That's it, lover, that's it. Come for me, come for Vanessa. Shoot it in me. Oh, but shoot it on me, too. I want your hot come. Give me all your come."

Jake grabbed Vanessa's ankles and spread her legs wide apart as he entered the final stages, pounding his cock into her wet cunt, grunting as he did so.

"That's it, baby! I want it all," she whispered. "Give it all to Vanessa."

"Get ready, Vanessa. I'm going to come for you, baby. It's all for you!"

Jake slammed his dick home three more times, shouting with each thrust, and then he held himself inside her. He shot one thick spurt of hot come into her pussy, and Vanessa squealed when she felt it flood her insides. He fired another thick spurt, and she squealed a second time.

Jake quickly pulled out, grabbed his shiny cock, and jacked himself off, aiming his third shot at Vanessa's taut stomach and nearly reaching her breasts. It spattered, and she mewled her appreciation. It was followed by a fourth jet of come that landed around her navel, and the fifth one nestled right on her lightning bolt thatch.

"Holy fuck, that was incredible," he said, his body slick with sweat. He released his cock and grabbed her ankles one more time, pressing her legs together with his cock resting on her leaking pussy.

"Fuck yeah, it was," she agreed. She was covered in sweat as well, her hair matted to her forehead, sweat pooling between her breasts. She scooped up his come with her finger again and stuck it into her mouth. "Still good the second time around."

Jake helped her up and carried her back to the couch, where they sat as they had before, her on his lap, resting her head against his chest.

"I haven't been fucked that hard in a long time," she said. "That was amazing."

"Me either," he agreed. "That was so fucking hot."

"I hope you're not done," she said, grinding her pussy against his now-soft dick.

"No, no, I just need some time to recover first. Then I'll be happy to fuck you again, Vanessa."

"I love the way you say my name, Jake-Jake."

"Same here, Vanessa. Same here."

And the two lovers drifted off to sleep, at least until Jake's cock realized where it was and woke them both up again. Vanessa reached under herself, positioned his head right at her opening, and then impaled herself on his thick dick.

"I'm ready for the next round, Jake-Jake."

Piper
in Portland

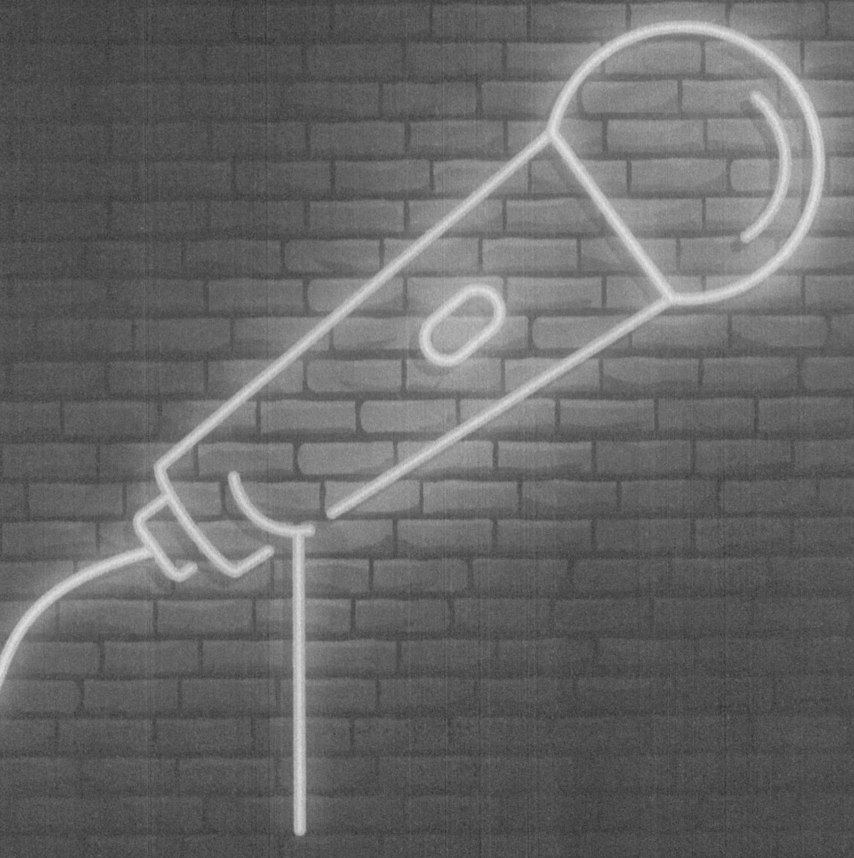

TABLE OF CONTENTS

CHAPTER 1

"Hi, I'm looking for Caitlin," Jake Nilsen said to the guy behind the bar. Jake was at Waffle's Comedy Club in Portland, Oregon, having recently finished a long weekend gig at Doughnuts in Vancouver, British Columbia. He left early on Sunday morning because he was hoping to experience Portland. He'd heard great things about the city and wanted to spend a few days exploring before his gig started on Thursday.

"She's upstairs," said the bartender, pointing at a door marked "Employees Only. This means you. Or doesn't."

Ah, Portland, thought Jake, reading the sign. *You're so quirky.*

The stairs creaked like Jake was in a horror movie, and he was trying to figure out where the weird screams were coming from. Jake walked down a short hallway to an old wooden door and knocked.

"Come in," shouted a woman on the other side.

"Hi, I'm Jake Nilsen," said Jake. "I'm your headliner this weekend."

"Niilsen?"

"No, Nilsen. With just the one i."

"Hi, I'm Caitlin. With, uh, two i's."

"Two eyes?" said Jake.

"No, two i's. Letter i. There are two i's in Caitlin." She was short, with platinum blonde hair and thick dark eyebrows, wearing a black Metallica t-shirt and ripped jeans. She held up a small plate of brownies to Jake.

"Would you like a brownie?" she asked.

"Are they special Portland brownies or just regular brownies?"

"Regular brownies."

"Ah, okay. Sure, thank you." Jake selected a corner brownie because those are the best ones, and I will fight anyone who says differently.

"Do you, uh, partake in special brownies?"

"Not usually," said Jake. "It's just something I never got into. The last time I did it, I got really paranoid."

"Ah, you must have had the wrong brownies then. You can get good brownies that won't make you paranoid. There's a marijuana dispensary next door, and they teamed up with a local bakery to make pot brownies."

"Cool, I'll stop by."

"So, your agent tells me you're on your Wacky Wild West Tour," said Caitlin.

"Fuck, I told him I'm not calling it that."

"Yeah, but it's cute," Caitlin said with a laugh. "You could call it the Wacky Tabacky Tour while you're here. It would play big with the potheads."

"I mean, it plays in some of the smaller towns, but it makes me sound like one of those morning DJ 'zoo crews.' I feel like a prop comic or like I should have one of those fake arrows through my head."

Caitlin laughed. "That's a classic, but yeah, it sounds a bit hackneyed. I was going to give you some shit about it, but as long as you recognize it makes you sound like a doofus, I'd feel kind of guilty."

"Oh, no, fire away. If there are any good ones, I'll steal them for my show."

The two riffed on Wacky Wild West Tour jokes and jokes about Jake's agent, Kurt, for the next five minutes, cracking themselves up in the process.

"I think I may have gotten one of your special brownies," Jake said, wiping tears from his eyes.

"No, those are in my fridge at home," said Caitlin. "I think." The two broke into peals of laughter again.

"No, they really are," she reassured him.

They began talking about some of the different things to do around Portland, and Caitlin gave a few recommendations for places to eat, bookstores to visit (Powell's Books being at the top of the list), plays to see, and other attractions and sights to see around the City of Roses.

After another 30 minutes, Jake thanked Caitlin and headed off in search of lunch and the city's local alt-weekly. He figured that he would have the latest listings of events that he wanted to see while he was in town. He was already planning his itinerary in his head—galleries during the day, live music at night when he wasn't working. Maybe catching a late-night band on Friday or Saturday night.

Jake stopped off at a local brewpub for a late lunch/early dinner and enjoyed his favorite kind of cheeseburger: peanut butter, jalapeños, and pepper jack cheese. The server gave him a weird look, but he reassured him that it tasted wonderful.

"I'll take your word for it," said the server, rolling his eyes.

Jake perused the paper and saw there was an art show at a gallery just a few blocks away. He checked his phone for the time and saw that it had just started. It was the second day of the show, so he thought he might be able to find a piece for his art collection, not that he had seen it in a while.

Jake was a working comic, which meant he was on the road roughly 40 weeks per year. He had been doing this since he left college, slowly working up to the point where he could travel the country in his pickup, which was equipped with a locking lid. He didn't live out of his truck, although he sometimes envied the van dwellers who had tricked out their vans and lived out of them full-time.

"Houseless, not homeless" was the nomad's mantra, and Jake sometimes thought about switching to a rolling home for his tours. But he preferred taking hot showers every day and being able to poop in a real toilet. So that alone kept him staying in hotels and club apartments during his travels.

He also occasionally bought artwork as he traveled and shipped it home to his parents' house in Mankato, Minnesota, Jake's hometown. He did the same with his collection of books, which he amassed whenever he visited a new city. He loved visiting used bookstores and finding lost treasures. He would read them, and when his truck was nearly overrun with books, he shipped them home as well.

Most people didn't realize that Jake was already wealthy. Not from comedy, of course. (Don't be silly!) Jake had made some smart investments in rental properties while he was still in college and plowed all his profits back into more properties.

Since then, his financial advisor and former swim teammate, Alan Johansen[17], had turned him onto a couple of other investments, including two car washes in Miami and a strip mall in Savannah, Georgia. His latest investment was as a part-investor in a hotel being converted into luxury condos outside Chicago.

Jake wasn't quite rich, but he could have retired from the stage and lived off his earnings for the rest of his long life. But he didn't want to. Jake loved comedy, he loved making people laugh, and it gave him something to think about besides money.

Instead, he was free to see the country, support his book habit, and get paid to do it.

That, and he got to have a lot of sex. I mean, *a lot* of sex. That's why you're reading this book.

Another notice caught Jake's eye, a literary open mic at a coffee shop just a few miles away that evening. Jake was intrigued. He had never been to a literary open mic but had heard about them from writer friends.

---

[17] We met Alan in *Stand Up, Lie Down: Betty In Birmingham.*

"Excuse me," Jake asked his server, pointing at the very small notice in the alt-weekly. "Do you know where this is? Cup of Jitters?"

"Oh, sure. That's a couple of miles east of here in Mount Tabor on Belmont. It's a pretty good place. Are you going to the open mic?"

"Yeah, I was thinking about it."

"Awesome. You should get there a little early. It can fill up kind of fast, especially in the fall. All the Portland State creative writing kids decide they want to be poets and they flood the place. I do some poetry there myself."

"Really? Anything in particular?"

"I'm a slam poet," said the guy, puffing his chest out a little bit.

"Cool, cool," said Jake, not quite knowing what slam poetry was. *Something to do with wrestling?* he thought.

"You don't know what that is, do you?" said the server.

"No, not at all," admitted Jake. "I'm Jake, by the way."

"Brian," said Brian. "Slam is performance poetry, usually about some social injustice or current events. It's sort of like the protest songs of the Sixties. They were singing about ending the war and ending racism and sexism. Slam poets talk about that stuff, too."

"Looks like the protests didn't take."

The server scowled and grew red in the face.

"Sorry, I'm a standup comic. I'm a professional smartass."

"Ah," said Brian, cooling off. "Yeah, that's funny. Anyway, slam poets are really passionate, you know. We care about a lot of things. And when we get on stage and spit—"

"You spit on the stage?" Jake's mouth hung open.

"No, man, no. We spit our rhymes. We say our poetry."

"Why don't you just say 'say?'"

"It doesn't sound as cool."

Jake assumed this was some new meaning of the word "cool" that he wasn't previously aware of. "Ah, so you all get up and spit about society."

"Yeah, you got it, man. I'll be there tomorrow. You should come check it out."

"I will," said Jake. "I'll definitely be there."

CHAPTER 2

"Hi, are you here for the reading?" the woman asked.

"Uh, yes," said Jake Nilsen. He looked a little nervous and said as much.

"Don't worry, this is a safe space," the woman said, patting his arm. The space in question was a coffee shop a few miles from the club. He had read about the literary reading in the city's alt-weekly earlier that day.

"Read your short stories, poems, and essays at Portland's oldest monthly open mic," the announcement said, and Jake was intrigued. Jake had secretly been working on a few short stories while he was on the road—so secretly that the author wasn't even aware of it until just now.

Look, you don't have to watch everything *I do,* thought Jake. *It's nice to have some private time where everyone isn't looking over my shoulder.*

What's wrong with people knowing you write stories? asked the author.

Some things are just personal and private.

WE LITERALLY WATCH YOU HAVING HOT MONKEY SEX! shouted the author

My therapist says I have to set boundaries in my life.

You're seeing a therapist?? It's like I don't even know you anymore!

Can we talk about this later?

Oh, we'll talk about this later, said the author, stomping off to her kitchen for a sandwich.

Jake turned his attention back to the woman standing before him. She was 5'6", in her late 30s or early 40s, with a real nurturing, Earth Mother vibe about her. She had curly strawberry-blonde hair pulled back into a loose ponytail, and she wore round, gold-rimmed glasses. She was curvy, with a well-endowed bust, curvy hips, and a round backside—some might call her "Rubenesque," as if she might appear in a painting by Peter Paul Rubens.[18] She wore a deep-plunging rusty-orange blouse that showed off her ample cleavage and an olive skirt that nearly reached her ankles but was slit up both sides to her knees. She also wore a bright and colorful scarf over her shoulders. Jake imagined himself in her warm embrace, her arms and legs wrapped around him as he slowly screwed her.

"I'm Laurel Maguire," she said, extending her hand and shaking Jake out of his reverie. "Is this your first time here?"

"Yes, it is. I'm Jake. Jake Nilsen."

---

[18] The 16th century Flemish painter, not Pee Wee Herman.

"Niilsen?"

"No, Nilsen."

"That's what I said."

"No, you said Niilsen, with the second 'i.'"

"Wow, I didn't even hear it. My apologies."

"Oh, no need. I get that all the time. Nelson, Nielsen, Knellson. And God forbid, Nilson?"

"What's the difference between Nilson and Nilsen?"

"Basically, the Nilsons are pig rustlers and sheep fuckers. Except on weekends, when they're sheep rustlers and pig fuckers."

Laurel snorted and clapped her hand over her mouth. "That's hilarious." She cleared her throat and tried to appear more serious. "So, what brings you here?"

"Well, I'm in town for, uh, work, and I saw the notice in the paper about the reading, so I thought I would check it out."

"Do you have anything you'd like to read?"

"Maybe, if I can work up the courage to do it." Jake wiped the sweat from his forehead as his eyes darted around and took in all the people who were at the event. A number of people were standing and talking or sitting at tables, nursing a coffee drink, or eating a light snack.

"Oh, I'm sure you can." Laurel rested a comforting hand on Jake's wrist. "It's pretty easy. Just focus on your work and pick one or two people to make eye contact with, like me. Just focus on me." She moved her hand to his forearm and left it there. "Stage fright is perfectly normal. Have you ever done any public speaking?"

"Nearly every day. I'm a standup comic."

"Then what the hell are you worried about?" Laurel said, laughing. "This should be easy for you."

"Yes, but I'm working when I do that. I write things that are funny in order to make people laugh. This is more personal. I'm putting my inner self out there. When I do comedy, it's like I'm performing as a character. It's not really me. But this is me being vulnerable."

"That's a good way to think about it," said Laurel. She moved her hand on Jake's biceps, and her eyes widened a little bit when she discovered what was underneath. "Just think of your story as another part of your character. It's not 'your' story, it's the comic's story."

"Huh," said Jake. "That makes a lot of sense." He relaxed almost immediately. Laurel still hadn't removed her hand, and Jake's imagination drifted back to him laying on top of her, her powerful legs wrapped around his narrow waist.

Jake was wearing what he called his "work clothes," blue jeans, a button-down Oxford shirt, and a gray sports coat. It hid his swimmer's physique, washboard abs, and well-developed pectorals and arms. Jake had blond hair and wore the same kind of glasses as Laurel. People often compared him to Tony, the first terrorist in *Die Hard* to die at Bruce Willis's hand.

Laurel gave his biceps a harder squeeze, and her nostrils flared imperceptibly. She imagined Jake thrusting himself inside her and felt herself getting wet at the thought. "Tell you what, Jake. We'll get you on the list. If you feel up to it, tell your story, and if you don't feel like it, you can do some of your standup if you're more comfortable."

"Thank you, Laurel, I appreciate that."

"No problem. Can I get you a drink?"

"Oh, no, that's okay. I can get it."

"No worries. I own the place and you can consider it a welcome drink."

"Well, then, thank you very much." Laurel led Jake to the front counter and told the barista to get Jake whatever he wanted; it was on the house. Jake ordered an iced latte. As they waited, the two chatted a little longer until an argument broke out between two slam poets about cultural appropriation, and Laurel marched off to fix the problem.

Drink in hand, he signed his name to the sign-up sheet and found an empty seat at a long table near the back of the room with two other people already seated there. He pointed at the chair and raised his eyebrows, and they welcomed him to their table.

A guy with long hair and a scraggly beard tapped on the microphone and welcomed everyone to the monthly open mic event. Laurel sat down in the empty chair next to Jake, sliding a bit toward Jake to fit into the tight space. She moved her leg to rest against his, but Jake didn't move his leg to see what she would do. She left her leg pressed up against his, and so he slid his leg over a little more, so it was more firmly pressed against hers.

Jake turned and looked at Laurel, who smiled at him. He winked at her. She slid her hand under the table and squeezed his knee. Jake tried not to look surprised but didn't stop her, either.

The two chatted between readers because talking while someone is reading on stage is rude. Jake asked how she became a coffee shop owner ("My husband and I started it about 23 years ago and then I caught him grinding his beans with one of the baristas"), whether she had any kids ("no, just a cat and a parakeet"), and whether she was a writer herself ("mostly erotica and some murder mysteries").

Jake leaned back in his chair and rested his arm on the back of her chair. He occasionally stroked his fingers on her shoulder or upper arm. Whenever he did that, she would look at him and smile.

Jake was so lost in their flirting and light touching that he nearly didn't hear his name being called. When they called him a second time, he jumped up and whacked his thigh on the table. He limped up to the stage.

"Is this your first time here, Jake?" asked the emcee.

"It is," said Jake, red in the face. He worried he might throw up.

"New meat! New meat!" chanted the crowd.

Using his comedy skills to punch it up, Jake read a segment of his story of his first meeting with a bookstore owner in Milwaukee, Wisconsin, their relationship, and how she threw him over for a successful tax lawyer her prudish aunt had introduced her to. He read the third chapter in the *Stand Up, Lie Down #1: Molly in Milwaukee* saga, but without the sexy bits.

When he was finished, the audience cheered and applauded, and he returned to his seat. Laurel stood up and hugged him. "That was so great, especially for your first time. I'm so proud of you." She pressed her ample breasts against him, and when he wrapped his arms around her, she rested her head on his chest. She sighed contentedly and might have stayed there for several minutes if the next reader hadn't started.

"I may have to congratulate you a little more. Are you busy later?"

"I'm yours for the night," Jake said.

"I'm going to hold you to that," said Laurel, smiling. The lines around her blue eyes showed she smiled and laughed a lot, which Jake appreciated. He loved a woman's laugh lines and loved being able to make them appear.

"I'm going to hold you to a lot of things," she added, squeezing his arm.

"I can't wait." The two sat down and scooted back under the table. Laurel ran her hand up Jake's thigh toward his already-hardening cock. He made no move to stop her and opened his legs a little more to invite her upward. She encountered his thick shaft with her fingers and explored it as if trying to size up his eight-and-a-half-inch prick.

She squeezed with her fingers and looked up at him, a questioning look on her face. *Is that real?* her expression said.

He smiled back at her and gave a small nod. *Oh yeah, it's real.*

"I have to check something in my office," she whispered. "Come with me."

He nodded, and the two moved quietly so as not to disturb the reader on stage. She led him through the kitchen into a small six-by-eight-foot room and shut the door.

"What did you have to check?" he asked.

"Whether your cock will fit in my mouth," she said and dropped to her knees. She undid Jake's belt, opened the zipper, and pulled down his pants. His cock sprang free and pointed itself at her face.

"Ohhh fuck, is that all for me?"

"As much as you can take."

"I'm going to be a greedy girl then," she murmured and kissed the tip of his cock before sucking it into her mouth. Jake gasped and watched as she worked more of his cock into her mouth. He admired her oral technique and stroked the side of her face, feeling his hard shaft through her cheek.

Laurel bobbed her head up and down on Jake's cock, holding it between her lips delicately, not sucking or scraping it with her teeth. It felt to Jake like she was fucking his cock with her mouth, which was wet, warm, and gentle. Laurel stuck her tongue out so it slid along the underside of his shaft, adding to the sensation. She continued to bob on his dick, shoving nearly six inches into her mouth without any effort.

Jake groaned and rested his hands against her cheeks, watching her expert ministrations. She grabbed his hands and moved them to rest on her head.

"I want you to fuck my mouth," she said. "Fuck my mouth and come in it, Jake."

He held her head gently and complied with her commands, sliding his hard dick in and out of her soft mouth, already close to giving her what she wanted. Laurel rested her hands on Jake's legs to make sure he didn't drive in too deeply, but he was being careful. He knew how much she could take, and he wanted to make sure he didn't cause her any discomfort.

"Laurel, I'm going to come," he said, figuring anyone who hosted a literary event would pronounce it "come" instead of "cum."

"Mm-hm!" Laurel moaned, receiving Jake's thrusts. She popped his cock out of her mouth for a moment. "Do it. Come in my mouth, lover."

She returned his dick to her mouth, and he resumed fucking her face.

"Ungh! This is it, Laurel. I'm going to come."

"Mmm! Mmm! Mmm!" she grunted with each thrust. Her lips were wrapped tightly around his dick; it shone with her spit each time he slid it out and back in.

"Here you go, baby. I'm going to come just for you. You're making me come, baby. Here it—UUNNNNNGGGGHHH!"

Laurel pulled Jake's cock deep into her mouth as a powerful jet of come blasted out, and she swallowed it quickly, knowing more was to come. It was hot and a little sweet, and she moaned in appreciation at the taste.

A second jet shot out, followed quickly by a third. Laurel's eyes widened at the amount of come Jake was feeding her. Some of it dribbled out of the corner of her mouth and down her chin as she swallowed twice to take what he had given her. She continued sliding her mouth on his cock and worked out a fourth and fifth spurt of his man juice, which thankfully was not as voluminous as the previous two. She kept Jake's dick in her mouth in case there were any stragglers. And she slid her tongue over his cockhead to catch the little dribbles.

Jake twitched when she did that and said, "Oh, you have to stop. I'm really sensitive now."

Laurel smiled and sucked hard as she slid his dick out of her mouth, releasing his head with a *pop*. "That was amazing," she said, smiling up at him. "Your come tastes so good. You must eat a lot of fruit."

"And drink a lot of water," he said.

"Well, whatever you're doing, it's working. Do you feel like going to my place so we can continue this, or do you have someone waiting for you back home?"

"No, I'm totally available. And willing."

"Good, because I want you to eat my pussy, and then I'm going to take you back to my place and fuck you until we both pass out."

Laurel stood up, stepped out of her skirt, and leaned against her desk, spreading her legs. She wasn't wearing any underwear, and Jake saw she had a trimmed bush that was the same strawberry blonde as her ponytail, and her labia were swollen and glistened from her juices.

"Eat my pussy, lover."

"I thought you'd never ask."

Jake helped Laurel hop up onto the desk and slide back so her ass was resting on the edge, and she laid back, ignoring the various papers and writing instruments. Jake spread her legs and draped them over his shoulders so her heels were resting on his back. He licked at her folds, slipping his tongue between her lips as if he were enjoying an ice cream cone.

"Mmmm, you taste sweet," he said, his chin already covered in her fluids. He returned to her cunt and drove his tongue deep inside her while sucking on her lips, pulling them into his mouth.

Laurel cried out and clapped her hand over her mouth. She yelped a few more times, but managed to keep it down. Jake enjoyed the sounds, and any time he made her yelp, he repeated that move.

His hands massaged her fleshy thighs while she squeezed them against his head, but not too hard. He found her clitoris and sucked on it while he flicked it with his tongue, which made her shriek into her hands several times.

She moved her hands and whispered, "Oh, Jake, I'm going to come in your mouth. Eat my pussy while I come!"

Jake lifted his head and looked up at her, smiling. "Give me your come," he said. "I love your pussy." He sucked her lips and flicked her clit with his thumb, and she lifted her hips to drive her cunt against his expert mouth.

"Mmmmhh!" groaned Laurel into her hands. "Mmmmhh! Mmmmhh! Oh, God!" Laurel's body wracked and contorted as a jet of juice flooded Jake's eager mouth. He continued to lick into her folds to get all of the fluids as Laurel's orgasm subsided. When she slumped back against the desk, Jake released her and raised up, his face shiny with her wetness. He moved around the desk and kissed her deeply, their tongues running over each other, where she could taste herself on him.

"I definitely want you to fuck me now," Laurel said.

"Do you want to head back to your place?"

"Absolutely not. Fuck me here, right now." She reached down for Jake's dick, which was already hardening. She directed Jake back to her pussy, and he lined his rock-hard prick with her eager cunt.

"Now! Do it now. I need you inside me!" she groaned as he slipped the head of his cock in between her swollen, meaty lips. Suddenly, someone was banging on the door and shouting, "Laurel, the poets are rioting. We need you out here right now!"

And that's why you don't keep secrets from me, said the author, slamming her laptop shut.

CHAPTER 3

Jake paid for his burger and left the server a nice tip, despite her sneering doubt about Jake's burger order. He consulted his phone's map app and walked to the gallery.

It was a pleasant day, a bit chilly, but at least it wasn't raining. When Jake reached the gallery, he was the only one there.

"Hi, can I help you?" asked a woman. She was short and slender, and her thick brown hair was knotted up into a bun in the back, with a couple of artists' paintbrushes holding everything in place. She was wearing black slacks and a sleeveless Prussian blue blouse with black pumps. She looked up at him with wide, brown eyes. Jake felt like he could get lost in those eyes.

"Oh, no thank you," he said. "I'm here for the showing."

"Ah, you're the first one."

"Am I early?"

"No, we opened 20 minutes ago, so you're right on time. Sundays are usually kind of slow, especially after a big opening. We had the opening last night. We may even have some wine left, if you're interested."

Mmm, art gallery wine, thought Jake half-sarcastically. "Sure, I will if you will," he said.

"Okay, I'll be right back."

The woman walked to the back of the gallery as Jake followed her, glancing only occasionally at the woman's tight ass and slender hips, because a gentleman never stares.

"We keep a wine fridge under the counter, and I know we didn't go through all the bottles from last night." She pulled out a bottle of red and a couple of glasses before retrieving a corkscrew from a drawer. She popped the cork from the bottle with a squeak and poured a full glass of wine for each of them.

"Cheers," she said, raising her glass. Jake clinked his to hers.

"To a successful run."

"Thank you."

"Who's the artist?"

"A local artist. He's up-and-coming but still needs some time to really find his artist's voice. He's starting to catch people's attention, but his work needs some, well, work. Another couple years, and he should be showing in New York and LA."

"That's interesting. Are any of his pieces for sale?"

"Yes, all of them. We had a few people interested in pieces last night, but no sales. So, if you see anything you like, you can certainly buy it and then just pick it up after the showing in a few weeks."

"Ah, I'll be gone by then. I'm only in town until next Sunday."

"What do you do?"

"I'm a standup comic?"

The woman smiled. "And you can afford to buy art as a standup comic?"

"I'm a very good standup comic," said Jake.

The woman laughed at that. "Touché," she said.

"I'm Jake Nilsen."

"Niilsen?"

"Nilsen, with only one i,"

"I'm Piper," said the woman. "Also with one 'i.' I own this gallery."

Jake extended his hand, and Piper reached out to shake it. Her hand was slender, and Jake could see the bones and tendons as his large hand enveloped hers.

"So, which pieces do you like the best?" he asked. Piper guided Jake around the gallery and showed him the best pieces, including a few of her favorites. They were abstract pieces, using bold lines and bright, vivid colors, sort of like a Where's Waldo puzzle with mismatched pieces. Jake felt like he could study each piece looking for different shapes and combinations. It didn't hurt that Piper was there to tell him about the different paintings and what the artist had intended by each piece.

She stopped in front of one particular piece that looked like the artist had let paint run down the canvas in a rainbow of bright colors and then painted outlines of stick figures over it. "This one is my favorite. This is the start of what's going to take him to bigger and better things."

Jake could see why she liked it. Something spoke to him about it as well, and he could sense the playfulness of the piece.

"Are you going to buy it?" he asked.

"No, I already have enough art in my apartment," she said. "I live above the gallery, and my walls are covered with art. I love it, but not enough to find room for it."

"I know someone who lives above a gallery she managed in Louisville," said Jake, remembering back to a wonderful weekend he spent with a redheaded artist named Lydia.[19] "She's an artist as well. Oh, and I have a sculptor friend in Jacksonville, Jackie Taylor."[20]

"Ooh, I love her!" gushed Piper. "She's so amazing. We've got one of her sculptures in Mount Tabor Park. She was here for the unveiling, and I got to meet her very briefly. You said you're a friend of hers?"

"Uhh, sure," said Jake. He didn't want to mention that he had lived in Jackie's building for a month while he took a brief hiatus after his Midwest/Southeast tour that took place over eight fuck-filled books, now available in a single volume on Amazon.[21] He decided he'd better not mention any of that, especially the fact

---

[19] See *Stand Up, Lie Down 3: Lydia In Louisville.*

[20] See *Stand Up, Lie Down 8: Jackie In Jacksonville*

[21] "Jesus, Chastity, can you just give it a rest for once?"

that he and Jackie had fucked like rabbits nearly every day during that month.

He tried to divert the conversation before he shared too much information. "Are you an artist yourself?" he asked.

"Guilty as charged," Piper said, smiling.

"Well, if you're not going to buy it, then I will," he said. "Would you be able to ship it to me when the showing is over?"

"Absolutely. We ship anywhere in the U.S. We'll box it up in high-density cardboard and send it wherever you'd like."

Jake pulled out his credit card, and Piper returned to the counter to run it. Jake gave her his parents' address, and she said she would ship it in 29 days when the show ended. Two more people, a man and a woman, drifted in and waved at Piper like they knew her. She waved back.

"What kind of art do you create?" asked Jake.

"I paint, and I do photography," said Piper. "I went to Pacific Northwest College of Art for my undergraduate, and then I finished my Masters of Fine Arts at Oregon College of Art and Craft a couple of years ago. I started working here when I graduated and was able to snag the apartment upstairs. I was able to sell some of my work to major collectors back East and was able to buy this place when the owner was looking to retire."

"Have you shown any of your work here?"

"Sometimes, but I try not to make this gallery about myself. It's too masturbatory." Jake blushed at that. He always had trouble with talking dirty unless he was actually in the throes of having sex.

"I've had a couple of showings around town," Piper continued, "and I've exhibited in Seattle and San Francisco a few times."

"So, you're pretty good then?"

"At the risk of sounding immodest, I am. I've been doing serious art and photography since I was a teenager, and I get asked to do commissions by some of the West Coast tech bros. They may be dickheads, but they're willing to pay top dollar."

Jake threw his head back and laughed. "I've been fortunate," he said. "I only know East Coast dickheads. They're usually investment bros, not tech bros. Still, a dickhead's a dickhead, no matter which side of the country you're on."

Piper snorted. "Are you free later this week before you leave?" she asked, grabbing his hand and slowly caressing the back of it with her thumb. "When does your show start?"

"I'm actually free tomorrow. My first show doesn't start until Thursday. Would you be free for lunch tomorrow?"

"Absolutely," said Piper. She bit her lower lip. "We're closed on Mondays and Tuesdays, so I can be wide open."

"Could I see some of your artwork?"

"Are you inviting yourself upstairs to see some of my etchings?"

Jake laughed again. "No, really, I'd like to see some of your work, and maybe buy something."

"You must be a very good standup comic. Or very rich."

"Something like that."

"Sure, that would be great. I'd love to show you something of mine." Piper bit her bottom lip again.

"Excellent," said Jake. He pulled out his cell phone and sent her his phone number. "Do you want to meet somewhere, or should I pick you up?"

"There's a place a couple of blocks from here, if you like Thai food. You can park in the gallery lot behind the building, and we can walk there."

"That sounds like a plan. I'll see you then."

Piper held out her other hand, and Jake shook it again, cradling it gently. She let her grip linger and held his fingers. She leaned up for a quick kiss, planting a soft one on Jake's cheek, and then hugged him. She could feel Jake's dick hardening as she pressed her full, firm breasts into his chest.

"I'm looking forward to seeing you again," she said. "And thanks for buying the painting. I'm sure you'll love it."

Jake turned and walked out the door. As he walked, he turned around and waved, and could have sworn Piper was watching his ass as he left. He stopped at the door and flexed his ass for a second and thought he heard her and the other two visitors breathe in sharply.

CHAPTER 4

Jake pressed the buzzer outside Piper's apartment at the back of the gallery. He heard a window slide open above him; he stepped back and looked up.

Piper stuck her head out the window. "Hey! I'll be right down."

"Sounds good," said Jake. A few minutes later, the door opened, and Piper emerged wearing a lavender button-down blouse and a long black flamenco skirt with black boots. Her bra pushed up her ample breasts, and the top few buttons of her blouse were open, so her ample cleavage was tight, deep, and inviting; Jake fantasized about burying his face between her beautiful breasts. Her hair hung loosely and came down to the middle of her back.

"Hi, you look great," said Jake, as Piper reached up and gave him a quick hug.

"You, too." Jake was wearing his jeans and a polo shirt that accentuated his swimmer's build and did not hide his biceps. Piper squeezed his biceps lightly as she released the hug as if confirming that they were real.

"Are you still up for Thai food?" she asked.

"I've had the urge ever since you mentioned it, so I'm looking forward to it."

It was a warm fall day in Portland, but a cool breeze would blow occasionally, so Jake excused himself and grabbed a light jacket from his truck, just in case.

"Are you going to be warm enough?" he asked.

"I'll be fine," said Piper. "I actually enjoy the cold weather."

"I usually do, too, but I like to be prepared. What makes you enjoy it?"

"I'm from northern Idaho, and we have some brutal winters. Winters are mild, but wet here in Portland. Lots of rain, lots of gray skies."

"I'm from Mankato, Minnesota, and we get brutal winters, too. I miss the cold, but not that much. These days, I prefer to be a little warmer than I was when I was a kid. I used to go outside in shorts and a sweatshirt when it was in the 30s."

"But not anymore?"

"No, not anymore," said Jake. "I spent a few months down south last year, and now I find I don't enjoy the cold the same way I used to."

The two chatted as they walked to Thai One On, Piper's preferred Thai place.

"Hello, Piper!" greeted the woman at the hostess stand when they entered. "So good to see you again. Stephen and I really enjoyed the gallery show this weekend."

"I'm so glad," said Piper. "It was great to see you both. Oh, where are my manners? Mae, this is Jake. Jake, this is Mae. She and her husband own this place."

"Oh, my, looks like you found yourself a Viking," said Mae. She held her hand out, and Jake carefully took it in his own. Her hand was much smaller than Piper's. He wondered how his cock would look with her fingers wrapped around it. Would she even be able to wrap her fingers around it? He smiled and blushed a bit, hoping his face didn't betray his thoughts.

Mae smiled up at him and—*Did she just bat her eyes at me?* Jake thought.

Mae was short and slender, with small breasts and a tiny waist. She wore a black cotton wraparound skirt with white bamboo designs and a blue long-sleeved tunic with embroidered flowers. She was a few inches shorter than Piper. Her jet-black hair was tied up in a bun with two chopsticks holding it in place, much like Piper's hair had been styled with two paintbrushes the previous day. Her bangs tickled her eyelashes, and she would occasionally brush a red-lacquered nail across her brow to get them out of her eyes.

"I love your hair," said Piper. "I did something like that over the weekend."

"I know," said Mae, smiling. "I decided to wear mine like that today after I saw yours." Mae grabbed a couple of menus and said, "It's pretty slow today, so you can sit anywhere."

The restaurant looked like it had 20 tables, but there were only three occupied. Jake wondered how a business like this could stay afloat with such a light lunch crowd.

"They do a booming business at dinner and on weekends," said Piper, as if reading his mind. They sat down in a booth across from each other.

"I'll give you a chance to look over the menus, although I'm pretty sure I know what you want, Piper."

Piper looked over at Jake and smiled, biting her bottom lip. "Yeah, I think I know, too."

Mae smiled and winked. "I'd join you, but there are people here. So I'll just service you. Serve you! I mean, to serve you!"

Jake and Piper laughed, and Mae left them alone.

"Did I miss something?" Jake asked.

"She was flirting."

"Really? I didn't notice. She barely talked to me."

Piper laughed, a light, tinkling laugh. "With me. She was flirting with me."

"Oh. Oh, really? Does she usually do that?"

"Sometimes, especially when she's feeling lonely or neglected."

"I thought she was married," said Jake. "Does he not ... meet her needs?"

"No, not always. They have a pretty up-and-down relationship. Of course, he's down more than he's up, so she sometimes likes to explore other options."

"I see," said Jake. He paused for a second. "No judgment, of course."

Piper laughed. "No problem. Mae and I have … spent some time together in the past. Sometimes it's just the two of us, sometimes we'll share. Do you like sharing?"

He thought back to his trip to Birmingham and his special crossover visit to Abraxus Tasker College[22], where he did quite a bit of sharing. He felt his cock stiffen under the table and was glad the tablecloth covered his lap. She leaned back, kicked off her shoe, and rubbed her foot against Jake's calf. He smiled and winked at her.

"So, what's good here?" he asked.

"I'm trying to find it."

"Really? What are you in the mood for?"

"Something with beef, I think. Maybe something creamy."

Jake pretended to study his menu intently. "Do they use a lot of cream in Thai food? I mean, I know they use coconut milk, but do they actually—whoa, hello."

Piper's small foot found Jake's crotch and rubbed his hard cock. "Are you trying to be funny?" she said, smiling.

"Sorry, force of habit," he said. "I'm actually bad at talking about, you know, it."

Piper giggled. "It? What do you mean, it? Do you mean 'doing thingy?'"

Jake's face grew red. "I'm really bad at talking about … sex."

------

22 See *Stand Up, Lie Down: Betty In Birmingham* and *Stand Up, Lie Down: Carrie On Campus*

"That's disappointing. So you haven't had much sex?"

"No, not at all. I mean, yes, I have—goddammit. Let me start over. Yes, I have had sex, and I'm pretty good at it. But I grew up in Minnesota, and we didn't talk about it, so I get very shy about talking dirty when I'm not actually doing it."

"And what about when you're actually doing it?"

"I sound like a fucking sailor on shore leave."

"That's a relief. I'd hate to think you sounded like a sailor still on his ship," said Piper. "No judgment," she added with a smile.

"So do you know what you want?" Mae asked, gliding silently up to the table, making Jake jump.

"I'm so sorry, honey. I didn't mean to scare you," she said with a giggle, putting a hand on his shoulder. "Oh," she murmured when she felt the hard cannonball under Jake's shirt. "You definitely found yourself a real Viking, Piper. Have you felt his arms?"

"Once or twice," Piper said, smiling shyly. "I'm hoping to feel them more."

"Oh, really?" said Jake, winking at Mae. "How about you? Would you like to feel them some more too?"

Mae's eyes widened. She looked over at Piper, who smiled and nodded. Mae looked around to make sure no one was watching and put her hand on Jake's shoulder, caressing it and squeezing it before letting her hand drift down over his pectorals.

"Wow, he's a good one," Mae whispered. "Have you guys...?"

"Not yet," said Piper. "I was thinking about taking him back to my place after lunch."

"Oh, really?" said Jake. "Was I going to get a say in this?"

"Do you not want to go back to my place?"

"Oh, no, I absolutely do. I just wanted to play hard to get."

"It's not working," said Mae and Piper in unison.

"I'd better get your order in," said Mae. "Otherwise, my husband will come out to see what I'm doing."

Jake and Piper placed their orders—masaman curry for him, pad thai for her—and Mae rushed off to enter them into the computer and ring up the three other tables. The two continued to chat about art and comedy even as Piper rested her foot on Jake's crotch, rubbing it against his raging hard on. He was worried he was going to come in his pants, but she was careful not to create too much friction on his cock.

Ten minutes later, Mae set their plates in front of them and left them in peace, giving Jake's shoulder one more appreciative squeeze.

"Enjoy your meals," she said with a wink, "and each other."

They tucked in and made the appropriate yummy noises, sharing bites with each other.

"How is it?" Piper asked.

"This may be some of the best Thai food I've ever had."

"Thank you," said Mae as she approached the table. "I'll be sure to let my husband know." She sat down with them, sliding her chair closer to Jake. "So, my friend seems to be enjoying herself. I can see where her foot is resting, and she hasn't set her leg down for ten minutes. She must like what she found."

"I'd like to think so," said Jake.

"Do you mind?" she said to Piper.

"I don't mind if he doesn't," said Piper.

"Mind what?" asked Jake. "Oh, that." Mae slid her hand over Jake's thigh and in between Piper's foot and his cock. She squeezed it gently, probing it to see how much he was working with.

"Oh! Oh my! That's ... uh, that's a lot. Oh, honey, he's going to split you wide open with this thing. How big is this monster?"

"Eight-and-a-half inches," Jake said.

"Seriously?" said Piper, her eyes opening wide.

"He's not exaggerating," said Mae, who still hadn't released his cock from her grip. "It's thick, too!"

"Do you think it'll fit in my mouth?" asked Piper.

"Well, it feels a little bigger than my purple strap-on, and you were able to get that in your mouth last month."

Piper blushed furiously and smiled at the memory. "I remember that night. God, I came so many times."

"You and me both," said Mae.

"I might come right now," said Jake, making the two women cackle. Mae gave his cock a final squeeze.

"I'll let you save it for Piper," said Mae. "Maybe I can get a sample tomorrow."

"That's up to her, I guess," said Jake. "I'm just along for the ride."

Piper snickered. "Yeah, you are. And yes, you can absolutely get a sample. Just text me and come by my apartment. I'm sure we can fit you in."

"I just hope I can fit *him* in," Mae giggled. She leaned over and kissed Jake full on the lips, slipping her tongue into his mouth. Then she stood up and leaned over to kiss Piper. Piper reached her hand up and grabbed the back of Mae's head, and the two Frenched for several seconds before Mae stood back up.

"God, I'm so wet right now," she said. "I'm going to the bathroom and get myself off. But I'm going to be thinking about you two the whole time. Lunch is on me, and tomorrow, I want you both on me."

"I can't wait," said Piper. "Now, my Viking lover, take me back to my place and fuck my brains out good and proper. I'm as wet as Mae, and I can't wait for you to fill me up with your jizz."

Jesus, thought Jake, *are all Portland women this horny?*

CHAPTER 5

The weather was still warm when they left Thai One On, and they slowly walked back to Piper's apartment over the art gallery. They didn't want to rush, but they didn't want to dawdle. They both knew what the other wanted, but they also knew the joys of delayed pleasure, so they were willing to meander back. Besides, they were a little full from lunch and didn't want to fuck on a full stomach.

Before they had left, Mae had returned from the bathroom and returned to their table. She held her hand up to Piper, who sucked on her middle finger. Mae turned to Jake and raised her eyebrows questioningly. He nodded, and she gave him her index finger to suck. Jake could taste the tang of Mae's pussy, and he swirled his tongue over her finger. She kissed them both again, slipping in a little tongue for each of them.

"See you soon," she whispered.

They eventually reached Piper's building and made their way upstairs. She closed her door behind them and locked it. Then she turned to Jake and wrapped her arms around his neck. He had to bend over so she could reach him, and he planted a soft, wet kiss on her eager mouth.

"I've been so wet ever since I rubbed your cock under the table. And I thought I was going to cum when I knew Mae was groping you."

"Me too," admitted Jake. "If it hadn't been in public, I would have bent you both over the table and fucked you silly."

"Oh, my, you do know how to talk dirty," Piper said, smiling before kissing him again. "Where would you have come?"

"I'd play pussy roulette. Ten strokes in each pussy, and I blast my come in either of your pussies."[23]

"Fuck, that's hot," she gasped. She drove her tongue into his mouth and explored as deeply as she could. Jake straightened up and lifted her with him. Piper wrapped her legs around his slender waist and dry-humped him as their tongues twisted around each other's.

He cupped his hands on her pert little ass and held onto her while shuffling his feet toward her couch in the middle of the living room. When he reached it, he carefully sat down and slid his hips forward so Piper could grind against his hard shaft. She lifted up her skirt to reveal a black thong and smiled at Jake as she lowered herself until she landed on him and moved back and forth along his hardness.

She moaned deep in her throat, and he pulled her blouse out of her skirt before sliding his large, soft hands up her blouse and cupping his hands over her breasts. He squeezed and massaged them through her bra, and could feel her nipples harden at his tender ministrations.

---

[23] To be clear, Jake meant either woman's pussy; Piper does not have two pussies by herself. This is erotica, not science fiction.

Piper breathed harder as she slid her hips over Jack's rock-hard dick, her black skirt pooling around her waist. She unbuttoned her blouse, shrugging it off before removing her bra.

"Mmmmm," moaned Jake as he saw Piper's full breasts. They were shaped like teardrops, and her nipples and aureoles were brown; her nipples were hard and eager for attention. Jake flicked his thumbs over them, making her coo in appreciation.

"Do you like seeing my breasts?" she asked.

"Yes, very much. They're perfect."

"What would you like to see about them? What would you like to do to them? Tell me five things you want to see my tits do, Mr. Can't Talk Dirty. But be dirty."

Jake continued rubbing her nipples, and he kissed each of them, first one and then the other. "Hmm, okay. First, I'd love to see how they look cupped in my hands. So far, they look pretty good." He kissed her again as he thought for a moment. "Next, I'd love to see how shiny they get after I covered them in my saliva from licking and sucking them."

"Oooh, you are pretty good at dirty talk."

"I'd love to see them wrapped around my cock as you squeeze them together while I fuck your tits."

"I think we can do that. That's three."

"I'd love to see them sway and swing while I fuck you from behind. I'll bet we can make them twirl."

"Ohh, fuck, I would love that."

"And five, I'd love to see them covered in my come after I fucked you."

"Ohhhh, God, I'm going to come. That was hot, and my pussy is so wet." Piper gripped Jake's shoulders for support as she ground on him harder and faster. "Jake, I'm going to come. Ohh, shit, I'm going to come. Ahh! Ahh! Ahhhh!"

Sweat dripped down Piper's cheek as she threw her head back. Jake wrapped his arms around her waist to keep her from falling and watched enraptured as her tits wobbled with her rocking motion.

"OHH, FUCK! THAT'S IT! OH, FUUUUCK!" Piper collapsed against his chest, breathing heavily, sweat running down her face. She stayed there for a minute before she raised up.

"Your turn," she said. "I don't want you to think I'm selfish."

"Oh, are you a giving person?" he said, grinning.

She kissed him deeply before answering, "Yes, I'm very giving. I'd love to give you something to remember."

She helped him take off his shirt and ran her hands over his muscular chest and shredded abs. "Mmm, I think I'm going to love this."

Jake pushed her gently so she was sitting upright and then leaned up and licked one breast and then the other before returning to the first one, sucking her nipple into his mouth. He licked, nibbled, and lightly bit it as she clutched the back of his head to pull him to her.

Jake sucked as much of her tit flesh into his mouth as he could, pulling a few inches of it into his eager lips. He then switched breasts and repeated the process, paying close attention to her nipples, getting them wet and hard. He licked between her tits on her breastbone, and she squeezed her tits together, wrapping them around his face against his cheeks.

"God, I love how you suck my tits. My nipples are so sensitive, and your mouth feels so good."

"You have gorgeous breasts," said Jake.

"I want to see your cock now," said Piper. She stood up, and her skirt fell back into place. She stepped out of it and threw it onto a nearby chair. She put her thumbs inside the waistband of her panties and slowly worked them down her slender hips. She turned to the side as she bent over so Jake could see the profile of her smooth ass. Piper clearly worked out and was proud of her petite ass. Jake reached out and ran his hand over her ass cheek.

"Now you," said Piper. She pulled him to his feet and kneeled in front of him. She helped him remove his socks and shoes first because guys look ridiculous when they're completely naked except for their socks.

Then she worked at his belt, opening it, before turning her attention to the button on his jeans. She unzipped his pants slowly to delay the pleasure even further. "I want to see if Mae was right," she said. When she unzipped his pants, she pulled them down over his hips, exposing his blue skin-tight boxer briefs with a spot of pre-cum on the front. Jake's hard prick bulged and begged for release. Piper rested her hand on it and squeezed.

"Oh, God," she gasped. "She wasn't kidding." She reached into Jake's briefs and fished out his cock. "This looks gorgeous." She gripped it with both hands like she was holding a baseball bat and jacked him off, putting the head into her mouth.

"This is so fucking big. I want to suck it, but I want to fuck you, too. I don't know what to do first."

"We have plenty of time," Jake reassured her. "We can do both."

"Which would you rather do first?"

"Well, I take a lot longer to come the second time than I do the first. Do with that what you will."

"Perfect. I want you to fuck me for a long time." With that, she slurped his dick into her mouth, fitting about four inches into it before hitting her gag reflex. She fought it and coughed, holding him as deep as she could before releasing him and coughing.

She giggled and stuck his dick back in her mouth, reaching her depths again. This time she was able to hold him without coughing, so she pushed herself a little farther, swallowing another half-inch before she had to release again. Thick ropes of saliva hung between his cock and her mouth; she wiped it off her chin and used it as lubrication to jack his cock with both hands.

"Oh, God, I love watching you suck my cock. You look so beautiful with my dick in your mouth." She returned it to her mouth, bobbing her head back and forth, sucking as deep as she could before sliding back and collapsing her cheeks from the pressure.

She rocked herself that way for several seconds and then popped his dick out of her mouth. "Fuck my face with that big cock," she commanded.

Jake held her head steady and slowly began to drive himself in and out of her eager mouth. Piper grabbed his ass with one hand and kneaded it while she massaged his heavy ball sack with the other.

His cock hit the back of her throat, and she went, "Gluk, gluk, gluk" with each thrust. Then he pushed his cock into her mouth and held it for a few seconds. She patted his thigh, and he withdrew. She took a few deep breaths before gasping, "More!"

Jake held his hands on the top of her head and chin, holding it perfectly steady, resuming her face fucking. Piper reached down and played with her pussy, teasing her clit, and sliding a finger into her wet folds.

"I'm gonna come, baby," Jake groaned, using his preferred pronunciation. "You're making me come."

"Come on my tits, like you promised," she said before jamming his cock back into her mouth. She drove her head back and forth like a piston, sucking and slurping his cock, massaging his ball sack with one hand, jacking and twisting her other hand over his shaft. When she felt his sack tighten, she released him and jacked him off, pointing his cock at her chest.

"That's it, baby, come all over me. I want you to come on me."

"Fuck yes!" agreed Jake.

Piper continued stroking him with her hands until Jake grabbed his dick from her and began pumping furiously. "Here you go, Piper. I'm coming for you."

"Ohh, say my name when you come!"

"I'm coming, Piper. I'm going to come on your beautiful tits. Oh, fuck, Piper, you're so gorgeous and I want to come all over you."

"Do it! Give it to me!"

"Oh, God, Piper. Here it comes. It's all for you, all over your gorgeous tits. OHHH, PIPERRRRAAUUUGGGGHHHH."

White come shot out of Jake so hard they could hear it splatter on her chest, stream after stream landing on her tits and dripping onto her thighs and the floor.

"Ohh, fuck, your come is so hot on me," said Piper. "It's so hot." She scooped up the different jizz blasts off her tits, thighs, and stomach and popped them into her mouth. "Mmmm, you taste sweet and creamy."

She licked off the head of his dick, sucking the last few drops into her mouth. "So good," she groaned. She used her fingers to scoop his hot jizz off her tits and sucked it off her fingers.

Jake collapsed onto the couch, sweat running down his face and chest. "I think you need a turn," said Jake after a few minutes. "Where's your bedroom?"

"This way." Piper walked toward her bedroom, giving her hips a little extra wiggle. She turned and beckoned him with her finger. Jake popped up off the couch and quickly followed her.

Once they reached her bedroom, Jake gathered her up in his arms and held her close, reveling in the feeling of their skin touching. He kissed her deeply before settling on her bed.

"I want you to straddle my face," he said. "Sit so you can look down and see my eyes."

Piper smiled, and her eyes widened at the command. Jake laid back, and Piper quickly kneeled over his face, resting her feet on his shoulders. He reached up and massaged Piper's tits, her nipples still hard all this time.

He raised his head up and licked at her folds, sliding his tongue up over her clit. She shuddered and gasped at the contact. "Ohh, yessss," she hissed.

Jake grabbed her hips and pulled her lower to his face so her shaved pussy was riding his face. He slid his tongue in and out of her cunt, feeling her wetness trickle into his mouth and onto his chin and cheeks.

"You taste so good. You have such a sweet pussy."

Piper arched her back and massaged her own breasts, tweaking her nipples as Jake ate, licked, sucked, and tongue fucked her. "Ohhhh, fuck, Jake, you eat pussy so good. This is amazing."

He flicked his tongue over her clit several times, and Piper yipped with pleasure. "Oh! Oh! Oh! Oh!" she shrieked. "I'm going to come again. Keep doing that! I'm going to come!"

"Say my name!" Jake said in between licks.

"Jake, you're making me come! I'm going to come in your beautiful mouth, Jake. Oh, fuck, this is it! Oh, my God, I'm—AAAAAAHHHHH!!!"

Piper fell forward, breathing heavily and resting her hands and head against her headboard. "Oh, fuck, that was amazing. No one has made me come like that in a long, long time."

"I'm glad I could help," said Jake, smiling, his face shiny from her juices.

"Now I want you to fuck me and make me come again."

"As you wish," said Jake. Piper quickly scrambled back and grabbed his cock, pointing it at her opening.

"I'm so wet for you," said Piper. "I just want this in me—OH FUCK!" Jake had grabbed her hips and pulled her down onto him, impaling her on his thick cock, driving it all the way into her.

"Oh fuck, I'm so full! You're so deep in me!" Piper rocked back and forth as Jake massaged her tits, driving his cock inside her over and over. She grunted as she raised her hips and dropped back onto him. "Ungh, ungh, ungh, ungh."

Jake propped himself onto his elbows and sucked her nipples as she fucked her Viking lover. She held the back of his head so he would pay more attention to her tits.

After several minutes of riding him, she wanted to change positions. "I want you to fuck me now," she said. Jake grabbed her waist and flipped her over without ever pulling out. She thrust her legs into the air as he drove himself into her, jackhammering her wet pussy and breathing hard. Their sweat mixed together as Piper gave little grunts and moans every few seconds. Their bodies slapped together as Jake propped himself up and thrust into her. She grabbed the back of her knees so he could drive in as deeply as possible.

"Do you still want to see my tits swing?" she asked. Jake grunted in the affirmative. "Fuck me from behind then."

He kissed her deeply and then raised himself off of her, reluctantly slipping his dick out of her. Her pussy lips were swollen and wet, and her juicy cunt gaped open from where his massive invader had just left. She ached for him to return, so she quickly scrambled to her hands and knees, pointing her delicious ass at him.

"Quick, get it back in me. Fuck me hard. Pound me, goddammit," she ordered.

Jake slid back into her sweet opening in one smooth motion, burying himself to the hilt. "OHHH!" yelped Piper.

He grabbed her hips and thrust himself deep into her, his pelvis slapping into her pert ass, causing it to ripple with each slap. He sped up his tempo and used his grip on her waist to help pull her back to meet him before using his thrusting hips to shove her forward again.

The slapping noise filled the room, and, as Jake wanted, her tits swung in time with his thrusts, swaying in circles, one turning clockwise and the other counter-clockwise.

Piper leaned forward so her ass continued to point up at Jake even as her face pushed into her quilt. Her cries and moans were muffled by the bedclothes, and she worked up to another orgasm.

"I'm going to come again, Jake. Ohhhh, God, I'm going to come again. Fuck me, goddammit. Fuck me harder! Faster! Harder!"

Jake eagerly obeyed, and their bodies slapped together louder and faster than before. His knuckles were white from gripping her waist, and her ass cheeks were bright red from the impact of their bodies.

"I'm going to come, too, Piper. Where do you want my hot come?"

"In my pussy! Fill up my pussy."

"Oh, Piper!" cried Jake. "Oh, fuck, I'm going to come deep in your cunt, Piper. I'm going to fill up your pretty pussy."

"Ohh! Ohh! Ohh!" she shrieked. "Come inside me, Jake! Fill me up with your hot come, Jake!"

Jake felt his balls boiling, so he banged into Piper one, two, three more times before shoving himself in as far as he could go and unleashed a rocket of come that, if he hadn't already been on his knees, would have made him collapse.

"FUCK!" Jake shouted.

"OH, GOD!" screamed Piper, her voice still muffled.

Jake withdrew and thrust again, sending another jet of sperm deep into Piper. "UNNGGGHHH!" he shouted again. A third thrust sent another come blast, and Jake held steady as he sent a fourth and a fifth jizz jet up into his new lover.

He shuddered, sweat running down his face, and slowly leaned over Piper, who moved forward so she was lying on her stomach, Jake lying on top of her. The two panted and breathed deeply as they came down from their orgasmic high.

Neither said a word. They just lay there even as Jake's cock shrank and slipped out of her.

"That was fucking amazing," said Piper.

"It was," agreed Jake. "I haven't come that hard in a while. That was amazing."

He rolled over onto his back, and Piper laid her head on his chest. "Holy fuck, that was just ... amazing," she repeated.

The two didn't speak as Jake stroked her damp hair out of her face, planting kisses on the top of her head. They dozed slightly.

After thirty minutes, Piper asked, "How late do you want to stay?"

"I don't have a show until tomorrow night, and I don't leave until Sunday, so I can stay for however long you want."

"Good," said Piper. "Because Mae wants some of this and I can text her and tell her to come over. If you can give a repeat performance, she definitely needs it."

"I'm up for anything," said Jake agreeably, who was getting turned on at the thought of taking on both women.

She ran out to the living room and returned a minute later with her phone before ducking into the bathroom. A few minutes later, she emerged and climbed onto the bed. She put her phone back on the nightstand.

"She'll be here in an hour. In the meantime, I want another turn first," said Piper, climbing up onto Jake's muscular frame, resting her pussy right on Jake's re-hardening dick. "So tell me, what are the rules to pussy roulette?"

Randi
in Reno

TABLE OF CONTENTS

Chapter 1

[Hey, lover. I was thinking about you. I've got some good news for you.]

Jake's phone read the new text messages over his truck speakers. It was Sunday afternoon, and Jake was driving from Portland, Oregon, after his show in the City of Roses. He had his phone set to a British female voice, so it sounded rather sophisticated and sexy when she read his text messages.

The message in question was from his lover in Birmingham, Alabama, Betty Abernathy. Jake smiled at the memory of bedding her and her good friend, Sheila Goodwin, in the apartment above Sheila's yoga studio. The three had spent an entire weekend sucking and fucking one another and declared their love for each other.

Jake remembered the scene as if he had just copied and pasted it from his very own copy of *Stand Up, Lie Down 6: Betty In Birmingham*, now available at your favorite online bookstore.

"Ohh, I'm coming too, Jake! Fill me up! Fill up my wet pussy with your hot come. I'm coming for you! Oh, Jake, I love yoooooooouuu!"

"I love you, too, Betty! I love—GAAAAAAAHHHHHH!!!!"

Later, as the three were lying together, bodies still slick with sweat, chests heaving from intense orgasms.

"That was the deepest orgasm I've ever felt, and I think your come reached my liver, Jake. I can feel it inside my pussy," said Betty.

"I know I haven't come that hard. And I've never done it with two women," said Jake.

"I've never been in a threesome before either," said Betty.

"This wasn't my first, but it's by far my favorite," said Sheila

"I'm sorry for what I said, though, Jake," said Betty. "I was caught up in the heat of the moment. I didn't mean to say it. It doesn't count, and I don't want to scare you away."

"Oh, no, don't apologize," said Jake. "I was caught up too, and I said it too. I know we said something that we maybe won't feel tomorrow, but we felt it today. This was very special, and it stirred up some emotions in both of us.

"So, for right now, for as long as I'm here and you'll both have me, we can feel this way, and we can say it this weekend, even if it doesn't last. We'll be a temporary couple—well, a throuple—and say it whenever we feel like it, and it'll be true. It will be true for us for as long as we're with each other. And when I leave, we'll go back to the way we were before. But for the next three days, I love you, Betty Abernathy."

Hearing Betty's voice again brought the memories back, and Jake's eight-and-a-half-inch dick swelled at the memory, and the feelings of love swelled in his heart. The two had talked on the phone occasionally, giving each other phone sex, masturbating together, and listening to each other's orgasms over the phone.

Jake hit the voice button on his phone. "Call Betty Abernathy," he said.

"Hey, lover," she said after two rings. "That was fast. Couldn't keep away from me?"

"No, I couldn't. I was remembering our weekend together with Sheila," Jake said, smiling in a way that Betty could hear through the phone.

"I still think about it, too," she said. "Mmmmm. In fact, I'm thinking about it right now. My pussy is so wet. Oohhhhh, fuck, I wish I could feel your cock inside me." Betty cleared her throat and spoke a little more formally. "But that's not why I called, lover. Or, it is, but not to have phone sex."

"What's going on?" Jake asked.

"I wish I could flick my pearl and hear your deep, sexy voice, but I don't have time right now. My husband will be home from work in a few minutes."

"Tease."

"Yep." Jake could hear her smiling, too. "No, actually, I called because I'm inviting myself out to your next gig. I remembered that you're heading to Reno, right?"

Jake felt his heart beat faster, and his cock swelled up. "Yes! I'll be performing there this weekend at one of the local clubs. I'm actually getting there tonight and hanging out for a few days before my show. I've got a few free days, so I figured where better to spend it than 'The Biggest Little City in the World.'"

"Excellent; I got your text last week and was hoping that was still your plan. My husband is traveling to Germany for a trade show for a week, and he flies out tomorrow morning. So, I wanted to fly out for two days and then come back before he gets home."

"Can't you stay for five days and go home on Friday?"

"I would, but I'm chairing a meeting of the Daughters of Alabama Society Thursday morning. And then Sheila and I are spending the weekend in her apartment again."

"How is Sheila?"

"Delicious," moaned Betty. "Ohhhh, fuck."

"What are you doing?" Jake asked.

"Fingering my pussy thinking about you and Sheila."

"Any chance she can join us this time?"

"No, she's got a full schedule at the studio, and she's in the process of hiring an assistant manager."

"So, I get you all to myself for two days? Why the short notice?"

"Because my husband just called me and told me about the trip. He had to swing by the dry cleaners on the way home from golfing. Uhhhh, oh God..."

Gene Abernathy was a corporate executive who often had to travel for work. Betty had immersed herself in different clubs and organizations to distract herself from the fact that her husband was cheating on her with members of his staff. He often took "unexpected" trips that would last for several days or a few weeks.

Sheila's husband worked for the same company, and both men had their favorite mistresses who would accompany them on their little trips. Betty finally figured what was good for the gander was also good for the goose, so she took Jake as her first lover and Sheila as her second. Even after Jake left Birmingham, the two women often met while their husbands were traveling and would sometimes involve another man in their lusty adventures. But Jake had been, and would always be, her favorite.

Betty continued, "Personally, I think he's taking his little 'marketing coordinator,' some 20-something bimbo with perky tits and a deep throat, on a European cruise. So I started thinking about your big cock, and I—I—I—ohhhh, fuck! Oh, God, Jake, I just came." She breathed heavily for a few seconds and then continued, "So I figured I'd get away for a couple of days and get you inside me. It's better than my fingers and dildos."

"You know I'd love to have you any time, Betty. What day are you coming?"

"I can be there tomorrow, just in time for chapter 2."

Jake was silent for a few seconds. "I'm the only one who's allowed to break the fourth wall, Betty," said Jake, seriously.

"Sorry! I'm sorry," said Betty. "Anyway, I can be there tomorrow morning around 9 a.m. And my flight home won't leave until 9:00 the following night. It's a direct flight, so it's just a few hours."

"Perfect! Do you need a ride from the airport?"

"No, I'll take an Uber," said Betty.

"I'll text you the hotel information then. I'm really looking forward to it."

"I love you," Betty said quietly. "I still love you, Jake."

"I still love you, too, Betty. You're an amazing woman."

Jake pulled his truck into the parking lot next to Brownie's Comedy Club and wandered inside.

"Hey," he said to the bartender, a young, rangy guy who looked a bit like a weasel. He looked like the kind of guy who knew where most of the action was, legal or illegal. "I'm looking for Kaitlin."

"Oh, yeah?" said the bartender, looking around him as if he was going to tell a secret. Jake looked around as well. "Who wants to know?"

"What?"

"I said, 'Who wants to know?'"

"No, I heard you. It was just unexpected. Like, who says that?"

"What?"

"No, who? Who says that?"

The bartender looked bewildered. "I don't know."

"Third base!" Jake shouted.

"Ah, fuck! You got me, man. That was great." The bartender reached across the bar and offered his hand. Jake shook it.

"Jake," said Jake.

"Gabe," said Gabe, with a laugh. "Sorry about that. I love fucking with the comics when they check in. I thought I was going to get you, but you were a step ahead of me."

"Yeah, I usually get that kind of shit from all the bartenders, so I'm always on my toes."

"Right on, man. Anyway, Kaitlyn is in the back." He pointed at a door to the left of the bar marked "Employees Only." Jake opened it and walked down the hallway to the door marked "Manager." It was partly open, so he knocked.

"Come in," called a woman. Jake pushed the door open and saw a woman sitting at her desk. She stood up and saw she was about 5'6" with wide hips and a generous chest. She had light brown hair cut in a page bob and had honey-green eyes.

"Kaitlyn?"

"Depends. Who wants to know?"

"Gabe already got me," said Jake.

"Bummer. He gets all the good ones," said Kaitlyn.

Jake snickered. "Sorry. I'm Jake Nilsen,"

"Nillsen?" said Kaitlyn.

"Nilsen," corrected Jake.

"What's the difference?" Kaitlyn asked.

"You said Nillsen, with two l's."

"Ah. Anyway, you want some pancakes?" Kaitlyn held up a plate of pancakes. "We're going to be doing a 'Breakfast for Dinner' special this weekend, and the cook is trying to perfect her recipe before then."

"No thanks, but they look good. I love pancakes. I'll definitely make sure I eat here for dinner."

"Excellent. I've got the keys here for the comic's apartment. You're the only one there this weekend. The opener and middle are both locals, so you're going to be on your own until you leave next Sunday morning."

"Perfect. I've got a guest who's going to come visit for a couple days. Would it be alright if she stayed?"

"Shit, I don't care. Just don't trash the place, and try to keep it clean. I hire a cleaning lady who comes in after each comic, and she charges me more if the comics trash the place. And if it's too bad, I just don't have them back, plus I tell the other clubs in town."

"No, no problems from me," said Jake. "I'm pretty tidy."

Kaitlyn tossed a set of keys to Jake, and he caught them in his large hand. She caught the length of his fingers, and her nostrils flared. Jake thought she would have made a great Chapter 2 sex partner, except Betty was arriving tomorrow, and he wanted to save his energy and come all for her.[24]

"And there's a washer and dryer if you need to do laundry," she said. "You're probably in need of some clean laundry. There's also a dry cleaner on the same block in case you dress up for your shows."

"That would be great. I've been on the road for a few weeks and was running out of clean clothes."

"Sounds good. We don't have any open mics or anything this week, so your first show is on Thursday night at 8:00. Be here about an hour before if you want dinner."

"Sounds good. I'll see you in a couple days."

---

[24] Oh, don't act all surprised like I just spoiled something. If you've been reading these books, you know Jake *always* has sex in chapter 2. And hold onto your hats! He's going to have sex in chapter 5, too! With a woman named Randi! Ooooooohhhh!

Jake followed the GPS directions to the apartment and let himself in. The apartment was clean, decorated, and nicely furnished, which was rather surprising for a comedy club apartment. But then again, this is the twelfth consecutive book about a secretly rich, muscled-up standup comic who has sex with two women in every city, so don't start complaining that this isn't realistic.

He changed clothes and went out for a run, heading to one of the 24-hour fitness chains just a couple of miles from his apartment. He hit the weights for two hours, pushing his muscles in a way he hadn't for a few weeks. Life on the road makes it hard to maintain a chiseled physique like Jake's, so he was always careful to find time to run, swim, or lift weights to keep it up.

Jake showered and booked a massage at a massage spa next door to bring some relief to his sore muscles. He knew that without it, he would be sore in the morning, and he couldn't have that. Not with his favorite lover visiting.

He capped off the evening with dinner and another mystery paperback at a burger joint nearby.

The following morning, Monday, Jake was up early and made sure to tidy the place up and make sure everything was clean and put away. He threw yesterday's workout clothes in the washing machine and changed into jeans and a tight t-shirt. He had no illusions that Betty would be impressed by such an apartment—she was the wife of a millionaire and lived in a big house in the tony part of Birmingham, after all—but that didn't mean he didn't want to make an effort.

Jake was in the middle of writing some new jokes on his laptop, drinking from a small bottle of orange juice, when there was a knock at the door. He quickly closed the lid and almost skipped to the door.

He took a breath and composed himself, making sure his t-shirt was tucked in tightly to show off his narrow waist and huge pectorals.

He peeked through the peephole and opened the door.

"Hello, my love," he said.

CHAPTER 2

"Hello, lover," said Betty Abernathy, beaming. She leaped into his arms and wrapped her legs around his waist, kissing him hard on the mouth. Jake held her up by her ass and backed into the apartment, slamming the door shut and locking it with his other hand.

She was 5'3", slender from years of yoga, and had short blonde hair with every strand perfectly sprayed in place. She was wearing a long-sleeve crisp white blouse with black pants and bright red designer pumps. She wore a white pearl necklace and a gold tennis bracelet.

She crushed her breasts against Jake's chest as she drove her tongue as far into his mouth as she could manage, and Jake carried her over to the table where he set her down, careful not to set her on his laptop.

"How was your flight?" Jake asked between tongue thrusts.

"I'll tell you after you fuck me," Betty said. "My pussy has been aching for you for weeks."

Jake pulled away and started unbuttoning Betty's blouse as she fought to pull his t-shirt out of his jeans and over his head. Once her shirt was off, Jake reached behind her and expertly flicked her bra open, making her gasp and smile, her pearly-white teeth dazzling in the morning sun. When her exquisite breasts were free, Jake sucked one nipple into his mouth as he massaged her other globe. Thanks to the miracles of modern surgery, Betty's breasts were about the size of softballs and firm, and he loved putting his mouth on them and cock between them.

"Hello, old friends," he murmured between kisses and sucks. Betty ran her fingers through Jake's thick, blond hair, moaning at his ministrations.

"Take my pants off. Now!" she commanded. Jake removed her red shoes and helped her take off her pants, but left her panties.

"As you wish," he said, smiling. He ran one of his thick fingers up her pussy, rubbing it through her silk panties, which were sopping wet.

"Oh, God, I need you so bad." Betty undid Jake's belt and yanked his shorts and underwear down, using her foot to push them down to his ankles, and he stepped out of them, kicking them out of the way. "Now, take off my panties, Mister Literal."

Betty raised herself up a few inches, her cannonball shoulders flexing, strengthened from her years of yoga practice. Jake removed her panties and kneeled down to give her pussy a quick lick.

"No!" she commanded again. "I want you inside me. Don't make love to me, fucking fuck me! I need you to fuck me so bad."

Betty laid back on the table, her hips on the edge, and Jake lined his throbbing cock with her dripping cunt. He slid his cock head up and down between her lips a few times, getting it wet, before he thrust himself inside her.

"AHH, FUCK!" Betty yelled as he drove himself home, burying himself completely inside her clean-shaven pussy, his balls slapping into her asshole. "OH, FUCK, I'VE NEEDED YOU SO BAD!"

Jake started pounding her pussy, rocking the table, and causing the empty orange juice bottle to fall over. "I need you too, Betty. I've missed you so much."

Jake put Betty's legs on his shoulders and grabbed her arms at the elbows, pulling her onto him and pushing back as he pulled his cock back out, only to pull on her arms again as he slammed himself into her welcoming pussy once more.

"I've missed you, baby. You have no idea. Oh, fuck me, baby. I need this. Uhh—uhh—uhh—uhh, fuck me, Jakey," Betty moaned. Sweat formed on her forehead and plastered her hair to her scalp.

"Your pussy is so wet and smooth. I love being inside you, Betty." Sweat dripped down Jake's cheeks and into his eyes, even as his smooth chest was covered in perspiration. Betty wanted to massage his chest, but he was still holding her forearms and pulling on them as he plunged himself into her over and over until they both felt the pressure building.

"Jake, I'm going to come," she gasped.

"I am, too, baby."

"Come with me, Jakey. Tell me you love me and fill up my pussy."

"Look at me when you come," said Jake. "Look into my eyes, and let me see you come." Jake drove his cock as deep as he could with each thrust, feeling Betty's wet cunt gripping his shaft as he slid in and out, pulling almost all the way out before slamming himself back inside her, their bodies slapping in rhythm, the table rocking, threatening to collapse.

"I will, lover. Oh, God, you make me feel so good. Oh, fuck—this is it—oh, God, I'm going to—I LOVE YOU, JAKE! OH FUCK...!" Betty wrapped her ankles around Jake's neck and squeezed as the first orgasm washed over her, quickly followed by an aftershock. She fought to keep her eyes open, her face turned scarlet, and she opened her mouth in a silent scream as a second orgasm crashed into her.

"I love you, too, Betty! OH, GOD, I LOVE YOU TOO!" Jake's orgasm quickly followed Betty's, and he jetted his come into her eager pussy. He drove himself to the root one more time and held still; she felt the first blast deep inside her, and then the second, and a third. Jake thrust a couple more times and squeezed out the fourth and fifth weaker, but no less welcome, shot of his man juice.

Jake stood, still inside her, knees trembling, as the two recovered and regained their breath, chests heaving, dripping sweat.

After a minute of gazing into each other's eyes, caressing each other's chest, and Jake running his fingers through Betty's hair, he said, "So, how was your flight?"

Betty burst out laughing. "I'll tell you in the shower."

Jake pulled his deflating prick out of her, and some of his come dribbled out of her raw pussy. Betty ran her fingers through it and tried to scoop some of it up, popping it into her mouth and smiling.

"Mmmmm, still delicious, lover. I can tell you're still eating lots of fruit."

"And staying hydrated," Jake said, smiling.

He picked her up and carried her into the bathroom, where he already had two towels set out, as well as some scented soaps and Betty's favorite massage oil, something he discovered when he, Betty, and Sheila had spent their Sunday afternoon giving each other sensual massages, topping it off with masturbating each other to a satisfying orgasm and falling asleep for a couple hours, arms and legs intertwined. Sheila was never quite able to get the oil stains out of those sheets afterward and only used them when she and Betty repeated the occasion.

The two soaped each other off in the shower, taking extra time to clean each other's best areas. Jake soaped up Betty's tits three times, even as she soaped up his cock for several minutes. Jake took the removable shower head and blasted Betty's cunt, giving her another orgasm, and then fingered her until she grabbed his wrist and begged for mercy.

Jake turned the AC down—or do you turn it up to make it colder?—and the two lay in bed, snuggled under the blankets. Jake was on his back with his right arm around Betty, her naked breasts pressed against his chest.

"I love being this close to you," said Betty, brushing her fingers through Jake's hair, and looking deeply into his eyes. She kissed him on the mouth and then on his chin.

"I do, too. I've missed you greatly."

"I've missed you," she said, kissing him again. The two swirled their tongues together, and Jake could feel his cock stirring again.

"Do you ever feel bad saying you love me?" Betty asked after a few minutes.

Jake thought for a moment. "No, not at all."

"Not even if I'm married?"

He thought again. "No. Because that doesn't change how I feel."

"Even though we can never be together?"

"Well, never say never, but even then."

"And do you mean it?" she asked, her eyes brimming with tears. "You're not just saying that to make an old lady feel better?"

"First, there aren't any old ladies here," Jake said. Betty smiled as one tear spilled down her cheek.

"But I'm old enough to be your mother."

"Well, my young mother," said Jake.

"That's not one of your fantasies, is it? Do you have a mommy fetish? Do you want to have sex with mommy?"

"Shhh!" Jake hissed, covering her mouth with his hand. "The publisher says we're not allowed to do those kinds of stories!"

The two looked around to see whether anyone from the editorial department suddenly popped into the room. After a tense minute, they decided the coast was clear and continued on.

Jake cleared his throat. "Second, and more importantly, I do love you. I know we agreed the last time we were together[25] that we only meant it for that weekend. But I still think about you, and I still have those feelings for you even now."

---

[25] Still volume 1, book 6, *Stand Up, Lie Down: Betty In Birmingham.* It's my favorite book of the series!

Betty nodded and stroked her fingers down his pectorals.

Jake continued, "But just because we can't be together forever doesn't mean we can't say it when we *are* together. I enjoy talking with you, I love it when we have phone sex, and I think about you often. Sometimes, I'll smile when I'm alone because I thought about you. Or I'll get a hard-on because I thought about our amazing weekend, and I'll masturbate while I fantasize about fucking you again.

"Being with you here now is a bonus because I actually get to see your beautiful eyes, feel your amazing body against mine, and feel our bare skin touching. Even if we were never going to have sex again, I just love being with you, and that would be enough for me."

"But we're still going to have sex, right?" asked Betty.

"Oh, absolutely," said Jake, and he glanced down toward his hard cock, which was making a tent under the blanket.

Betty giggled and said, "Good. Because that's the second-best part of you."

"Really? What's my best part?"

"Your heart," said Betty, climbing on top of Jake and kissing him deeply. "You're a good man, Jake Nilsen. And that's why I love you. You make an—that is, a slightly older woman feel beautiful. But I don't want you to be good right now. I want you to be bad. I want you to be naughty and fill me up with your thick cock as many times as we can until I have to leave tomorrow night."

"Okay, but first I want to eat your sweet pussy. Come up and straddle my face."

Betty kissed him once more and then spun around, doing as Jake asked. She settled her hairless cunt over his eager mouth, and she sucked Jake's cock into hers. The two lovers explored their feelings for each other once more.

Actually, Jake would like me to point out that they explored each other three more times that night.

Good going, stud!

CHAPTER 3

It was Thursday morning, the first night of Jake's show at Brownie's. He and Betty had spent Monday and Tuesday together, going out to eat, visiting bookstores, going to casinos, and seeing some of the sights of Reno. They held hands, put their arms around one another, and made out at stoplights and between courses at dinner.

Jake topped it off by fingering Betty to an orgasm as he drove her to the airport Wednesday morning.

Still, he had a bit of a bangover after two days of fucking, and so needed to do something different to get his blood pumping. Thursday morning, he went out for another run and appreciated the dryness of the Reno climate. His phone said the temperature was in the mid-80s, but he barely broke a sweat because it was evaporating off his body quicker than it could collect. This was a lot different from the Midwest, or even Florida, where he had spent a month staying with another woman, Jackie[26], getting sweaty for other reasons.

---

[26] See *Stand Up, Lie Down 8: Jackie in Jacksonville*

He ran five miles before heading back to the gym and lifting weights again, hitting all his major muscle groups. He showered in the gym and then booked another massage at the spa next door.

He did that for the next two days, working himself hard in what he called a sexual detox. On Friday, he was at lunch, paperback mystery in hand, having just finished a taco salad. He was engrossed in the book when a shadow spilled across his book, and he looked up.

"What are you reading?" said the woman standing at his table.

Jake held up the book. "*The Girl with a Secret*, Charlotte Armstrong," Jake said.

"Interesting. Is that like *The Secret Garden* or something?" said the woman.

"No, it's a mystery. Charlotte Armstrong was a mystery writer in the 40s and 50s. I picked up a few of her books on a trip to Portland a couple weeks ago. A friend recommended them."

"No kidding? Do you read a lot of old mysteries?"

"I do. I'm on the road most of the year, and I'd rather read a good mystery than watch TV. So, I look for authors with a lot of books, and I've been trying to read books from the last century lately," said Jake. "I'm Jake, by the way." He stood up and extended his hand. "Jake Nilsen."

"Nillsen?" said Randi.

"Nilsen," corrected Jake.

She shook his hand with a firm grip. "Hi, I'm Randi."

Several jokes immediately popped into Jake's head, but he was positive she had heard every single one of them many times over her life, so he held back. Randi was tall, about 5'10", and curvy and voluptuous, with wide hips and a full, heavy chest. Her hair was black and cut short, combed back behind her ears. She had tattoos on her biceps and her calves, and she was wearing a white patterned t-shirt and faded denim cutoffs with white socks and black Doc Marten shoes. She looked like she was in her late 20s or early 30s.

Jake noted the laugh lines around her eyes and knew she was going to be a lot of fun. He loved people with laugh lines—often ungraciously called crows' feet—because it meant they laughed a lot. He didn't trust people who didn't have laugh lines.

"Would you like to sit down?" he asked.

"I was actually on my way out, but why not?" The two sat down, and Jake waved to his server for a refill on his water. "I've got nowhere special to be," she continued. "Oh God, that makes me sound like such a loser. Just a crazy lady and her cats."

Jake threw his head back and laughed.

"I didn't think you meant that. Unless you do have a lot of cats. How many cats do you have?"

"Three," Randi said, trying to hide an embarrassed smile.

"You're okay then. You're not a crazy cat lady until you have seven."

"So I'm only half-crazy."

"I don't know you well enough to say yet."

"Yet," Randi said, laughing. "So, are you a big mystery reader, Jake?"

"It's mostly what I read. I read a lot of different things, but I love old murder mysteries. What about you?"

Randi looked embarrassed. "Oh, I don't like to say."

"Oh, come on. It can't be that bad."

"It's not. I just feel like people judge me when they hear what I like."

"I promise not to judge you," Jake said.

"Okay." Randi took a deep breath and mumbled, "Erotica."

Jake snorted.

"You said you wouldn't laugh!" Randi protested, laughing herself.

"No, I said I wouldn't judge," he corrected. "But I'm not actually laughing at you, I'm—well, I'm laughing at you, but not at your reading choice. I laughed that you were worried about what I would think."

"You don't think that's weird?"

"Not at all," said Jake, in a very positive and affirming way. "A lot of women—and it *is* mostly women who do it—read erotica because they're looking for entertainment and escapism, as well as a relief from stress and anxiety. And people who read romantic fiction usually have higher empathy levels than people who don't. So don't feel ashamed for reading erotica. I happen to enjoy reading it myself from time to time."

"Wow, I appreciate you saying that. So do you read it?"

"From time to time," said Jake, blushing a little despite his speech.

"Really? Who are some of your favorites?"

"Emily Bunney is good," Jake said. "Also, Dalia Lance and Nova Embers."

"No kidding? I love Dalia Lance! Have you ever read Lynn Chantale's *The Baker's Touch*?"

"That was a great book! I just finished it on my Kindle a couple weeks ago," Jake said. "It was, umm, very … effective."

"No kidding. It was effective for me, too," said Randi, blushing again. "Twice."

"Have you ever read Ali Whippe?"

"I love Ali Whippe!" Jake exclaimed. "I even got to visit Abraxus Tasker College last year."[27]

"Visit it? You were actually on the XTC campus? How can you do that, unless... Wait... are we... are we in an erotica novel right now?"

Jake half-closed his eyes and shook his head imperceptibly. He put his finger over his lips and made a quiet *shhhhh*.

"Fourth wall," he whispered.

"Ah, got it," whispered Randi.

She continued in a louder voice. "That is, I mean, I love reading Ali Whippe."

"So, what do you do, Randi?" asked Jake, desperately trying to get the story back on track.

"I'm a Ph.D. student in English literature."

"No kidding? Do you have a particular focus?

"American Literature of the 40s and 50s."

Yawn, thought Jake. "That sounds … interesting?"

---

[27] See *Stand Up, Lie Down 7: Carrie On Campus*

"Specifically, pulp novels—mostly mysteries."

"Oh, no kidding?" Jake retracted his unspoken sarcastic yawn. "So you already know about Charlotte Armstrong?"

"Yeah, I was yanking your chain with that *Secret Garden* joke."

Smart *and* funny? *And* tall? Jake mentally swooned. "Be still, my heart," he said.

Randi laughed. "How about you, Jake? What do you do?"

"I'm a professional standup comic."

"Really? I've never met a professional standup comic before," she said. "I know plenty of people who think they're funny, but ... they're not. So not funny." She shook her head at the pained memories.

"That's okay," he said. "I've never met anyone who studied mysteries for a living."

The two talked about her work and compared favorite mystery authors from different eras—Golden Age mysteries, *noir* mysteries from the 1940s, pulp mysteries, and the resurgence of the locked room mysteries in the last several years.

"I have a show tonight," Jake finally said. "I'm playing at Brownie's all weekend. Would you like to come? I can leave your name at the door, and you can get in for free."

"Sure. I've been on a Cornell Woolrich reading binge, and I could use a break."

Jake shared the details of the show with her and then texted Kaitlyn to make sure Randi was on the guest list.

"So, what else do people do for fun around here?" asked Jake.

"Do you mean besides the casinos?" said Randi. "I'm not much of a gambler."

"Yeah, me either. The house always wins, and I'd rather just use my money somewhere more productive. Like the lottery."

Randi snorted. "Well, there's the Nevada Museum of Art, the National Automobile Museum, and if you had come in the summer, there's a minor league baseball team in town."

"I haven't seen a ballgame in years," said Jake.

"And you won't today," teased Randi. "The season ended in August."

"So, what are you doing today?"

"I was taking a day off from studying and just finished lunch, then I was going to the automobile museum. I've lived here for three years but haven't been there yet, so I thought I would go. Do you want to join me?"

Jake checked his watch—it was just after 1:30—and said, "Sure. I don't have to get ready for my show until 6:00. My first set is at 8:00, and my second is at 9:30. If you'd like, we can grab dinner afterward. Would that work?"

"Sounds like a date," said Randi. "Er, that is, not a date-date. I didn't mean to be so forward. This would just be a, um, just a casual outing. Right? Right. I mean, no point in putting pressure on this. Oh, God, what am I doing? I just get so tongue-tied when I get nervous."

Jake put his large hand on Randi's, covering her small hand, and gave it a gentle, reassuring squeeze. He murmured, "Remember where we are."

"Huh?" said Randi before she realized his meaning. "Oh, right! I mean, yes, sounds like a date! That's what we'll do. You'll do your show, I'll laugh my ass off, and then we'll go to dinner. And then, who knows what will happen afterward?"

"Who, indeed?" said Jake. He and Randi stood and headed out of the restaurant.

Chapter 4

"Oh my God!" exclaimed Randi, grabbing Jake's arm with one hand and holding her stomach with the other. "That was hilarious. I haven't laughed that hard in months!"

The two met up after Jake's second set when he wrapped it up, left the stage, and headed back to the green room. He sent the opener out to the audience to bring Randi back to the green room, which was really just a small room where extra chairs were stored, plus two chairs and a table for the comics.

Then she reached up and gave him a full hug with her whole body, pressing the length of her body against his. Jake could feel her full, natural breasts on his chest and imagined how they must look in the full light of day.

Randi had gone home to change after their museum visit and was now wearing a low-cut, deep blue summer dress and a banana yellow sweater, plus white sneakers. Her long legs looked much longer in the short dress, and her skin was milky white. Jake fantasized about what they would feel like wrapped around his narrow waist, and he tried not to stare at the deep cleavage before him. His prick started to stir as he fantasized about sliding it inside that deep cleft.

Jake was wearing his usual work clothes: blue jeans, striped blue button-down shirt, gray herringbone sports jacket, and tan Oxford shoes.

"Thank you so much," said Jake. "I really appreciate that. I'm glad you had fun."

"I really did. I feel like I could watch it again and still laugh at all the same jokes. They weren't just funny, they really made me think."

"Thank you again," Jake said, blushing. Like most Midwesterners, he was uncomfortable with praise and receiving compliments. That made it tough to be in entertainment, but it was a burden Jake was willing to bear, especially when coming from beautiful women like Randi.

"Are you still interested in dinner?"

"Sure, that would be fine. I know a little French bistro near here if that strikes your fancy. Or we could have sushi if you'd prefer that. There's a sushi place down the street a couple of blocks that I love. We could walk there."

"Sushi would be wonderful. I love sushi."

"Sushi it is, then."

"See you tomorrow, Jake," called Gabe the bartender as they walked out. "Good show tonight. I was laughing my ass off!"

"Thanks, man!"

"Third base!" hollered Gabe.

"Third base!" Jake hollered in return.

"What was that about?" asked Randi, as the two walked out. She had linked her arm through his and was pressed up against him, which made Jake appreciate her height even more. He couldn't do that with shorter women, since he was 6'3". There was something about walking arm-in-arm with a tall woman that made him appreciate them.

"Oh, he was trying to play a trick on me when I first got here, but I managed to swing it around to the old 'Who's on First' routine by Abbott and Costello."

"I know that one! I think," said Randi. "What was the name of the pitcher?"

"No, What's on second."

"No, who's the pitcher?"

"No, Who's on first."

"Dammit!" Randi laughed. "Jake, tell me the pitcher's name."

"Tomorrow."

Randi stared at him for a second.

"His name is Tomorrow," Jake clarified. "The guy's name is Tomorrow."

"Okay, that's what I thought. I couldn't remember it."

They chatted about Jake's work as a standup comic and some of the different places he had performed. They talked about his agent, Kurt, and how he kept calling this Jake's Wacky Wild West tour.

"I'm still not calling it that," said Jake. "I do thoughtful humor, not wacky bullshit. Calling it wacky makes it sound like I'm a prop comic with a bike horn and an arrow-through-the-head trick."

The restaurant was mostly empty, and Jake asked for a booth in the back. Before they sat down, Randi inspected the seats, pulled out a sanitizing wipe from her purse, and wiped down one of the seats. She slid into one and then said, "Sit here next to me."

Jake slid in next to her, Randi on his right arm.

"There's a big split in that seat," said Randi. "I hate sitting on broken vinyl seats. Besides, I'm a bit chilly in here."

"No problem," said Jake. "I'll keep you warm." He put his arm around her and squeezed her close. "You know who has good sushi?" continued Jake. "I had some great sushi in Vancouver, Canada. They're close to the ocean, so the fish is absolutely fresh. I went to a place that was right on the beach, and they had a day special that whatever they caught from the docks could be turned into sushi within an hour. They paid fishermen to bring their catch to the restaurant right away and pay them fifty bucks for a 5-gallon bucket of perch or flounder. I went back twice. I had the perch one night and the flounder the next."

"Those don't sound like typical sushi fish," said Randi.

"No, but they make great sashimi."

"Have you ever had freshwater fish sushi? Is that a thing?"

"Eww, no," said Jake, making a face. "Never eat freshwater fish raw. I'm from Minnesota, and you learn quickly that you cook the shit out of that stuff."

"Really? I'm from Wisconsin! I just moved here for grad school."

"Ah, wuh-Scahnsin! I taut dat I detected a little Up Nort accent dere," said Jake, exaggerating the Upper Midwest accent prevalent in their home region.

The server came by to take their order, and they decided to split three rolls—spicy tuna, firecracker, and a spider/soft shell crab.

As they ate, they talked about some of their favorite books and took turns feeding each other sushi bites with their fingers, sucking on each other's fingers as they did so. Randi pressed her leg up against Jake, who was resting his hand on her bare thigh, and she would occasionally press her left breast into his arm.

Once, after she sucked his long index finger completely into her mouth, she pulled his face close to hers and said, "I want you to come over to my place, and I'm going to sit on your face."

She kissed him long and deep and then looked up at him again, staring into his icy-blue eyes, reaching down and squeezing his already-hard cock. Jake slid his hand up her thigh until he encountered her pussy. He felt her silky panties and ran a finger along the wetness that was soaking the material.

Randi gasped and shuddered as his finger made contact with her, separated only by a very thin layer of fabric.

"What color are your panties?" Jake whispered.

"Yellow," said Randi, her eyes searching his. "Like my sweater."

"Take them off," he said.

Randi looked around to see if anyone was looking their way, raised up, and slid her panties off. "I wouldn't do this if I hadn't wiped down the seat," she said with a smile. She handed Jake her panties, and he tucked them into his jacket pocket.

"Thank God for disinfecting wipes," Jake said. He slid his finger back up toward her wet pussy, nestling his middle finger between her lips, running lengthwise like a hot dog in its bun. He crooked his finger so the tip of his finger entered her pussy just a little and then slid upward so his finger ran over her clitoris.

Randi gasped and then moaned when he removed it and slid his finger into his mouth to taste her wetness.

"I definitely want you to sit on my face, and I'm going to lick your cunt until you come," Jake said in a low, rumbly voice that made Randi even wetter. The kind of low rumbly voice you might hear in a 4 Horsemen erotica audiobook, now available on our website.[28]

"Oh, fuck. I definitely want that."

The server had brought their check by a while ago, so Jake dropped a $100 bill on the table, and the two left as quickly as they could.

"I live in a house just outside of town in a new development," said Randi. "I didn't want to be in town because I like having my own space without a lot of people around. My uncle bought it as an investment, but he's renting it to me for pretty cheap while I'm in school."

"Where's your car?"

"At home. I took a Lyft just in case things worked out this way." Randi smiled mischievously.

"Ah, so you knew we were going to have sex?"

"No, I knew you were going to fuck me silly," said Randi. "I just wasn't sure if we were going to do it at my house or your place."

"Let's go to your place."

---

[28] https://4horsemenpublications.com/our-authors/chastity-veldt/

When they reached Jake's truck, Randi punched her address into his GPS and selected the longest possible route that would take some of the more secluded streets on the outskirts of Reno.

As Jake pulled out of the parking lot, Randi unbuckled his belt, unzipped his jeans, and fished his dick out of his pants. She leaned over and sucked him into her mouth, taking a few inches of him at once, and pulling back off his cock, sucking with some pressure.

"Turn left on 4th Street," said the GPS.

Jake appreciated the long route she chose and was pretty sure he was going to come before they got to her place. Jake smiled because he always lasted longer for the second and third rounds than for his first round.

"Oh, baby, you taste so good," she said before returning to her task. She slid her mouth over his cock again, sliding a few more inches into her mouth, reaching about six inches of his eight-and-a-half-inch prick before she hit her gag reflex. She pulled out and slid back, stopping just short, and held it for several seconds before it became too much. She fought against the gag reflex, and her body curled up as Jake's cockhead tapped the back of her throat.

Randi pulled her mouth off of his dick and looked into Jake's eyes. "Such a great cock. Come into my mouth, okay? I want your hot come in my mouth," she begged. "Shoot your seed in my mouth."

Jake appreciated that she pronounced it "come" and not "cum." But then again, he expected nothing less from a woman getting a Ph.D. in English literature.

"Turn right on Keystone Avenue," said the GPS.

"I'll give you whatever you want, as much as you want," said Jake, resting his hand on the back of her head and guiding her back down until her wet lips were wrapped around his cock once more. She bobbed her head up and down, fucking him with her face, making his shaft glisten with her saliva in the dashboard lights.

She stopped for a rest and breathed deeply as she jacked him off for a few seconds. Then she returned to his dick once more and resumed her oral ministrations. She sucked his dick deep into her mouth and then pulled off with a dry pop and repeated the motion and sound. Then she would noisily slurp it back into her mouth, her lips and cheeks vibrating from the loose suction. And then once more with the hard suction and pop.

Soon, Randi could feel Jake's balls tighten up, and he bucked up to fuck her face. She drove her mouth deep onto his thick meat and let him fuck her face.

"Oh, God, Randi, I'm going to come," he warned. "I'm going to fill your hot mouth with my come."

"Turn right in one-quarter mile," said the GPS.

"Mm-hmm," she said, her mouth full of his cock. "Mm-hmm," she repeated.

"Fuck, do that some more," said Jake. "The vibrations tickle my dick."

Jake's radio was playing a local rock station, and Randi hummed along with the song that was playing, a song about two friends becoming lovers for just one night. The rumbling in the back of her throat tickled Jake's cock head as he continued thrusting into her mouth until he reached the inevitable conclusion of her eager and willing suction.

The first shot hit the back of her throat with such force that it made her cough. She pulled his cock out of her mouth just as the second shot hit her on her left cheek and her eye, which she had fortunately closed just a half second before.

She quickly shoved his cock back into her mouth and took the third, fourth, and fifth shots of jizz, savoring its salty-sweet taste. Randi held Jake in her mouth until she was sure he had fired every delicious load and wasn't going to surprise her with a sixth.

After he stopped shuddering and had relaxed, Randi released him with another *pop!* and looked up at him, his come still plastered over her left eye. She opened her mouth, showed him the contents, and then closed it again to swallow. She opened her mouth one more time, and it was empty.

"You have arrived at your destination," said the GPS.

"Just in time," said Randi. "We all arrived at the same time," she added, laughing.

Jake handed her a napkin from his glove compartment, and Randi wiped the strand of Jake's jizz from her eye and cheek.

"Let's hurry inside because I still want to eat your pussy," said Jake.

"I can't wait, big boy."

CHAPTER 5

Once inside, the two began taking each other's clothes off, leaving them on the floor, littering their way to the bedrooms in the back of the house until they were clad only in their underwear. They walked awkwardly back, Jake's hands cupping Randi's tits as she rubbed his hard-on through his boxer briefs.

On the way, Jake spotted three cats sleeping on the couch and an easy chair. The cats raised their heads to consider the new human who was groping their human who provided them food, ignored them both, and went back to sleep.

The two passed the bedroom that Randi had turned into an office. It was lined with bookshelves; there was a desk, a chair, and what looked like a kind of camp chair suspended from the ceiling.

"Whoa, what is that?" Jake asked, stopping in his tracks and letting go of Randi's globes. It looked like an outdoor nylon chair hanging from the ceiling by four ropes, one on each of the four corners.

"That's a chair hammock."

"A what?"

"You know, like a regular hammock strung up between two trees? Only this is a chair that hangs from a tree or a ceiling. I like to sit in it and read. I give it a little shove, and I rock while I read."

"So, it's not a sex swing?"

"Not … technically?" Randi's face turned red, along with her upper chest.

"Not technically? You mean you have had sex in it?"

"Well, I masturbated in it a few times. I put my legs between the ropes on the sides and fuck myself with my vibrator."

"That's so fucking hot. So you've never had sex in it?"

"No... not yet?"

"Let's christen your chair."

Randi grinned and kissed Jake hard. "Okay, let's."

Jake ushered her into the office and turned her around to face him. She ran her hands over Jake's washboard abs and huge pectorals, and Jake was thankful he had been working out so hard the last couple of days.

Jake kneeled, kissed Randi's flat belly, and licked as deeply as he could into her cleavage between Randi's heavy, natural breasts. She had a front-clasp bra, which she reached up to unhook, slowly lowering the cups so her breasts could finally breathe.

"Oh, God," murmured Jake. Randi's breasts were long, heavy, and full, and her nipples were already hard. From where he was kneeling, Jake sucked her left nipple, trying to take in as much of her beautiful tit into his mouth as he could. He let it fall out with a loud popping sound and repeated the sucking on her right tit to balance her out. His cock was already stiff again, despite having filled Randi's eager mouth with come just moments before.

"Fuck, that feels so good, Jake," moaned Randi, running her fingers through Jake's hair as he switched back and forth between her eraser-long nipples. "My tits are so sensitive. I love having them sucked and fucked."

"Your wish is my command," said Jake. "Especially that last part." He buried his face between her breasts and licked the entire cleft for several seconds. Randi squeezed her breasts together with her elbows, smothering Jake in her wonderful tit flesh. If he died at that moment, he would not have been more satisfied.

"Get on your knees. Give my cock a few sucks to get it good and wet," Jake commanded. "Please," he added, because good manners are important.

Randi smiled as she realized what he was thinking. She popped his cock into her mouth and bobbed her head up and down a few times, coating it with her saliva. She jammed it as far into her mouth as she could, nearly gagging as his head hit the back of her throat, and then pulled off, leaving long ropes of her thick honey saliva. She stroked Jake's cock with her fist to spread it around and get the shaft good and wet, then straightened up her spine, offering her breasts up to her Viking lover.

Jake spread his legs and bent his knees so his massive prick was on the same level as her beautiful chest, then laid his meat between her tits. Randi squeezed them together, and Jake began sliding his cock between her tits. She lowered her head and kissed his head as it peeked out with each thrust.

"This is so fucking hot; my pussy is soaked," Randi told Jake. "I can't wait for you to eat my pussy."

"I can't either," he said. "I don't want to come just yet. I want you to come in my mouth first."

He thrust between Randi's bountiful breasts for a few more minutes and then stopped, pulling her to her feet. He bent down and kissed her deeply for several seconds and then said, "Get in the chair and spread your legs."

"Ooohhh," moaned Randi when she realized what he was going to do. She tossed a throw pillow onto the floor, settled into the chair so she was nearly sitting up, and snaked her legs between the ropes, putting her glistening cunt on display. Her pubic hair was black and trimmed short, shaved into a triangle that directed Jake's eye down to her pink pussy lips, which were thick and full. Randi opened her lips with her fingers and spread her labia apart, exposing her inner folds and clitoris.

Jake grabbed the pillow, dropped it on the floor, and kneeled on it before Randi. He rested her hands on the insides of her powerful thighs and put his nose just an inch from her shiny cunt. He inhaled deeply, looked up at Randi, and smiled before burying his face in her wetness.

He drove his tongue deeply inside her with no preamble. No kissing of her thighs or licking around her pussy. He was on a mission and couldn't wait to eat her and hear her scream. He shoved his tongue straight into her moist folds and licked upward, hard, like he was trying to get as much ice cream as he could off of a melting cone.

"Holy fuck," moaned Randi as Jake continued to lick and lick and lick. He was selfish for her juices, which were flowing from her pussy, and Jake could barely keep up. Every few licks, he would stop and suck her clit into his mouth, flicking his tongue over it before drilling his oral muscle back into her gash.

After several minutes of devouring her deliciousness, the area around Jake's mouth was slick from her juices. He ate her like a starving man seeing his first meal in days, and Randi moaned under his attentions.

She began to feel that familiar tingle in her belly, and she tightened her thigh muscles to drive her ass up, pressing her snatch deeper into Jake's mouth.

"Oh, fuck, Jakey. You're eating me so well." Jake caught that she said "well," instead of "good," so he drove his tongue in harder. "That's so good. Eat my fucking pussy, you beautiful fucking Viking!"

She grabbed the back of his head and pressed him harder into her cunt. Jake opened his mouth and sucked as much of her cunt lips into his mouth as he could and rubbing her clit with his thumb.

"Fuck, that's it, Jake! I'm going to come. Oh, fuck, you're making me come! Oh, God! Oh, God! Oh, God! Here I—FUUUUUUCCCCCCK!" Randi threw her head back and wailed as her body shuddered from her orgasm. Jake hooked her legs with his forearms and held on as Randi bucked and thrashed while he devoured her beautiful pussy and she came in his mouth.

As she rode out her orgasm, she finally had to pull on Jake's hair and shout, "Ow! Ow! Fuck, please stop! I'm sensitive after I come."

Jake released her and rocked back, sitting on his heels. His cock was at full mast, pointing upward, and his face was covered in her juices. He wiped his fingers along his cheeks and lips, wiping off her fluids, and then licked his fingers clean. Randi watched him and breathed heavily as she recovered.

"Fuck, I actually came in your mouth," she said. "I've never done that."

"I definitely want to do that again. You're delicious," said Jake. "Only I want you to sit on my face next time."

"I can do that. Now, stand up and fuck me with your beautiful cock because my legs are too weak to try to make it to my bed."

"Your wish is my command," Jake said, rising to his feet. He held his mammoth prick in his hand and stroked it a few times with his fist. He moved his feet apart to lower himself to the best level and lined his tool up with her opening.

"Let me see you do it," moaned Randi. "Let me watch you enter me."

She grabbed the ropes and pulled herself forward. Jake slid his head into her velvety opening and held it for a few seconds.

"Can you see it? Can you see my cock entering your pretty pussy?"

"I see it! I fucking see it! Oh, please put it in me. Put it in further.[29] Go slowly. Let me see you go in me—ohhhh, shit!—but make it last."

Jake grabbed onto the ropes and pulled Randi toward him, controlling his entrance into her gorgeous slit. Slowly, as his cock slid into her, they both watched her lips spread and shift as more and more of him filled up her eager pussy, rearranging her muscles for this new invader.

---

[29] Or is that "farther"? Jake and Randi discussed whether it should have been one or the other between their marathon fucking sessions. Ultimately, they agreed "farther" was the better option, but when you're fucking, who cares? I'll bet you don't get grammar lessons in your other erotica, do you? Take THAT, Honey Cummings!

"Oh, fuck, you're so big," Randi marveled. "You're bigger than my fucking vibrator, that's for sure. God, I haven't been this full in years."

Jake held himself three-quarters of the way inside her so she could get used to his thickness before he pulled himself back completely out.

"Put it back in!" begged Randi. "Please, put it back in me!"

Jake did as he was told, pushing slowly again so Randi could watch him repeat his entrance. Then he pulled out again and pushed back in once more to the same depth as before.

"I need you to fuck me, Jake. Don't tease me, pound the shit out of me."

Jake slid his cock out again and then slid back inside, this time driving himself into her all the way to his hilt, his massive tool buried deep inside Randi. She threw her head back and wailed, "FFFUUUCCCKKKK!"

Jake held himself there for a few more seconds before withdrawing and plunging, pulling out, shoving in, over and over, slowly at first. As she got used to his thickness splitting her apart, he pushed himself hard into her, which pushed her back on her not-a-sex-swing chair. Jake held onto the ropes and pulled her back onto his cock, pushing himself completely into her. It was a slow-but-study rhythm, letting the swinging of the chair drive their pace until she demanded that he well and truly plow her.

"That's it, Jake. Fuck me hard. Pound my pussy. I haven't had a good dicking in years, and now I've got you. Fuck me, goddammit!"

That sent Jake into frenzied action. He grabbed Randi's thighs to keep her from swinging at all and jackhammered himself into her eager cunt, their bodies slapping together and Randi grunting with every thrust.

"Ohh! Ohh! Ohh! Ohh! That's it! That's it. Fuck me hard. I'm going to come again. Please keep fucking me! I'm going to come."

"Randi, your pussy feels amazing!" Jake gasped as sweat ran down his face and hairless chest; Randi's hair was plastered to her scalp, and her body shone in the low light of her office. "Oh, fuck, I'm going to come, too."

"Come on my tits! Spray your hot seed on my tits, Jake."

Jake reached down and started rubbing Randi's engorged clit as he continued to thrust himself into her, which was enough to start her second orgasm of the hour.

"Oh, God, Jake! That's it, please keep doing that! Ohh! Ohh! I'm coming, Jake! I'm coming for you! AAAAHHHHHHHH!!"

Randi gripped Jake's forearm as she shuddered and came once more. Jake continued drilling her pussy a few more times before he felt the tingling in his balls as well. He pulled out of her wet snatch and stroked his cock, using her juices as lubrication, until he gave her what she asked for.

"Oh, fuck! This is for you, baby! I'm coming for you, too. Ahh! Ahh! Ahh!"

The first jet splattered Randi's full tits, the impact so hard, it splattered and was followed by a second shot equally as powerful as the first one. Randi moaned as each hot blast of jizz landed on her sweaty chest.

Jake fired a third rope of come, followed by a fourth, and finally, a weak fifth shot landed on Randi's pubic region. She used her fingers and scooped up Jake's come and looked him in the eye as she slid it into her finger and sucked it clean. She repeated the process until she had cleaned herself up. Jake admired her attention to detail and stood watching her eat his come, while he breathed heavily, sweat dripping from his chin and brow.

"That was amazing," Jake finally said when she finished cleaning herself.

"It was for me as well. I haven't been well and truly fucked like that in years. I sure hope you're up for a second round soon."

"Absolutely," he said, helping her out of the now-it's-a-sex-chair chair. He wrapped his arms around her and pressed her naked, sweaty body to his own naked, sweaty body. "What do you say to a shower first, and then we'll try another room in the house?"

"You're on, stud. But I want to try it doggy style in this chair, too."

"Mmmmm," moaned Jake. "Now that you've put that image in my head, we may not make it to the shower."

Randi stood up on her toes, and Jake kissed her, then she jumped up and wrapped her legs around his waist.

"Carry me to the kitchen first. I need a drink, and I want to see if my kitchen table will take a good pounding."

Jake smiled. "Your wish is my command."

Tracy
in Tucson

Table of Contents

CHAPTER 1

"Now entering Tucson," said the sign along the highway. "The Old Pueblo welcomes you."

"Meh heh heh," snickered Jake, imitating Beavis & Butthead. "Entering."

Of course, no one was in the car to hear him, but that didn't stop Jake from making a running commentary on everything he saw on his travels. He was on the second day of driving from a trip to Reno, Nevada, where he had done a week at Brownie's Comedy Club. It was over 850 miles from Reno to Tucson, but Jake wasn't in any hurry. He was a little bored though, so he talked to himself, yelled at road signs, practiced Norwegian on his foreign language app, and voice-dictated texts to friends and past lovers.

"Hey, babe, thinking about you. I wanted to thank you again for visiting me. I had a great time," he said to Betty, his lover from

Birmingham, Alabama,[30] who had visited him while he was in Reno so they could renew their relationship.[31]

"Hey, Kurt, Reno was great. Had a good time, the crowd was a lot of fun, and Kaitlyn said she would love to have me back," he texted to his manager.

"Hey, jackass, you're not funny, and everyone secretly hates you," he texted to his best friend and fellow comic, Curtis Sanders.

"Hey dickweed, every1 openly h8s u. Got the call I'm going 2 Tucson. They need The Kid to carry your unfunny ass," Curtis responded a few minutes later.

"You couldn't carry my ass with a bucket and two hands. Plus, I'm much funnier and handsomer. Also, I have a new story for you," Jake messaged back. He was very careful to even dictate the punctuation in his messages because he was a nerd about language and grammar.

He had stopped in Henderson, Nevada, the night before, so he wouldn't have to actually stay in Las Vegas. He hated Las Vegas for its flashing lights, glitz and glamor, and emphasis on riches and success. Everyone thought they were a high roller and did their best to live up to the reputation of Sin City. It's not that Jake was a prude—far from it. (You *are* reading an erotica novel, after all.) But he didn't like the false front everyone put up, trying to appear richer and more successful than they actually were. He hated the fakery of it all.

Which was odd since Jake was an entertainer. He was a professional comic on the fifth stop of his Wacky Wild West tour.

---

[30] See *Stand Up, Lie Down, vol. 1, #6: Betty In Birmingham*

[31] See *Stand Up, Lie Down, vol. 2, #4: Randi in Reno*

Jake hated the name of the tour and wouldn't actually say it out loud, even though his agent had been calling it that, and sent out dozens of posters to all the comedy clubs along his tour, as well as launching a large-scale social media campaign.

His hatred of the glitz was also odd because Jake was actually rich. He had made some smart investments while he was in college, using money a rich uncle had left him. He further invested in a shopping center in Savannah, Georgia, and a couple of car washes in Miami, so now he was worth a couple million dollars.

But rather than staying home in Mankato, Minnesota and swimming in a pool filled with money, he was pursuing his true love of stand-up comedy. He was good, too, which meant he was able to support himself with the money he made rather than dipping into his investments. Jake's goal was to actually get his own comedy special on one of the streaming services. He had already gotten a few looks from some of the talent acquisition people, and Kurt had had a few "feeling out" phone calls with them, but nothing yet.

He also liked fucking. Jake got to have sex with a lot of women on the road, which is, again, why you're reading this book in the first place.[32] Jake could have had a lot of sex at home in Mankato, too, but it was not a large city, so he would have run out of available women. Plus, one or more of them would have wanted to get married. He wasn't opposed to getting married, but he wanted to see a lot more of the world first. He also hadn't found the right woman yet, although he had gotten pretty close to a few of them, especially Betty.

But Jake loved life on the road, loved being a nomad, loved touring the country in his pickup truck. He considered getting a cap put on his truck back so he could convert it to a sleeping space if he ever felt like truck camping, but he never followed through on

---

[32] Pervert.

it. He just had a flat cap on the back that he could lock up to keep his stuff safe.

He sometimes thought about trading up to a high-top delivery van like the Amazon drivers drove, converting it into a camper, and living out of that. Jake often watched #vanlife videos on YouTube and dreamed about being a van lifer himself. But then he woke up in the morning, used a proper working toilet, took a hot shower, and realized he didn't really want to lead that kind of life. Van life looked cool until you had to take a shit.

He followed his GPS for 30 more minutes, as it guided him to the Pancake's Comedy Club less than a mile from the University of Tucson. He parked in the parking lot, stretched, hit the button on his key fob, checked to make sure the truck bed was locked up, jumped up and down a few times to get the blood circulating in his legs, and looked around to take in his surroundings.

It was after 4:00 on a Monday afternoon, and Jake could see the traffic building up to leave downtown and head back home. This was another reason Jake loved life on the road. He was pretty much on his own throughout the week, only working a few hours a night on the weekends.

One of Jake's fears was that he would be consigned to a life of commuting back and forth from a job he didn't like. He didn't think less of the people who did it—they were taking care of their families, making sure they had a home and enough to eat. He just knew that if that were his life, he would hate every minute of it.

Maybe that would change once he found a woman he wanted to settle down with, but for now, he was happy to be a nomad, living out of his suitcase and his truck.

It was in the mid-70s at that moment, not too warm. And it was a drier climate, so he didn't immediately start sweating the moment he got out of his truck, not like the month he spent in Jacksonville[33] where he would start sweating just looking outside.

Jake found the door and walked inside. The place was empty, which you would expect on a Monday afternoon. He wandered back to the manager's office, where he heard a radio blasting country music and a female voice singing along.

"Hello?" Jake called so as not to startle the person inside. "Hello?" he called again.

The music shut off. "Hello?" came the response. "Back here."

Jake pushed the door open and saw a woman seated at a desk, laptop open, and a spreadsheet on display.

"Hi, are you Katelyn? I'm Jake Nilsen." He stepped forward, hand extended.

"Nilssen?" asked Kaitlyn. She stood up and shook Jake's hand.

"Nilsen," said Jake. "With one 's.'"

"Ah," said the woman. "My name is actually Kaitlyn, not Katelyn."

"Got it," said Jake. "You probably get that a lot."

"You have no idea," said Kaitlyn. "So, you're our headliner this weekend? What are you doing here so early? We weren't expecting you until Thursday."

---

[33] See *Stand Up, Lie Down, vol. 1, #8: Jackie in Jacksonville*

"Sorry. I just got tired of Reno, so I thought I'd head down. Everything up there is all about gambling, and I got bored. I figured I'd come here, do some sightseeing, maybe some hiking."

"I get that," said Kaitlyn. "I lived in Las Vegas for three years after college and worked at one of the casinos. I got so jaded about the whole thing that I left. I went to college here, so I just came back and opened this place. It's been around for twelve years, so I think we're doing pretty well."

Kaitlyn turned around and grabbed a plate with some fried dough balls on it. "Fritter?" she offered. "It's actually one of our specialties in the kitchen, and we make them fresh every day. They're made with corn and jalapeños, and the dipping sauce is a mango habanero sauce, our chef's own creation."

"That does sound pretty good," said Jake, taking one. He dipped it in the sauce bowl she held up.

Jake took a bite, and his eyes widened. "These are amazing!" he said between chews. He finished chewing and regarded Kaitlyn. She was average height, about five feet, five inches, with black hair, brown eyes, and horn-rimmed glasses. She was wearing black yoga pants and a white sweatshirt with her black hair tied back in a short ponytail. She was curvy in all the right places, and her sweatshirt mostly hid her sizable breasts. Mostly. Jake had boob radar—*boobdar*, he called it—and could spot the outline of large breasts no matter how well hidden.

He finished his fritter and took another one when it was offered. He and Kaitlyn chatted about life in the comedy business, the acts she had seen come through there, and some of the bullshit and shenanigans the other comics had gotten up to over the years.

She talked about how a young comic told a couple of jokes about Native Americans and had his ass kicked out in the parking lot after his show. Or how a male and female comic—the opener and the headliner—ended up hooking up in the club apartment and were now married and running a marketing agency in St. Louis.

"Oh, by the way, our other middle dropped out this morning, so we called in Curtis Sanders. He said we should have dropped you and let him headline because he's funnier."

Jake threw his head back and roared with laughter. "He might be, but I've got a better agent." He wiped his eyes and continued, "He texted me a few hours ago and told me he was coming. He's one of my best friends, and we say that shit to each other all the time."

Kaitlyn snickered and popped the last bite of fritter into her mouth. "The apartment won't actually be cleaned until tomorrow, I'm afraid. You're welcome to stay there tonight and deal with the last comic's mess, or we can put you up in a hotel tonight."

"Uhh, how about a hotel?" said Jake. "I'm a bit of a germaphobe."

"Well, it's a good thing you're Curtis' best friend because you guys are sharing the place for the rest of the week."

"Not a problem. We're used to staying together."

"Excellent. Head over to the Holiday Inn Express on Grant, and I'll have a room reserved by the time you get there. Here's the keys for the apartment, but don't go until after 3:00 tomorrow. My cleaner usually gets there before noon."

"Sounds good. Say, can I get an order of fritters to go? Those are amazing."

"Sure," said Kaitlyn, and the two walked back to the kitchen where she put in the order. They talked some more while they waited for the chef, Enrique, to fry up the tasty corn balls, and handed him a styrofoam container.

"They're on the house if you do the open mic tomorrow,"

Jake hesitated. "I usually hate open mics, but for an order of these, I'll do it. Plus, another order tomorrow night."

"Done," said Kaitlyn, a big smile on her face. Jake grinned at her—they *were* amazing fritters, after all.

Jake shook Enrique's hand and then Kaitlyn's and said his goodbyes.

"Open mic's at 8:00. See you tomorrow."

CHAPTER 2

"Jake the Snake, you in here?" boomed Curtis Sanders. Curtis entered the apartment and set his bag on the floor. Curtis was a tall, skinny Black man with an afro, grown out longer than Jake had last seen him. He was wearing jeans, a plain t-shirt, and horn-rimmed glasses.

"Yo!" hollered Jake from the bathroom. "Be right out." A few seconds later, Jake left the bathroom, waving his hands dry after washing them for twenty seconds with soap and warm water. Because that's what you should do after you use the bathroom.

"The cleaner forgot to leave us new towels," he said, explaining his hand waving. The two men embraced, and Jake wiped his hands a little on Curtis's back.

"Dude, I need a shower after that drive. I drove in from Albuquerque this morning. I was doing a show there and was all set to go back to Cincinnati for a couple weeks when Katelyn called me."

"Kaitlyn," corrected Jake.

"What'd I say?"

"Katelyn."

"Ah," said Curtis. "Yep, I hear it." Curtis looked around the apartment and nodded. "Pretty nice for a club apartment," he said. It was your normal apartment, decorated with art from local artists. The sofa and two side chairs looked like they had come from a Swedish DIY furniture store but were comfortable enough. "Anyway, I have a new story for you."

"Excellent. I think I've got a winner today," said Jake.

Curtis took his bag to the other bedroom and went into the bathroom as Jake fixed himself a drink and got a second one ready for his friend. The two had a friendly competition whenever they were together, where they would tell each other a story of their sexual adventures and whoever told the hottest story won, and the loser bought dinner. The score was currently 5—3, with Curtis in the lead.

After he finished his shower and settled onto the couch, drink in hand, Curtis launched into his story:

So this happened when I was in Kansas City a few weeks ago. I was middling a show, and for whatever reason, there were some protestors outside the club. Turns out the headliner there was being hassled because he had told some sexist jokes back in the late 90s and they had shown up on YouTube. So a bunch of students from the University of Kansas came out to protest. There were about fifteen or so people, and they had signs and shit. Men, women, and non-gender people. Of course, none of them were even born until about ten years after the fact, but whatever. There's still rampant racism in this country, but sure, the 28-year-old jokes are the most pressing matter.

Anyway, I was walking into the club, and one of the women, her name was Katie, accosted me and starts getting in my face about how I'm a misogynist and sexist and all that shit. I said, "Do you even know me?"

She said no, and I said, "You just assume I tell sexist jokes because I'm a dude? Any other assumptions you want to make about me based on my race, too?" That set her back on her feet, and she fumbles out some apology.

I laughed and said, "I'm just giving you shit," and I let her off the hook. We stood there talking, and I told her about my comedy and said that I wasn't one of those comics that need to denigrate people and blah blah blah. I mean, I tell off-color jokes, but they're about family dysfunction. I hate those fucking, "women be shopping, men love sports" comics. Anyway, we talked for a while, and her friends got bored and dispersed. They just left without her, but she had driven herself, so I invited her to the show.

She was pretty cute, too. Kind of curvy with curly, light brown hair and big brown eyes. She had big tits and a beautiful round ass. She was one of those Midwest farm girls. You know the type, being from Minnesota. I love women with meat on their bones, so I was in love. Well, at least Little Curtis was in love. She was wearing a low-cut shirt that showed off her deep cleavage, which I tried sneaking peeks at, plus some tight jeans. Little Curtis was screaming at me to let him out.

Anyway, she thought I was really funny, and we met up after the show—you know what they say about humor being the ultimate aphrodisiac. So we went out for dinner afterward, and then we Ubered back to the club apartment. She was holding onto my arm in the car, pressing her tits up against me and whispering in my ear. Then, when we got close, she licked me on the ear once and said, "I want to suck your cock."

No, I'm not lying, man! I was just as surprised as you. Here I'm thinking this is some innocent college girl who's all jacked up about feminism and shit, and it turns out she's horny as fuck and is down for just about anything. So we start making out in the backseat—yeah, I know that's what happened last time[34]. Coincidences happen, man!—and she's grabbing at my cock through my jeans.

We get back to the apartment, and as soon as I close the door, she's pulling at my belt like she's been poisoned and my cock is the antidote. She immediately drops to her knees and slurps my cock into her mouth.

Yeah, I hate that word too. That and moist.

Anyway, this girl had some suction! She was pulling my cock into her mouth like she was a vacuum and getting it wet and slick. She managed to take off her jacket while she was on her knees, and she stopped long enough to pull her shirt over her head and then undo her bra.

She had some massive tits—36G, because I checked her bra later when she was in the bathroom—and I fucked them for a couple of minutes before she took me back in her mouth. She was slurping so loud, which I love, and fucking her mouth like she was angry at it.

It wasn't too long before I had to come, so I said, "Baby, I'm gonna come. I'm gonna fucking come." She just kept going without breaking motion. If anything, she sucked even harder. She grabbed my ass and fucked my dick with her face. It was so hot that I shouted when I fired my first rocket. Katie went, "Mmmph!" and held on like a champ. She pulled back enough so just my dickhead was in her mouth, and she jacked me off with her fist. I fired three more rounds

---

[34] See *Stand Up, Lie Down, vol. 2: Vanessa in Vancouver*

into her mouth, and she looked up at me with those big brown eyes as I gave her a mouthful.

When I finally stopped shooting, she popped me out of her mouth and held it open so I could see my come on her tongue. Then she closed her mouth, swallowed, and showed me that it was empty. My fucking knees almost buckled.

I helped her up and got her over to the couch, and she took her pants off while I got completely undressed. She sat down and scooted her ass to the edge, and I knelt down in front of her. She was wearing a red silk thong, and they were soaked with her cunt juices. I rolled them off her and put her legs over my shoulders. I immediately dove into her wet pussy and started licking up her slit and grinding my tongue on her clit as hard as I could. She was panting and moaning, grabbing the back of my head to make me go harder.

I sucked on her clit as hard as she sucked on me and she was wailing, "Ohh, fuck, Curtis! That's so good! Suck my fat clit!" She's thrusting her ass up at me like she's trying to fuck *my* mouth now, and I'm trying to hold on so she doesn't give me a bloody nose or something.

After a few minutes, she's shouting, "Oh, fuck, baby! I'm gonna come! I'm coming! Oh, fuck!" and she tenses up like she's being electrocuted and she screams, "AHHHH!" and floods my face with her juices. I hold on while she's riding the wave, but I don't let go of her clit until it's over and she pulls me up by my face.

"I'm so sensitive after I come," she says, and then she kisses me deep, pushing her tongue into my mouth. Then she licks my face to clean her cunt juices off. It was so fucking hot that I got hard again.

She saw my cock and said, "Fuck me, baby. I want you to fuck me with that big cock." So I make her stand up and bend her over the arm of the couch. She has to put her arms straight down to hold herself up, and I line up behind her.

I swipe my cock up and down her pussy a few times, and it's so wet that my cockhead is shiny. She goes, "Put it in me, Curtis. Fuck me with your big prick. I want you to shove that fat prick in my pussy."

So I do as the lady says, and I jam myself in there. She was so wet that I made it all the way inside on the first thrust. I buried myself up to my balls, and she shouts, "OHH!" I grab her hips, pull out again, and then slam myself back once more.

She goes, "OHH!" again, and then every time I shove myself into her.

I start out slow and work up to a faster rhythm. She bends her head way down so she can see what I'm doing, and she says, "I can see your cock, Curtis. It's going so deep inside me. Fuck, I love seeing your cock slide into my cunt." So I slow down a little bit so she can see me sliding in and out of her.

Then she says, "Harder. Fuck me harder." I start thrusting into her faster and harder, and her ass cheeks are jiggling every time I slap into her ass. Her tits get to swinging and are going in circles as I get a steady rhythm going.

She's grunting every time I bury myself into her, going, "Unh! Unh! Unh!" and I'm getting all sweaty. Sweat's running down my face and my back, and she's getting sweaty too.

So I'm pounding her, and she's pushing back into me, telling me "Harder! Fuck me harder!" when I reach back and slap her on the ass. Not hard, but not gentle, either.

She screams, and I think she's about to stop, but she says, "Do it again! Spank my ass!" so I'm happy to do more. I'm holding her hip with my left hand, and I spank her three more times, Whap! Whap! Whap! Each time I do, she shouts, "Yes! Yes! Yes!"

Then she drops down to her elbows so she can reach up with one hand and rub her clit. I'm still fucking her, and I'm holding on with both hands while she's flicking her bean and moaning.

Then she says, "I'm gonna come, Curtis. Fuck me until I come!" I'm all too happy to give her what she wants. She grabs one of the throw pillows, buries her face in it, and goes back to frigging her clit. Then she screams into the pillow and collapses on the arm of the couch, but I manage to stay inside her. I go a little slower but keep sliding my prick inside her. She's moaning now, and we're both covered with sweat when I feel like I'm about to come, so I tell her.

"I'm gonna come for you, Katie. Where do you want it?"

"On my ass, baby. Paint my ass with your hot come. Oh, fuck, please come on me."

I thrust inside her a few more times, driving myself as deep as I can, and she's still rubbing her clit and moaning, and then I can feel my balls start to boil. I pull out and jack myself off, and blast four solid ropes of my come on her back and her ass. My first shot landed up to the middle of her back and drew a straight line down to her ass. My second one fired a little harder, and it landed between her shoulder blades. The third one matched the first, and I spread the fourth and fifth ones to her ass cheeks.

After that, we took a shower together, and I fucked her once more against the shower wall, and then she spent the night before we Ubered back to our cars the next morning.

So what do you think, Jakey? Was that one a winner?

CHAPTER 3

"Meh," said Jake. "You've had better ones. The one about you and Anna and Debi was my favorite.[35] Those photos you sent me of Debi were pretty hot. Short, blonde, grapefruit tits. She may be my favorite story of yours."

"Yeah, she's pretty great. I'm still living with her and Anna, but they let me sow my wild oats when I'm on the road, and they'll fuck one of Debi's old high school friends. So what've you got? What's your winner of a story?"

Jake thought for a minute. He wanted to tell the story about Betty but decided against it. He liked the relationship he had with Betty and wanted to keep it private. So instead, he told the story of Piper in Portland, Oregon[36], including a previously unpublished scene where Mae, the owner of Thai One On, had joined them.

---

[35] See *Stand Up, Lie Down, vol. 1, #5: Alyssa in Atlanta*

[36] See *Stand Up, Lie Down, vol. 2: #3: Piper in Portland*

"Oh, shit!" said Curtis when Jake was finished. "That's pretty hot. You won that one. I think it's true what I said last time: stories are much better when we fuck two women."[37]

"Excellent!" said Jake. "I've been dying for some Mexican food, and there's a place near the club where we can go."

The two drove together in Jake's truck and enjoyed their dinner, and true to the rules of the competition, Curtis was more than happy to pay.

"Do you ever think about settling down?" asked Jake as they were enjoying their desserts.

"No," said Curtis. "I mean, maybe? I don't know. I'm living with Anna and Debi, but I get to screw around while I'm on the road. Ours is a relationship built on fucking and economics. We have a pretty good house that's pretty cheap, especially when you split it three ways. But we've never talked about marriage or anything. Why?"

"Oh, no reason. I've just been wondering whether I should settle down and stick with one woman."

"Do you have anyone in mind?"

"No. Well, maybe. Possibly, but I don't know. She's married, and she's older. We got together last week while I was in Reno[38], and that's the first time I've ever done that with any of the women from my past. I just like her, and we still talk from time to time."

---

37 See *Stand Up, Lie Down, vol. 2: #2: Vanessa in Vancouver.* Look, this isn't grad school. Why do I have to keep footnoting every goddamn past reference??

38 I'm not citing this one. You should just know! It was the previous book! Or are you reading these out of order, like some kind of monster?

The two men were silent for a few minutes until the author reminded Jake that he had an eight-book deal and shouldn't think about quitting or settling down until he actually finished his Wacky Wild West Tour.

I'm not calling it that, said Jake.

I don't care what you call it, said the author. *You've got three more books to do, so don't think about packing it in until we're done.*

Jake was suddenly overcome with a feeling of satisfaction at his situation and eagerness to continue his tour without question, fucking every woman he could get his dick into.

That's better, said the author.

Friday Night

"Hey, Jakey, these girls invited us out to a club," Curtis said after Jake had finished his second set. He was seated at a table with four other women. It was one woman's 25th birthday party, and the four were celebrating with a comedy show and then dancing all night.

"Sure, I'm game." Jake wasn't sure how he was going to spend his Friday night. He had run out of books, having spent the entire week reading the ones he had in his luggage, but hadn't picked up any new ones. He didn't feel like watching TV, and he had already worked out, so he wasn't sure what he was going to do.

The women stood up, and Curtis introduced them all: Kelsey, Trish, Amber, and Tracy. They all thanked Jake for a good show and began to ask him questions. How long had he been doing comedy? Where was he from? Did his wife or girlfriend mind all his touring?

"Six years. Mankato, Minnesota. No, because I'm single."

The four women all *ooh*ed and *aah*ed and took turns getting selfies with the two comics before they were ushered out by Kaitlyn, who was eager to clean up and go home.

Kelsey was a project manager with straight brown hair and brown eyes and wore an olive-green skirt and a white blouse, while Trish was a dental assistant with platinum blonde hair, thin eyebrows, and a wide mouth with pearly-white teeth, which gave her a beautiful, if unlikely, smile.

Amber was a bartender with black, curly hair cut short and several tattoos. She wore a short denim skirt and sleeveless black blouse with the top button undone; Jake could see a Betty Boop tattoo peeking out over the top of her shirt.

But it was Tracy Higgins, the marketing coordinator, who captured Jake's attention. She was the birthday girl, celebrating her 25th. She reached out to shake Jake's hand, and her tiny hand was engulfed in his. She held on for several seconds and wondered if it was true about men with big hands. She inadvertently glanced down at his crotch and hoped it was.[39]

Tracy stood close to Jake and touched his forearm and biceps as they talked, so he knew she was interested. Whenever she touched him, he didn't move, hoping to signal that he was receptive to her touch. The two flirted, and Jake surreptitiously glanced up and down at his new friend. They talked for a while, even while her three friends joked, laughed, and flirted with Curtis several feet away.

---

[39] It is. It totally is.

Tracy was barely an inch over five feet tall, slender, with thin arms and legs. She looked sinewy without being muscular. She had a ballerina's grace and reed-like appearance. Her light brown hair had blonde streaks, was curly, parted in the middle, and hung down the sides of her face. She wore a black sleeveless, backless halter top tied behind her neck, stopping a few inches above her waist, showing her navel. She also wore a short, dark green skirt with booty shorts underneath and black, thick-soled patent leather shoes with white ankle socks with lacy cuffs. She had small breasts, and her skirt and shorts showed off a pert, tight ass, and Jake imagined squeezing those tight buns in his big hands.

The women had all Ubered to the club and were planning on Ubering to the next club, but Curtis and Jake offered to drive them. They walked out to the parking lot, which was now mostly empty. Curtis's rental car and Jake's truck were parked farther away from each other, and the six of them stood in the middle, trying to decide the logistics of driving five minutes away.

"There's only one seat in the truck," Jake said.

"I'll ride with Jake," Tracy said quickly.

"But it's your birthday, Tracy-y-y-y-y," Trish wailed. "You shouldn't have to ride by yourself."

"Trish, it's okay. It's literally five minutes from here. I think I can be alone for five minutes."

"I'll miss you, Tracy!" shouted Kelsey, who was a bit drunk and hanging onto Curtis's arm for support, pressing her tits against his bicep. She and Amber, who held onto Curtis's other arm, laughed wildly.

"I can take two of you if you want to sit on someone's lap," said Jake.

"We can talk about that later," Tracy murmured to Jake, squeezing his biceps. She said to the others, more loudly, "No, that wouldn't be safe. Plus, Jake might get a ticket for it, and that would just put a damper on the evening. We'll just follow you all in Curtis's car, and we'll see you in five minutes. I'm sure he can handle all three of you at once."

"You know that's right, baby!" hollered Curtis, and the three women cackled.

"We're just going to the Pink Noodle on Broadway, Curtis," Tracy said. "The girls can tell you how to get there, and we'll follow you."

Curtis quickly ushered the three women to his car, and they all climbed inside. Curtis put the car in gear and drove off. Jake walked Tracy around to the passenger side and opened the door for her. It wasn't a big truck, but it did take a little extra effort to climb in if you weren't six feet tall.

"Jake, can you give me a boost up?" Tracy asked sweetly.

"Uhh," Jake stammered, not sure of what to do. If they were dating, he would have just planted his hands on her ass and helped her up, but they had only known each other for half an hour, and he didn't want to seem forward.

Tracy snorted, grabbed the handle, and hoisted herself in. "I'm just teasing you. My dad had a big truck like this, and I had to scramble into it all the time."

Jake punched the address for the club into his GPS, and they made their way to the club. When they arrived, they pulled up next to Curtis's car in the parking lot and spotted him making out with Kelsey.

Jake held his finger to his lips. "Shhhh."

The two crept out of the truck and very quietly shut the doors. Then they walked over to the driver's side door, bent down, and looked in. Then Jake pounded on the window and shouted, "What're you doing with my girlfriend?"

Curtis jumped like he had been jabbed in the ass with a stick and shrieked. He turned and shouted at Jake, "Not funny, motherfucker! I about peed!" Tracy and Jake laughed uproariously and wandered into the club. They showed their IDs and were granted entrance. They found Amber and Trish at the bar and ordered drinks. Trish ordered rum shots for the four of them and then frozen margaritas. Jake paid for everyone's drinks, and they waited for Curtis and Kelsey, who showed up a few minutes later. Curtis flipped Jake the middle finger and then told the others what they did.

It was 80s night at the club, so they went out on the dance floor and grooved to the Clash, Prince, Human League, and Men Without Hats. The six friends danced together as a group until the deejay finally slowed things down with Cyndi Lauper's "Time After Time."

Tracy melted into Jake's arms, and they swayed together. Tracy held her arms around Jake's narrow waist, and her head came up to his chest. She rested her cheek against him and listened to his heartbeat. He could feel her small breasts against his stomach, making his prick harden.

Oh, shit, Jake thought. He tried thinking of unsexy things to make it go back down, but it was no use. Tracy could feel it hardening, so she squeezed Jake to her tighter to feel it.

"Somebody seems to like dancing," Tracy said, smiling and looking up at Jake.

"Er, sure, yes, dancing is pretty great, especially with someone who's so graceful."

"I used to be a dancer with the ballet company in Houston. We toured around Europe and Latin America a few times, but I finally had to retire. I'd been doing it for ten years professionally and eighteen years total when my knees gave out. My doctor said I have the knees of a football player, and I'll probably need to get replacements when I'm in my 40s."

"Wow, that sounds... well, I'm not sure what I should say. I used to be a swimmer, but that's a low-impact sport, so I've been fortunate. I do know a couple of former swimmers who have shoulder issues, but I've been lucky."

"Do you still work out?"

"I do. I like to run and swim whenever I get the chance."

"I can tell," Tracy said, smiling up at him. "Your chest feels massive, but you've got such a narrow waist, I'm able to wrap my arms around you."

"What are you doing tomorrow?" Jake asked, trying to change the subject. He didn't want his boner poking her in the stomach. "Would you like to get lunch and maybe spend the day together?"

"That would be great. I'll text you my address and you can pick me up. I know a great café near my apartment."

The song wound to a close and the deejay got back on the microphone and shouted, "A little birdie tells me that it's someone's birthday today. Everyone wish ... TRACY a happy birthday!"

The crowd clapped and whistled, the deejay played an old children's version of "Happy Birthday" over the speakers, and the crowd sang along. After it finished, the deejay dropped some Peter

Gabriel, the dancing resumed in earnest, and Jake and Curtis stayed with their new friends until two in the morning.

Although Curtis, Kelsey, and Trish disappeared out to Curtis's car for about twenty minutes.

When they walked back in, Curtis mouthed to Jake, "I've got a new story for you, and I think this one's a winner."

CHAPTER 4

"These guys do an amazing jazz brunch on Saturdays," said Tracy as they settled in. Jake had picked her up from her apartment and brought her to the café for a late breakfast.

He suppressed a shudder. He had never heard the words "amazing," "brunch," and "jazz" used together successfully in the same sentence. Still, he was interested to see how this went.

He was not a fan of most jazz. He liked the older stuff—the classics, the standards, the stuff from the 40s and 50s. But when he thought of jazz, he usually thought of jazz fusion and smooth jazz, which he felt was a punishment from God, on par with a plague of locusts and frogs. In fact, after the plagues of locusts, pestilence, boils, and hail, there was the plague of smooth jazz. So he tried to avoid it unless he listened to a jazz standards streaming station during his travels.

Jake wondered if his love of old pulp mysteries from the 40s and 50s had anything to do with his interest in old jazz from the same era, and wondered if he should appear in a sci-fi time travel series where he got to have sex with a lot of women from that era.

Let's just get through this series first before you commit both of us to any other projects, said the author.

He was imagining what that series might look like when Tracy interrupted his thoughts of 1940s nookie.

"Jake? Jake?"

"Huh? Oh, uh, sorry, I was, uhh, lost in the music," he said.

"Uh-huh," said Tracy, smiling. "I said, do you want some coffee?"

"Sure, that would be great." The server, who had been standing there while Jake was in his retro reveries, poured a cup for him and left cream and a tiny box of sweetener. They were at a small round table near the back, tucked into a little alcove. Jake was seated to the side while Tracy had her back to the wall. A white tablecloth draped over the table. The restaurant was half full as brunch was winding down.

"I love your dress," Jake said to Tracy after the server had left. Today, she wore a sheer orange, yellow, and brown patterned tube top dress that showed off her sinewy back and defined shoulders. "It reminds me of autumn in Mankato."

"I'm guessing that's where you're from," she said.

"Yep, born and raised. How about you?"

"I'm actually from Kansas City. Missouri, not Kansas. I studied ballet and started dancing professionally with the Kansas City Ballet when I was still in high school. I did that until I was seventeen and then took a role with the Houston Ballet. We toured regularly, and I got to dance at both the Vienna State Opera House and the

Vienna Volksoper. I even stayed in Vienna for half a season because the Vienna Ballet wanted me in their chorus, but I tore my ACL during a rehearsal, and that was it. The doctors over there were able to reattach it, and I spent months in physical therapy to strengthen it again. I did all that before I ever came home because healthcare is so much cheaper over there."

She scooted back in her chair and put her left leg up on Jake's lap. "You can see the scar." She slid her dress up, and Jake admired her scar.

"Do you want to feel it?" She took Jake's hand, placed it on her knee, and began moving it up and down slightly. He gently squeezed and massaged her leg, sliding his hand a few inches farther up her deceptively strong thigh.

"They did a nice job," said Jake. "It looks sexy, as does everything else."

"Mmmm," she moaned lightly and parted her legs slightly. Jake continued to massage her leg, inching halfway up her thigh and under her dress. Tracy inhaled sharply and licked her lips. A server walked past, and they quickly snapped back to their normal positions.

"Can you still dance?" Jake asked.

"Sure, but I don't have the leaping ability that I did. Plus, it gets really sore after just a few hours, which is a terrible way to spend your days as a professional dancer. So, I hung up my toe shoes and went back to college. Got my degree in marketing and became a marketing coordinator for a social media agency here in Tucson."

"That sounds interesting."

"It's not," Tracy said with a laugh. "I mean, it is, but all I'm really doing is writing social media updates for bars and restaurants in town. I don't even get to work on the big accounts because I'm still new at the job."

The server returned and took their orders. Tracy ordered blueberry pancakes with a side of bacon, while Jake ordered a sausage and salsa omelet with cheese and avocado.

"I hike a lot," said Tracy. "Now that I don't have to watch my figure the way I used to, I can enjoy carbs more. But I still work out and go for a lot of hikes to burn them off. Or maybe you can help me think of some other creative ways to burn energy."

"Sure!" said Jake, agreeably. "We could take a walking tour downtown, go for a swim, rent some bicycles, or now that you mention it, a hike sounds nice."

Tracy snorted. "Funny guy. You ever think about doing comedy?"

The two talked about Jake's work and his Wacky Wild West Tour.

"Your social media person does good work," Tracy said. "I looked you up this morning, and they're doing a good job. They're hitting all the right social networks. I even saw some of your TikTok videos. You're really good. Do you really do this professionally?"

"Yes. It's still a fledgling career, but I'm able to earn enough money to put gas in my truck, buy food, and pay for hotels when I don't get to stay in a club apartment."

"What's a club apartment?"

"Most comedy clubs own an apartment, and they let their traveling comics stay here. A lot of them are shit holes, but I've been fortunate that the ones I've stayed in are relatively clean and well-kept. It doesn't hurt that I get booked into the good clubs. I suppose I have my agent, Kurt, to thank for that. He seems to know which clubs have good apartments. But if I had to, I could always sleep in my truck."

"You sleep in that thing? It's like a coffin with the cap on the back."

"No, I sleep in the cab. I can lean the seat back enough, so it's like sleeping in a recliner. It's certainly not a great way to get a refreshing sleep, but it's enough to take the edge off. The times I did it, I made sure to get a hotel the next night so I could really sleep. But I'm thinking about putting a proper camper cap on the back and putting a bed in there."

The two talked about life on the road and what it was like to share the road with other comics who didn't understand hygiene or share a hotel room and bathroom with five other girls. They talked until their food came, and they shared bites with one another, feeding each other and flirting.

"I was a nomad for a while," said Tracy. They had finished their breakfasts and were sitting, enjoying the music—*"enjoying" is a strong word for it*, thought Jake—as he caressed her leg, from her knee to her inner thigh.

"I had just finished my rehab and decided to tour Europe before I came back home," she continued. "I had heard about it from a friend who did this, so I did it, too. I bought a Eurail pass that gave me unlimited rides anywhere in Europe.

"So, I would get on an overnight train for the longest distance I could find and sleep on the train. Then I would spend the day visiting the city, going to museums and cafes, doing laundry when I needed it, and then get back on another train to another far-off city.

"Once in a while, I would spend a few nights in a hostel if I really liked the city, like Amsterdam or Lisbon or Milan. Ooh, and Brussels was great.

"Anyway, I did that for six weeks and then came back home and started school a week later."

"And now you're in marketing," said Jake.

"And now I'm in marketing."

"So, would you like to do anything else today?" asked Jake. He looked at his phone—it was nearly 1:00 in the afternoon. "I have a show tonight, so I need to get ready around 7:00."

"I can think of a few things we could do for the day." She smiled and put her hands over Jake's, sliding it farther up her thigh.

Jake felt his cock getting harder. "Oh yeah? Like what?"

Tracy leaned over, half-closed her eyes, and looked at Jake's mouth like she was about to kiss him.

She fought a smile. "We could go for a swim, rent some bicycles, or go for a hike," she said.

Jake laughed at that. "You got me there," he said.

"Or we could just go back to my place and see what happens next," Tracy said, still leaning over as if she wanted to kiss Jake.

"I think that's my favorite idea," said Jake. He paid the bill, and the two walked out to Jake's truck, and he punched her address into his GPS.

CHAPTER 5

"You've got a great place," said Jake as they walked in. Tracy dropped her keys into a pottery bowl on a table by the front door and removed her shoes. Jake followed suit and left his shoes next to hers. He marveled at how small her feet were compared to his.

"You know what I'd like for my birthday?" said Tracy, standing close to him in the living room.

"What's that?"

She reached for one of his hands and held it up in her two tiny ones. "You've got such big, powerful hands. I'd love a massage. Would you rub my shoulders?" She kissed one of his fingertips.

"I'd love to. Do you have any lotion or oil? It makes things easier."

"Sure, I have a lavender-mint oil I sometimes use instead of lotion. I love the way it smells. It feels great on my skin after a shower."

She glided gracefully back to her bathroom and returned a few seconds later with a blue pump bottle.

"Here you go," she said, handing Jake the bottle. "Have a seat on the couch, and I'll sit in front of you."

She sat down and expertly tied her hair into a bun with the motions of someone who had done it every day for eighteen years.

Jake poured a little oil on his hands, rubbed them together, and then smelled it. "Mmmm," he said. "That smells good. I can smell the mint." He put his hands on her shoulders and worked the oil into her skin.

He kneaded her shoulders and neck with his strong thumbs, trying not to dig too sharply into her muscles. Despite being so slender, her muscles were still strong, so Jake spent time working out the knots and tight spots.

"Mmmmmmm," moaned Tracy, moving her head around as she felt Jake loosening up her neck muscles. "Your hands are magical."

"Thank you. I endeavor to provide satisfaction."

Tracy bent over and said, "Can you do my back, too?" She rolled down her tube top so her back was exposed, as well as her small breasts. Jake couldn't see them, but he also noticed she didn't try to cover up or hide them. She pulled her knees up and leaned forward until she could rest her chest on her thighs.

He poured some more oil into his hands and rubbed them together again. He continued rubbing her back, adding more oil as needed, making sure to massage every inch of skin. He also worked his fingers around the sides of her rib cage, making sure to stay away from her armpits. He didn't want her to jump, so he said, "I won't tickle you."

"I know," she murmured, eyes closed. "I trust you."

After several minutes, she asked, "Can you do my lower back?"

"Sure, but you'll need to sit on my knees so I can reach that low."

Tracy stood up, her dress down around her waist, the elastic of the tube top holding it in place. She kept her arms at her side and didn't cover herself up. She turned her body to the side, turned her head back, and smiled at Jake, giving him a glimpse of her pert breasts.

Jake's cock was pressing against his zipper, straining to be released. Tracy glanced down and admired the bulge growing in his jeans. Jake pressed his knees together but didn't bother to hide his growing erection.

Tracy lowered her dress even farther down her hips and sat down on his knees. Jake added more oil to his palms and began rubbing her lower back, pressing his thumbs into either side of her spine and digging in, her muscles firm and pliable.

"Ohhhhh," moaned Tracy. "That feels so good, Jake. I've needed this for weeks."

Jake moved up to her upper back again before working on her shoulders and arms, massaging first her right arm and then her left.

"I'm melting," she said. "You're making me feel so good."

"Thank you. Is there anything else you'd like me to massage?" Jake asked, hoping for a reason to touch her front.

"How about you let me give you a massage?" said Tracy.

"That would be great," said Jake. "Where do you want me?"

Tracy snickered. "How about my bedroom? The couch is too short for you to lie down comfortably." She stood up and led him into the bedroom; he couldn't see her breasts, but she still didn't cover up or pull up her dress. She turned into the bathroom and said, "Strip down to your underwear and lie down on your stomach. I'll be right out."

A few moments later, she came out wearing a short, deep-blue satin robe with wide sleeves. The bottom of the robe barely covered her tiny tush, and it was tied loosely at her waist.

"Are you ready?" she asked. "I've been looking forward to this."

Jake said he was, and Tracy grabbed the bottle of lavender oil from the nightstand where Jake had set it, and then set it back down.

"I should probably make sure I don't get any oil on my robe," she said, disrobing. She tossed her robe onto a chair, and Jake turned his head and saw that she was wearing bikini-cut panties that matched her robe. It looked more like a bikini with a small patch of material covering her pussy and ass crack with thin bikini straps holding the patches in place. The patch covered what seemed to be her hairless pussy, and he admired the small gap between her thighs.

He also got a look at her beautiful breasts. They were small and teardrop-shaped, and her nipples were already erect. Jake licked his lips and said, "You look beautiful."

Tracy smiled and twirled her finger to tell him to turn around and lie down. She poured some oil on his back, and he started from the chill; she giggled.

She climbed onto his ass and began to dig her small but strong fingers into his back. She found the knots and painful areas, kneading her knuckles into the spots, loosening up the tight areas.

While she dug into his muscles, Tracy was grinding her pussy on Jake's ass, rocking her hips back and forth, and making her pussy get wetter and wetter.

She poured some more oil onto Jake's back and then leaned forward and pressed her naked front to him, sliding back and forth, rubbing their bodies together and spreading the oil. Jake reached an arm behind him, keeping it straight, and was able to cup her beautiful ass.

"Would you like me to do your front?" she asked.

"Like this? Absolutely. Are you sure I won't get oil on your quilt, though?"

"It's an old quilt from Target. I'm not too worried about it."

Tracy stood up and slid off her panties. She then helped Jake remove his underwear; he raised his hips as she pulled them down and then slid them down over his ankles. She tossed them onto her floor, where they landed near her panties.

Tracy took up the oil once more and poured some on Jake's chest, and he jumped again from the chill. Tracy kneeled beside him and rubbed the oil into his torso, admiring his pectoral and abdominal muscles. She didn't touch Jake's raging erection, though, even as it pointed skyward. Whenever she would rub the oil into his pubic region, lingering over the Adonis belt, she would come close to his cock, but not actually touch it.

Jake fought the urge to grab his cock and stroke it, but instead just laid back and let Tracy perform her ministrations, rubbing her hands over his chest and abdomen. This was a massage of relaxation and touching, not tension relief and digging in.

"I can't get good pressure here. I need to sit on top of you," Tracy said, her voice hoarse with desire. She threw a leg over his legs, sat down, and then slid forward, pressing Jake's cock down until it was trapped under her pussy. She resumed her massage with the added action of grinding her pussy on his hard shaft, the underneath side between her wet lips.

Jake could feel the heat of Tracy's pussy and could feel her wetness sliding against him. He loved the friction of her slit and breathed heavily at the heat building up between them.

"That feels so good," he murmured.

Tracy leaned forward and kissed Jake deeply. Then she took one of his hands and placed it on her breast, and squeezed it, signaling that she wanted him to massage her tits. Jake brought his second hand up and started massaging both of them, cupping them in his large hands.

"Mmmmm, that feels so good, Jake," Tracy whispered. "I love having my breasts touched."

Jake continued rubbing her precious mounds and lightly pinching her nipples between his fingers, even as Tracy maintained the friction between her wet snatch and his hard shaft.

"Ohhh, yes, that's so good." She leaned down and kissed him, driving her tongue deep into his mouth. Jake wrapped his long, strong arms around her and held her. The position lifted her pussy off his cock, and she felt the cool air between her legs.

"I want you to eat my pussy," said Tracy. "Eat my wet pussy, Jake!"

"I would love to eat you," said Jake. Tracy lifted herself off of Jake and spun around on the bed, positioning her hairless cunt over Jake's face, holding it just a few inches over his mouth. Jake gripped her thighs where they joined her pelvis and pulled her down to him. He licked gingerly at her slit, causing her to moan quietly. He repeated the action, and she moaned again.

Jake pulled Tracy down hard so her pussy was directly on his face, and he jammed his tongue as far up into her as he could go.

"Ooh, Jake, that's so good. Fuck me with your tongue," she commanded. Jake eagerly obeyed and licked her as deeply as he could, giving long tongue lashings from her clit to her ass and then back again with the underside of his tongue.

Tracy's cunt leaked her tangy juices, and Jake lapped at them like a hungry man at a feast, getting them smeared on his lips and cheeks. He sucked at her clit and sucked her pussy lips into his mouth.

"Oh my God, Jake, that feels amazing," said Tracy, completely forgetting about her end of the bargain. She closed her eyes and threw her head back, and pressed her pussy into Jake's mouth. He pushed his jaw into her bald cunt and continued to feast.

"Oh, I'm going to cum, Jake! That feels so good. Keep doing that. Keep eating my pussy like that. I'm going to cum on your face! Oh, you're making me cum, Jake! I'm going to—I'm going to—oh, fuck, I'm cumming! AAAAAHHHHHHH!!"

Tracy bucked and writhed as Jake clamped her into place on his face as he licked and sucked, and she rode out her orgasm on his face. He was so caught up in the moment, he didn't even notice she pronounced it "cum" and not "come."

"Oh, fuck, Jake, that was amazing. I've never had anyone eat me to an orgasm."

"Really? That's a shame. I'll be happy to do it again," he said from under her pussy. He massaged her pert ass with both hands, kneading and squeezing her muscular dancer's cheeks.

"I'll hold you to that, but first, I want to suck your cock. I just hope I can fit it in my mouth." Tracy climbed off his face and situated herself between his legs. She gripped his eight-and-a-half-inch cock and was barely able to wrap her fingers around it. "Holy fuck, you're so big."

"Take your time," he said. "Do whatever you're comfortable with."

"I love to suck a big dick," she said, smiling, "but this is a lot." She stroked his shaft with both hands and took a few licks at his dickhead. A fat drop of pre-cum leaked out, and she smeared it on his shaft for lubrication. Then she licked up one side of his hard meat and down the other before putting the head in her mouth again. She was able to manage about two inches of it before she gagged. She drove it back into her mouth one more time, reaching the same length and holding it in place before her gag reflex took over, and she was forced to relinquish her oral grip on his cock.

She gave a small giggle and tried a third time, holding it in her mouth once more until she gagged and released one more time.

Tracy continued to jack him off with both hands, and she smiled up at him. "I want this cock so many ways, I don't know what to do with it. I want to possess it, and I want it to own me. Just fucking own me with your cock, Jake."

"Give yourself to me, Tracy," Jake rumbled, his voice deep in his chest.

"I'm all yours, baby," she said.

"Come back up here and sit on my cock." Tracy's eyes widened as she smiled. She scrambled up Jake's torso, dragging his dick under her belly as she went. She felt its hardness trace a line from between her tits down to her clit until it sprang free when she cleared it.

The two kissed deeply, tongues entwined, as Jake's hands returned to Tracy's ass. He cupped her round cheeks and squeezed them tightly, slipping one finger into her slit again.

"Ohh," gasped Tracy. She closed her eyes and savored the feeling. "That feels so good."

Jake slipped in another finger and gently pushed them deeper inside her. She pushed back on Jake's fingers and fucked herself on his middle and index finger. "Unhh," she groaned. "That feels good, but I want more. I need your cock inside me."

"I do, too," Jake said. He removed his fingers and licked them off. Tracy sat up and raised herself up, positioning her dripping twat above Jake's massive prick. She grabbed it and lined it up with her slit, sliding the head between her lips a few times before settling herself gingerly on his cock head.

"Uhhhhh," gasped Tracy as she felt Jake's width slide inside her, pushing her pussy lips apart, feeling like it was rearranging her insides. She managed to get a few inches into her before she stopped. Jake held onto her waist to support her.

"I just need a minute to adjust," she said, her eyes screwed shut. "I've never had anything this big inside me." She raised up again and pushed back down, reaching the same spot as before. "Hooo, fuck! You're so big!"

She raised herself slowly and lowered herself once more, pushing one more inch into her. Tracy's legs began to shake, so Jake held her up to support her. "Take your time, baby," he said. She repeated the motion a few more times until she was able to manage half of Jake's thick meat into her tight little pussy.

"Come down here, but keep me inside you," Jake said. Tracy leaned forward so she was crushing her chest to Jake's, keeping him inside her. He started thrusting slowly, sliding his cock until just his head was still nestled between her lips before slowly pushing himself back inside her. Each time, he returned to the same depth as before, making sure not to shove himself too far inside her. He worried he could injure her if he weren't careful.

Soon, she was rocking back and forth on his chest, driving herself onto his cock, controlling the depth. With each push, she was able to take more and more of him into her until she was taking two-thirds of his giant prick into her eager slit. It was warm in Tracy's bedroom and sweat beaded on their smooth, hairless bodies covered in lavender-mint oil.

"Ohh, fuck, Jake! This is so good. You're so fucking big, I can't believe your big dick is inside me," Tracy shrieked. She continued to rock back and forth onto Jake's fleshy invader, grinding her clit on his pubic bone.

"Oh my God! I'm going to cum again! Jake, I'm going to cum on your cock! This is so good! Oh, fuck me, Jake! Fuck me with your big dick! Ohhh! OHH, FUUUUCK!!" Tracy's whole body clenched up, and her pussy squeezed Jake's cock like a vise. He nearly blew his load right then, and it was only sheer willpower and a frantic mental recitation of the 2008 Minnesota Twins lineup that kept him from blowing his hot load inside Tracy's steamy pussy.

Tracy collapsed on Jake, breathing hard, his hard dick still inside her.

"That's twice. You've made. Me cum," she said, kissing him every other word. She licked his chin and kissed him. "But now it's your turn. I want you to fuck me until you cum. Take me any way you want and shove your cock in me as far as it can go and fuck me."

"I know what I want," Jake said, smiling broadly. He kissed her once more and licked her chin back. Tracy climbed off him, groaning as his thick cock slipped out of her. It was still hard and pointing upward.

She gave it a little peck on the head and said, "How do you want me?"

"Eagerly," he said, smiling. "But lay on your stomach and spread your legs a little."

"Oh, God, Jake, you're not going to fuck my ass, are you? That'll kill me."

"Oh, no, no," said Jake. "Even if I managed to get in there, I don't think you would ever come off, and I'd have to live my life with you on my dick."

"Well, when you put it that way, it doesn't sound *so* terrible," Tracy said. Jake snorted.

"No, just lay down. I've been admiring your beautiful ass since I saw you last night, and I want to watch it when I fuck you."

"So, doggy style?"

"No, I'm going to fuck you from behind while you're lying flat."

"Ah," said Tracy, finally getting it. "I'm going to love this. I've never been fucked like that. Hell, I've never been fucked by something this big ever," she added.

Jake parted her thighs and saw Tracy's hairless pink pussy glistening and already looking like it had been well-fucked. He straddled her legs and remained sitting up, positioning his cockhead at her beautiful entrance. Once he was lined up, he slid himself inside.

"Ohhhh!" Tracy groaned as Jake's dick was re-introduced to her pussy. He slid himself in until he felt resistance and held himself for a second.

"Is that good? Is that as deep as I went last time?"

"That's it. Oh, that's it!" Tracy gasped. "Try a little more."

Jake pushed a little farther, and Tracy opened her mouth as wide as it could go, but no sound came out. He managed to get another inch inside her but didn't want to hurt her, so he held himself in place. After a few seconds, he pulled himself out and returned to the same depth.

"AAAAH!" shrieked Tracy.

"Is that hurting you?" Jake said.

"A little, but don't stop. I love it! Keep doing it."

Jake slid out and back in again, once again returning to the same imaginary line on his shaft.

"Ohh, that's better," Tracy said, her pussy getting used to the feeling of being opened so deeply.

"That's it, claim my pussy, Jake. Take me. Fuck me silly with that giant prick!"

Jake eagerly complied. He continued to pump into her tight little cunt with a slow-but-steady rhythm, in-out. In-out. In-out. Tracy moaned with each entrance, "Unh. Unh. Unh. Unh."

"You've got such a tight little pussy, baby," said Jake. "I love fucking your beautiful cunt."

"You feel so good filling me up, Jake. This feels sooooo good." Jake continued to push inside her, picking up the pace, but still holding back.

He felt the familiar sensation in his huge nut sack and knew he was reaching his limit.

"I'm going to come, baby. Your pussy is so wonderful, I'm going to come. Where do you want me to shoot it?"

"Oh, God, Jake, you feel so good. You've got a magic cock. I'm going to cum with you."

"Oh, fuck, get ready. I'm going to fucking come because of you. Your beautiful pussy is making me cum." He switched to her favored pronunciation so it wouldn't be awkward; one does not correct his or her lover during sex, after all.

"Cum inside me, Jake! Claim my pussy! Mark it with your hot cum! I want to feel it shoot inside me!"

"I'm going to cum in you!" Jake shouted, now thrusting with everything he had. "I'm going to cum in that sweet cunt!"

Tracy buried her face in her pillow and screamed as Jake pounded her delicious cunt. "AAAHHH! AAAHHH! AAAHHH!"

Jake thrust himself into Tracy one last time, and a flood of come—er, cum—fired out of his cock. The feeling of the first blast of hot jizz in her pussy set Tracy off, and she screamed, "OH, FUCK! THAT'S IT! AAAAAAHHHHHHHH!" and she rode her third orgasm of the day.

Jake fired a second, third, and fourth burst into Tracy's eager cunt. He continued thrusting much more slowly, and a fifth one pushed out. Jake gave a shudder as his orgasm subsided, and he pulled out and dropped next to Tracy, who rolled over onto her side and put her arm on his chest.

"Oh, fuck!" she exclaimed. "Today is just a day of firsts. I've never had a simultaneous orgasm like that, either."

Jake smiled. "Sounds like you had a momentous day."

"You're telling me. That was incredible."

Jake wiped some sweat off her forehead and kissed her on the lips. "So, have you just not had much sex?"

"No, not much. I had a boyfriend who was another dancer in the troupe and then two different guys when I was in college, but nothing like this. The college guys were just a couple of one-and-done guys, and I dated them at different times. The dancer was average size and didn't like to go down on me. So this was the first big cock I've ever had."

"Well, you're the first ballerina I've ever been with," said Jake.

The two kissed deeply again, and Jake rolled onto his side so he could look Tracy square in the eyes.

"What are you doing for the rest of the day?" she asked.

"Well, I've got to take a shower and do my show tonight, but other than that, nothing else."

"How about we shower together, and then you fuck me once or twice? Then, after your show, you can come back here and fuck me again. What do you think?"

Jake pretended to mull it over and said, "Yeah, I think I could arrange that."

"Excellent. This is turning out to be a wonderful birthday. I'm glad I met you."

"Me, too," said Jake. "Me, too."

"I may not make it to the shower, though. I want another round before we get in there. Do you think you can manage?"

"I need a little time to recover," said Jake. "But, in the meantime, hold me closer, tiny dancer."

Tracy snorted. "You're so fucking corny."

Ellen in El Paso

Table of Contents

CHAPTER 1

"Thank you for everything, Jake," said Tracy. "I enjoyed spending time with you."

"No, thank you. You're an amazing lover," said Jake. He leaned down, wrapped his arms around the former ballerina, and raised back up. She wrapped her legs around his narrow waist and kissed him deeply.

The two had spent the last six days fucking and sucking, and it was time for Jake to head on to his next destination.

"My pussy is so sore," Tracy said. "I feel well and truly fucked."

"Me, too. I lost count of how many times we did it."

"I stopped counting after eight." She kissed him again, nuzzling his neck and giving him a gentle bite before licking him. "But if I don't let go of you, I may never let you leave."

"I may not want to," he said, smiling. He kissed her once more. She unwrapped her legs, and he set her back down.

"I'll never forget you, Jake Nilsen."

"I'll always remember you, too, Tracy Higgins." He turned and climbed into his truck, started the engine, and rolled down the window.

She hopped gracefully onto the running board and kissed him once more.

"Now get going," she said, "because my pussy really is sore, but I'm going to want to fuck you one more time if you don't leave."

"Bye-bye, love-ah," he said in that weird way that makes people cringe whenever someone says it like that. She kissed him once more and hopped down. Jake drove away and watched her get smaller—even smaller, because she was already tiny—in his rearview mirror as he got farther away.

That was two weeks ago, on Jake's last day in Tucson. Now he was in El Paso, where he was going to headline a show this weekend. He was originally supposed to perform in Albuquerque last weekend, but when he arrived Wednesday afternoon, he arrived in time to meet the manager as she was closing the club for the last time.

"Sorry, kid, turns out five comedy clubs in Albuquerque is one too many. We just couldn't cut it, especially after the asshole landlord doubled our rent. So, we're shutting down, and I'm heading back to Idaho to lick my wounds and figure out what to do next. You can stay in the club apartment for the weekend, but I have to get it ready to rent back out on Monday."

So that's what Jake did. He explored Albuquerque, went for a hot-air balloon ride, went for a run each day to enjoy the beautiful sunrises and sunsets, worked out at a local franchise of his favorite 24-hour gym, and spent his days hanging out at coffee shops and bookstores, writing more comedy, and living like a tourist.

He wasn't too worried about money because he was nearly rich. ("Comfortable," he would say, his Minnesota humbleness not letting him admit he had $2 million in business investments, plus another $1 million in stocks and cryptocurrency.)

However, his goal was to be financially successful in his comedy; he made almost enough money to support himself but had an American Express black card to bail himself out whenever he wanted to pay for a nice dinner or stay in a nice hotel.

Jake had also made an Airbnb reservation in El Paso, and when his time in Albuquerque was up that Monday morning, he made a leisurely drive to the city four hours away. He also double-checked and made sure Fritters was still open.

"Yeah, we're doing fine," the hostess said on the phone. "Why do you ask?"

"Just checking," said Jake, hanging up.

He spent another four days in El Paso playing tourist before heading over to Fritters to check in with the manager.

Jake parked his truck in the parking lot on Thursday afternoon and wandered into the club. They were setting up for a comedy showcase and competition of local talent that night. The hostess pointed him back to the manager's office, and Jake knocked.

"Come in!" a voice called from inside. Jake opened the door and saw a woman sitting at a desk, looking at a spreadsheet on her laptop, a video playing on a tablet propped up next to the screen. She was munching on a snack from a bowl on her desk.

"Hi, I'm Jake Nilsen, your weekend headliner," said Jake.

"Nilseen?"

"No, Nilsen." The woman stood up. She was average height, about five feet, five inches, thin, with short brown hair that hung to her jawline. She was wearing a black tank top, ripped blue jeans, and white sneakers.

"Sorry, you caught me with my mouth full. Hi, I'm Katelynn," she said. She shook Jake's hand and finished chewing whatever she had been eating.

"Caitlin?"

"No, Katelynn. With a K instead of a C." She retrieved the bowl from her desk and held it up for Jake.

"Would you like some crumbles?"

"Some what?"

"Crumbles. Our chef invented them. Well, sort of. They're actually a bit bad for you. We serve fish and chips, and he takes the last of the batter and pours it into the hot oil, and cooks up the droplets into little nuggets. We thought about selling them, but right now, it's just a little treat that we share with the staff."

"That sounds good, actually," Jake said, and he took a few, crunching on them like peanuts. "Wow, these are excellent!"

"Thank you. We're trying to figure out the price and whether it's worth making them. For now, it's just a little treat the cook makes for us."

"I'd pay five or six bucks for a bowl of those, if that helps," said Jake. "Those would be something good to snack on if I wasn't very hungry or didn't have anyone to share with."

"Good to know. Anyway, what can we do for you?"

"Nothing, really. I just wanted to let you know I was in town. I saw you have a comedy showcase tonight. What's going on with that?"

"Oh, not much. We're hosting a regional comedy show as a way to get some bookers in to look at our local talent. It's a comedy competition, and the top three finishers will get to middle at different comedy clubs in Austin."

"Austin's got a great comedy scene," said Jake. "I'd love to play there one of these days. My agent just wasn't able to get me a slot on my tour this time around."

"Well, let me see if I can get any of the bookers to stick around to see your show. I already know you're going to be funny because I've seen a lot of your YouTube videos. Plus, you come highly recommended by my friend, Shari, from Chips in Birmingham, Alabama.[40] She said you brought the house down and wants to get you back into town one of these days."

"She's not the only one," Jake said with a smile, thinking of his repeat lover, Betty Abernathy.[41] "I'll let my manager know."

"I'm guessing you'll be wanting the keys to the club apartment then?"

"Actually, there's no need. I got an Airbnb because I got here a few days ago. If it's all the same to you, I'll just extend my stay and keep my stuff there."

"That would be fine. We need to do some painting and steam clean the carpets, so we might as well get that started sooner rather

---

[40] See *Stand Up, Lie Down volume 1, #6: Betty in Birmingham.*

[41] Who reappeared in *Stand Up, Lie Down volume 2, #4: Randi in Reno*

than later. That's a big help. Tell you what, I'll let you emcee the showcase tonight if you're interested. I'll give you a hundred bucks and all the crumbles you want. That way, you can do some of your act for the scouts, too."

"You had me at 'too,'" said Jake, and Katelynn laughed.

"The show starts at 8:00, so get here around 7:15 for sound check and earlier if you want dinner."

"Sounds good. I'll be here."

CHAPTER 2

"Excuse me, Mr. Nilseen?" Jake felt a tap on his shoulder. He turned and saw a young woman, about five feet, six inches tall, with long black hair that hung to her shoulders. She looked to be in her late 20s or early 30s and was voluptuous and curvy, with large breasts and wide hips.

Her jeans hugged her hips and ass like a second skin, and she wore a plaid shirt that was buttoned up except for the top two buttons, with a deep-cut tank top underneath showing off cleavage that went on for days. She had big brown eyes, an innocent, eager look, and a shy smile. The way she looked up at Jake made his heart melt.

"Nilsen," said Jake.

"What did I say?" said the young woman.

"Nilseen."

"Also, you can just call me Jake. Mr. Nilsen is the milkman."

The woman looked confused. "I don't get it."

"Most people say 'Mr. Nilsen is my father,' but there's also the joke some people say about 'my kid looks like the milkman.'"

"Ah, I get it." The woman smiled but didn't laugh. "That's what I wanted to talk to you about."

"The milkman? I don't really know him all that well. I only see him on my birthday and Father's Day."

She snorted at that. "No, I want to talk about comedy."

"Ah, that's different."

"My name is Holly Hernandez." She stuck out her hand, and Jake shook it. "I've been thinking about getting into comedy, so I came to the showcase to see some different talent and to support a friend. I live in Albuquerque, but I heard about this on the internet, so I thought I would check it out."

"No kidding? I was just in Albuquerque last week. I was supposed to play a show there, but the club closed down."

"I heard about that. I used to go to shows there once in a while. I did an open mic there once about three weeks ago."

"How'd you do?" Jake asked.

"I bombed. It was my first time ever, and I was really nervous."

"That's okay. Everyone bombs their first time out. What's important is that you go out for a second time."

"I will. I just need to get my nerve up again and work on my material."

"Excellent, good for you!"

"And I was hoping I could pick your brain for a little bit. I wanted to come to the showcase because a girlfriend of mine was in the show. Shelly, the blonde who talked about road trip food?"

"Yeah, she was really good. I thought she should have gotten higher than fifth, but I wasn't a judge. She's got some good stuff."

"Well, she's heading back to the hotel, but I figured I'd see if you were free for a little bit. I'm her ride home and we're leaving tomorrow afternoon."

"Sure. I was just about to get dinner. Why don't you join me?"

"That would be great." Holly lowered her gaze and shifted her eyes up to look at him, biting her lower lip. Jake could never resist a woman who bit her lower lip at him.

Ohh, fuck, Jake thought. *I'm in trouble now.*

"I'll just tell Shelly and then we can go."

Two hours later, after Jake had paid their tab, Holly had several pages of notes in the composition book she carried around.

"Good thinking," said Jake. "Always carry a notebook because you never know when inspiration might strike. But take photos of everything in case you lose it."

"I already do," she said, smiling. "I save everything to a note-taking app and use that to transcribe my notes."

"Smart. So, is there anything else I can help you with?"

"Well, I'm a bit buzzed from those margaritas. I shouldn't drive just yet."

"I shouldn't either; those strawberry margaritas hit hard. My Airbnb is just a couple of blocks away. Do you want to walk over? We can talk a little more, and when you feel up to it, I'll walk you back to your car."

Holly smiled up at Jake, biting her lower lip again. "I'd like that," she said, her voice a little husky.

Yep, definitely in trouble, thought Jake. "Excellent. It's this way." He held out his arm, and she linked hers through it. The two strolled down the block, enjoying the cool night air. The night felt much cooler than it was because of the lack of humidity; their sweat evaporating as soon as it appeared.

They chatted about Holly's life growing up in Albuquerque, studying at the University of New Mexico, and working at a construction supply store as the inventory manager. They talked about Jake's life on the family farm, and how he went to the University of Minnesota on a swimming scholarship and nearly qualified for the Olympic swimming team before turning his attention to comedy.

He talked about his last tour through the Midwest and Southeast[42] before starting his Wacky Wild West Tour a few months later. ("I'm not calling it that, though," said Jake. "My stupid manager insisted on that stupid name.")

When they arrived at Jake's place, he poured a couple glasses of red wine. They sat down on the couch. Jake sat on the end, and Holly sat next to him, both turning to face the other.

---

[42] See the entire *Stand Up, Lie Down, Volume 1* series. *Betty In Birmingham* is my favorite.

They talked some more, drinking their wine, before Holly said, "I think I'm more buzzed than I was before." She laughed and snorted. "Mr. Nilsen, are you trying to get me drunk?"

Jake laughed. "No. Is it working?"

"Maybe a bit." She leaned forward and closed her eyes. Jake leaned forward and met her in the middle, softly kissing her. They pressed their lips together, and Holly touched his lips with her tongue. Jake opened his mouth and welcomed her tongue in to explore. He slid his tongue into hers, and the two kissed deeply, tongues writhing around each other. Jake tried not to think about how weird the word "tongue" sounded, especially since the author was overusing it on purpose.

They made out for several minutes before they finally broke and came up for air.

"This wasn't my intention in coming here," said Holly.

"It wasn't mine in bringing you here," said Jake. "Do you want to go?"

"I just don't want you to get the wrong idea about me," said Holly. "I don't normally chase celebrities."

"Good thing I'm not one." He kissed her again.

Holly giggled. "And I certainly don't go with strange men back to their place."

"Well, I *am* a bit strange, so I can't help you there."

"But no, I don't want to go." She scooted closer to Jake and wrapped her arms around his neck. "Kiss me some more. I love how your lips feel, and I'll bet your tongue is magical in more than just a girl's mouth."

Jake pulled her even closer as he mashed his mouth onto hers, their tongues getting re-acquainted after wasting all that time talking and not kissing. Now the word "tongue" was really getting in his head!

He ran his hand on Holly's ass, squeezing her ample cheeks, massaging them. She reached back and grabbed his wrist, which Jake thought meant she wanted him to stop. Instead, she guided his hand to her full, heavy breast, and he started kneading that instead.

Next, Holly rested her hand on Jake's thigh, a few inches from his hardening cock, and massaged his thigh. She slowly slid her hand up his thigh, squeezing and massaging until she reached his cock. She squeezed it and moaned into his mouth.

"How big is this thing?" she asked.

"Would you like to find out?"

"Very much. But tell me. Every guy measures his dick."

"Eight-and-a-half inches."

"I'd say you were a liar, but I can feel this thing. Let me see it now." She sat up, undid Jake's belt and pants, and reached in to fish his hard cock out. It sprang to attention, and she gave a sharp intake of breath.

"You weren't kidding," she murmured. Holly took Jake's shaft into her hand and slowly began jacking him off.

"How big are your tits?" Jake asked hoarsely.

"36E," she said.

It was Jake's turn to groan. "I'll need to see them to be sure," he said with a sly wink.

"You can do the honors then," Holly said. She put her hands down at her side and pushed her chest out. Jake unbuttoned and untucked her shirt. She took it off and flung it across the room, and then unclasped her bra from the front. Then she leaned forward and slid her bra straps off her shoulders, flinging her bra to land on her shirt.

Her heavy, natural breasts hung down, full and long, her brown nipples erect and waiting to be kissed. Jake leaned forward and sucked her left nipple between his lips, flicking his tongue over it.

"Ohhh," moaned Holly. "I love having my nipples sucked. That feels so good."

Jake switched over to the other nipple and rolled the first one between his fingers. She pulled Jake's head down harder. "That feels so good, Jake. Suck it harder."

Holly reached down and wrapped her hand around his dick, stroking it.

"My pussy is getting so wet for you," Holly moaned. "Please touch my pussy."

Jake looked up at Holly, eyes hungry for her. "I'd love to put my tongue in your pussy." *Fuck, now you've got me doing it!* Jake said to the author, who cackled.

"Oh," Holly gasped. Jake slid his hand onto Holly's crotch and rubbed her mound hard through her jeans. She moaned and lifted her hips to meet his hand.

"Touch me," she begged. "Please touch my pussy. And drive your tongue into it." Jake unbuttoned her jeans, and she raised her hips as he slid them and her panties down over her hips and past her feet, throwing them on the floor. Holly's bush was full and thick, but trimmed. She had shaped it to a neat little oval, and her wet lips glistened with her dew.

Jake slid his middle finger down along her cunt and laid it the length of her lips, curling his finger as it pushed between her lips, the tip of it slipping into her opening. He slid his finger up, dragging it over her engorged clit, which made her gasp and grab his arm.

"Holy shit!" she said. "Do that again."

Jake leaned in and kissed her again, repeating the motion on her pussy with his finger once more. The next time, he slid his middle finger into her pussy and wiggled it around a little. Holly breathed in sharply and moaned into his mouth.

"Oh, fuck, that feels so good," she moaned, barely breaking from their kiss. He continued to slide his finger in and out of her pussy as she stroked his dick.

After a few minutes of Jake's tender finger fucking, she pulled away from his kiss and looked at him, her eyes wide. "Ohh, God, that feels so good. I'm going to cum! Jake, you're making me cum!"

He continued sliding his finger over her clit and into her pussy, over and over.

"Oh, fuck, Jake! I'm cumming! I've never felt one this hard! Oh, shit! Oh, shit! Oh fuck, here I ... CUUUUMMMMM!!" Holly tensed up like she was being shocked, and she squeezed Jake's hand between her thick thighs. She stayed frozen like that for a few seconds as she came down from her orgasm. She heaved several breaths, like she had just run a mile at top speed.

Jake held onto her and kissed her sweaty forehead.

"Holy shit, Jake, I've never cum like that before."

"Seriously?" he asked, ignoring that she had been pronouncing it "cum" and not "come." *Oh well, when in Rum.* "Never? Not even by yourself?" he asked.

"Not that hard."

"And not with a partner?"

"No, I've only been with two other guys, and they were pretty inexperienced, which means I am too. My last boyfriend rarely made me cum, and when he did, it was only by accident. I'd finish myself off in the bathroom after he fell asleep."

"Ouch, that's pretty rough."

Holly reached down for Jake's stiff manhood again. "Can I ask you something?" She blushed furiously, looked down, and mumbled something Jake wasn't able to hear.

"What's that?" he said.

"I said, can I suck your cock?"

"You don't have to ask, you know. It's perfectly all right."

"I just... I just have never properly done it before. My first boyfriend only lasted for a week. I tried sucking him off once, and he immediately came in my mouth after five seconds, and I didn't like the taste. My second boyfriend—the one who could never make me cum—thought oral sex was dirty, and he never ate me or let me suck him."

Jake said, "Do you want me to teach you?"

"Wellll... yes. I've only ever learned it by watching porn, and I see these women shoving a dick into their mouths, all the way down their throats like they're mad at it. The dick or their throat, I can't tell.

"Or they spit on the guy's dick and slap themselves in the face with it. I don't know how much of that is for show and how much is actually real. I'm not supposed to slap my face with your dick, am I?"

Jake laughed. "No, I think it's demeaning, so don't do it unless you really want to. And I don't know where the spitting thing came from either, but that didn't start in porn until the last ten or fifteen years. Porn stars in the 80s and 90s never did that, and suddenly in the last ten years, everyone's spitting on cocks?"

Holly kneeled down on the floor in front of Jake and wrapped her hand around his dick. "So, what do I do with it?"

"To start, just lick it like an ice cream cone. Use your tongue—" *GodDAMN it!* thought Jake "—and lick the head and the sides. Explore it and get it nice and wet."

Holly did as Jake asked and licked the front of Jake's cock with one long stroke and then repeated the sides. She licked his cock head a few times, too, and kissed it.

"Fuck, that feels so good, Holly. You're a natural," said Jake. "Now, just take me into your mouth. Gently and slowly. Get used to the thickness."

"It is pretty thick. Do I have to shove the whole thing in my mouth?"

"No, just the head, maybe a little past it. Only what you're comfortable with."

Holly kissed the tip of Jake's cock, and then flicked her tongue on the slit. Then she popped the head into her mouth and sucked on it, popping it back out of her mouth after a few seconds, his head glistening with her saliva. She returned it to her mouth and sucked it again. She slid another inch into her mouth and then slid it back out again, the cock popping out of her mouth with a sound like a cork.

"Like that?" she said, smiling up at him, biting her lip again.

Jake's heart fluttered at her lip-biting again. "You're doing great," he said. "That feels so good."

Holly slid Jake's shaft into her mouth one more time, this time getting nearly three inches into her mouth before sliding it back out.

"Can I give a little bit of constructive feedback?" said Jake. "Try it without so much teeth.[43] Let your lips slide on my dick, but keep your teeth out of action. Think about how you'd suck on a popsicle."

"That makes sense," said Holly, and she tried one more time. She managed to take in four inches until she went "Gulk" and then slipped it out with another pop.

"God, I love that sound. That sound when my dick hit the back of your throat."

"I remember seeing a woman do that in some of the 'training videos' I watched."

Jake laughed at "training videos," and stroked her hair back out of her face. Holly returned to her task, bobbing her head up and down on Jake's dick, hitting the head in the back of her throat and going, "Gulk, gulk, gulk, gulk."

---

[43] Yes, it *should* be "so many teeth," but Jake's not too picky about grammar when getting a blowjob. It's not like you're reading this for the grammar either, but I couldn't just let it go without saying something.

"That sounds amazing. And you look so hot with my cock in your mouth," Jake groaned. Holly looked up at him without removing his dick from her mouth and began to massage his balls with her other hand. "Oh, fuck, that's incredible. You're a natural."

"I've got a good teacher," Holly said, smiling, and then returned her attention to Jake's tool once more.

His dick was slick with Holly's saliva as she jacked him off. "I'm going to cum in a minute," he warned. "It's always a good idea when you start sucking a guy to have a game plan about where you want him to cum. Plus, he should be considerate enough to warn you, but you need to be prepared in case he doesn't."

"I don't want you to cum in my mouth," she said, continuing to slowly stroke him.

"What else sounds good?"

"Well, you could cum on my breasts. I liked seeing that in the videos."

"I would love to cum on those beautiful tits," Jake rasped.

"Then let me know when you're about to cum," said Holly, sucking him into her mouth one more time. She resumed her sucking and stroking, hitting the back of her throat with his cock head: "Gulk, gulk, gulk."

"Oh, this is it, baby. You're going to make me cum. Get ready. Let me take over."

Holly raised up and held her heavy tits in her hands, offering them up to Jake for his hot cum, several inches away from him. Jake fisted his cock and groaned as he did it. "This is all for you, Holly. You made this, and I'm going to gush all over those great big beautiful tits. Here I cum, baby. It's all for you—AAAAAGHH!"

Jake's first blast of cum splattered on her chest, followed by a second, more powerful blast that caught her on the throat and chin. The third one landed next to his first, and the fourth one was a little weaker, landing on the meat of her tits and running down over her nipples.

Jake pulled her forward by her shoulder and rested his cock on her left breast, with his fifth shot spurting out onto her beautiful tit flesh.

"Oh, God, it's so hot," Holly whispered. "Your cum is so hot on my skin. That feels so good." She reached for Jake's manhood one more time and stroked it some more. She leaned down and flicked the last drop of cum at the tip with her tongue. She raised up and looked thoughtfully as she tasted it, rolling it around her mouth with her tongue.

"It's a little sweet," she said. "And salty."

"It helps that I eat a lot of fruit and stay hydrated," he said. "A guy can change the taste of his cum by what he eats and how much water he drinks."

"I think I like it," she said. She used her finger to wipe the cum off her chin and licked it off. "Mmmmm. I definitely like it." She wiped off some more from her tits and sucked it off her fingers. She cleaned up every drop of Jake's jizz that way.

"I'd love to eat your pussy next, and when I've recovered, I'd love to fuck you."

"I want that so bad!" Holly said eagerly. "And I want to do it doggy style. Can you fuck me doggy style?"

"I'll fuck you however you want me."

"A big cock like that? The only way I want you to fuck me is 'hard' and 'a lot.'"

"I can manage that. Now, let me taste that beautiful pussy of yours."

"Oh, God, Jake, use your tongue on me. Lick me with your wonderful tongue."

Jake sighed inwardly. *GodDAMN it!*

CHAPTER 3

"Jake, have you ever gone horseback riding?" Greg asked. It was Friday afternoon, and Jake was having breakfast with Greg Corcoran, the middle comic of the weekend. He was from Houston, Texas, and was starting to make his name in the region as an up-and-coming comic, although his day job was as a graphic designer at a sign shop. He and Jake had known each other for a few years, having met at previous comedy festivals and attending the Abraxus Tasker comedy college together last year.[44]

"Well, I grew up on a farm, and rode on occasion because friends had horses, but nothing too serious. Why?"

"My cousins own a dude ranch outside of town, and they're looking for some help over the weekend. They need some extra riders to help work the horses. They lost three of their staff to food poisoning, and so they're short-handed in exercising the horses and cleaning up."

---

[44] See *Stand Up, Lie Down, vol. 1, #7: Carrie On Campus*

Holly had already gone home after she and Jake had fucked and sucked until three in the morning when they fell asleep together in Jake's bed. Holly had given Jake a final blowjob before she left, swallowing his entire load and then smiling up at him, looking entirely pleased with herself.

"Your cum is so yummy," she said. "I think I like swallowing now."

"I'm glad. Let me return the favor one more time before you go." He slid down and buried his face between her thighs, hearing her moans and cries of delight, before he raised up and placed his cock at her velvety entrance once more.

"So, are you up for it?" Greg's voice brought him back to the present.

"Huh?"

"I said, do you want to ride some horses today and tomorrow? We could ride for a few hours, shower at the ranch, and then get back here in time for our first set at 8:00. They'll pay us $200 apiece for the two days."

Jake thought for a minute. "Well, I don't have much else going on this weekend. I've already seen all the bookstores I want to see."

Greg scoffed. "You and bookstores, man. Why do you read so fucking much?"

"So I don't become a graphic designer at a fucking sign shop."

Greg threw his head back and roared with laughter. "Ow, fuck, you got me with that one." He wiped a tear from his eye.

"Sorry, man, I couldn't resist," said Jake, chuckling. "And yeah, I'll be happy to go riding. Do I need to wear anything special?"

"If you've got some work boots or cowboy boots, that will be fine. Other than that, jeans and a long-sleeve work shirt."

"Yeah, I don't have that kind of stuff. Do you?"

"I'm from Texas. That's part of the state uniform. Tell you what, they don't need us until noon, so that gives us time to go find you some boots and a work shirt. There're a few farm stores near here. We can go pick up some gear and head over there."

"Alright, let's go." Jake paid the bill, and the two climbed into Jake's truck.

They pulled up to the El Paso Equestrian Experience right at noon. It was a large working farm with a corral, riding arena, and stables ringing a gravel parking lot. Jake parked and noticed that every vehicle in the place was a pickup.

Greg was wearing gray cowboy boots, blue jeans, and a denim work shirt that looked like it had seen more than its fair share of heavy workdays.

Jake was wearing a brand-new pair of brown Ariat riding boots and a crisp, new gray work shirt that looked like it had been tailored to fit Jake's streamlined swimmer's body. That's because he had tucked the shirt into his pants, folding the extra material at the sides so it showed off his large chest and narrow waist.

Greg rolled his eyes at Jake. "Fucking pretty boy," he grunted.

"Cousin!" came a shout from the horse barn.

"Cousin!" Greg hollered in response. A woman ran over and gave Greg a quick embrace. She was tall, about five feet, nine inches, well-built, not too slender, not too curvy. She was wearing the requisite blue jeans, cowboy shirt, and cowboy boots, with a mouse-colored cowboy hat that was sweat- and weather-stained. Her blonde hair was pulled back in a ponytail, and Jake wondered if she was a natural blonde until he noticed her eyebrows were much darker. *Ah well,* he thought, *maybe it's only us Minnesotans who are the true blondes.*

Jake took a quick glance at the woman without being too obvious. Her tight jeans showed off muscular thighs and a well-toned ass. Her plaid work shirt disguised her large breasts, but Jake was enough of a tit aficionado that he could spot the telltale swell of great tits under a shirt. She smiled at Greg, and Jake saw that it reached her eyes because they crinkled in the corners.

Her mouth was wide, and her teeth were pearly-white, which made Jake go weak in the knees. He always loved women with wider mouths for some reason. Whether it had something to do with their oral abilities, he didn't know. He just loved their big smiles because they covered their entire face.

Given that she spent a lot of time in the sun, Jake couldn't begin to estimate her age but guessed her to be in her late 20s or early 30s, although she looked a little older.

"And you must be Jake," said the woman. "I'm Ellen Corcoran, Greg's cousin. Our dads are brothers. He told me you were joining us. Uh, Greg did, not my dad."

She stuck out her hand, and Jake shook it. Her grip was very strong, and her hands were callused and rough, so Jake knew she was a serious horsewoman.

"Welcome to the Riding Experience. It's a family venture. My parents started it, and now I run it with my sister, Becky, and her husband, Earl."

"It's good to meet you," said Jake. "I grew up on a farm in Minnesota, and I've ridden a few times on friends' horses, but I don't know much about them. So I'm hoping you can show me the ropes."

"Wow, you're good-looking *and* humble," Ellen said. "I can appreciate that. Most guys come in here and see a girl, and they get all puffed up and think they're going to show me a thing or two about horses. 'Cept I've been riding since I was four, and I'm one of the best barrel racers in the region."

"Barrel Rider? Like Bilbo Baggins from *The Hobbit*?" Jake said.

"Jee-ZUS," laughed Greg. "You and your fucking books. Fuckin' egghead."

Ellen snorted and said, "No, barrel racing. Trick riding in a rodeo."

"I know, I was just kidding," said Jake. "I went to a rodeo once in high school." He stared off wistfully into the distance. "It was my first rodeo."

Ellen laughed again and clapped Jake on the shoulder. "You must be Greg's comedian friend. He said he was going to invite a couple friends to join us, and one of them was a standup comic."

"Guilty," said Jake.

"Anyway, these horses ain't gonna ride themselves," said Greg, turning on the Texas twang. "We've got to be back in town by 8:00 for our first set."

"Are you the opener?" Ellen asked.

"No, he's the headliner," said Greg. "He's on his *Wacky Wild West Tour.*"

"Please don't call it that," said Jake. "My manager came up with that name. I fucking hate it."

"Alright, cowboy, we won't call it the Wacky Wild West Tour. No one here will say the phrase Wacky Wild West Tour at all today. You got that, Ellen? Don't say Wacky Wild West Tour around Jake."

"You got it. I will refrain from saying Wacky Wild West Tour around our guest."

"You're both hilarious. You should go into comedy."

"Alright, let's go. I've got three horses saddled up. We'll ride them for an hour and then come back, clean them, and ride three more. If there's time, we might take out three more. After that, we have to ride six or nine tomorrow, depending on how many we do today. Sound good?"

"Sounds good, boss," said Jake.

"Ooh, boss. I like this one, Greggy." She put her arm through Jake's and guided him into the stables.

"Don't call me Greggy, Elly," Greg called after them.

At a few minutes before 7:00, the three rode back to the stables on their fourth round of horses. They had managed to squeeze in a fourth round because Becky and Earl agreed to clean and brush all the horses so they could ride longer.

The three had spent the last several hours talking, getting to know one another, and sharing stories about their lives growing up. And Jake felt a spark of attraction to, and from, Ellen.

"Since we got twelve of them ridden today, there are only three left to exercise tomorrow, and the three of us can handle them. You won't need to come back. Then, the other hands will be back on Sunday, and we'll resume our normal schedule."

"Why can't you do them tonight?" Jake asked.

"We don't want the horses to injure themselves. They could step in a gopher hole and break a leg."

"Ah, that makes sense. Still, I'd like to come back and ride, assuming my thighs will recover."

Jake dismounted from his horse and nearly collapsed when his feet hit the ground.

"I withdraw my previous offer," he said. "Now I see why cowboys are always portrayed as being bow-legged." He held onto the saddle for support and wobbled like a newly born fawn taking its first steps.

"Yeah, riding horses really puts a strain on your thighs," said Greg. "I only ride on weekends in Houston, and I'm always sore on Monday mornings."

"I ride every day, so I'm used to it," said Ellen. "Beats working out at a gym."

"I don't know. I've never been trampled by a leg press machine."

"You do look like you take pretty good care of yourself, though," said Ellen.

"I was a swimmer in high school and college, and I still work out and run while I'm on tour," said Jake.

Greg took the three horses and led them into the stable, leaving Ellen and Jake out in the yard.

"I'm serious, though. I'd like to come back out tomorrow. I enjoyed it, and I'd be happy to help out some more."

"I appreciate it. I'd pay you the $200 either way, though. Just having you out here helped us out immensely."

"It's not about the money," said Jake. "You don't need to pay me. I had a wonderful time, and I know I would normally have paid for this experience, so considering I got to enjoy several hours of free horse riding and lessons, I think we're even."

Ellen looked up at him and smiled that million-watt smile. "I'd like to be able to make it up to you some way, though." She put her hands on his arms like she wanted to hug him.

"How about dinner tomorrow night?" said Jake. "My first set isn't until 9:00. We could ride in the morning, get cleaned up, and have dinner around 5:00."

"That is eminently doable. Or, if you'd like, come out here tomorrow morning, we'll ride, eat lunch, and then go into town for dinner. What do you think about that?"

"I'd love that," said Jake, smiling.

"And depending on how the day goes, we'll see what happens." She looked at his mouth and bit her lip.

Ooh, fuck, another lip-biter, Jake thought.

"I'd definitely love that," said Jake, moving closer. He leaned down and kissed her tenderly. She flicked her tongue against his lips, and he opened his mouth and touched his tongue to her tongue.

Please don't start this again, pleaded Jake.

Fine, said the author.

Jake's thick oral muscle wrestled with Ellen's oral muscle. *Happy now?*

Goddammit, thought Jake.

CHAPTER 4

"You know, for someone who doesn't ride that much, you're doing really well," said Ellen. She and Jake were out on a riding trail a couple miles from the ranch. Her sister Becky had taken one of the other horses out that morning so Ellen and Jake could take the last two and have the time to themselves.

"Thank you," said Jake. "We usually went out once or twice each fall for a long ride to see the leaves change color and enjoy the last days before the snow."

"Yeah, we don't get the leaves changing color around here, so I'm a bit jealous that you got that every year. I bet it was gorgeous."

"Oh, yeah, it was beautiful. I miss it because I've been on the road in the fall for the last couple years. But right now, near the end of October, we'd be freezing our asses off already. It would be in the low 30s by now, and we'll start getting snow in a couple of weeks. I definitely don't miss that."

"We've gotten snow a few times here in El Paso. Not much, and not for long, but it happened."

"I'll bet that was pretty unusual for you all."

"Oh, people freaked the fuck out," said Ellen. "There were so many traffic accidents because people didn't know how to drive in it. Even though there was a light dusting on the roads, some people drove super, super slow and would end up getting rear-ended."

The two rode on in companionable silence for a time before Ellen said, "Do you think you're ready to start galloping?"

"Uhhh… sure?" said Jake, brow furrowing.

"We'll try trotting first and see how you do. Just be aware that trotting is actually a little bumpier than a gallop, so hold on."

Ellen kicked her horse's flanks and flicked the reins. "Let's go, Star." The horse, a chocolate brown Arabian, obliged and began to trot. Jake didn't have to do anything; his horse, Drum, a brown-and-white American Paint Horse, followed Star, matching her stride.

He realized how right she was as he started bumping up and down. He looked over and saw that Ellen was riding smoothly and naturally.

"H-h-how d-d-do y-y-you d-d-do th-th-that?" he hollered.

"Lift your ass off the saddle. Raise up in the stirrups a little bit."

Jake did as she said, and the ride was immediately much smoother.

"There you go! Nicely done." They trotted for a few more minutes before Ellen sat down and gave a quick kick and flick, and Star broke into a canter. Jake mirrored her motions, albeit less smoothly, and Drum matched Star's pace again.

"Excellent. You're a natural!" Ellen called. They cantered a little while longer before she said, "I think you're ready."

She kicked her heels once more and said, "Go, Star! Go!" The horse immediately broke into a gallop, and Ellen leaned forward, urging it onward. Jake matched Ellen and said, "Run, Drum! Run like the wind—OH MY FUCKING GOD!!"

Drum didn't need to be told to run; he'd been itching to run all day and couldn't understand why this stranger was so afraid. He was an excellent horse and took good care of his riders. Still, he hated losing to Star, so he broke off into a gallop after her.

Jake leaned forward and held onto the reins for dear life, his heart pounding as his blond hair was whipped back by the wind. As Drum thundered after Star, Jake realized the horse knew what he was doing and wasn't actually out to kill him. *That would just be a lucky bonus for the horse*, Jake thought.

When Drum felt Jake relax, he put on another burst of speed and was nearly matched up with Star. Ellen spotted a river about three hundred yards ahead and slowed up. Drum shot past her, so Ellen spurred Star into a gallop again, not sure whether she would be able to stop Drum or if she would just arrive at the crash site that much sooner.

"Oh, fuck, horse! Where are you going? What are you doing? Please God, stop horse! Drum, whoa! Whoa, goddammit! Whoa!"

Drum finally pulled up about twenty yards from the river and looked back at the human on his back. "I know what the fuck I'm doing, dumbass," he seemed to say, rolling his eyes.

Ellen caught up, out of breath, and said, "Sorry, I should have warned you. Drum is super competitive, especially when he's riding with Star."

"I think he hates me. That's what it is."

Ellen laughed. "No, he's a sweetheart. He just loves to run. He thinks he knows more than his riders, and so you have to be firm with him and let him know you're the boss. What do you say we take a break here? Let the horses get a drink and rest and we can have some lunch."

"What river is this?"

"The Rio Grande."

"No kidding? It doesn't look that, well, grand."

"It varies along the entire length. I think it's nearly three hundred-thirty feet at its widest, but it's only about sixty feet here."

The horses slowly walked up to the river and drank for several seconds before Ellen hopped off and led them away. Jake climbed down from Drum as well.

"Whoa, fuck," he said. "I thought my thighs were sore yesterday, but holding on during that gallop and standing in the stirrups really did a number on me. It feels like I've been doing leg day for a week."

Ellen laughed. "I'll help you with that in a minute," she said. She pulled a couple of tent stakes out of her bag and drove them into the ground with her heel a few feet apart. She tied each of the horses' reins around a stake.

Next, she pulled out a Native-style blanket from its position behind her saddle, plus a few plastic food containers from the saddlebags, and a couple of insulated water bottles. Ellen spread out the blanket several feet away from the horses and sat down. She patted the blanket, and Jake sat down with her.

She opened the container, and Jake saw that she had brought two sandwiches on hoagie rolls, Twinkies, and six apples.

"Road food," she said. "You need things you can eat with your hands and don't require any preparation."

"Yeah, but Twinkies?"

"I love Twinkies, and I found some heavy-duty plastic containers at the farm store a few weeks ago, so I wanted to try them out. Let's see if our little treasure survived." She popped open one of the containers and showed Jake the prize inside, which was already unwrapped. "Looks good! Check the other one."

Jake opened his container, and it was similarly undamaged. "We're grown-ups," he declared. "Let's eat dessert first."

"Salut!" said Ellen, and she and Jake clinked their Twinkies together and ate them. When they were finished, Jake had a little cream filling on his lip.

"Op, you've got something on your lip," she said. She moved toward him on her hands and knees and licked it off his lip before kissing him. She quickly pushed back and sat down again.

"Let's eat our sandwiches before we get too distracted," she said. "Then I'll see what we can do about your thigh muscles." She winked at him and held up the two containers. "I've got ham and roast beef. Which one do you want?"

"Ham, unless that's what you wanted," said Jake.

"Nope, that's perfect. I was hoping you'd pick that."

The two talked and ate, taking drinks of water from their insulated bottles, which were still surprisingly cold.

Afterward, Jake lay back, propping himself on one elbow, and Ellen moved closer to him. He lightly rubbed his fingers on her knee as she told him about how she had gotten into barrel racing, what the competitions were like, and how she was taking the fall off to recover from a shoulder injury she had suffered over the summer.

"Now, let me help you recover a bit. We'll take it easy on the way back, but I bet you could use a good massage."

"I'd love that."

"Well, we won't do too much right now, but I can relieve some of the pain and then give you a better one when we get back to the ranch."

"Whatever you say. I won't argue with a horsewoman's wisdom."

Ellen snorted a laugh. "Just lie back, and I'll start." Jake did as he was told, and she started massaging his right thigh with her powerful hands.

"Gaah, fuck! You've got strong hands. That almost hurts."

"Really? I can go easy if you want."

"No, it sounds weird, but it's a good hurt. You know, like after you do a big workout or work on a big project?"

"Uh-huh. Are you sure you're not just a masochist?"

Jake laughed. "No, I'm actually a big baby. But we used to get rubdowns from our massage therapists in college. I'm used to having people with big, powerful hands dig into my muscles."

"Big hands, eh?" said Ellen, clamping down on Jake's thigh with an iron grip.

"Ah! Ah! Ah! I meant delicate hands! Delicate, tender hands!"

Ellen laughed again and eased up on the pressure. She kneeled between Jake's legs and bent over, focusing on his thigh, seemingly unaware that her shirt was unbuttoned at the top couple of buttons. Jake looked down and could see the inside curves of her large breasts and the deep cleavage that invited him to fall into it.

Ellen's hands worked their way up Jake's thigh and got closer to his dick. Her beautiful breasts and her close hands caused the blood to rush to his cock, and it grew harder and filled out against his pant leg.

"Ohh, my," said Ellen, sitting up. "That's, uh, that's a nice surprise. Did I do that?"

Jake could only smile and nod. She looked down and saw that leaning over had caused her breasts to swell in her bra.

"Oh, I see. You were admiring the view?"

"A gentleman never stares," he said.

"Who said I wanted you to be a gentleman?" She unbuttoned her shirt and untucked it, tying it back behind her, exposing her still-covered breasts. Then she reached up and unclasped her bra from the front and slowly uncovered her big tits, tucking her bra behind her back into the shirt.

Jake's cock reached peak hardness. Her nipples were hard and pink, and her breasts were pearly white.

"I don't want to have sex out here," she said. "We're both sweaty and gross, and we'll get sunburned, but I wanted you to have a preview." She reached down and squeezed Jake's cock through his jeans.

"Good God, how big is this thing? It feels huge!"

"Eight-and-a-half inches," he said, a bit sheepishly.

"And it's all for me tonight, right?"

"All weekend, if you're up for it," he said. He sat up and reached for her. Ellen climbed into Jake's lap, straddled his lap, and began grinding on his hard-on.

"Oh, I'm up for it. I want you to fuck me six ways to Sunday."

"We've only got about eighteen hours then, so we'd better get started." He massaged her massive mammaries and kissed her deeply. Ellen moaned as she dry-humped him.

"Oh, fuck, I'm going to forget myself in a minute if we don't stop. Let's go right now. We can shower in the house, and you can fuck me in my room. Becky and Earl went into town this afternoon, so we'll have the place to ourselves."

"Can you come to my show tonight? We can go back to my place afterward and I'll fuck you for as long as you want then, too."

Ellen raised up and put her tits right in Jake's face; he started sucking and kissing her nipples as she ran her fingers through his hair.

"Oh, God, I want that so bad. Now, let's go before I take off our clothes and ride you like I stole you."

CHAPTER 5

Jake's already-hard cock continued to throb as he soaped Ellen's full tits. The two were standing in the shower, and the beating spray was rinsing the dirt and dust from their bodies. It was a large walk-in shower with jets in the walls as well as overhead.

"It's actually therapeutic," Ellen had said by way of explanation. "Working with horses can be really taxing, so we had these showers installed in the master suite and in my bathroom for a nice massage."

"It feels great," said Jake. "I can't get enough of it." He didn't raise his eyes or his hands from her breasts once.

Ellen squirted some soap onto her hand from the soap dispenser mounted to the wall and used both hands to soap off Jake's cock and balls. Then she kneeled down and stroked his cock with one hand, gently massaging his balls with the other.

"Have to get you good and clean," she said with a smile. She moved aside so the spray could rinse his cock off, and then she returned and kissed the head a few times. Jake combed his fingers through her hair as the water continued streaming down on her scalp.

"Mmmmmm," she moaned as she slipped the tip into her mouth, swirling her tongue around it.

"Ohh, fuck, that feels amazing," groaned Jake. In response, Ellen slowly pushed more of his shaft into her mouth, working it deeper and deeper. She lifted her head off with a small gasp.

"Your cock is so big. I can barely get it in my mouth."

She returned it to her mouth again, opening wide so his dick slipped in and made it four inches in before it tapped her gag reflex. Ellen held on for a few seconds before she had to relinquish her hold on it. "Oh, that's so big," she gasped before shoving her mouth back on it and bobbing back and forth.

She didn't apply any pressure, just letting the hot, wet friction of her mouth tease him. She also used her tongue to apply gentle pressure to the underside of his shaft, which got him breathing heavily.

After a few minutes of fucking him with her mouth, she popped her mouth off his prick and raised up a bit, putting his shaft in line with her large, wet tits.

"Fuck my big wet titties, Jake. Lay your pipe right there and fuck me." Jake did as he was told, spreading his legs a little so he could line his dick up with her cleavage. She squeezed her breasts together with her hands, and Jake rocked his hips back and forth, sliding his cock in her heavenly valley.

"I love having my tits fucked," moaned Ellen. "Your big cock feels so good in my tits."

"Your tits feel amazing on my cock," answered Jake, smiling. "Two great tastes that taste great together," he said, repeating the old candy commercial slogan from the 80s.

Ellen looked up at him, confused. Then she leaned her head forward and kissed Jake's dick each time it poked out of her cleavage. After a few minutes of being pummeled by the shower as he slid his dick along her chest, she released his hot prick and stood up.

"Eat my pussy now. Get me good and wet."

Jake lowered himself to his knees, and Ellen put her foot up on a bench on the wall. He positioned his head underneath her pussy, which was clean-shaven, and began licking like there was no tomorrow. He grabbed her hips to steady her and leverage himself so he could lick harder.

"Ohh, fuck," Ellen gasped. Jake pushed his mouth on her cunt and sucked as much of her labia into his mouth as he could, licking deeply into her slit. He sucked hard on her pussy and drew her lips into his mouth. He could taste it as her cunt got wetter and her juices filled his mouth.

"Mmmmmm," Jake growled. He released the suction and licked all over Ellen's slit and lips. The shower was still running, or Jake's face would have been shiny from her juices.

Jake released one of his hands and slid a finger into her wet pussy, even as he sucked and licked her clitoris.

"Ohh," gasped Ellen. "Oh, that's wonderful. Please keep doing that, baby. Do that with your finger and your mouth. That feels so good. Unh, unh, unh!"

Jake eagerly complied, flicking his tongue over her clit and finger-fucking her snatch, her labia swollen and red, hanging loosely. Jake gave her clit a break and sucked each lip into his mouth in turn.

"Ohh, fuck!" screamed Ellen. "That's so fucking good! Make me come, baby!"

Jake returned to her clit and slipped two fingers into her wet slit. Ellen's leg buckled, and she nearly collapsed. She draped a leg over Jake's shoulder, leaned back, and braced herself against the shower wall, balancing herself on her other leg.

"That's it, baby. Eat my wet cunt. Make me come with your mouth. I want to come in your mouth."

Jake pulled Ellen's ass toward him with one hand and reached up to massage her beautiful tit with the other.

"Ohh! Oh, God, I'm coming! This is it, Jake, I'm coming! Ahh! Ahh! Ahh! OH, FUCK, HERE I COOOOMMME!!"

Ellen would have collapsed if she hadn't braced herself against the shower and Jake hadn't been holding her up. She shuddered and shook as the wave of orgasm crashed over her. Jake continued to flick her clit and finger-bang her until she gasped.

"No more! Oh, fuck, stop! My clit is so sensitive." Jake released her and leaned back. Ellen took her leg off Jake's shoulder and kneeled down next to him, holding onto him so she didn't fall on the floor.

"That was fucking amazing," she said. "I haven't had my pussy eaten like that in a long time."

"I loved it," said Jake, kissing her on her cheeks and forehead. "You have such a beautiful pussy, and it tastes so good."

He stood up and lifted her up; he wrapped his arms around her. She leaned up and kissed him, tasting herself on his tongue.

"Poor baby, we still haven't made you come yet. Let's fix that now." Ellen turned around and adjusted the shower, which had been cooling off. "I want you to fuck me now and come for me," she said. "Give me your come, baby."

"I'll give you as much as you want," Jake rasped. Ellen turned around, pointing her ass at his cock. She bent over at the waist and looked behind her. "Please, Jake, slide that monster inside me. Fuck me hard."

Jake pointed his cock at her swollen pussy lips, whose tang he could still taste on his tongue. He lined himself up as she spread her legs and pulled her ass cheeks apart, granting him full access to her.

"Put it in me," she demanded. "Put that monster in me and fuck me now—OW! Holy fuck!" Ellen pushed back against the hard intruder, splitting her still-engorged lips and shifting her insides.

Jake was able to get himself halfway inside her before he felt a little resistance. He slowly slid back out, pushing himself back in a second time. He was able to slide in a little farther and repeated the out-and-in once more, getting even deeper.

"You've got such a big dick, Jake! I haven't been this full in forever. Keep going. I want all of it inside me."

He drove himself forward one more time, and that was all he needed before he bottomed out in her eager cunt.

"OH, FUCK!" she squealed. He was fully and deeply inside her. He waited a few seconds while she adjusted to having a big cock in her hot pussy. Once he was sure she could handle it, he began sliding in and out of her, slowly at first, but getting faster every few seconds.

"God, what a great pussy," Jake groaned. "You're so tight and hot. Your pussy is amazing!"

"Years of riding horses," she said. "My thigh strength is amazing." To prove her point, she tightened up her Kegel muscles, squeezing Jake's cock and making him gasp. He grabbed onto her hips and slammed himself as hard as he could into her cunt.

"Fuck me hard, goddammit! Ride me! Slap my ass and fuck me!"

Jake spanked Ellen's right ass cheek, making her cry out. "AHH!" she yelled. "Again!" He was only too happy to comply, and she shrieked when he smacked her ass two more times.

"Now, fuck me hard and fuck me fast. I haven't been fucked in such a long time. I just want you to nail me. We can make love later, but fuck the shit out of me, Jake!"

Jake grabbed onto her hips one more time and drove himself as hard as he could against her beautiful ass over and over. He pulled himself almost completely out before plowing back into Ellen's wet pussy, hearing her moan each time he filled her back up.

"Ohh! Ohh! Ohh! That's so good, Jake! That's it! Fuck me! Fuck me! Fuck me! I'm gonna come again. Jake, make me come on your cock." She reached down and rubbed furiously on her clit even as Jake continued pummeling her cunt.

"I'm coming, Jake! I'm coming again! Oh, God, here I ... COOOMMME!!" Ellen would have collapsed on the shower floor if Jake hadn't lifted her up by her hips to keep her from falling. Even so, he continued thrusting into her.

"I'm going to come, too, baby. Your pussy is so good, I'm going to come in it!"

"Later, cowboy. Right now, I want you to come on me. Come on my tits. I want to feel your hot jizz on my beautiful tits."

"Get ready then." Jake pulled out, Ellen whirled around, and held her big, beautiful tits up to her lover, offering them up for his hot seed.

"Come on me, cowboy. Give me your hot come!"

Jake's fist was a blur as he fisted his thick cock, still wet from Ellen's cunt juices. He used that to lubricate his stroking until he felt the pressure boiling up in his nut sack.

"Here we go, baby. I've got a hot load for you. Here it is. Oh, God, here you GOOO!!" A hot stream of white jizz shot out and landed on both of Ellen's tits.

"Ohh fuck," she said. "That's so fucking hot.

A second blast fired out and caught Ellen on the chin and went into her mouth. She quickly swallowed it and opened her mouth in case she got lucky again. "Again," she said.

Jake lifted his cock a little, and the third blast landed on her cheek, chin, and in her mouth. Then he pointed back at her tits so the fourth and fifth blasts could coat her beautiful tits. He shook his cock to make sure he milked out every drop, and they landed on their intended target.

Jake groaned his appreciation as Ellen scooped the come on her cheeks into her mouth, and then she licked the slit in his cock to catch the last little bit of come at the tip. Then she stood up and rinsed herself off in the shower, soaping herself down one more time. Then she kissed Jake and wrapped her arms around him, pressing her wet breasts against his chest.

The two stood there, the slowly cooling water still beating down on them. *Her water bill is going to be outrageous this month*, Jake thought.

They embraced and let the water wash over them, Ellen's face resting up against Jake's firm chest and Jake running his hands up and down her bare back, the water making it slick and smooth.

"I hope you're not done," she said after a few minutes. "I think we have time for one more round before we go to your show. I want to try my favorite position today."

"What's that?" he asked.

"Cowgirl, of course."

Debra in Dallas

TABLE OF CONTENTS

CHAPTER 1

"The stars at night are big and bright!" Jake sang at the top of his lungs.

Clap clap clap clap!

"Deep in the heaaaaart of Texas!" he responded.

It was Tuesday afternoon, just two days before Thanksgiving, and Jake had been driving for roughly nine hours from El Paso to the Crumbles Comedy Club in Dallas. And whenever he got bored—which was constantly—or a little sleepy, he would sing the opening line to Texas' state anthem, made famous in *Pee Wee's Big Adventure*. It was a little silly, but Jake loved doing silly shit when he was alone. It made him smile and sometimes made him laugh.

He had even gotten so bored that he called his parents and chatted with his mom for a few minutes.

"I saw in the paper that Rachel Hagen[45] got married," his mother said. "Some guy she met in The Cities."

Well, shit, thought Jake. He had been in love with Rachel in high school and had fantasized about her repeatedly. The two hooked up at their 10-year reunion, and Jake finally made his fantasies come true. Several times that weekend, in fact.

In fact, she even went above and beyond his fantasies, as she did things with him he had never dreamed of and only knew how to do because he'd learned over the last few years of sleeping with different women while he was on tour.

"Mom, you don't need to tell me about it. Mom. Mom! *MOM!*" His mother had been reading the wedding announcement in the newspaper, but Jake didn't want to hear it. To him, Rachel hadn't been the one who got away, she was the one he never had a chance with. And now he would never get a chance to do anything more than remember a sexy weekend with her at his 10-year high school reunion.

And, it turned out that she'd had a crush on him as well, but neither acted on it because they were both too shy and awkward to admit anything stronger than a friendship forged over years of being in the theatre program together—not "theater," because theatre kids are nerdy that way.

Jake had been one of those weird kids in high school who was both an excellent swimmer and a decent actor. As a result, he never quite fit in with either crowd, as they both saw him as "one of *them*." He had friends in both theatre and swimming, but he wasn't one of the core members of either friend group.

---

[45] Jake's old high school crush from *Stand Up, Lie Down, vol. 1: Jackie in Jacksonville.*

If someone had made a TV show about either group, he would have been one of the extras you saw over and over but rarely heard speak.

Still, he was an excellent swimmer, and he attended the University of Minnesota on a swimming scholarship; he nearly made the Olympic team after he graduated from college.

His love of acting sent him to the arms of a college improv troupe, which awakened his love of standup comedy, which is why he found himself driving past a "Welcome to Dallas" sign in the middle of November, following his GPS to Crumbles for a weekend gig as the middle comic—the comic who's between the opener and the headliner.

"When are you coming home again, Jakey?" asked his mom, interrupting his mental stroll down memory lane.

"I'm not sure yet, Mom," he said. "I've got a show in Dallas next weekend, and then I've got a show in Shreveport, Louisiana the week after. I was just going to stay here for the week over Thanksgiving and skip the cold."

"Well, we'd love it if you could come home and see your family."

Jake mentally reviewed his calendar. He was just planning on renting a condo for a couple of weeks, working out, running, and reading. It was a perfect vacation, but Jake felt the tug of home and decided on the spot that he would go.

"Alright, Mom. I can fly up on Monday and fly back here on Saturday to get my truck." If nothing else, he could get an Airbnb and salvage a few days of his personal vacation.

"Well, we're not doing it at our house this year. Your dad and I decided we needed the break. So, we're all having it at your cousin

Caroline's house this year. Remember, she and Derek moved to Rochester so their kids could go to the public schools there?"

"Yes, Mom, I remember. You've told me for the last six years."

"Well, you don't talk to your family that much now that you're a big shot, so I don't know what you remember. I just want you to be nice to Derek this time. I don't want a repeat of last year."

"Me? What the hell did I do?"

Caroline was almost ten years older than Jake, and she and Derek were physicians working at the Mayo Clinic; he was the chief of anesthesiology, she was an OB-GYN. Derek looked down on his wife's family for being farmers and blue-collar workers from Mankato. Never mind that Caroline's mom and Jake's dad were siblings who had grown up working on the same farm that Jake's father owned now.

The last time the family had gotten together for Thanksgiving last year, Derek—who had grown up in one of the wealthy Chicago suburbs—had bragged about his career successes and rode Jake for his career as a stand-up comic, saying it wasn't a real job.

The rest of the family enjoyed a chuckle at Jake's expense because they wanted him to either come back home and take over the family farm, or at least go into finance, like he had majored in.

Most of them didn't realize that Jake was already fairly wealthy, thanks to some smart real estate investments he had made starting when he was a senior in college and had purchased some student rental homes. They assumed he was just barely scraping by, living out of his truck, and working like a performing monkey for a few hundred bucks a week.

Most of them also didn't realize that one of Jake's stage specialties was dealing with hecklers, and he had honed his chirping game to a razor's edge. After a few scotch-and-sodas, Derek had made a few too many passive-aggressive remarks about farmers—"I hope we didn't just eat the family pet," he had said, laughing loudly—when Jake unloaded and gave Derek a taste of his anti-heckler work.

"Do you really use anesthesia or do you just tell patients the stories you told us? I swear to God, I'm gonna gnaw my arm off just to leave the fucking table. I'll bet your diary spontaneously combusted just to kill itself. You're so fucking boring, your love language is a Vicodin."

Derek's face reddened, and he sputtered a response. "Yeah? You're just a fucking comic. What the hell do you know?"

But Jake wasn't done.

"Is it true that you faked a jellyfish sting at the beach so Caroline would pee on you again? Did she tell you there were no jellyfish in Minnesota? You know, you could just pay women to pee on you. You don't need to lie to your wife. You already lied to her about the size of your dick. Why would you lie about a fucking jellyfish sting?"

Caroline, who was used to years of Jake's insults, could only sit and laugh at the chirping Derek was receiving. Even she had grown tired of Derek's superior attitude and thought he could be an asshole sometimes.

Derek finally stormed off to sulk in the basement and lick his wounds. As he thudded downstairs, Jake let fly with one more, "You're so uptight, you need one of Caroline's speculums just to take a shit."

"Promise me, Jakey," said his mom. "Promise me you won't lay into Derek this year."

"The guy was asking for it, Mom!"

"I know, but promise me. Derek apologized over Christmas, and we forgave him."

"Funny, he never said shit to me," said Jake.

"Hmmm, I wonder why. Anyway, if he apologizes to you, I want you to do the same," said his mother.

"Fine." He knew Derek wouldn't apologize, so he wasn't worried.

"And you have to be nice to him."

"As long as he's not a major dickhead."

"Jacob Nilsen! Watch your mouth."

"What, major? I can't say major?"

"No. You know what word I mean."

"No, Mom, I don't know what you're getting at. What word is that? He? Not?"

"Oh, now you're just being an asshole."

Jake burst out laughing. "Okay, Mom. I'll come home for Thanksgiving. And I won't call Derek a dickhead, even though he's a dickhead. Love you."

"Love you, Jakey!" His mom disconnected the call, and Jake stared out at the empty highway again.

"The stars at night are big and bright!"

Clap clap clap clap!

"Hi, I'm looking for Kaytlin," said Jake, knocking on the manager's office door at Crumbles an hour later. He had already arranged a plane ticket for tomorrow afternoon and a return trip the following Wednesday.

"I'm Kaitlynn," said a voice from behind a filing cabinet.

"What, the cabinet? You sounded more like a photocopier on the phone."

"Smartass. You must be Jake Nilsenn." Kaitlynn popped up from behind the cabinet.

"Nilsen," said Jake.

"What did I say?"

"Nilsenn," said Jake. "With two N's."

"Nilsen has two N's," said Kaitlyn.

"No, two N's at the end. So, you said three N's, I guess."

"Muh-huh. Anyway, before this turns into a 'Who's On First?' routine, what are you doing here? You're not performing until next week."

"I know. I just got into town and was going to hang out until next week, but I decided to fly home for Thanksgiving. I wanted to see if it was safe to leave my truck in the parking lot until next Wednesday or if I should pay to park it at the airport."

"No, you can leave it here. This is a pretty safe neighborhood, and we have security cameras overlooking the parking lot."

"Excellent, thank you. I'm flying out tomorrow, and I'll be back next week."

"I'll let you do it if you give me a hand. I dropped my favorite pen behind the cabinet, and I was trying to get it, but my hands aren't small enough. Can you help me?"

She stepped forward and extended her hand. Jake shook it and said, "I don't see how. My hands are way bigger than yours."

"Fucking smartass."

Jake laughed. "Thank you. I'm a professional. Anyway, yes, I can help you."

Kaitlynn was a few inches over five feet tall, curvy with large breasts, and had short brown hair with loose curls. She had large brown eyes, an upturned nose, and a full mouth with plump lips. Jake quickly flashed on those lips wrapped around his cock and felt his face get hot.

Kaitlynn didn't seem to notice as she said, "Great, I just need you to pull the cabinet back a few inches so I can get my hand in there."

Jake looked at the filing cabinet, moved a couple delicate-looking knickknacks onto the desk, and grabbed the back corners with both hands. He leaned it back a bit and pivoted the filing cabinet a few inches. Kaitlynn quickly grabbed her pen and a few papers that had fallen back there and stood up triumphantly.

"Got it!" she said, holding her pen up.

"What kind of pen is it?" Jake asked after he returned the cabinet to its previous position. Jake had recently developed an interest in notebooks since he kept a travel journal about his life and sexual exploits on the road.[46] He began collecting special notebooks and was partial to a couple of specialty brands. He had also started paying closer attention to pens. While he wasn't very particular about the pens he used, he had also stopped using ballpoint and other junk pens.

"It's an old fountain pen that used to belong to my grandfather. He showed me how to fill it with ink and I still use it for writing notes and signing order forms. I still manage to get ink on myself when I fill it."

She held up an ink-stained hand. "I filled it yesterday," she said by way of explanation. She showed it to him. It was a brown tortoiseshell pen with a gold clip. It looked like it had been used for a lot of years, but was still in good shape.

"Wow, I've got a couple disposable fountain pens in my truck, but nothing this nice," said Jake. He handed the pen back to Kaitlynn.

"So, you're my middler next weekend?" Kaitlynn asked although she knew who he was. "I've been looking forward to meeting you. I hear good things about you. By the way, would you like some cobbler? I made some apple cobbler last night and brought it in for the crew today. We still have some left."

"I love a good apple cobbler," said Jake, grinning. "My mom makes great apple cobbler every fall."

Kaitlynn dished some up from the pan on her desk onto a paper plate and handed it to Jake along with a plastic fork. She motioned for him to sit down. The two talked about the different comics who had come through Crumbles in the last few years that Kaitlynn had managed the place, taking over from her mother and father, who were now retired and living in The Villages in Florida.

---

[46] *Stand Up, Lie Down, vol 2: Francis in Fargo*

"I hear they have the highest incidence of STDs per capita in the world," said Jake.

"I try not to think about it," said Kaitlynn. "I enjoy sex and think people should be free to do whatever makes them happy. Just not my parents."

"That's fair. My parents are a little freer with their discussion about their sex life than I'd like," said Jake. He told her about an awkward discussion with his mom when she shared how she and his father loved to practice hot nude yoga that often led to[47]... Jake shuddered. "I try not to think about it either. I figure my parents had sex four times, which is how my sisters, brother, and I were born, but I like to believe they stopped right after and never had sex again."

"Kaitlynn, we're normal, healthy adults who like to do normal, healthy things," she said in a stern, nasally voice in imitation of her own mother.

"My mom has said that before!" Jake said, laughing.

The two continued talking for another hour before Kaitlynn's phone beeped. Jake looked at his watch and saw that it was 3:00.

"Do you have somewhere you need to be? I've taken an awful lot of your time," he said.

"No, that's just my alarm to remind me to eat lunch, especially because that apple cobbler's not going to cut it. I usually forget and just work straight through to showtime. Then I end up getting a headache and really cranky. So I set an alarm to remind myself if it gets too late. We've got a showcase tonight, so I don't have to do

---

[47] *Stand Up, Lie Down, vol. 1: Jackie in Jacksonville* again. Wow, two mentions in one chapter!

much. That also means the club apartment is empty, so you could spend the night there instead of getting a hotel room."

"That would be amazing," said Jake, meaning it. He may have been rich, but you don't get rich by skipping opportunities to save money.

"Anyway, I was going to go out for lunch. If you want to join me, I can take you to the apartment afterward."

"That would be great. What's good around here?"

"There's a place on the way to the apartment that does some good Texas brisket. They've won a few awards. One of the waitresses is a friend of mine. Does that sound good?"

"Lead the way," said Jake. "I'll follow you anywhere for brisket."

As Kaitlynn walked out of the club, Jake paid close attention to her voluptuous ass, her jeans clinging tightly to her curves, and Jake imagined holding onto those hips as he drove himself home, his taut pelvis slapping against her gorgeous flesh.

Kaitlynn turned around and nearly caught Jake staring, but he had flicked his gaze up to her face just in time. Still, she smiled because she could feel his eyes on her ass, so she put a little extra wiggle into her hips.

Jake saw that he had parked next to her truck, so he followed her to the barbecue joint.

Lunch was amazing—she had a brisket basket, and he had a burnt ends sandwich—and he was well satisfied when they pulled into the parking lot of the small apartment complex just a few miles from the club.

"Our headliner has his own RV, so you've got the place to yourself."

"His own RV?" said Jake. He had been toying with the idea of converting a van or small delivery truck into a tiny home and touring in it, but wasn't sure. He liked being able to shower whenever he wanted to and didn't like the idea of pooping into a bucket.

"Yeah, he's kind of a dickhead and can be a bit pretentious, but he's fucking hilarious, and he really brings in the crowds. The last time he was here, our middler got discovered by a couple of Netflix guys, and she got her own special." Kaitlynn told him the name of the comic.

"That's awesome," said Jake. "I met her once at a club a couple years ago. I was still coming up, and she had just started middling. I opened that night and she middled. She's great."

"Anyway, here's the apartment," Kaitlynn said, drawing a set of keys from her jacket pocket and handing them to Jake. "Let me show you inside."

CHAPTER 2

"This is a, uh, nice place," said Jake when they got inside. Kaitlynn closed the door behind him.

"Thanks. I know it's a shit hole," she said. "We're having it repainted and getting all new carpet this weekend, so it will actually look nicer when you get back. That was one of the reasons I picked our headliner for this weekend. He had his own RV, so we could get the work done over the weekend. Some friends and I are painting the place on Thursday night as a working Friendsgiving. I promised them all a huge dinner if they would help me paint the place. Then, on Friday, my brother and his husband are re-carpeting the place for me."

"Do they lay a lot of carpet?" asked Jake.

"Actually, my brother used to be a carpet installer in college. That's how he met his husband. Baylor installed the carpet in Kelvin's apartment, and then the two started seeing each other. They've been married for six years."

"Your brother's name is Baylor?"

"Yeah," sighed Kaitlynn. "That's where my parents met. My grandmother had to talk them out of calling him Waco."

"I mean, I had a whole joke about laying carpet all geared up, but the Baylor thing took the wind right out of my sails."

"Save it. We've heard 'em all." She walked into the kitchen and opened the refrigerator. "Hey, there's a bottle of white wine in here. Do you want some?"

"Sure, that would be great," said Jake. He sat down on the couch, which was surprisingly clean, given the condition of the rest of the apartment.

"The couch is new," said Kaitlynn, as if she was reading his mind. She walked to the couch, handed him a glass, and sat down next to him. The two turned to face each other, each bending a knee and putting their leg on the couch, the other leg hanging over the edge.

Jake tried not to steal glances at Kaitlynn's low-cut shirt, which was stretched over her ample tits, or her jeans that hugged her curvy hips and gorgeous ass. Jake always tried to be a gentleman and make eye contact with women, but he did manage to sneak a couple of glances when Kaitlynn looked around or closed her eyes for a second.

The two talked about Kaitlynn's time as a club manager and how she hoped to own it one day. The current owner was an old friend of her parents, and she started working there ten years ago while she was still in college.

She started as a server before becoming a bartender, and then finally became the manager when the owner got tired of the late nights and retired to a beach cabin in Galveston. He would drive up to Dallas to check on things once a month, which left Kaitlynn alone to run things, which she preferred.

Still, it hardly left her any time for a personal life because whenever her friends were going out, she was working. And when she was free at the beginning of the week, her friends all begged off going out, citing work the next morning.

"That means most of my friends are in the business, either in food service or they're comics. I haven't even had sex in six months!" Kaitlynn said.

"Wow, that's … a lot?" said Jake, unsure what to actually say.

"Have you ever gone that long without sex?" she asked.

"Well, I once went seventeen years without having sex," he said.

She snorted. "Childhood doesn't count."

"Ah, then…" Jake thought about it for a moment. "Yes, I have. Once."

Kaitlynn drained her wine glass and set it on the coffee table.

"And how was it?" She rested her hand on Jake's thigh. His cock started to stiffen and swell.

"Oh, it was hard," Jake rasped. "It was very, very hard."

"I'll bet it was," murmured Kaitlynn, leaning in to kiss him. She slid her hand up to Jake's dick and squeezed it through his jeans.

"Mmmm," she moaned. "That's a big one you've got there."

"I haven't had any complaints," he said, between kisses. He put his left hand on her shoulder and pulled her closer to him before sliding his hand down her front and massaging her right breast through her shirt.

I've never fucked one of the club managers on my tours, Jake thought to himself.

I thought it would make a nice little treat to thank you for all your hard work, said the author.

This could be fun, or it could bite me in the ass, Jake thought.

Uhh, you don't want her to bite you in the ass, do you? asked the author. *This isn't that kind of story.*

No, that was just an expression. No ass stuff, please.

"I can't wait to ride this fucking thing," she said as she rubbed his cock through his jeans like she was rubbing a lamp to get the genie to pop out. "I want you to fuck me with this monster. I just need to be jammed."

Jake responded by pulling her on top of him so she was straddling his lap. He lifted up her shirt, and she took it off, exposing her heavy breasts contained in a navy-blue bra with three straps at the back. He unhooked them with ease, and Kaitlynn slipped her bra off her shoulders, letting her large globes hang free.

"Ho fuck, your breasts look amazing," rasped Jake.

"Suck on them. Suck my big titties, Jake."

Kaitlynn ground her crotch on Jake's thick package while he sucked her nipples and massaged her breasts with his large, strong hands.

"Ohhh, that's so good, baby," she said, running her hands through his thick blond hair, pulling him harder to her tits. "I love having my titties sucked."

"They taste so good," he said, barely lifting his mouth from her hard nipples. He licked and sucked each one in turn, switching between her left and right tits. Then he moved to lick the deep valley between her breasts, and she squeezed them together, suffocating him between them.

"I munh to hive muh ceck memeen beez," he mumbled, muffled by her tit flesh.

"What?" she said, leaning back a little.

"I said, I want to slide my cock between these."

"I want that, too," she said. She climbed off of Jake's lap and worked at his belt and zipper. "Let me see this big boy."

Jake raised up and helped her remove his pants. He took off his shirt, showing off his rippled abs and huge pectoral muscles. She let her fingers drift over his abs and down to his hairless cock, which he had thankfully shaved the night before. His eight-and-a-half-inch cock was fully erect, and Kaitlynn could see that Jake didn't have any hair on his body, including his dick and balls.

"Oh, my, is that all for me?" she said. Her pussy was wet now, and her panties were soaked. She stripped off the rest of her clothes so they were equally naked. She had a hairy pussy that was trimmed close. "Do you want me to suck your cock or fuck you first?"

"Well, I last longer the second time, so you decide."

"Cock sucking it is!" she said, smiling. She kneeled down, wrapped her tits around Jake's cock, and rocked up and down, bending at the waist and tit fucking him like she was pumping for oil.

"That's so good, baby," he said. "God, your tits look amazing, and they feel so great around my cock." Jake put his hand on her shoulder to hold her still and then pumped his hips up and down so he could drive his cock up higher between her tits.

As big as her globes were, he was still able to poke his head up a couple inches past her gorgeous globes. Kaitlynn bent her head and sucked at his head as it appeared, making a little popping suction sound with each thrust.

Soon, she released her mammaries and let them fall and focused on getting as much of Jake's cock into her mouth as she could. At first, she only managed a couple of inches, but as she bobbed her head, she was able to relax her throat and work more of it into her mouth.

After nearly a minute of pistoning on Jake's meat, she had almost two-thirds of his throbbing prick probing the back of her throat.

"Gluck! Gluck! Gluck!" She continued to fuck her mouth with Jake's dick and the sound turned him on even further.

"I fucking love that sound," Jake groaned. "I love hearing my cock hit the back of your throat. That's so fucking hot."

Kaitlynn responded by driving herself down on his dick even farther. "Gluck! Gluck! Gluck!"

As she lifted her head each time, she used her hands to jack off the lower part of his shaft and worked at his meat, eager for his salty reward.

"Holy fuck, that's amazing, Kaitlynn," said Jake. "You sound really hot, and that feels so fucking good. I'm going to come in a minute."

Kaitlynn looked up and met Jake's eye, but never broke her rhythm or her grip. She continued to suck him off and stroke his dick.

"Do you want me to come in your mouth?" he said. "Can I shoot my come in your hot mouth?"

"Mmm-hmm," moaned Kaitlynn. She let go of his dick for just a moment, continuing to jack him off. "Shoot that big fucking load in my mouth. Then I want you to eat my wet pussy and fuck me."

"I'd love to," he said, and she returned to her work. After several more seconds, Jake could feel his come boiling up in his balls.

"This is it, baby. I'm gonna come for you. I'm gonna shoot in your hot mouth." Kaitlynn began sucking harder and stroking faster. "Oh, get ready, baby. Here it comes. Get ready."

Kaitlynn locked eyes with him and massaged his ball sack with one hand. "Oh, fuck, I'm gonna come, baby. Right in your fucking mouth. Oh fuck, here it comes. I'm gonna come for you, baby. I'm gonna—COME! OH! FUCK!"

Jake thrust his hips up one final time, and Kaitlynn clamped her mouth down on his dick, sucking out every drop. He fired one, two, three rockets of hot jizz into her eager mouth, shuddered, and then fired two more.

Kaitlynn moaned with every shot that hit the back of her throat and nearly gagged as number three was especially powerful. But she held on like a champ and kept his dick in her mouth without spitting out the white gold flooding her mouth.

She waited to make sure nothing else was coming out before she released her oral grip and showed him her prize. She then closed her mouth, swallowed hard, and opened it again to show him that she had swallowed it all.

"I learned that watching pornos," she admitted. "Plus, you taste really good. It was sweet and salty."

"I eat a lot of fruit and stay hydrated," Jake said, more than a little proud.

"Well, it's working." Kaitlynn patted Jake's dick as it slowly deflated. "I'll see you again in a little bit," she said, giving it a small kiss.

"Now I'd love to eat your beautiful pussy," Jake said.

"I thought you'd never ask." She stood up, put a foot up on the coffee table, and pulled her pussy lips apart. Jake could see them glisten in the light. He kneeled in front of her and began to lick at her slit, lapping at it like he was starved. He pressed his mouth fully to her sweet cunt and licked deep inside her, tongue-fucking her. He then sucked her lips into his mouth and rubbed her clit with his finger.

"Oh, fuck, that's so good," she moaned. "I don't think I can keep standing up; my knees are going to buckle."

She sat down on the couch, lifted her legs, and held them apart with her hands as Jake dove back into her cunt. He sucked at each of her swollen lips, slipping a finger into her wet snatch, and finger fucking her even as he licked, kissed, and sucked all around her beautiful pussy. She moaned with delight as he increased the friction on her hard clit and sped up his motions.

He slipped a second finger into Kaitlynn's waiting pussy, and then a third, and her moans increased. He slid his three fingers in and out of her slippery snatch and felt her sweet juices flow as his activity increased.

Jake switched tactics and began licking the length of her pussy, from bottom to top. He held her lips apart, exposing her clit, and he made sure to drag his tongue over the aching bud with every lick.

"Oh, fuck, Jake, that's so good. That feels so fucking good!" He continued to lap at her wet cunt like it was an ice cream cone melting on a hot summer day. "Oh, Jeeeeeezus!" she moaned. "I'm going to cum now! You're making me cum!"

Jake ignored her pronunciation of the word "come," because he knew it was rude to correct someone, especially with his mouth full. He drove his tongue deep in between her lips as he licked, making sure to keep sliding his tongue over her clit.

"Holy shit!" she yelled. "Oh, fuck! That's so good. Lick my wet cunt, goddammit! Keep licking my pussy! Aaaahhh! Aaaahhh! That's it, Jake! I'm fucking ... CUMMING! OHH, SHIIIIT!"

Kaitlynn's hips bucked like she was in the rodeo and she slammed her heels into Jake's back as her thighs clamped around his ears. Jake tried to pry her milky thighs apart even as he continued driving his tongue into her sopping pussy and she orgasmed into his eager mouth.

After several seconds of writhing in ecstatic agony, she slumped back into the couch and released her death grip on Jake's head. He had already decided that if he was going to die at that moment, he wanted the taste of a sweet cunt on his lips. But it was not his day, and he would live to fuck again. Even so, he continued to lick at her snatch, savoring the flavor.

Kaitlynn grabbed Jake's hair and lifted his head. She studied his face, which was shiny with her juices. "Slow down, lover. My cunt is so sensitive after I cum."

"Well, let me know when you're ready," Jake said, rising to his feet, his thick cock fully erect again. "Because I still want to put my dick inside that beautiful pussy of yours."

Kaitlynn smiled, walked around the couch, and bent over one arm, putting her wet and swollen cunt on display. Jake moved into position behind her and put his hands on her hips. She looked over her shoulder at her new lover. "How about now? Will now work for you?"

"I think I can make now work," Jake said with a smile.

Jake lined his massive tool up with Kaitlynn's pussy and slid it up and down between her lips a few times. Then he laid his cock so it was directly underneath Kaitlynn's pink pussy, between her thighs, and began to saw back and forth, the topside of his cock sliding against her clit.

"Oh, shit, don't tease me with it. I need to get fucked right now!" Jake grabbed his cock, and lined himself up again with her beautiful cunt.

"I haven't had a cock in me for six months," she continued to moan. "I need you to fuck me right no—OH, MY GOD!"

Chapter 3

"The captain has turned off the seatbelt sign, so you are free to move about the cabin," said the flight attendant. "But we ask that you keep your seatbelt fastened in case of unexpected turbulence. And in a few minutes, cabin attendants will be by to serve drinks and snacks."

"That's all a bit disconcerting, isn't it?" said Jake to the woman next to him.

"What, the drinks? They do that all the time," said the woman. She was Black, her hair tied in box braids, and looked to be in her mid-40s, although Jake couldn't be sure. Her eyes were wide and clear, and when she looked Jake directly in the eye, he felt like she was looking for something deeper. She smiled at her little joke.

Jake chuckled. "No, not the drinks." He looked around as if he was about to share a deep secret and leaned in. "The cookies! If they don't have the cookies, I'm going to be awfully sad."

The woman smiled and looked out the window. They were sitting in the business section on a two-and-a-half-hour flight from Minneapolis to Dallas. It was Wednesday afternoon, the week after Thanksgiving, and Jake was flying back so he could start his weekend show at Crumbles.

It had been an uneventful Thanksgiving with his family. Derek was on his very best behavior, and he even embraced Jake and welcomed him into his home. He apologized for his behavior the previous year and said he had been drinking too much in the weeks and months leading up to last Thanksgiving. He was now sober for an entire year and realized how much his drinking had affected his behavior.

Jake, being a born-and-bred Minnesotan, thanked Derek and apologized in return, even though he hadn't wanted to. It was just another case of Knee-Jerk Politeness Syndrome that affects most Minnesotans.

After spending a week with his family and seeing his friends, he was ready to get back out on the road. He loved his family, but he loved life on the road. He wanted to spend a few more years out there before he decided what to do next. Maybe he would decide to settle down in one of the cities from his travels.

He thought back to Betty and the intensity of their "casual" relationship. He did love Betty and sometimes thought about moving to Birmingham so the two of them could spend more time together, especially as her husband traveled on a regular basis.

Maybe he could open up a financial advising practice and hire Betty to "work" there. That would at least give her an excuse to come to his office every day. He started fantasizing about how he would have a private office with a couch or even a daybed, and how they could fuck while they were supposed to be working.

"It's the Gardetto's for me," said the woman next to Jake, interrupting him from his office/sex den fantasies.

"I'm sorry?" said Jake with a start. The snack cart rolled past them to the front of the plane, and the attendants began handing out snacks and drinks.

"The snacks they give out. I love the Gardetto's snacks, and they don't always have them. That's my favorite airplane snack."

"Ah, I love Gardetto's," said Jake. "Especially the little rye crisps."

"Yep, me too," said the woman. "All that other stuff is just cheap filler. I wish they would just sell bags of the rye chips."

"They do," said Jake. "I bought a bag while I was on the road once."

The woman's eyes widened, and she smiled. "Seriously? I've never seen them!"

"Oh, sure. If nothing else, you could always order them online. I can only find them by accident because I'm rarely at home."

"You mentioned that," said the woman. "What do you do? Are you a consultant?"

"Something like that. I'm a strategic wit analyst?"

The woman smiled uncertainly. "What is that?"

"I'm a standup comic."

The woman laughed. "No kidding? I've known a couple standups in my day, but only in college. They weren't very good. You must be pretty good if you're riding in business class."

Jake snorted. "My family would disagree. They want me to go to work in finance."

The woman turned in her seat to face Jake. "Really? Why is that?"

"That's what I majored in in college. Except I got bit by the improv bug in college and from there, I went into standup. My family agreed to let me try it for two years, and I'm on year five now."

"No kidding? I'm an economics professor at the University of Texas at Dallas. Where did you go to college?"

"University of Minnesota. I was also on the swim team there."

"That would explain your—" she looked him up and down once more, "—fitness level."

"I still work out," he admitted. "What about you? Where did you go to school?"

"UCLA for undergrad and a master's and Ph.D. at University of Georgia."

"Really? I was a B student at best, so I'm always impressed whenever I meet a Ph.D."

"Don't be. A Ph.D. just means you're tenacious and a glutton for punishment. You were an athlete, so you know what that's like. And you still work out to maintain your, uh, physique, so you still know what that's like."

As the two talked, the flight attendants brought them their drinks and snacks of choice, including an extra pack of cookies for Jake and Gardetto's for—

"Debra Dawson, by the way," said the woman, extending her hand. Jake reached over and shook it carefully, noting her long, slender fingers and bright red fingernails, which she looked like she had just gotten done in the last couple of days. She held Jake's hand for a few seconds longer than normal.

"So, Dr. Debra Dawson? DDD? Sounds like a pro wrestler's name—Triple D!"

Debra snorted. "It definitely sounds like a wrestler's name. I used to watch pro wrestling with an old boyfriend in the 90s. He was crazy for it, and I got sucked into it a little bit."

"That's understandable. I watched it when I was a kid. I'm Jake Nilsen."

"Nilsenn?"

"No, Nilsen."

"Ah, I see," said Debra, not actually seeing.

"So, were you in Minneapolis for the holiday?" Jake asked.

"I was taking care of my late uncle's estate for the last few days." She nibbled a few more pieces of her Gardetto's.

"I'm sorry to hear that," said Jake, finishing the last bite of his cookie.

"Thank you. He died several months ago, and my cousin needed help settling the final details. She wasn't close to her father—he was an asshole—but he left her everything, including quite a mess. She needed help getting it all straightened out. So, I went up a week ago to help out, and I'm coming back home today. We're still on fall break for another week at the university, so I thought I'd get a few days to myself. Anyway, what are you doing in Dallas? You don't strike me as a native Texan."

Jake snorted. "I'm not sure how to take that," he said with a laugh.

Debra smiled and touched Jake's forearm. "It's just we don't get many Vikings in Texas unless they're playing the Cowboys on Sunday afternoon."

"Ah."

Debra left her hand in place, and Jake didn't move, like she was a doe in the woods and he didn't want to spook her into running away. She looked like she was trying to make a decision about something important as she licked her lips and flicked her gaze down at his crotch.

Jake pretended not to notice that she was continuing to steal glances at his cock. "No, I'm originally from Minnesota. I have a show in Dallas this weekend. My mom wanted me to fly home for the holiday and make amends with my cousin-in-law."

"And did you?"

Jake thought for a minute. "Yes, actually. Turns out he's not such a bad guy when he's not drinking."

"That was my uncle's problem," said Debra. "What made him quit?"

"I, uhh, chirped him."

The flight attendant came over the public address system. "Ladies and gentlemen, we are beginning our descent into Dallas/ Fort Worth International Airport and should be on the ground in about ten minutes."

"You what? What's chirping?"

"Shit talking. Athletes do that to each other. When hockey players do it, they call it chirping. He was getting kind of obnoxious during Thanksgiving dinner last year, and when I'd had enough, I kind of went after him. One thing I'm good at in my comedy is dealing with hecklers, and I worked on him."

Debra laughed. "And the power of your chirping made him quit drinking? You must be quite the chirper."

"I was, but I wasn't directly responsible. When I was done, he stormed off into the basement and sulked. After we all left, his wife—my cousin—read him the riot act. I guess she was really sick of his shit, too, and I sort of shocked her into it. She helped him quit drinking, and it changed his entire personality."

"Wow, the power of the chirp," said Debra. "It's kind of like the 'Yo Momma' show on MTV in the early 2000s."

Jake laughed. "A bit. I watched that when I was a kid when my parents weren't home. My classmates and I would bust on each other at recess with some of the lines we'd heard. I think that's where I started developing how I deal with hecklers."

Several minutes later, as they continued talking, the plane had pulled up to the gate and was waiting for the ground crew to unload the plane and bring the jetway up to the exit doors.

"So, what does your girlfriend think about you being on the road so much?" Debra asked, speeding up her conversation a little bit as if she wanted to keep talking to him before they separated.

"Oh, uh, I'm single. Er, very single. How about you? Do you have someone, uh, special waiting for you at home?"

"No. No, I don't. Just my fish, and I don't even think they realize I was gone. I had someone feed them for me, and they probably think we're the same person. So when does your show start?"

"It's at Crumbles Comedy Club, and the first night is tomorrow night. Would you be interested in coming to a show?"

She nodded as if she had made the decision she was mulling over. "If you promise not to chirp me, I think I can make it."

Jake and Debra stood up to retrieve their bags from the overhead compartment. Debra stood about five foot, ten inches, and the top of her head came up to Jake's chin. She was in good shape and looked like a runner. She had full breasts, narrow hips, and a juicy ass. She wore a white blouse with the buttons undone and a blue tank top that showed off her cleavage, with olive green slacks tucked into dark calf-length brown boots. Her box braids had black, red, and white-colored extensions; University of Georgia colors, Jake guessed.

Jake reached up for their bags, and his t-shirt came untucked from his waistband. Debra's eyes widened a little as she saw Jake's taut abs and a bit of his Adonis belt[48] hidden under his actual belt.

"Oh, uh, do you have any plans tonight?" she rushed to get out. "I'd love to show you around town a little, and maybe we could have dinner? I don't live too far from the club, so I could drive you around, maybe?"

Jake held her bag out and gazed into her eyes. "I would love that," he said. "Would I be able to shower first? I hate flying because I always feel so funky afterward."

"That would be fine, I need to do the same. Let me text you my phone number, and then I'll send you a couple of suggestions about where we could eat."

Jake smiled warmly at Debra. "That's perfect." Their hands touched as she reached for the handle, and neither of them pulled away. "I'll walk out with you. I'm going to catch a Lyft to the club because that's where I left my truck."

---

[48] That's that sexy V on a guy's torso that guides your eyes downward to his groin.

"I'm catching a Lyft home. I hate trying to park at the airport," said Debra.

Jake looked at his watch; it was nearly 3:30. "How is 7:00? Is that enough time?"

Neither Jake nor Debra had let go of the suitcase handle yet. "That's perfect. Do you like Mexican food? There's a great place a few minutes from, uhh, my house."

"I love Mexican food," said Jake. He released her bag, and the crowd began to move forward. When they cleared the gangway, Jake offered his arm to Debra. She put her hand into the crook of his elbow, and the two walked to the ride-sharing stand.

They stood outside the ride-share stand and selected their rides from the app. Once Debra's car pulled up, she moved in for a hug from Jake, who squeezed her to him. He could feel her heavy breasts resting against his stomach, and she could feel his hard cock pressed against her body. She laid her head against his chest and sighed.

After a few seconds, she leaned back. "I'm, uh, really looking forward to seeing more of you," said Debra. "Uh, for dinner!" she added quickly. "I'm looking forward to seeing more of you for dinner."

Jake leaned in. "I can't wait to see more of you either," he murmured into her ear.

Debra quickly stood on her toes and kissed Jake full on his mouth before turning and darting to her ride. As she drove away, Jake tried to will his hard cock to relax so he didn't look like he had an obvious hard-on.

After a couple minutes of trying to will his hard-on to go away, he remembered the time his mom told him about how she and his dad practiced hot-naked yoga, and that deflated him right away. His car arrived right after, and he rode back to the club, imagining Debra underneath him or straddling his face, and his erection returned.

He retrieved his truck from the parking lot and drove to the club apartment.

Chapter 4

"Is that the college football stadium?" asked Jake. "Weird that it's way out here."

Debra snorted. "No, that's the local high schools."

"*That's* a high school stadium? It looks like a stadium for a small college."

"Yeah, high school football is practically a religion here in Texas. I don't even bother driving around here on Friday evenings because the place gets packed out—people are tailgating hours before and after the game. You'd think Florida State was playing University of Georgia or something."

"Minnesota's stadium holds like 50,000 people, but we're so bad at football, it's easy to find a seat."

"Yeah, people are crazy for football in Georgia, too. I went to a few games, but I wasn't that excited by it."

Debra in Dallas

The two were riding in Jake's truck, and Debra was directing him around her area of town in Garland, a Dallas suburb. When he arrived to pick her up at her house, he had stopped by a florist and picked up a bouquet of irises.

"Here you go. I hope you like irises. I saw them, and they made me think of you," Jake had said when he arrived at her house. He didn't tell her he had spent an hour trying to track down a florist who had irises. The first one was closed and the second one was out. Who runs out of irises? *thought Jake.*

"Thank you! I love irises," said Debra. She was wearing a maroon dress with black floral designs. The skirt was cocktail length, coming up to mid-thigh, and the material hugged her tightly, making Jake think it had nylon or spandex as part of the material. It hugged her body, accentuating her large breasts and a little pooch in her tummy. Jake admired the dress, and he was turned on by what he saw.

I bet it'd look good on her floor, too, *he thought, repeating the corny pickup line.*

She hugged him and gave him a lingering kiss. "Let me put these in water."

"Here, the florist recommended you put this in the water, too. It helps them last a little longer." Jake held out a small pouch the size of a sugar packet.

Debra took it and poured the contents into a vase and then filled it from the sink. She unwrapped the purple flowers and then placed them in the vase as well. She fluffed them up a little and then stepped back to admire them.

"*They look lovely,*" *she said. "Thank you so much." She embraced Jake again. "No one has given me flowers since my husband passed five years ago." She laid her head against Jake's chest and sighed as he squeezed her in his powerful arms. She squeezed him back and held on; Jake didn't let go either, savoring the moment.*

The two stood for several seconds without moving, which Jake loved. Her breasts crushed against him, and she felt wonderful. She was tall enough that her pelvis was grinding into his erection. She pressed her entire body up against his so there was no mistaking the hardness pressing against her; he couldn't have hidden it if he'd tried.

"We should probably go to dinner," said Debra, not letting go. "If we don't go now, we're never going to go."

"I'm fine doing whatever you decide."

She squeezed him harder one last time and stepped back, her eyes welling up with tears. "I'm sorry. I'm so sorry. I don't mean to do this to you. I can't ask you for that."

"Do what to me?" Jake asked. "Ask me for what?" He was confused; it was going so well, and it was like she had a change of heart about everything. Oh, God, did he smell? "What's wrong?" he said.

Debra sighed and stared off into the distance for a few moments. Finally, she said, "My husband died five years ago, and I really haven't been with anyone since. I mean, I had a short fling a couple of years ago, but the guy turned out to be cheating on his wife with me. I never wanted to be the 'other woman' so I kicked his ass to the curb.

"But I've had a strong urge to be with a man. Someone to hold me and make me feel beautiful again. To make me feel like a woman. I've had this ... skin hunger and I want to feel a man's skin against mine. To feel his embrace. And to feel him inside me. Your beautiful flowers brought up some emotions and made me want all that even more. But

I barely know you. I can't ask for that. I'm sorry, I didn't mean to dump all of… this onto you. We just met, and I'm asking too much of you."

Jake put his hands on either side of her face and gazed into her eyes. "You don't even have to ask. I would love to be that for you."

"But I'm old enough to be your mother!"

"Hey, I'm 28."

"And I'm 49. That's not weird to you?"

"Not at all. I love older women, and I would love to give you whatever you need. I felt a connection when we were on the plane, and I was hoping you felt it too. That's why I'm here. I want to see what happens next."

Jake leaned in for a kiss, and Debra wrapped her arms around his neck as their tongues explored each other's mouths, both of them thankful they had brushed their teeth and used mouthwash earlier.

After a few minutes, Jake pulled back. "Tell you what, let's go to dinner and make this a real date. I brought you flowers like a real date, and we were already going to have dinner, so let's make this a real date. And when we're done, we can come back here and satisfy your skin hunger, however—and however much—you'd like."

Debra kissed him one more time and said, "I would love that. Because I've been feeling this lovely dick pressed against me, and I'm curious about what it can do." She reached down and squeezed his cock through his pants. She breathed in a little and smiled. "But yes, let's go to dinner first, because I haven't eaten since breakfast, and if I don't eat, I'll get hangry. You won't like me when I'm hangry."

"Take a left and Chico's is a few blocks on the right," said Debra. Jake followed her directions and arrived at a small Mexican restaurant in a half-full parking lot.

"It doesn't seem to be very busy."

"It's usually not on a Wednesday night. This is normal, but it gets packed on the weekend. I love coming here after a long day of classes. I'll get a margarita and a few street tacos or a burrito. It's a nice treat for myself."

"I haven't had good Mexican food in a while," said Jake. "This will be a treat."

The two walked inside, and the hostess greeted Debra. "Buenos noches, Miss Debra. It's good to see you again. I see you have a handsome young man with you. I have just the table."

She took them to a booth in the back, set down the menus, and rattled off the specials. Debra ordered a strawberry margarita, and Jake ordered a Dos Equis.

As they perused the menu, Jake told Debra about life on the road while Debra talked about what it was like to teach business students.

"You don't strike me as a business major," Debra said. "Most of them are money-hungry and soulless. They're eager to get rich, make it big, and are willing to grind down whoever they need to to get there. Not you though. You're kind and caring, and you chose a career in the arts, not in finance. Why did you even go into finance as a major?"

Jake thought for a moment. "Well, I grew up on a farm, and my parents saw what farm life was becoming. Luckily, my parents and grandparents never bought into the 'expand or die' philosophy of the 1970s and 80s that killed so many family farms. It was definitely tough and lean in those years, but we managed to hold on.

"Then, when organic food became such a big deal, my family was one of the first ones to embrace organic farming. Still, even that has been tough, and so my parents wanted my siblings to have something else we could do instead. They pushed me into finance since I was always fairly good at math. I got my degree in finance but ended up loving improv in college. I even acted in a couple of student plays. I got interested in stand-up when I graduated and managed to do pretty well at it."

Their food arrived, street tacos for Debra and a chicken burrito for Jake. She continued, "But do you make enough? It doesn't seem like a stable lifestyle. You either succeed or wash out. There doesn't seem to be a middle ground. Am I right about that?"

Jake smiled. "You sound like my family. They were definitely worried about me my first year, but I actually made some smart investments. That's one thing my business degree helped me with.

"I had an uncle who left me a lot of money when he died, so I bought a few rental properties at the U. Then I bought a few more. And then I made a couple of real estate investments in Savannah and Miami, and now I'm making enough money off of those that I don't need to actually work. I do standup for fun, but I've gotten good enough that I can support my life on the road.

"My goal is to be so successful I never have to dip into my investments to live. And I want my investments to be able to carry me if I ever leave comedy."

"And you don't want to be a real estate investor? Those guys make millions."

Jake shook his head. "No, because the ones I've met are assholes. They sound like the students you were describing, but worse. They're locusts that swarm over a field and strip it bare. Besides, I've already got enough money. The only real estate development I'll ever do is when my parents retire from farming. They want me to develop their farm into a suburban residential development. We'll split the profits, and they'll get a nice house to live in. But we're several years away from actually doing that."

They finished their meal, split a dessert, and Jake asked for the check.

"Let me at least pay for my half," offered Debra.

"Oh, no. This is a real date. I would never make a date pay for her half."

"Don't you think that's sexist?"

"Nope," said Jake. "It's how my parents raised me. If it helps, I recognize that you are an independent woman with her own job and money and are fully capable of paying for dinner. But I asked you on this date, which means I get to pay."

"Technically, I asked you," Debra reminded him. "On the plane, I mean."

Jake thought about this and then slid the check across to her. "That you did," he said. "It's all yours."

Debra laughed loudly and snatched the check from under his fingers. "You make me laugh, Jake Nilsen," said Debra. "Whatever else happens, I haven't had a good time like this with another man in a long time. Thank you."

Jake rested his hand on Debra's, and they interlaced fingers. "Oh, we're not done yet," he said. "I still want to take you back to your place and, uh, do things with you."

"Do things?" Debra snorted. "Is that how they do sexy talk in Minnesota?"

Jake turned bright red and stammered; Debra laughed again.

"Yes," he sighed. "I'm actually really good at sexy talk. I just get embarrassed when I do it, and it's not the actual, you know, sexy time. When we're together and naked, I can be as dirty as you want. But when we're not, and we're at a place like this or just talking on the phone, I get very flustered and nervous about it."

"Well, my lovely Viking, I want you to take me home, pull out that big cock I've been fantasizing about, shove it deep into my pussy, fuck me until you shoot your come in me, and talk filthy while you do it. Can you do that?"

Jake looked her dead in the eye, face reddening, and said, "I, uh, I would, uh that is, I'd love to do all of that with your, uh, pussy."

Debra snorted. She stood up and held her hand out to Jake. "I sure hope you can fuck better than you dirty-talk."

CHAPTER 5

"Hold me," whispered Debra. The two were sitting on her couch. She had put a fireplace video on her TV, and her stereo streamed some smooth jazz, which Jake normally hated. But when you're about to have sex, you don't quibble about music.

Jake was sitting on the right side of the couch, and Debra was snuggled up against him, her feet underneath her. Jake ran his fingers on her upper arm and planted little kisses on the top of her head, admiring the braids in her hair.

"I love your hair," he said. "I love the colors."

"Thanks," said Debra. "I do it myself. Hair is very important to Black women. I never go out without it looking put together."

She laid her head on his muscled chest and stroked his flat stomach, listening to his heartbeat, the long, slow thump of each beat.

"I can tell you work out," she said without raising her head. "You have such a slow heartbeat."

"Mmmmmmm," hummed Jake so she could hear his voice.

"Let me see if I can speed it up." Debra smiled and reached down to rub Jake's dick through his pants; she felt it immediately harden. She also heard his heart beat faster.

"Yep, there it goes."

She climbed up onto his lap and faced him. The two kissed deeply, tongues sliding over one another, exploring each other's mouths once again. Jake loved the wetness of her mouth on his.

He broke off and licked and kissed her long neck, inhaling her faint perfume and sucking softly where her neck and shoulders met.

"Ohh," Debra whisper-moaned. "That's so good. That feels so good." She closed her eyes and threw her head back as Jake licked and kissed both sides of her neck, trailing his tongue up to her ears, which gave her goosebumps.

"Ohhhh," she moaned a little louder. "You're driving me crazy."

He drove his tongue into her deep cleavage, and she ran her fingers through his blond hair. He massaged her breasts and pinched her nipples through the fabric, making them hard.

Debra pulled his head up and slipped her arms out of her dress, exposing a black lacy bra that strained to contain Debra's beautiful breasts. She slid her dress down to her waist and then unhooked her bra clasp from the front, holding the two ends together with her hands.

"Don't forget, I'm an old woman. Things tend to ... sag with age."

"You're beautiful, you're not old," said Jake. "I don't care how old you are or what may ... sag. I want you. I want to be with you and to be inside you."

He kissed her on the mouth and then down her chest. He gently pulled her hands away and slowly slid the cups apart. Her breasts spilled out and sagged a few inches, but they were so full and heavy that Jake nearly came right there.

"So fucking beautiful," Jake said and kissed them once each before taking off his own shirt. Debra ran her hands over his huge pectorals and washboard abs. She leaned down and kissed his pecs and sucked on his nipples before raising back and laying against Jake, their naked chests touching.

Jake wrapped his arms around her and held her close. She sighed and closed her eyes as he ran his fingers lightly over her smooth back. The two stayed like that for several minutes, enjoying the feeling of their skin together. Debra planted small kisses on Jake's neck, and he began rubbing both hands on her back, trying to touch every inch of her skin.

"This feels amazing," said Debra. "I've needed to feel a man's skin against mine. To feel his heartbeat against my chest. To press my breasts against him. Even if we don't do anything else, this is wonderful. For the first time in years, I feel ... complete."

"Does that mean I should stop?" said Jake, smiling.

"If you try to leave, I'll throw you on the floor by your dick and fuck you until we both pass out."

"I wouldn't dream of it." He pushed her so she was sitting up straight, leaned over, and latched onto one of her nipples. He licked and sucked on it, and Debra moaned with pleasure.

"Ohhhhhh. Suck my titties, baby. I need your mouth on me. It's making my pussy wet. I'm so wet right now."

Jake squeezed and massaged them as he gave them equal amounts of attention, lapping first at one beautiful breast and then the other.

Debra was grinding on Jake's cock while he plied his tender oral ministrations to her heavy breasts and the friction on her snatch was making her breathe heavily and moan with delight.

"My pussy is on fire for you, Jake," Debra groaned. "I'm so fucking wet for you."

"On fire, eh?" Jake said, smiling. "I'd better put you out then."

He stood up and lifted her with him. She felt a moment's fear and grabbed onto his shoulders with both hands. She didn't need to worry, as he had wrapped his arms around her and gripped tightly.

He helped her stand and lifted her dress over her head, throwing it on the floor.

Huh, it does look pretty good there, he thought when it landed.

Jake kneeled before her and licked at Debra's nipples one more time. He slipped his thumbs beneath the waistband of her black lace panties and slid them down her runner's thighs, helping her step out of them, even as he kept his mouth latched onto her brown breasts and hard nipples.

He stayed on his knees and ran his hand over her thatch of short pubic hair. She had trimmed it when she got home anticipating this very moment, and he could smell her musky scent. He tipped his head back and slipped his tongue into her crevice, drawing it up like he was licking an ice cream. She shuddered and gave a little moan.

"I want to eat your beautiful cunt and feel your sweet juices all over my face," he said before diving back into her sweet snatch and licking deeply into her slit.

"Ooh, you *can* talk dirty!" she squealed. "But enough talking, more pussy licking."

Jake guided Debra back to the couch. She sat down, scooted her ass toward the edge, and opened her thighs, exposing her beautiful vagina. She opened her legs as wide as she could, grabbed her ankles, and pushed her knees apart with her elbows.

Jake licked at her dark brown labia, and she moaned with pleasure. "Ohh, shit. Eat my pussy, Jake. That's so good. I love feeling you eating my pussy."

He flicked his tongue up and down her clit and slipped one of his thick fingers inside her slippery cunt.

"Oh, shit!" she gasped, grabbing his hair with one hand. She froze, not pushing him down or pulling away. She held on like a lifeline as a small orgasm washed through her. "Oh, fuck, you just made me come a little," she moaned.

Jake was pleased to hear that she pronounced it as "come" and not "cum," but he knew he could rely on a woman with a Ph.D. to say it the right way.

"That's only the first one," Jake said, smiling up at her, his face already slick with her fluids. He returned to his task, increasing the speed on her clit with his tongue and sliding his middle finger in and out of her tight pussy. When she had relaxed a little, he introduced another finger, and she gave a little squeal.

"Your fingers are so thick!" she cried. "I don't know if your cock is going to fit inside my little cunt."

"We'll do whatever is comfortable for you," he said.

"No, I want you to shove that fucking thing inside me no matter what," she said. "I haven't come this far to turn back now."

Jake slid his two fingers in and out of her juicy slit and watched Debra's face contort with pleasure.

"Oh, shit, make me come on your hand, Jake. I'm so close, I'm going to come. You're making me come. Oh, fuck, Jake, here I come, baby! Oh, fuck! Oh, fuck! Oh, I'm coming for you! Aaahhh! Aaahhh! Aaaaaahhhhh!"

Debra wailed and grabbed Jake's wrist as an even bigger orgasm overtook her. She clenched her body and thrust her ass into the air as she felt her first serious orgasm in more than three years.

Jake slowly slid his fingers out of her sopping cunt, licked up the juices that were glistening on her swollen lips, and then sucked both of his fingers clean, looking his lover in the eyes the entire time. He watched her as she breathed heavily, recovering.

She watched him stand up, unbuckle his belt, and slide his pants down over his ankles, before stepping out of them and throwing them next to Debra's dress.

Hmm, those pants look pretty good there, Debra thought. She didn't know why that popped into her head.

Jake slipped his socks off because naked men look totally ludicrous in socks and then slid off his underwear. His eight-and-a-half-inch cock sprang out and stood out at ninety degrees from his body.

"Holy shit," breathed Debra. "That. Looks. Amazing." She leaned up and wrapped her fingers around it. Her bright red nails looked sexy against the backdrop of Jake's cock skin. Her fingers were a little cold as the blood had left her extremities during her orgasms, and Jake flinched a little as he felt them on his member.

"Sorry, my hands are cold. Let me warm you up, baby." She leaned forward and kissed the tip of Jake's penis and flicked it with her tongue. She kissed it a few more times and then slipped the head into her mouth and sucked it, flicking her tongue over it.

She pulled it back out of her mouth with a pop and then repeated the motion. She pushed her head forward a little more, slipping a little more of his dick into her mouth, before sliding it back out once more.

A third time, and she was able to fit more than half of it in her mouth. She moaned her pleasure, and Jake felt the vibration in his cockhead.

"Talk dirty to me, baby," she ordered.

"Ohh, that feels so good when you suck my cock, baby. I love seeing you take my cock in your hot mouth. I want you to wrap your big tits around my dick so I can fuck them and come all over them. And I'm going to fuck the shit out of you doggy style so I can watch them swing."

She bobbed her head back and forth and slurped loudly each time she withdrew it from her mouth.

"Fuck, that all sounds great. You're going to do that. But don't come yet," she warned. "I want the first time I make you come to be inside me." She stood up and wrapped her arms around him, pressing her nude body against his again. "Make love to me, Jake. Make love to me and fill me up with your hot come. You can fuck the shit out of me later, but right now, I need you to love me. Love me, Jake."

"I do. I mean, I will." Jake swept her off her feet and carried her toward the back of the house.

"Where is your bedroom?"

"Third door on the right," she said, pointing down the hall.

Jake followed her directions and found her bedroom. He laid her gently on her bed, which was made up, and threw the throw pillows on the floor.

Huh, those look pretty good there, they both thought, independently of the other.

Jake bent over and sucked Debra's nipples one more time, and she ran her fingers through his hair, her bright red nails gently scratching and massaging his scalp. Jake felt like he could suck her tits for days just for that feeling alone.

He reached down and slid a finger into her pussy, which was still wet, and brought it up to his mouth, licking it clean once more.

"Please, Jake. Love me," she whispered. "Make love to me."

Jake climbed onto the bed and kneeled between her legs. He grabbed his rock-hard shaft and aimed it at her shiny slit. He slid the head between her lips, pushing them apart and wetting the head. Debra lifted her legs and put them on Jake's shoulders so he could more easily line up with her opening.

He gently eased the tip into her and pushed forward.

"Mmmmmmmmmm," she moaned, her voice a raspy whisper.

He watched her pussy reshape and reform around the fleshy invader, pushing deeper inside her. He was halfway in when Debra's face contorted in a silent scream as he continued to push forward.

"Ooooohhhhhh!" she groaned. "So good! It's so good!"

When he felt like he couldn't push any farther without hurting her, he stopped and let Debra get used to the feeling. He slowly slid back out and pushed back to the same place as before, and she relaxed as he returned.

"Ohhhh, yessssss!" she hissed. "So fucking good!"

He slid back out a little faster and slowly eased himself back in a third time. Once he reached the same depth, he paused. Debra nodded, so Jake pushed in deeper, just a couple more inches. She put her hand on his stomach, and he stopped once more, waiting until she could get used to his thickness.

"Be gentle with me, but don't stop. I need all of you in me."

He repeated his motions a few more times, getting deeper with each push until he buried himself fully into her.

"Oh, fuck! You're so fucking big!" she wailed. "Holy shit, I'm so full. I don't think I've ever been this full! Ever!"

Debra gasped as Jake eased his cock back out of her tight pussy and she felt empty. He immediately returned to his full depth.

"Ooohhh!" Debra squealed as he hit bottom one more time. "Again! Do that again!" she commanded.

Jake did as he was told, pulled out of her hot folds, and then shoved himself back inside.

Tears welled up in Debra's eyes. "Lay on top of me, Jake," she pleaded. "Let me feel your skin against me again. I want to feel you on top of me."

Jake lowered himself onto Debra's lovely body. He loved its curves, sagging breasts, and slightly squidgy tummy and wanted to do more than just fuck her. He wanted to merge with her; to meld their bodies together so they were a part of each other. They were experiencing the ultimate closeness, but Jake wanted to coalesce together with her to get even closer.

Debra kicked her legs up and wrapped them around his narrow waist, clamping him to her so he could barely move. He lay on top of her and slowly moved in and out of her just a couple of inches.

"You're so beautiful to me. You're a gorgeous woman, and I feel so right being inside you," he said. "I love feeling you underneath me and feeling your hot skin on mine. I could do this for hours."

Debra looked into his eyes as tears spilled down the sides of her face. "I haven't felt this good in years, Jake." She loosened her legs' grip on his waist and said, "Push into me. Keep it slow so I can enjoy it. Make love to me."

Jake rocked his hips up and down, slowly gliding his thick cock in and out of her tight pussy, and she moaned with every thrust. She grabbed his head and kissed him hard, tears still flowing. "I love this. I love this. I love this."

Jake raised up and looked into her eyes. "I love this, too."

"I just love this," she said, not hearing him. She closed her eyes and smiled. "I love ... this. I love ... this so much."

Jake silenced her with another kiss. "Say it," he whispered. "Say it to me. I know what you want to say." Jake flashed briefly to another time and city. He knew he was feeling a love that might be temporary but was no less real. His heart overflowed with love for Debra Dawson and, at that moment, he didn't want to be anywhere else.

"I can't," she said, opening her eyes, tears still streaming. She smiled at him, but it was a sad smile of loss and regret. Regret at not being able to say or do the things you most wanted to.

"You can," he said, still gliding in and out of her. "It's okay to say it. I'll say it back." He increased his pace slightly but still maintained his slow and steady lovemaking. His animal instinct was to pound away and make her shriek with every thrust, but she wanted to be loved, needed to be loved. He would love her like she needed.

"I love this," she said. "I love ... this."

He continued sliding in and out of her, filling her up, leaving her empty, filling her up, leaving her empty, filling her up.

"Say it," he repeated. "Say it for me."

In. Out. In. Out.

"Ohh, God," she said as another orgasm started to build.

He kissed her deeply once more and then looked at her.

"Uhh. Uhh. Uhh. I'm going to come for you, Jake."

"Me too, Debra. I'm going to come deep inside you. Say it when you come."

"Okay," she breathed. "Make me come, and I'll say it. I love this so much." Jake sped up a little more, and Debra repeated it like a mantra each time he slid home. "I love this. I love this. I love this. Oh God, I'm going to come again."

Jake picked up the pace once more, still restraining, still looking into her eyes even as Debra pulled him down with her heels.

"I'm going to come, too. I'm going to come for you. Say it for me!"

"Oh, God! Here I come! Jake, I'm going to come again! Uhh! Uhh! Uhh! Oh fuck, I love you, Jake! I love you! I love yooouuu!"

"I love you, too, Debra. I love you, too!"

Jake drove as deep as he could into Debra's tight pussy and blasted his first come shot deep into her. He pulled out and thrust himself into her once more and fired a second shot. He pulled out and shot his third as he shoved his dick back inside, and held himself there as his fourth and fifth spunk blasts exploded into her.

"Ohh, yes! Yes Yes!!" Debra cried, clawing at his back, shouting as she felt each burst of Jake's seed inside her. "I feel your come inside me!"

Both lovers were drenched with sweat and breathing hard as they recovered from their mutual orgasms and professions of love. Jake stayed on top of Debra and kissed her mouth, cheeks, and eyes, even as he wiped her sweat so it wouldn't drip into her eyes.

"I love you," they murmured to each other between kisses.

"You were amazing."

"No, you were."

"I love you."

"I love you, too."

As his dick softened and slipped out of her, he rolled off and pulled her on top of him. He tried not to think about his come dripping out of her onto him. Come was great when you were fucking. But when you were done, it was just a slimy mess.

"I can't believe I said that to you," said Debra, not quite looking him in the eyes as tears spilled from her brown eyes. "I'm so embarrassed. I'm usually not that needy or emotional."

"Don't be. I said it, too." He wiped his thumb on her cheeks, where her sweat mixed with her tears. She looked unconvinced.

"Hey," he said, turning her chin so she looked right at him. "I love you, too." Jake's eyes turned a little red and welled up.

Debra buried her face in the crook of his neck and cried softly. Jake wrapped her up in his arms and held her tight without squeezing too hard.

"Is that so bad?" he asked.

"No," she said, her voice muffled. "I just feel silly." She turned so he could hear her better. "I mean, I know we don't actually love each other, but I got to feel it for a few moments. I haven't felt loved or so thoroughly... well, fucked, in such a long time. I enjoyed the sex, and I want to do it again. But the love thing was unexpected. It just welled up in me when you entered me and I couldn't help it. I felt like my heart was going to burst with love if I didn't say it."

Jake flashed back once more to his time with Betty Abernathy, who had said she loved him the first time they were together.[49] That profession of love actually turned into something more than just a heat-of-the-moment shout.

"I loved that we said it," said Jake. "It made the sex so much more ... exciting. It felt better, like it was something deeper and more meaningful. But I won't hold you to it when I leave. It's not a promise we made and we're not committed to anything," he said.

Debra said, "I appreciate it, and you're right, the sex was a *lot* more exciting, especially when you said it and came inside me. But I just feel weak. I just wanted to have some great sex and feel wanted by another man. I didn't expect ... *this* to be the result."

---

[49] See *Stand Up, Lie Down, vol. 1, #6: Betty In Birmingham*. That's my favorite book of the whole series because of that scene. This may be a close second.

"You're not weak for needing to be loved," Jake assured her. "We all want to love and be loved. Sex is great and a lot of fun, but it's the best when there's a real emotional connection like this. And I felt that when we were, uh, together."

"Together?" Debra laughed. "You really can't do dirty talk when you're not fucking, can you?"

Jake chuckled. "Told you."

They kissed a few more times. "I was serious though," she said. "We can love each other for the night. Not just make love, but actually love each other. No matter what we do, or where and how we make each other come, we'll love each other. But I won't hold you to it. We won't move in together, I'm not moving to Minnesota, and we don't need to maintain a long-distance relationship."

"And when it's time for me to go, we'll have one last good fuck and say it several more times."

"Deal," said Debra. "I really just need some physical intimacy, but I'm not ready for a relationship." She kissed him once more and laid her head back on his chest. The two lay together, her on top of him, listening to each other breathe, and enjoying the feeling of their skin being together.

After several minutes, Debra said, "Now, I believe you said something about pounding the shit out of me doggy style so you could make my tits swing. Do you still want to do that?"

"Uhhh, yes. I want to, um, do *that*," said Jake.

"Uh-uh," Debra said, smiling. "I want to hear you say it."

"I can't."

"Yes, you can. It's okay to say it tonight." Debra covered her mouth with her hand so she didn't laugh out loud.

Jake's face turned bright red as his cock surged back to life. "I want you to get on your hands and knees and point your hot ass at me so I can fuck your sweet cunt and make your tits swing from my pounding."

"Oh, shit!" Debra fanned herself with her hand and spoke with a southern accent. "Mr. Nilsen, ah do declayer! And wherever shall you cum!" she said, switching pronunciations with her accent.

"I'm gonna flip you over and plow your tight little cunt until I pull out and shoot all over your tits."

Debra's eyes shot wide open. "Oh, fuck, I want you to fuck me like that and then cover me with your come."

Jake smiled. "I love you, Debra Dawson."

"I love you, too, Jake Nilsen."

Shannon
in Shreveport

Table of Contents

CHAPTER 1

Jake's phone pinged as he was driving on U.S. Highway 190, heading east to New Orleans. "Are you ready for the 4 Musketeers' Bachelor Cruise??" his speaker said in his phone's Irish voice that wasn't really very Irish.

It was a text from his former swimming teammate and one of his three financial advisers, Alan Johansen.

Jake hit the reply button on his heads-up display and dictated his reply. "You bet. Looking four ward to it. No, fore word goddammit. Forward, you fucking phone, forward like the opposite of backward! No, fuck!"

A few seconds later, Alan replied with several laugh-crying emojis followed by a phone call.

"My phone sucks," Jake said after he poked the answer button on the display three times.

"Dude, how you survive in the 21st century sometimes just amazes me," Alan said, roaring with laughter. "So, when will you get here?"

"My GPS says I'll be in New Orleans in about two hours. See, I'm not bad at technology."

"That's fine, except we're meeting in Houston, remember?"

"What?" Jake shouted.

Alan laughed again. "I'm just messing with you. We're in New Orleans. That's where the ship departs from."

"Asshole."

Alan snorted again. "I just got here a little while ago, and Tod and Clams are down by the pool drinking margaritas. We're figuring out where to go for dinner tonight. How does Mexican sound?"

"Hard pass. I was eating Mexican food all weekend." Jake had just finished his weekend doing comedy in Dallas. He had also hooked up with a beautiful Black woman named Debra. It was a torrid, steamy romance with professions of love. And a lot of Tex-Mex food.[50]

It turned out Debra really loved Mexican food, and Jake did too—although not as much—so they ate Tex-Mex every night they were together and took turns running to the bathroom to "freshen up," which was code for "try desperately to fart quietly." There was a lot of flushing to cover the farts, which wasn't always successful.

Afterward, Jake had spent most of this trip driving with his windows down, even though the temps hovered in the 40s because four days of refried beans and seasoned ground beef were playing havoc on his GI tract, and he was in danger of suffocating otherwise.

---

[50] See *Stand Up, Lie Down, vol. 2 #7: Debra In Dallas*

"As long as I can get a salad, I don't care where we go. Plus, I'm going to go for a run first."

"Taco salad it is," said Alan.

"Asshole," Jake said again. "I should be ready to go at 6:00. Want to just meet in the lobby?"

"That'll be good. Tod and Clams will probably be hammered by then. Serves them right. See you soon."

Alan hung up. He was a good guy but could be an uptight stick-up-the-butt Christian at times. He didn't drink and was married to a woman who was, if possible, more uptight than he was.

But the four men had been fairly close when they were on the swim team at the University of Minnesota, calling themselves The Four Musketeers. They were part of the relay team that won the Big 10 men's swimming championships three years in a row.

They had not been together since Alan's wedding two years ago. They were taking an early December bachelor's cruise to celebrate Tod's impending marriage to a physical therapist he met while rehabbing after a shoulder operation—one of the dangers of being a competitive swimmer for nearly sixteen years.

Tod and Clams had remained in Minnesota after college, Alan had moved down to Birmingham[51], and hopefully, you've been reading all the other books in the series to know Jake's story.[52]

---

[51] See *Stand Up, Lie Down, vol. 1 #6: Betty In Birmingham*

[52] Comedian. Minnesota farm boy. College swimmer. Nearly made the Olympics. Secretly rich after smart investments. Huge pectorals, washboard abs, and those muscles that guide your eyes down to his dick. Which is eight-and-a-half inches.

Tod and Chrissy chose to get married in February in Orlando, so everyone could escape the cold Minnesota weather for a long weekend.

David "Clams" Diggs was his best man, and Alan and Jake were his groomsmen, as was Tod's little brother, who was only eighteen and whose mother did not allow him to come on the cruise.

Alan's wife, Anna, had nearly ruined the entire trip when she first forbade Alan from going. Later, after he insisted, she "allowed" him to go, but said she was going with him in order to keep an eye on him.

Clams, Tod, and Jake all threatened that they would tie him up and leave him by the side of the road if Anna so much as set foot in Louisiana. So, Alan secretly got her appointed to give a talk at the Birmingham Baptist Youth Abstinence Conference that was happening that same week. It cost him a $1,000 donation to the First Birmingham Church, and a flurry of text messages between Alan, Jake, Betty, and Clarice Beauregard, the organizer of the BBYAC, to make it happen.

Finally, when Anna said she really felt God was calling her to keep Alan and his friends out of trouble, Alan put his foot down. He said he was not going to miss his friend's bachelor party because she didn't trust him and that maybe she didn't have as much faith in their marriage as he did.

This absolutely did not sit well with Anna, and she was about to double down, so Alan reminded her that if she missed the BBYAC, she would not be asked to join the Daughters of the Confederacy, a group she dearly wanted to join, despite its racist roots. So, she smiled sweetly and agreed to let Alan go, promising herself that he would pay for this later.

Jake knew nor cared about any of this, although he had warned Alan that despite Anna's "submissive wives" upbringing in the Baptist church, she was clearly not.

Oh well, he thought, shrugging his shoulders at no one in particular. He turned on the podcast he had been listening to, *Drinking With Authors*, put out by the editors of 4 Horsemen Publications, which you can find on your favorite podcast platform.

He was about to hit play when his phone rang with a number he didn't recognize. He hit the answer button on his heads-up display again.

"This is Jake."

"Jake Nilsen?" said a woman.

"No, it's—er, yes, that's right." That was weird. No one ever got his name right the first time.

"This is Kate Lynn, the manager at Cobbler's. I've got a slight problem. Our middle canceled on your weekend and I can't find anyone to fill in. All my go-to comics already have gigs. So, I wanted to give you an extra twenty minutes if you're okay with that."

"Sure, that'd be fine."

"Perfect. Thanks a lot. I really appreciate it."

Jake turned the *Drinking With Authors* podcast on and settled in to listen for a few hours. After catching up on the latest episodes, he switched over to one of his favorite streaming playlists and sang along until he pulled into the parking garage at the hotel eight minutes earlier than his GPS had predicted.

"Ha, I win again!" he declared, giving a little fist pump. He was one of those drivers who would race against the time the GPS calculated and declared himself the victor if he could beat it.

Twenty minutes later, he was following the running route suggested by Google Maps that would see him churn out eight miles in under an hour. It wasn't that Jake liked running; he hated it, if he were being honest.

But he noticed that his washboard abs were a little smoother after a couple of weeks of taking it easy and eating whatever he felt like, especially during his weekend with Debra. He promised himself as he ran that he was going to lay off the carbs for a few weeks, even on the cruise.

He wasn't sure if they had any treadmills or a running route on the ship, so he needed to get in as much exercise as he could before they left. A run tonight, a run tomorrow before the ship left at noon, and then time on a treadmill, or some serious yoga in his cabin.

Jake pounded out the miles, feeling more winded than normal, another sign that he had been neglecting his training regimen. He re-promised himself that he was running tomorrow morning and sticking with protein and veggies, no carbs. While he wasn't vain about his body, he was proud of it and loved it when women complimented him, or at least eyed him hungrily whenever he took off his shirt.

He thought back over this tour, Jake Nilsen's Wacky Wild West Tour, so named by his agent, Kurt, who he had originally met at the University of Minnesota when they were both in a student comedy troupe. When Jake went into comedy, Kurt was going into artist representation, so Jake became one of Kurt's first clients.

The tour had seen him travel all through the western half of the U.S.—Fargo, North Dakota; Portland, Oregon; Reno, Nevada; Tucson, Arizona; El Paso, Texas; and Dallas—not to mention a quick detour up to Vancouver, British Columbia, and Jake had met some wonderful women in each of the cities.

He replayed some of his favorite encounters and partners. There was Piper, the art gallery owner in Portland; Vanessa in Vancouver, the restaurant manager and competitive skier who called him Jake-Jake; and Tracy, the former ballet dancer turned marketing coordinator Jake met during her 25th birthday party.

But the woman who came back again and again to Jake was Betty Abernathy, the woman he met in Birmingham the year before[53] when he was there to meet Alan and perform over the weekend.

Betty was the only woman he had seen more than once in the last two years. She made a special trip from Birmingham to Reno for a visit. The two enjoyed a no-strings-attached relationship where they would have video phone sex, mutually masturbating until both of them came, crying out the other person's name.

A few months ago, for Jake's 28th birthday, she had arranged a special video call where she fucked Sheila Goodwin, the yoga studio owner from their first *ménage à trois*[54], with a strap-on dildo. For an added bit of sexiness, Betty made Sheila call her Jake as Betty fucked her from behind, grabbing her hips and slamming the fat dildo into Sheila's aching pussy.

"Ohh, Jake, you feel so good! Oh, fuck me, Jake! Slam into my wet cunt! I want to feel your hot come all over me!"

---

[53] Also in *Stand Up, Lie Down, vol. 1 #6: Betty In Birmingham*.

[54] Still *Stand Up, Lie Down, vol. 1 #6: Betty In Birmingham*.

When Betty slapped Sheila on the ass, Sheila pulled "Jake's cock" out of her dripping pussy, whirled around, and aimed it at her tits. Betty stroked it and shot several bursts of white come all over Sheila's martini-glass tits.

"Oh, fuck," Jake grunted, firing his own jizz at a paper towel just off camera. "That was fucking amazing! What the hell was that?"

"Happy birthday, lover," the two women chorused.

"I bought a squirting dildo online," said Betty. "We wanted to give you a little show for your birthday. Did you like it?"

"I loved it. That was so fucking hot," said Jake, still panting from his own orgasm. "That makes me want to do the same for both of you."

"Come visit us soon," said Sheila, "and we'll let you come wherever you want." She drew a line down her cheek with her finger indicating a possible target, and Jake gave a small groan.

"I definitely will."

That was a few months ago when Jake was spending a lonely birthday on the road in a hotel. In his most recent call, Jake had promised to visit Betty in Birmingham after his show in Shreveport this weekend.

It was, as we already said, the final weekend of the Wacky Wild West Tour—*I'm still not calling it that,* Jake said to the author—and then he was taking a couple of months off while he thought about what he was going to do next.

Take another sex-and-comedy tour around the Midwest? Perform on a cruise ship for a couple of months, sleeping with lonely wives ignored by their husbands? Travel back to a fantasy world where monsters lived in modern society and work as a 1940s hard-boiled private investigator who was as handy with his cock as he was his fists?

Whoa, whoa, there, slugger, said the author. *Let's get through this book and give ourselves both some time to think about what to do next. But I like that last one...*

Jake looked up and realized he was nearly back at the hotel. He returned to his room, showered, and put on a tight-fitting maroon polo shirt, jeans, and a pair of brown Ariat riding boots he had purchased on his trip to El Paso.

"Look at this pretty boy," Clams said when Jake showed up at the lobby, the third of the Four Musketeers to do so. "You still working out every day there, Muscles?" The two embraced, and Jake squeezed Clams so hard that he grunted.

"I don't know, you're looking a little pudgy there," said Tod, giving his own manly hug before patting Jake's flat belly.

"You don't have any room to talk, the way you're filling out those elastic-waisted pants," said Jake. The four men were all in excellent shape, thanks to being high-level athletes and not losing the habit once they left competitive swimming.

Clams was a triathlete, Tod had turned to marathoning, and Alan swam in a master's swimming club. Jake still swam and worked out, but had left the competitive life altogether.

"Alan, you look like you lost some weight, too, man," chirped Clams, the most ruthless one of the four. "You get a thinner stick up your butt?"

"As we gentlemen of culture say in the South, 'kindly fuck all y'all,'" said Alan. "Now, there's a wonderful steakhouse that's just a couple blocks from here, and I'm told they have some of the best jazz in the city. So, let's walk that way, and Tod can tell us all about his wonderful bride so we can properly begin the mourning process."

CHAPTER 2

"Excuse me, sir, can I refill your drink for you?" said one of the ship's waiters.

Jake looked up at the waiter, who had suddenly and silently appeared next to him. "I'm sorry?" he said.

"Another drink?"

Jake realized his glass was empty. "Uh, sure. Diet Coke, please."

"My pleasure, sir."

Jake and his three friends were seated in the dining room for their designated seating time. Many cruise ships seated people at certain times and combined smaller parties around larger tables. Jake and his friends were seated at an 8-top with a retired couple from Nebraska and their nieces who had not shown up yet.

"Ya know," said Bart, "one of the great things about cruising in the middle of the week is that it wasn't nearly as crowded as those four-day weekend trips."

Bart Parker, a retired trucking executive from Nebraska, and his wife, Grace, were regular cruisers.

"That ain't the same as swinging, mind you!" Grace had said with a cackle. "Although, for you, I might make an exception." She walked her fingers up Alan's arm.

The couple laughed uproariously at the same joke they made every time they met someone new. Jake had already heard them make it once before, when they were all waiting to be seated.

The two cracked jokes and laughed at themselves constantly, and talked about how all their friends thought they were sooo funny and someone should write a TV show about them.

Jake realized that they were going to be dining with the Parkers every night, and he glared at Alan, who refused to look up from his menu.

"So, what do you fellas do?" asked the retired trucking executive.

"Well, I'm a financial planner," said Alan. "Tod is a sales manager, Clams is a software designer, and Jake is a st—"

"Stockbroker," interrupted Jake. He was afraid of what his trip would turn into if the two found out he was a standup comic. People often shared their ideas for jokes with him, and he could tell that these two were the types to hound him constantly.

Alan looked at him, a bit puzzled. "And he's also a standup comic—OW!" He rubbed his shin where Jake had kicked him. Jake glared daggers at him.

"Comi-cow?" said Grace, and she and her husband cracked up.

"Standup comic," said Clams, helpfully. "He's not really a stockbroker, he's an up-and-coming standup comic who's on tour around the western U.S." Clams was sitting beyond Jake's reach and loved to stir up trouble for his friends.

"No shit?" said Bart. "You famous?"

"No, not really," said Jake. "I'm just getting started." This was a lie because Jake had been a standup comic for five years and was making a name for himself. There had even been some preliminary discussions with a couple of the streaming services about a comedy special.

"Clare! Clare, over here," said Grace, standing up and waving her napkin. Everyone turned and spotted a woman across the room. She spotted Grace and waved back before making her way over to their table.

"This is our niece, Clare," said Grace. "She just finished graduate school this past summer, so we're taking her on a cruise to celebrate before she starts her new job next month."

The Four Musketeers all stood up and shook Clare's hand. She was tall, about five feet, ten inches, with chestnut hair tied back in a bun. She was fair-skinned with high cheekbones, almost hidden by round gold-framed glasses. Her lips were pale pink and full, and her eyes were brown. She was lithe, svelte, and leggy, a yellow sun dress reached down to mid-thigh and flowed around her as she glided toward the table. She had a perpetual smile that looked like she might never look sad, even when she was.

Bart and Grace hugged and kissed their niece, then each of the four men introduced themselves.

"Hi, Jake Nilsen," said Jake, going last.

"Nilsen?" said Clare.

"No—er, yes, that's right. I think you're the first person in the last four months to get it right."

Clare smiled.

"Where's Marianne?" asked Grace and her husband as she sat down. Jake assumed that was Clare's sister.

Clare sat down in the seat between Tod and Grace. There was another empty seat between Clams and Bart.

"She said she had a headache. Too much time in the sun today."

"Oh, no. I'll bring her something when we're done. You got here just in time, we were just about to order," said Grace as the waiter showed up. Everyone ordered their food—steaks all around, because that's what you eat when you're from the Midwest—and settled in for the evening.

"What did you get your degree in?" asked Jake.

"I got my PhD in Classical Studies from Abraxus Tasker College," said Clare.

"No kidding, XTC? I spoke at a comedy conference there a couple years ago."[55]

"Really? I must have missed that one. I didn't get a chance to socialize much. They kept us really busy, and there wasn't much time for a social life."

"I don't think I've ever heard of Abraxus Tasker College," said Tod. "Where is it?"

Clare said, "Oh, well, it's nestled right in the heart of—"

---

[55] See *Stand Up, Lie Down, vol. 1, #7: Carrie On Campus*

She was interrupted by a crashing of plates and glasses behind her, which caused her to jump.[56]

"Idiot!" one of the passengers, an older man, shouted at a server who was standing with her face flushed and apologizing profusely.

"I'm so sorry, sir," said the young woman. "I wasn't expecting you to slide—"

"Do you know how much this shirt is worth?" he yelled, jabbing a finger at her, a heavy gold chain clattering on his wrist. "This is a vintage Tommy Bahama, and it costs more than you make in a week."

"Asshole," muttered Jake rising.

"Don't," warned Alan.

"Too late," said Clams. Jake had already walked over to the scene. Two other servers were helping to clean up the spill as the woman covered her face with her hands. A manager was rushing over to try to restore order.

Ugly Shirt Guy continued yelling. "I'm going to have you fucking fired! You're useless and stupid and you should—"

"I think you'd better take a deep breath," Jake said close to the guy's ear. The guy was five foot six inches, bald, in his late sixties, seventy-five pounds overweight, and was sweating heavily. "She said she was sorry even though this was clearly your fault."

Ugly Shirt Guy whirled around. "Who the fuck are you?"

"I'm the guy who thinks boasting about that shirt isn't the brag you think it is."

---

[56] If you had read *Stand Up, Lie Down, vol. 1, #7: Carrie On Campus*, this would have been hilarious.

Ugly Shirt Guy sputtered and waved his arms. He looked Jake up and down and realized he was outmatched.

"Now, we all saw you shove your chair back into this woman as she was walking past you. And we're going to tell the manager exactly that. So, you need to leave before you embarrass yourself any further." He leaned in closer. "Because if you don't, I'm going to feed that shirt to the sharks with you still in it."

Ugly Shirt Guy blanched at that. He mopped at his sweaty brow with his napkin, looked at the mess, and looked back at Jake. The manager arrived, apologizing and all but bowing.

"I'm so very sorry, sir. That was very unfortunate, and I promise you we will comp your meals and this young woman will be dealt with." He turned to the server, who was still crying behind her hands. "That's it, Cassie, you're done. When we get to port, we're going to—"

"It wasn't her fault," said Jake. "She was walking past him, and he pushed back without looking. We all saw it, right?" He gestured at his own table.

There was a chorus of agreement from his table. "Oh, absolutely. He wasn't watching. He pushed into her."

"Isn't that right?" Jake asked Ugly Shirt Guy.

„Uhh—" he looked at Jake, who narrowed his eyes slightly and then looked back at the manager before hanging his head. "That's right, it was my fault. I wasn't looking."

"Oh," said the manager. "Oh, I see. Well, I'm sorry, Cassie," he said to the server. "That is, you're not fired."

Cassie lifted her face from her hands in time to see Ugly Shirt Guy throw his napkin on his chair and stalk off. She helped to clean up the mess as the manager followed Ugly Shirt Guy and continued to suck up to him. Jake returned to his seat and slid up to the table.

"My hero," said Clams, clasping his hands and fluttering his eyes.

"Don't," said Jake.

"Jake always does this," Alan explained to their new friends. "He's everyone's knight in shining armor, always riding to the rescue."

"Knock it off," said Jake, clearly uncomfortable with the comparison. "Any one of us would have done the same."

"No, we wouldn't," said Tod. "Because we know you will." The others laughed.

"But what if she didn't want to be rescued?" said Clare. "Do you just go swooping in and rescuing people without waiting to see if they actually want to be rescued?"

"I didn't rescue her," said Jake. "I stopped a bully."

"What's the difference? Maybe she could have taken care of it herself."

"But why should she have to handle that alone?" responded Jake. "Why should she have to spend her energy dealing with a bully when she's just trying to do her job? I didn't rescue her, I dealt with a bully who was about to make life miserable for a whole lot of people."

"Tomato, potato," said Clams.

"Let's just enjoy our meals," said Grace. As if on cue, their server showed up carrying a tray, followed by two more carrying the plates that didn't fit on the original tray. After everyone's meal was successfully delivered, they all dug in and had a nice, casual conversation.

Jake could feel Clare's eyes on him, but whenever he looked up at her, she was studying her plate carefully and wouldn't look up at him. When she wasn't looking, he dabbed his finger into a blob of salad dressing and wiped it under his nose.

He continued to look down at his plate and felt Clare staring at him again.

"Uhh," she said. He looked up. "You have a, uhh..." She pointed at her own face. "...on your lip."

"Oh, excuse me." Jake wiped under his nose on the other side, purposely missing the blob.

"No, the other side," said Clare. He wiped too far over and missed again.

"No, toward the middle." Jake wiped once more and got the offending dressing.

Clare looked back down at her plate, not meeting Jake's gaze again, so he wiped some more dressing under his nose, but under the other nostril.

A few seconds later, he heard, "Uhh..." He looked up again. "You have more, uhh..."

Jake wiped in the wrong place again.

"No, over..."

He missed again.

By this time, Alan and Tod were laughing at Jake's antics.

Clare huffed. "Here," she said, leaning and wiping off Jake's lip with her napkin.

"Ah," said Jake, as if he finally realized the problem. "Thank you for rescuing me."

The entire table cracked up, and even Clare was forced to smile when she realized Jake had been messing with her.

With the mood lightened, the seven enjoyed their meal and drinks, chattering amiably about their lives back home. Clare and Jake talked about Clare's hunt for a professor job and where she had been applying. She warmed up to Jake, and the two talked about how hard it was to find a meaningful relationship in school or on the road.

"It's so nice to be able to talk to someone about something other than school," said Clare. "Every day, someone always wanted to have a meaningful conversation about the classic philosophers and writers."

"Oh, I love the classics," said Jake. "The Three Stooges, the Marx Brothers."

Clare stared at him bewildered before breaking out into a laugh. "Got me again," she said, briefly resting her hand on his. The two continued talking, but there was a definite shift in the conversation as the two flirted and touched each other's hands or arms as they talked.

The evening was topped off with complimentary desserts Cassie and the manager brought to their table.

After dinner, everyone had gone their separate ways. Alan, Clams, and Tod were heading to the ship's casino, and Bart and Grace went to the ship's karaoke night, which left Clare and Jake wandering the deck by themselves.

The deck was fairly empty, as most people were at one of the evening's entertainments. The night was a little chilly, and Clare hugged herself to keep warm.

"Aren't you cold?" Clare asked.

"No, I have my sports coat to keep me warm," said Jake. He was wearing his work clothes, a button-down shirt, sports coat, jeans, and Oxford shoes. "I mean, I would offer you my coat to keep warm, but I didn't want you to think I was rescuing you."

Clare stared at him open-mouthed, not sure whether she should laugh or kick his ass. Jake snorted, and took his coat off and put it around her shoulders.

"I'm sorry," said Jake. "I'm from Minnesota. This isn't very cold. Also, I'm just being an asshole."

She put her arms into the sleeves and snuggled into its warmth.

"Is that better?" Jake asked.

She looked up at him and smiled. "Mostly," she said.

"Can I put my arm around you?"

"Please," she said. Jake wrapped his left arm around her shoulders, and she leaned into him as they walked. She reached up her right hand and interlaced her fingers with his.

"You look like you work out," said Clare. "Are you up for some, um, 'meaningful exercise?'" She gazed deeply into his eyes so the meaning of the phrase was not lost on him. Jake felt his cock harden—it wasn't lost on Jake or Little Jake.

"I'd invite you back to my cabin, but my sister is there," she added.

"You could come back to mine," said Jake. "We each got our own cabin. Well, Tod and Clams are sharing, but I have my own."

This had originally been a point of contention among the Four Musketeers because Tod and Clams wanted everyone to share a single cabin to save money. Both Jake and Alan said they each wanted their own cabin, for privacy's sake—Alan so he could do some work and study his Bible in the mornings, and Jake in case he actually got lucky. But Jake and Alan said they would make up the difference for Tod and Clams.

Clare stopped, stood on her tiptoes, and grabbed the back of Jake's head to kiss him, letting it linger for several seconds. "Lead the way," she said.

Once safely locked away in Jake's cabin, Jake turned up the heat on the wall thermostat to a more comfortable seventy-four degrees. Clare gave Jake his coat, and he draped it over the desk chair.

"I'm still a bit chilly, so I'm hoping you can warm me up," said Clare. He took her in his arms and kissed her deeply. She was so tall that he didn't have to bend over very far to reach her. She wrapped her arms around his neck, and the two plunged their tongues into each other's mouths, exploring and tasting the other.

"You're so beautiful," said Jake between kisses. "I've wanted to do this all night."

"Oh, me too, baby, me too. I haven't been with anyone for three years. I hope I still know how everything works."

"I'll help you remember."

Clare unbuttoned Jake's shirt and kissed his pectoral muscles, flicking her tongue over his nipples, lightly sucking them. "Oh, my," she murmured. "You certainly take care of yourself, don't you?"

Jake peeled off his shirt, and Clare slid her sundress off her shoulders and down past her waist. She stood before him in her cherry-red bra and panties. She was lithe and sinewy, like a dancer. The nipples on her small breasts poked out under her brassiere, and Jake could see a wet patch in her panties.

Clare reached behind her back and unsnapped her bra. Jake gently licked and sucked at her breasts, and Clare gasped and gave a little moan.

"Ohh, that's so good," she breathed. Jake licked each breast and sucked as much of her tit flesh into his mouth as he could. "Ohhhhh," she moaned.

He stood up and gently guided Clare to sit on his bed. She leaned back, and he slid her panties off. He held them up to his nose and deeply inhaled her scent.

"Mmmmm. I can't wait to taste you," he said, his voice hoarse with desire. He saw that Clare had trimmed her pubic patch to a neat little triangle, the hair short and chestnut-colored. She reached up and pulled off the hair tie that was holding her bun in place, and her hair fell down to her shoulders.

"You know, we're mismatched," she said. "I don't have any clothes, but you're still wearing your pants."

"Can you help me with that?"

Clare licked her lips and reached up to Jake's belt. Her delicate fingers undid his belt and unzipped his jeans. She slid his pants down and gasped at the thick bulge waiting for her in his blue boxer-briefs.

"Holy shit, this is more than I was expecting." She slid his underwear off, and Jake's erection snapped to attention, nearly striking her cheek. Clare looked up at him. "This is going to take some work."

She wrapped her long fingers around his shaft and began stroking him slowly, with feather-light strokes. She kissed the head a few times before sucking it into her mouth. "It really has been a long time," she said. "I'm going to savor every moment."

Clare licked the underside of Jake's thick cock, from his cleanly shaved ball sack to the tip, and then rubbed the shaft against her cheek like she was reveling in feeling it against her skin.

Jake's breath was ragged and raspy as he watched Clare plunge her mouth over his cock, getting nearly half of his eight-and-a-half-inch shaft inside. She held it as deeply as she could get it for several seconds before she released it and breathed heavily. She smiled up at him and then repeated the motion, getting another half-inch into her eager mouth.

She released him once more and gasped as she released. "Oh, God, I want this so bad," she said. "I haven't had a good fucking in years, and certainly never by something this big. I just want you to fuck the shit out of me, but first, I want your hot come."

Jake appreciated that she pronounced it "come" and not "cum." But he expected nothing less from a Ph.D. He realized this was the second Ph.D.-holder he was going to fuck in two weeks, and he felt a little smarter for attracting beautiful *and* smart partners.

"I'll give you whatever you want," he said. "But I want to eat your hot pussy before I fuck you. I want to taste your come, too."

Clare attacked his cock once more, bobbing her head up and down, slurping and sucking loudly, her two hands pistoning and twisting as she moved. She wasn't sucking his dick so much as attacking it, determined to get every hot, salty drop out of it that she could.

After a few too-short minutes, Jake could feel his balls starting to boil, and he felt the familiar feeling once more.

"Oh, that's so good, baby. You're fucking amazing. I'm about to blow my load for you," he said. He rested his hands on her head, his fingers lightly caressing her scalp as she continued to work her magic with her mouth and hands.

She pushed his cock into the back of her throat, vocalizing with every thrust. "Gulk, gulk, gulk." Jake loved hearing that sound when women sucked his cock, and he knew he wasn't going to last much longer.

"Get ready, Clare," he said. "I'm going to come and fill up your hot mouth."

"Mmm-hmm," she said. "Mmm-hmm." Jake didn't think it was possible, but she moved her hands and her mouth faster.

"I'm gonna come for you, Clare. Look at my eyes when I come in your mouth. Here it comes. Here it COOOOMMES!" Clare looked up and met his gaze, looking as deeply into his eyes as she ever had. He fired a massive burst of jizz into Clare's eager mouth, and her eyes widened.

"Mmmph," she said and fought a cough. She swallowed just in time for the second shot to arrive, as powerful and full as the first. Jake grunted with each blast, and he fired a third and a fourth, Clare swallowing each of them as they rocketed from his cockhead.

Clare held the last mouthful for a few seconds even as a fifth, much weaker cumshot followed.

"Mmmmmm," she moaned, her mouth full of Jake's hot come. She swallowed deeply and then opened her mouth to show him it was gone.

"Holy fuck," she said. "I've never had that much come at once."

"I don't think I've ever come that much." He caressed her cheek and her hair. "You were amazing."

"And you're delicious. I definitely want to do that again."

"But first, my turn."

Jake pushed Clare onto her back and began to lick and kiss his way down her body, pausing at her pert breasts. He finally reached her closely trimmed pussy and parted her legs. Clare pulled her feet up and spread her knees, fully exposing her wet cunt.

Jake nestled between her thighs and immediately went to work, licking her sweet pussy and kissing her thighs. He sucked and pulled her lips into his mouth, slipping his tongue in between them.

"Oooooooh," purred Clare. "Eat my pussy, baby. That's so good. Eat my wet pussy." She ran her fingers through his blond hair and pushed her hips up to meet his magical mouth.

Jake pulled her lips apart and licked up and down the entire length of her slit, making sure to flick his tongue on her clit at each upstroke. Then he planted his mouth over her pussy and began licking at her hard clitoris, using an old trick he learned. He wrote the alphabet with his tongue, starting with A, then B, and C, and finally made it all the way to O as Clare moaned and groaned, clutching his hair in both hands.

"Oh, God, I'm going to come, Jake. Keep doing that, you're making me come!"

Jake decided to settle on the letter O and swirled his tongue around and around on her clit. He wrapped his arms around her thighs to keep her from thrusting her hips up so hard.

"Oh, shit! Oh, shit! That's it, baby. That's it, I'm going to come in your mouth! I'm gonna—I'm gonna—I'M GONNA AHHH! AHHH! AAAAAAHHHHHHH!"

Clare's body stiffened, and she thrust her hips up and held them there, as the first wave of her orgasm crashed over her like a storm wave on the shore, and Jake lapped at the juices that flowed from her sweet pussy.

Jake slowed his licks as Clare shuddered, then pulled him up by his hair.

"Slow down, baby. My pussy is really sensitive now." Jake looked up at her and smiled, his face shiny with her juices around his mouth. He stood up and lifted her in his arms. She held on to his neck as he stood up and kissed her.

"God, you're amazing," he said, smiling at her.

"Do you want to lay on the bed or sit on the couch? I could straddle you."

"Let's sit on the couch," he said. "I want to feel your skin against mine and I want to look in your eyes while you ride me."

Jake carried her over to the couch and sat down in the middle, while Clare straddled his lap, resting her dripping pussy on his half-hard cock. Jake leaned back, and Clare leaned her body against his, burying her face in the crook of his neck. He reached up and stroked her hair as the two breathed slowly and in sync with each other.

"I haven't come like that in so long," Clare said, her voice muffled. "We really were so busy in school that I never had time to find anyone.

Plus, most of my classmates were rather nerdy and doughy. I knew I wasn't going to get a good fuck out of any of them. So I had to resort to taking care of myself. But I was determined to find someone on this cruise so I could finally get my rocks off."

"Well, I hope I have provided satisfaction," said Jake. He lifted her head and kissed her again.

"You're close," she said. "I'll give you a three out of ten."

"A three?" Jake said, his eyes wide.

"Yes, but that means you get seven more tries," she said, repeating the old joke.

Jake smiled. "I think I'll be up for the challenge."

"I think you already are," Clare said, grinding her pussy against Jake's now-hard cock. "I know I am."

"Whatever you say, baby."

"Ah-ah. That's Dr. Baby, please."

CHAPTER 3

The rest of the trip was spent hanging out by the pool, getting drunk, and enjoying the various amenities the ship had to offer—gambling, buffets, talent shows, and even some stand-up comedy open mics.

Tod and Clams tried to get Jake to be a ringer for the talent show, but his sense of ethics wouldn't let him do it. Instead, he talked with the shipboard comic about some of the same people they knew, and Jake found out what it would take to be a cruise comic for a few weeks.

Jake and Clare tried to avoid spending so much time together since she was expected to spend that time with her aunt and uncle, and Jake was supposed to spend time with the boys. They also didn't want anyone to know about their relationship, so they tried to keep it a secret.

But each night, after dinner, Clare came to Jake's room, and the two fucked for a few hours before she returned to her cabin, fully satisfied and full of come. Their final night together was a marathon fuckfest that ended with them sweaty and gasping, Clare's legs wrapped around Jake's narrow waist, squeezing as he fired another load into her eager pussy.

When they docked the next morning, as the eight dining companions[57] were saying their goodbyes, Clare and Jake shook hands since no one else knew they were having sex.

"We totally knew you were having sex," Clams said after the Parkers had left. "Your cabin was right next to ours. Stud."

After Jake said goodbye to his friends, with many manly hugs and promises to get together a day early before Tod's wedding festivities began, he headed off to a nearby coffee shop to get a latte for the road.

The shop was a little crowded, but he managed to find a table. He opened his laptop to answer the emails he had neglected while he was on vacation. He looked up to see a woman standing next to his table, looking a little flustered and staring into the middle distance.

"Hi, are you okay?" he said.

"Hmm?" said the woman, looking down as if seeing him for the first time. "Oh, I'm fine. This is all just a little surreal to me." She was about five-and-a-half feet tall, with long, straight brown hair that hung down to her waist, and hazel eyes Jake could get lost in. She smiled, and the smile reached her eyes, crinkling up the corners. Jake's heart skipped a beat.

"The coffee shop?" Jake asked.

---

[57] We never met Marianne, did we? I toyed with a romance between Clams and Marianne, but this book is already running long. Ooh! Or maybe Marianne and Alan! He realizes what love truly is, so he dumps his wife and he and Marianne open a bar on some island beach! Ah well, if only.

The woman gave a bright, tinkling laugh, and she smiled broadly once again. "No, nothing seems real at the moment. I just—do you mind if I sit down?"

Jake gestured at the seat across from him. She gathered her skirt and sat down. It was a floral print skirt, and she topped it off with a blue-green sleeveless shirt. A pair of sandals completed the ensemble, and she looked like she was born to the summer. She draped her large bag on a corner of the seatback.

"I'm leaving on a cruise tomorrow morning," the woman said.

"No kidding? I just got off one. How long are you going?"

"I don't know," said the woman. Jake looked puzzled, so the woman leaned in as if she was going to share a big secret. "I just won the lottery."

Jake leaned in, too. "What, THE lottery?" he whispered.

"Mmm-hmm!" The woman nodded vigorously. "Last week. The Powerball. I quit my job, paid off my mortgage, and set my bills to auto-pay. I told my mom she could have the house, and now I'm going on a cruise for as long as I can. I just want to rest, relax, and not have to work, or deal with people ever again."

"There are people on a cruise."

"Yes, but I don't have to deal with them if I don't want to."

"True. So why are you telling me all this?"

"Because you have a friendly face. I feel like I have to tell someone because I won't be back in this country for many months, maybe a few years. And other than my mother and two good friends, no one knows where I'm going. So, I wanted to tell someone I was leaving, like I'm saying goodbye to the country. Is that weird?"

Jake considered that for a minute. "No, not really. What's your name?"

"Kelly," said the woman. "Kelly Aodann."

"I'm Jake Nilsen."

"Nilsen?" said Kelly.

"No, it's—er, yes, that's right. You're the second person in a week to get it right."

"Really? How hard could it be?"

Jake looked at his watch and said, "Well, I should get going."

Kelly stood up and wrapped her arms around him in a warm embrace that he never wanted to end. Without letting go of her, he said, "I have to be in Shreveport this weekend for a show. Do you feel like coming to Shreveport on a whim before you leave the country forever?"

"Sorry, I'm not that kind of girl," said Kelly, smiling sweetly once more, breaking Jake's heart. "Besides, we're in the wrong chapter."

It was Friday morning, and Jake was emerging from the club apartment. He was going on another run to get back into fighting shape. He had been pretty diligent, lifting weights, avoiding carbs and sugar, and running every day on the ship. His efforts were paying off because the smoothness of his belly was disappearing, and the ridges of his abs were returning.

He was wearing his earbuds, listening to the latest *Drinking With Authors* podcast episode, when he heard a muffled, "Watch out!" and something flew past him, knocking him backward into some bushes.

"Oh, my God, are you okay?" He looked up to see a woman on a bicycle, riding rather unsteadily. She wobbled to a stop and clambered awkwardly off her bike, letting it fall over. She looked horrified as she raced over to Jake.

"I'm so sorry!" she said. "Are you hurt? Oh God, I'm really sorry! I didn't see you. I'm not too steady on this thing, but I really didn't see you." She reached her hand out and tried to help Jake to his feet.

He scrambled from the bushes, brushing the broken twigs and leaves out of his hair and off his shirt.

"I'm okay," he said. "Really, I'm fine. It's alright." He was more embarrassed than anything, and he fought to keep the annoyance out of his voice.

The woman was just a little above five feet tall, delicate and dainty, with black eyes and black hair that hung down to her collarbones. Jake guessed she was Asian, but beyond that, he couldn't begin to guess her heritage. She was wearing a white T-shirt and red bike shorts with white ankle socks and white athletic shoes. She wore round glasses that framed her round face; her eyes were wide with concern for this attractive blond man she had just knocked over.

"I'm really very sorry," she said. She sounded like she had an Australian accent, although Jake couldn't be sure if she was from New Zealand. He didn't know many people from that part of the world, so he could never tell the difference himself.

She continued, "I just got a new bike, and I never learned how to ride when I was a kid, so I wanted to finally learn how to do it. Except I'm never going to ride this stupid thing. This was a mistake."

"How far have you gone?" Jake asked.

"From right there." The woman turned and pointed back the way she came, to the apartment two doors down.

"Oh," said Jake.

"I know," the woman said, hanging her head. "This was dumb. And now I've gone and injured someone."

"I'm not actually injured," said Jake. "More my pride than anything."

"Why, because you got knocked over by a girl?"

"No, because said girl saw me go ass over teakettle into the bushes."

The woman snorted. "My grandma used to say that. She was from England."

"I really am okay. I'm Jake." He stuck out his hand.

"I'm Shannon," said the woman. She reached out and shook his hand. She had small, delicate hands, and Jake made sure not to squeeze too hard. "I am really very sorry."

"No, if anything, it's my fault," said Jake. "I had my earbuds in, and I didn't even look when I stepped out. So I totally absolve you of all blame."

"That's very kind of you, but I feel like I should make it up to you."

"Well, I was just going to go out for a run. If you'd like, I can help you get started on your bike, and you can ride with me. And maybe we'll stop for a coffee on the way. I'll even let you buy."

Shannon smiled up at Jake. "Really? You'd teach me to ride?"

"Uh, sure." *How hard could it be?* Jake wondered. He remembered how his dad taught him to ride when he was six, so he figured it couldn't be that hard. Plus, Jake rode his bike all through college, because it was a great way to stay in shape when he wasn't swimming.

Jake held Shannon's bike for her, and she climbed on. He held the handlebars tightly and explained, "Now, the secret is to go faster rather than slower. Faster gives you the momentum you need to stay upright. Go too slow, and you'll fall over."

He moved behind her and grabbed the underside of her seat, making sure not to grab her ass because he wasn't a creep. "Now, I'll run alongside you and you start pedaling. When I push you and let go—"

"Don't let go!" she screamed.

"I won't. Except I'll eventually have to because I want you to go faster than I run."

"No! Just keep up."

"Uh, okay. I'll do my best." Shannon put her feet on the pedals, and Jake began to push and run alongside.

"Oh my God, I'm doing it!" she shouted.

"You are!" Jake cheered. He ran at a comfortable pace, enough that she could keep up the speed without wobbling. "Now, pick a spot about thirty feet in front of you. Point your wheel at that spot and focus on not wobbling. Just keep aiming at that spot."

"What happens when I pass it?" Shannon sounded a little panicked.

Jake snorted. "No, always focus thirty feet in front of you. Like when you drive, you always aim at a spot in front of you."

Shannon giggled. "Oh. Duh!"

She was kind of nerdy in a charming way. Jake looked over, and she was grinning like, well, a kid learning to ride her bike for the first time.

"Don't let go!" she yelled again.

"I won't," said Jake. "You're doing great."

Jake could see Shannon's confidence increase as she rode. Her line grew straighter with fewer wobbles, and she pedaled slowly to maintain her speed. Jake quietly let go and ran alongside her, dropping back a step so she couldn't see him.

"Don't let go!" she hollered once more.

"You're doing so well."

"Wait, did you let go?" She looked over at him, and her eyes grew bigger. "Oh, shit, you let go!" Her front wheel started to wobble, so Jake quickly clamped onto her seat and helped her stay upright.

"Go ahead and stop," Jake said. Shannon squeezed the handbrakes, and they both stopped.

"Did you know I let go of you for about thirty seconds? You were doing that all on your own."

"I was?"

"Oh, yeah. You were doing great. I think you're ready to fly solo."

Shannon looked scared again, but she climbed back into the saddle, and Jake coached her through starting up, turning, and stopping safely. She only tumbled twice, and he managed to catch her one of those times.

Through some trial and error, they made it to the coffee shop two miles away. By the time they arrived, Shannon was cruising right along and seemed more confident with every pedal stroke, and she was able to ride without wobbling. She even managed a couple of turns and could ride in a circle without falling over.

They ordered their drinks and found a seat outside. He had an iced tea, and she ordered an oat milk latte.

"That was really good," Jake said. "You did very well."

"Thank you," beamed Shannon. "I never learned to ride when I was a kid. We lived in Sydney, Australia—" *Australia!* thought Jake "—when I was a kid, and the traffic was too heavy to ride a bike. I never got to learn, and by the time I was in high school, I was too embarrassed to admit I couldn't ride. So, I decided I would learn. I bought myself a bike for my birthday last week and finally worked up the courage to try it."

"Well, I'm glad I met you then, so I could see your big win. So, what do you do when you're not learning to ride a bike?"

"I'm a research tech at a biotech startup in town," said Shannon. "We make different CBD-infused sports creams and gels. I've been there for almost a year. What about you?"

Jake told her about his career in stand-up comedy, worried that someone as smart as Shannon would look down her nose at his career choice.

"I love standup comedy!" she said. "Wait, are you playing at Cobbler's?"

"Yes, my first show is tonight."

"Oh, that makes sense then. I've been there a few times, and I knew they owned an apartment near me, but I wasn't sure where it was. So that's the club apartment you were coming out of?"

"Yep. Most clubs have one so they don't have to cover hotel costs for every comic coming through town."

"So, are you the opener?" Shannon asked.

"Actually, I'm the headliner. This is the last stop on my tour. Eight cities in twelve weeks, and then I'm taking some time off."

"Wait, you're Jake Nilsen?"

Jake looked worried. "Uh, maybe?"

"Oh, my God, I can't believe I didn't recognize you! I've watched your videos from your other shows. You're hilarious! I love how you deal with hecklers."

"Thank you," said Jake. This was weird because he had never met a fan out in the wild before, just after shows. He wasn't sure what to do. Was there an etiquette to this kind of thing?

"I was going to come to your show this weekend. I can't believe I crashed into Jake Nilsen. And he taught me how to ride a bike!"

Jake smiled shyly. God, this was uncomfortable.

He said, "If you'd like, I can get you in tonight, and maybe we could go get dinner afterward. That is, if you don't mind staying up late. I've got an 8:00 show."

"Sure, I'm usually a night owl, anyway. My work schedule is a little messed up this week because they're remodeling the offices, and they gave us two weeks off—paid! So, I went on a mini-vacation earlier this week and then came back to clean my apartment and try out my new bike. And then I've got all next week to myself, too."

"Great. I'd give you a ride to the club, but I have to be there a couple hours early."

"That's fine, but I'd like a ride home if that's okay. I'll just catch a Lyft there."

"Perfect. Now, we should probably keep going because I need to get four more miles in. Are you up for it?"

"Are you kidding? I feel like I could ride a hundred miles!"

CHAPTER 4

Jake showed up two hours early at Cobbler's and walked back to the manager's office. He knocked on the door.

"Come in," a female voice called from inside.

Jake popped his head in and said, "Hey, there, Kate Lynn." He had already checked in the day before to pick up the club apartment key and to confirm that he was filling in for the middle act who had canceled.

"Hey, Jakey," she said. "We were able to get the posters changed in time and I changed the website last Sunday after we talked on the phone."

"Great. I've got enough material for a ninety-minute set, but I can switch it around since I usually only do sixties. So, I can definitely drop in another fifteen minutes."

"You do? Hell, do the whole ninety minutes then. Our opener is only good for ten, and we'd like to go a little over two hours. People might buy one more round of drinks."

"Excellent. I've been trying to do my whole set together because I may get a streaming special here pretty soon. I need to hear the whole set in front of a crowd. Practicing it in the car just isn't cutting it."

"Good for you! Hell, we probably won't be able to afford you once you make the big time."

She held out a plate to him. "You want some cookies?"

There were huge chocolate chip cookies—his favorite—about as big as the palm of his hand. He sighed. "I probably shouldn't. I'm trying to get back into shape."

"You look pretty good to me," said Kate Lynn. "Besides, everyone knows weekend calories don't count."

"Weeeellll," Jake drawled. "I did run six miles this morning." He took one of the smaller cookies on the plate and headed toward the green room. "Hanks for de hookie!" he hollered, his mouth full.

Three hours later, Shannon and Jake were seated at a Cajun-Asian fusion restaurant, Wok The Bayou, that was doing a late-night tasting menu to preview their spring season next month. Shannon was friends with the owner, so he was able to squeeze them in. He asked everyone to taste the dishes and make notes so he could tweak the final menu.

They were seated next to each other at a four-top booth/table combo. The server had taken the two chairs for another group, which forced them to sit on the same side.[58]

Shannon had scooted closer to Jake and was pressing her thigh against his. She wore a dark blue blouse and an olive skirt that came up to mid-thigh. She wore her hair up in a bun with a tortoiseshell comb holding everything in place. And she must have been wearing contact lenses because she didn't have her glasses on.

Jake was drinking a Diet Coke while Shannon worked on a frozen strawberry margarita.

"To start, Chef has created a chicken dumpling gumbo," said the server, setting two bowls in front of them. They sampled the dish, compared their thoughts, and made a couple of notes on the notecards the restaurant had provided.

"You look beautiful tonight, by the way," Jake said. Shannon's blouse hugged her slim figure and narrow waist. Her breasts were small and firm, and her shirt displayed a small amount of cleavage. When Jake had hugged her hello that evening, he caught a faint whiff of perfume in her hair. He wondered if she had put perfume in her hair for that reason. It was only fair: he had spritzed a little cologne on the front of his shirt so she would smell it whenever they hugged.

"Thank you, so do you," said Shannon. "I mean, that is, you look handsome tonight." Jake was still wearing his work clothes. Tonight was a blue-and-black plaid sports coat with a black t-shirt, blue jeans, and a pair of oxblood wingtip shoes.

"So, what do you do for fun?" Jake asked after the server left.

---

58 Rather convenient, don't you think?

"Let's see. I like to read old mysteries and watch old detective movies and TV shows from the Seventies. Ooh, and I cosplay as old literary detectives whenever I can. There are some literary conferences I go to where people dress up as their favorite literary characters. There's one next weekend in New Orleans, in fact. I like to dress up like Ellery Queen or Hercule Poirot."

"Not Miss Marple or Mrs. Bradley?" asked Jake.

"No, not really. That's too on the nose, like I'm supposed to do that because I'm a woman. It's like saying I should go as Charlie Chan or Mr. Moto because I'm Asian."

"Yeah, but one is Chinese, and the other is Japanese."

"And...?" Shannon smiled and leaned over expectantly.

"And ... I don't know if I'm allowed to ask that."

"You want to know whether I'm Chinese or Japanese?"

"Um, yes. Am I allowed to ask that?"

"Sure. We Aussies aren't as hung up about that as you Yanks are. My family is from Japan, but my parents moved to Australia a few weeks before I was born. My mom is Aussie, and my dad is Japanese, which is why I have a Western name. My mom is an emotional force of nature, and my dad went along with whatever she wanted. What about you? Where is your family from?"

"I'm originally from Minnesota, but my family is Norwegian."

"And are all Norwegians as ... big as you?" Shannon asked. She seemed to breathe a little more heavily as she looked him over again.

"No, not really. I was a swimmer in college, and I still work out regularly to stay in shape even though I haven't competed in six years." Shannon licked her lips.

They were interrupted by the server carrying another plate.

"This next dish is Chef's take on sticky Asian chicken wings. He makes his own sweet-and-sour sauce and then grills the wings a second time to caramelize it. We call 'em Freddy Fryars, after the late, great NASCAR driver." The server set the plate down and walked away. Jake and Shannon chatted as they ate and then made some more notes. Shannon took another slug of her margarita.

"Do you have a wife or girlfriend back home?" asked Shannon.

"No, I'm very much single, I'm afraid. You?" said Jake.

"Also single," she said, licking her lips. "I broke up with my last boyfriend nine months ago and haven't found anyone worth ... being with. I can't believe you're single, though. Hot guy like you?"

Shannon clapped her fingertips over her mouth. "Ohmigod! I didn't mean to say that. That's the margarita talking. I think I'm drunk."

"How many of those have you had?" Jake asked.

"This is my first one."

"Really? You're not even halfway through it."

"They must have made it really strong."

"Are you sure you're just not a lightweight?"

Shannon snorted. "I know. I'm just really nervous. You probably can't tell, but I'm not very suave. I'm not one of those sexy Asian girls you see in the movies. I'm really just a big ol' nerd."

"What? No! I'm shocked. This is my shocked face." Jake stared at her, totally deadpan.

"Shut up!" Shannon said with a laugh. "You don't think I'm suave and alluring?"

"I never said that," said Jake. "I think you're very alluring. And very attractive."

"Now you're just being mean." She folded her arms and pretended to pout.

"No, I'm serious. You're very interesting. You're a scientist, you're a book nerd, and you don't just cosplay as a regular game character or superhero. You dress up as a character from books that are nearly a hundred years old. Of course, you're a nerd! And that's what I find so attractive and alluring about you."

Shannon uncrossed her arms and shifted in her seat to face Jake.

"Really?" she said. She looked up at him, her eyes open wide. "You really do think I'm attractive?"

Jake shifted as well. "Absolutely. When we met today, I was totally ready to be irritated at whoever knocked me on my ass. But you were charming and sweet, and I could already tell you were a little nerdy. I mean, who doesn't know how to ride a bike? But you decided you were going to learn it all on your own. That's impressive. Plus, you read old detective novels, which are my favorites. How could I not find you attractive?"

Shannon sighed and looked at her lap, wringing her hands in her napkin. "My last boyfriend used to gaslight me and tell me I was too skinny and plain."

"Your last boyfriend sounds like an asshole and an idiot."

"He was! It took me nearly two years to realize that, and I finally broke up with him. I had been seeing a therapist for a few months, and she helped me find the best way to do it."

"Well, I'm glad you got rid of him. He sounds like a terrible person."

"Oh, he was. I moved out of his apartment and got my own place while he was on a business trip. I left him a note that told him never to contact me. Then, I blocked him on my phone and on my socials. He sent me some pissy emails, but I blocked those as well.

"Once, he called from a friend's phone, and I told him that if he ever showed his face, I would gut him with my mum's big ol' hunting knife and throw him in the swamp."

"Gator tail fried egg rolls," announced the server, breaking the mood. She set a plate of six egg rolls in front of them. "We have three different sauces you can dip into, including a hot sauce, chili soy sauce, and a jalapeño hot mustard. We also have a crawfish etouffee over shrimp fried rice."

The two dug in and compared notes, saying this was some of the best Cajun-Asian cuisine—*Casian*, the server had called it—they had ever had.

"I want to ask you something, Jake, but I don't want you to think I'm weird or anything," Shannon said.

"Too late," Jake teased. He smiled to show he was joking.

"I'm serious," she said.

Jake stopped smiling and turned back toward her, putting his arm up on the seat back. "What's that?" he said.

"Would a guy like you," she looked down at her lap and wrung her hands in her napkin again, "ever be attracted to a girl like me?"

Jake hesitated, not sure how to answer.

Shannon's whole body seemed to slump. "That's okay, I understand. I'm sure you can have anyone you want, so why would you want me?"

Jake reached down and held her chin between his finger and thumb, tipping her head up to face him.

"Who says I'm not attracted to you already? Because I totally am."

He leaned in and planted a gentle, lingering kiss on her pink mouth.

"Ohh," Shannon gave a little moan of delight when he backed away.

"I've been attracted to you from the moment we met," he said. "And if you'd like, I can show you just how much." He kissed her again, slipping his tongue into her mouth.

They quickly broke off the kiss.

"Mouthwash?" he said.

"Mouthwash," agreed Shannon.

CHAPTER 5

The two returned to their respective apartments and quickly swished with mouthwash and brushed their teeth before Shannon knocked on Jake's door.

"Hi," he said, flinging open the door.

"Hi," said Shannon, getting a little red in the face. She looked nervous and excited at the same time.

"Come on in." Jake stepped out of the way, and Shannon stepped in. Neither had changed clothes, but Jake had hung up his coat and was now standing in his t-shirt and jeans. He had carefully tucked his shirt in so it was stretched flat across his belly, showing off his muscles and narrow waist.

He bent down and kissed her on the mouth again, slipping his tongue back in where it had been earlier.

"Better?" he asked.

"Better," she said.

He gathered her in his arms, she wrapped her arms around his neck, and the two resumed kissing. Jake slid his tongue into her mouth, and she moaned around it. He lifted her up to his level, and she wrapped her slender legs around his waist.

"Oh, God," she said, breaking off. "I'm so, uh, horny right now."

"Do you want to sit on the couch?" He led her to the couch in the middle of the living room, and she sat down next to him. Jake leaned in to kiss her again, but she put her hand on his chest.

"Wait, before we go any further, I need to tell you, I'm not very experienced."

"Oh, okay," said Jake. "Is there anything you don't like or don't want to do?"

"No, I just... I don't know what to do."

"Well, you dated your last boyfriend for two years, so I'm guessing you have *some* experience."

"Yeah, but he was my first and only. And he was rather vanilla about what he liked. He always had to be on top, he didn't like oral sex, and thought girls who did it were sluts. And he rarely let me come. If I wanted an orgasm, I either had to hide that I was coming or take care of it myself. He always made me feel dirty for wanting to feel good, so I never really got to explore what I liked other than watching it online."

"So, what would you like from me?"

"First of all, be gentle. He wasn't that big, but I had to act like he was. So take it slow with me, because you're probably a lot bigger. Second, teach me things and tell me if I'm doing it right or not."

Jake kissed her on the lips once more. "I'd be happy to. You're in charge, so you tell me what you want to do."

Shannon's face lit up. "Oh!" she exclaimed. She climbed onto his lap and straddled him. "I like kissing you, so let's start there." She wrapped her arms around his neck once more, and the two new lovers tasted each other, slipping their tongues together and exploring each other's mouths.

Jake reached up and lightly rested his hand on Shannon's right breast. He heard her inhale sharply through her nose and felt her lean forward to push it harder into his palm. He kissed the nape of her neck and gave light little sucks, which made her gasp and writhe under his tender ministrations.

Shannon reached up and unbuttoned her shirt, slipping it off of her shoulders. She was wearing a shiny, black bra that helped to lift her breasts. Jake slid his tongue down her cleavage and sucked harder on the swells of her breasts.

"Oooohhh," she moaned. She was breathing hard and running her hands through Jake's hair while he massaged both breasts through her bra. "That's so good. Already that feels so good."

Shannon had draped her skirt over her lap so she could rock her hips and grind her pussy against Jake's hard-on through his jeans. She panted as the friction rubbed against her clit.

"Let me see your breasts," he murmured, barely lifting his head from kissing her chest. She sat up and unclasped her bra from the front, slipping it off her shoulders and dropping it on the floor. Her breasts were small and full, about the size of tennis balls.

"Beautiful," said Jake before lightly kissing each breast. Then he very gently licked, sucked, and nibbled at her hard nipples, making Shannon moan again. He slowly sucked as much of her tit flesh into his mouth as he could and then flickered his tongue up and down onto her right nipple before switching to her left. As he kissed one, he rubbed her other nipple with his thumb, eventually making them both hard like erasers.

"Ohh, God, that's so good. You're making me so hot. Holy fuck, that's amazing."

Jake slipped his t-shirt off over his head and threw it on the floor. By now, Shannon was grinding hard into Jake's cock and creating a pleasant friction on her pussy. Jake held her by the waist so he could help with the rocking motion. The two resumed kissing once more, and Jake wrapped his long arms around Shannon's torso so they could feel their bodies pressing together.

"I'm so hot for you," she said. "What should I do now?"

"I don't know. You're in charge. What would you like?"

"I want you to lick my, um, me."

Jake licked her neck and chest once more. "You mean like that?" he asked, smiling.

Shannon giggled. "No, I mean lick my, um..."

"Your pussy? Do you want me to lick your pussy?"

"Yes, that. Lick my—" She took a deep breath. "Lick my pussy."

"I have trouble talking dirty, too," Jake said. "I can never do it without getting embarrassed unless I'm actually having sex. Then I'm really good at it. Just remember, you need to tell me what you want, so I'll do it. And be as filthy and dirty as you need to."

She nodded vigorously as if to say, "I trust you."

"Okay, Jake. Lick my hot pussy. Put your mouth on my hot lips and eat my, uh, cunt."

Jake smiled and helped her sit on the couch. He stood up and slipped off his jeans and boxer briefs. Shannon's eyes went wide when she saw the size of Jake's prick standing at full attention.

She reached up and wrapped her fingers around it and started caressing it, slowly jacking him off. "Holy fuck, that's so big. I don't know if I'll be able to manage all that."

"Let's fuck that bridge when we get to it," said Jake. "Right now, I want to taste your beautiful pussy.

He helped her slide off her skirt and panties. Onto the floor they went, along with his t-shirt and jeans. Her pussy was clean-shaven, except for a thin patch of pubic hair, trimmed neatly. She had made sure to shave herself that morning when she got ready for their date, not knowing he would be this close to her. She certainly never dreamed she would be getting ready to have this blond Viking about to devour her pussy.

Jake kneeled down before her and spread her legs. He slowly kissed and sucked her thighs, starting near her left knee, working up one thigh and back down the other. He let his mouth graze over her lips and blew his hot breath into her slit.

Shannon exhaled long and hard as the blast of warm air danced over her nether regions. She had never felt anything like that. Her pussy glistened in the low light, and Jake could smell her beautiful musk. He returned to the uppermost part of her thighs and sucked a piece of her tender flesh into his mouth, and then switched to her other thigh to balance her out.

"Oh, shit, Jake, my pussy is so wet. Lick my wet pussy!"

Jake smiled up at her and then did as she ordered, covering her entire gash with his mouth, slipping his tongue into her folds.

Shannon cried out, "Uhhhh! Oh, fuck!" She clamped her thighs against Jake's ears, grabbed the back of his head, and pushed him down to her slick cunt. He drove his tongue into her like he was trying to retrieve a prize, and she groaned with pleasure at his thrusts.

"Oh, shit, I can't believe this. I never knew being eaten out could feel this good."

Jake pried her legs apart a little and lifted his face, his mouth shiny with her juices. "There's more," he promised.

Shannon gave a little hoot of surprise and delight, and Jake spread her thighs as wide as they could go. He spread her lips open with his fingers and licked up her entire slit, dragging his tongue over her hard clitoris.

"OHH!" yelped Shannon. "What was that?"

"That was me licking your clitoris. Surely you knew about your clit."

"Oh yeah, I've rubbed my own clit, but I've never had anyone lick it. Do more please."

He licked up her slit and dragged his tongue over her clit again. Shannon yelped again, so Jake repeated it several more times, making Shannon yelp and squeal with each flick of the tongue.

He slid one of his fingers into her wet cunt, and Shannon moaned as it entered her. She closed her eyes and threw her head back while Jake slid his middle finger in and out of her wetness, licking her clit as he did so.

"Oh, fuck! I never knew! I never knew!"

"What's that?" Jake asked between licks.

"I never knew my pussy could feel this good. Oh, shit, you're so good at that. Eat my pussy, Jake. That's so good!"

Jake put his mouth over her upper cunt and licked her clit over and over as he put a second finger inside her. Shannon bucked her hips to drive his fingers deeper inside her.

"Ohh, shit! I'm gonna come, Jake! Oh, stop, I'm going to come. Stop or I'll come in your mouth."

Jake met her eyes to show he heard her, but he showed no signs of slowing down or removing his mouth. She grabbed his hair again and held on, trying not to push down on his head, but not pulling him up either; she needed to have something to hold on to when she rode out her building orgasm.

"Don't stop, Jake! I'll come in your mouth if that's what you want. Do you want me to come in your mouth?"

Jake nodded and increased the speed of his licking and finger fucking until Shannon could only wail, "AAAAHHHH! I'M COMING, JAKE! I'M COMING! YOU'RE MAKING ME COME IN YOUR HOT MOUTH! AAAAAHHHHHHHHH!"

Shannon slammed her heels into Jake's back and thrust her ass into the air, holding it there as she rode out the biggest orgasm of her life.[59]

When she came down, Jake slowed up and withdrew his fingers from her sodden cunt. Shannon was drenched in sweat, her tortoiseshell comb had come out, and her hair hung in sweaty

---

[59] Biggest orgasm of her life *so far*.

clumps around her face. Jake's face was sweaty and shiny from her sweet juices. He licked his fingers clean, savoring her taste.

"Ho, shit, that was amazing," she said, gasping for breath. "I never came like that before."

Jake sat on the couch next to her and let her catch her breath. He turned and feathered her breasts and stomach with his fingers, making her nipples harden again and raising goosebumps on her flesh.

"Let me know what you want next," he said, kissing her. He wiped her hair away from her eyes and forehead.

"I want to learn how to suck your, uh, cock, but first I want you inside me. Is that okay?"

"You're in charge," Jake said, smiling.

"Then, yes, I want you inside me, but I don't know if it will fit. I've got a small, uh, pussy." She smiled up at him. "See, I'm getting better."

"Yes, you are," he said. He grabbed her around her middle and hoisted her onto his lap so she was straddling him once more. He positioned her so his cock was under her pussy, but without his pants to hold him down, it was pressed directly against her dripping cunt. She rocked her hips back and forth again to feel it slip and slide between her engorged lips.

"I have an idea," he said. "You can lower yourself onto my cock and control the depth. That way, you won't get too much all at once."

She kissed him deeply. "Make love to me, Jake. I want to feel you inside me."

Jake held onto her and pivoted his body ninety degrees so he was lying on the couch and Shannon was lying on top of him. She leaned forward until she was horizontal along the length of his body, and his cock had sprung up and was now pointing straight in the air.

The two stayed like that for several minutes, kissing and caressing, Jake running his hands over her pert ass cheeks and squeezing them. She had a perfect ass, and he massaged it firmly, but gently. He knew he wanted to spend some time admiring and appreciating it later.

"Okay, Jake, I'm ready. I'm ready to take you inside me."

Jake kissed her once more, and Shannon sat up, sitting back on Jake's swollen dick. She raised up on one foot and centered herself over him. "I learned this online," she said with a grin.

She grabbed his dick and pointed it at her slit, sliding it back and forth a few times to get the head wet before she guided it to her hole. She slowly lowered herself and slid his member into her.

"AHH! Shit! That's fucking huge!" she wailed. She lowered herself a little more until she had a few inches inside her. She flailed her hands around for Jake to grab.

"Hold me up," she said. Jake grabbed her hands, and Shannon leaned forward so Jake was supporting her weight. She held her ass in position with Jake's cock a few inches inside her.

She scrunched up her face at the new sensation. "I just need a second to get used to this," she said. A moment later, she lowered herself a little more until he was nearly halfway inside her.

"Ohhh, fuck! You're so fucking big! I can't hold myself up much longer."

"Lay down on me," said Jake, "but don't take me out."

Shannon carefully lay forward on Jake again, making sure his dick didn't slip out. Part of her worried it might never come out, and she would be stuck like that forever.

That would certainly make work meetings awkward, she thought.

"Hi," said Jake, once Shannon was two inches from his face again. He wrapped his arms around her and put his hands on her perfect ass.

"Hi," said Shannon. She kissed him once. "Now what?"

"Now, just rock back and forth. This way, you won't fall and shove me all the way inside you. That could be bad."

Jake grabbed her hips and started moving Shannon to give her an idea of how to move.

"Ooohh," she moaned as she rocked. "Oohh. Oohh. Oohh." Shannon raised herself up a few inches, supporting herself on Jake's chest, and continued rocking.

"I feel so full, but I want more," she moaned. "Hold on." She stopped rocking and pushed herself backward a few inches.

"AAAAHHHH! That's so good!" she screamed as she slid Jake two more inches into her. She stopped and held still. Jake still had his hands on her ass, and he was lifting a little bit so she wouldn't fall.

"No more for a minute. Let me just get used to this," she said. She lay forward again, nearly six of Jake's eight-and-a-half inches inside her. Shannon looked at him again and kissed him.

"You're so big," she said. "This feels so good, but I don't want to get hurt."

"I'll never hurt you," he said. "I care for you too much."

Shannon snorted. "Ass! I meant hurt me with your giant horse cock." She kissed him deeply and said, "But I appreciate that, too. It means a lot."

She began rocking back and forth again, sliding Jake's cock in and out of her, returning to the same depth and sliding until his dickhead was all that remained in her. She wasn't slamming herself down, but she was pushing herself to her limit.

"AAHH! AAHH! AAHH!"

"You feel so good, Shannon," said Jake. "Holy shit, you feel amazing. Your pussy is so tight, and it feels like velvet on my cock. This is so wonderful."

The two lovers were sweating and panting as Shannon continued to ride Jake, wailing every time she drove him up inside her. The friction of his pubic bone on her clit began to build up another orgasm, and Shannon rocked a little faster as she felt it grow.

Jake was also getting ready to build up his own orgasm as Shannon increased her speed.

"Jake, I'm going to come again. I'm going to come on your beautiful cock."

"Me too, honey. I'm going to come. Where do you want me to come?"

"Oohh! Oohh! Inside me, baby. I'm on the pill. Come inside me, please!"

Shannon rocked faster and harder, pushing Jake's last two inches all the way home and she screamed in pleasure-pain. "OHHHHHHHHH! FUCK, I DID IT, JAKE! I GOT YOU INSIDE ME! AH, I'M COMING! UHH! UHH! UHH!"

"Look at me, honey. Look in my eyes when we come!"

Shannon snapped her eyes right on Jake's and continued rocking, pulling herself on his shoulders and then pushing herself backward. "I'M COMING, BABY! YOU'RE MAKING ME COME!" she cried.

"Me, too, honey! I'm going to come inside your tight pussy!"

"AAHH! HERE I COME! I'M—AAAAHHHHHHH!"

"I'm coming, too. This is all for you. I'm coming in your sweet pussy! Here I—GAAAHHH!"

Shannon quaked as the new biggest orgasm of her life[60] crashed over her body and led to a second one as she felt the first burst of Jake's hot come paint the walls of her cunt.

"Oh, I feel your come in me!" she cried out at each explosive blast of jizz that filled up her stretched pussy. "Oh, another! Oh, shit, another!"

She collapsed on Jake's chest as they both gasped for air, sweat mingling, kissing and caressing each other, gazing deeply into each other's eyes.

"That was amazing," said Jake. "You're fucking amazing."

"I've never felt that before. I came so hard, and then I came again when you started shooting in me. Holy shit. And looking into your eyes when we came together? Oh, my God, that was so fucking hot."

Jake kissed her again. "For me, too. That was perfectly timed. I wonder if we could get that lucky again."

---

[60] Told you.

"I don't know, but I'm happy to keep trying until we get it right."

The two lovers closed their eyes and fell asleep on the couch until they woke up a few hours later for a repeat performance. Shannon lay back on the couch, and Jake kneeled in front of her, carefully guiding his hard dick inside her pussy, thrusting deep inside her in a slow, steady motion. He wanted to cut loose and pound away, but worried that he would break his petite partner.

After another orgasm and filling up her pussy one more time, the two took a shower and washed each other thoroughly. While they were in the shower, Jake taught Shannon how to suck her first cock and educated her on the best way to bring a man to orgasm, how to use her hands when she couldn't fit the whole thing in her mouth, and what to do when he was ready to come.

Since she was in the shower, she let Jake come on her tits and rinsed it off, but not before scooping up a little taste first. She liked the taste and said the next time, she would be happy to let him come in her mouth.

"So, where do you go next?" Shannon asked on Sunday morning. They were lying in her bed, recovering from an early morning session that saw Shannon trying another first—laying on her stomach as Jake entered her from behind. He got to kiss and lick her perfect ass before sliding into her wet pussy.

Jake had finished his last show in Shreveport last night, and for the first time in a few months, he didn't have anywhere to be.

"I don't know. I don't actually have to work because I told my agent I want to take a break. My next show isn't until April. I'm thinking about going home to Mankato, Minnesota before I go on tour again, but I haven't decided."

"Would you be interested in staying here for a few more days? I'm still on vacation this week. I could show you around Shreveport, or we could go down to New Orleans for a couple of days. We just have to keep it cheap; I don't make a lot of money."

"I'd love to go to New Orleans," said Jake. "And don't worry about the costs. I've got a little money set aside. I've got you covered."

Shannon climbed onto Jake's stomach and kissed him deeply. "No, I've got *you* covered."

Jake snorted. "You're such a nerd."

Epilogue

It was the middle of February as Jake drove his truck north on I-35 and saw the sign: Kansas City, 250 miles. He was heading home to Mankato, another successful tour in the books.

He was well-rested and relaxed, having spent another week in Shreveport with Shannon. They had visited New Orleans and spent the nights visiting jazz clubs and the days visiting bookstores and museums. But they knew theirs was just a passing romance, and so they focused on having fun and as many orgasms as they could manage.

(It was a lot.)

As he drove, Jake thought back on the time he spent in the different comedy clubs he performed in and with the different women he, uh, performed in.

Each one was special in their own way, and he would remember them all.

But despite his rather productive eight-city tour, his mind continued to cast back to one woman in particular. One woman his thoughts returned to again and again. One woman who tugged at his heart in a way no one else had. One that he often wondered what she was doing and whether he might spend more time with beyond their occasional phone sex sessions and rare in-person hookups.

As if by magic, his phone rang, and he hit the answer button on his heads-up display.

"Hey, I was just thinking about you," Jake said.

"I was just thinking about you, too," said Betty Abernathy. "I only have a minute. You Know Who is flying to Australia for a sales trip for three weeks starting tomorrow, and that means I can meet you wherever you'll be. Maybe we can spend a couple weeks together. What do you think?"

"I can do you one better," Jake said. "I don't have to be anywhere. I was going to head up to Mankato for several weeks, but Minnesota in winter is too fucking cold. So how about I come down there? I can be there tomorrow afternoon."

"That would be amazing! But you can't stay here. The neighbors will talk when they see some blond Viking parking his pickup truck in the driveway for three weeks."

"What about Sheila's apartment above her yoga studio? I could stay there for as long as she'd let me, and I wouldn't have to leave town after three weeks."

"I love that." Betty lowered her voice. "I can spend the night there or smuggle you into the house here. And Sheila would love to have you inside her again. Almost as much as I would. I'd better go because Gene and I are going out to a bon voyage dinner. But I'll have you for dessert tomorrow. Bye, Jake. I love you."

"I love you, Betty."

Jake hit another button on the display and said, "Hey Siri, set a route to Birmingham, Alabama."

Author Bio

Chastity Veldt is a humor erotica fiction writer from Ohio. She loves to laugh and she loves to read smut books, so she figured, why not combine those two interests and let people laugh while they're getting freaky? (Literarily speaking, of course.)

Chastity loves to read and go for walks in the spring, or spend time with her cats. Chastity usually writes her books after watching a standup comedy special on TV and reading other erotica publishers. Chastity is involved in a couple of writing communities around Ohio, but no one actually knows about this secret side of her life.

Discover more at
4HorsemenPublications.com

10% off using HORSEMEN10